THE LADY DETECTIVE

Also published by the same Author
Robert H Fellows

Forced To Move. Part 1
Forced To Move. Bernadette. Part 2
Cold trip to the seaside.
The Health Shop Murders

THE LADY DETECTIVE

A MURDER MYSTERY NOVEL

ROBERT H FELLOWS

authorHOUSE®

AuthorHouse™ UK Ltd.
1663 Liberty Drive
Bloomington, IN 47403 USA
www.authorhouse.co.uk
Phone: 0800.197.4150

© 2014 Robert H Fellows. All rights reserved.

The right of Robert.H.Fellows to be identified as author of
This work has been asserted in accordance with sections 77 and 78 of
the Copyright, Designs and Patents Act 1988.

No reproduction, copy or transmission of this publication may be made
without written permission.
No paragraph of this publication may be reproduced, copied or
transmitted save with the written permission of the publisher, or in
accordance with the provisions of the Copyright Act 1956
(as amended).

Any person who commits any unauthorised act in relation to this
publication may be liable to criminal prosecution and civil claims for
damage.

This is a work of fiction.

Names, characters, places and incidents originate from the writer's
imagination. Any resemblance to actual persons, living or dead, is
purely coincidental.

Published by AuthorHouse   05/22/2014

ISBN: 978-1-4918-9285-5 (sc)
ISBN: 978-1-4918-9286-2 (e)

Any people depicted in stock imagery provided by Thinkstock are
models, and such images are being used for illustrative purposes only.
Certain stock imagery © Thinkstock.

This book is printed on acid-free paper.

Because of the dynamic nature of the Internet, any web addresses or
links contained in this book may have changed since publication and
may no longer be valid. The views expressed in this work are solely those
of the author and do not necessarily reflect the views of the publisher,
and the publisher hereby disclaims any responsibility for them.

DEDICATION

To: Violet Georgina Kent: Living in Jersey. Channel Isles.

To: Ann, who has for the past year made me endless teas & coffees and sandwiches whilst I was writing the novels. Bless!

To: Delilah my ever smiling happy contact at Author House, and Kim for most graciously having made the changes I wanted.

PART 1

CHAPTER 1

During my growing up years, I'd never had any romantic illusions that being a Private Investigator would have been anything like they had always so glamorously portrayed them to be on the Silver screen.

The Private detective would, in most of these films, always be seen to be going to an endless amount of parties, gambling for high stakes at casinos; or travelling to many exotic and sunny places.

Added to which, I'd somehow known that the cinema industry had always thought of the Private Investigator, as having a life of O'Reilly, and there'd always be luxury villas, yachts, and fast cars to have been always available for the investigator to enjoy whilst they were solving whatever it was they had to solve—and all on the wages/expenses he'd been allowed as a Private Investigator!

The films would always portray them as heroes, who were always involved in bucket loads of corruptness, endless dangers, many punch-ups and shootings, and this had of course, meant an endless amount of excitement. They had as well, always been attractive to the most beautiful of women, dames to some, and somehow involved with corrupt men.

Truth was, I had been previously informed by Stewart— my male friend—what the real world of being a private investigator/detective was going to be like; which he said was, 'ugly and unappealing', particularly for a woman.'

However had you told me I'd be getting a job that had meant I'd needed to go to brilliant parties, casinos, and sunny beaches to hunt down my quarry, I'd have certainly thought that would have made the job much more appealing or interesting! However my friend told me that in the real world of a PI would never be half as glamorous, or as exciting as the film makers had imagined.

And when I questioned my friend, why was it that to my knowledge, PI's were almost always men in both the films and in real life, and never women, he told me.

'Because of you being a female, that for any woman to succeed in certain aspects of the business, that'll mean you would first need to overcome all the prejudices of a man's world.' Charming!

He told me. 'Without doubt, there will be many more obstacles deliberately placed in your path for you *not* to succeed, than there would ever be placed before a man!'

'Gee thanks,' I'd said, 'there's no point beating about the bush then is there?'

Well at least I know now that my life as a sleuth was not going to be easy, although I hadn't been aware of just how quickly those difficulties would arise, even before I'd finally been given my PI license, or began to be a Private Investigator.

Truth was, that any prejudices about my being a woman PI hadn't bothered me one little bit, for I believed that I wasn't just any woman trying to do a man's job, I was going to be another wonder woman doing a man's job!

Although I'll secretly admit, despite Stewart's words, I knew it was going to take a lot more than my beauty and great charm for me to be a successful PI—though it would help of course. Also I wouldn't pretend I'd be any good at it, but at least I would try to be.

So ok, now I knew that even had I been a man, to be successful in this business, was not going to be a breeze; plain sailing; a doddle, or any of those lame expressions that

THE LADY DETECTIVE

people, even my friends might have used, had they thought something might have little or no difficulty involved with it.

However with my being a stunning looker—a fair piece of crackling, and having the ravishing looks that many, many men, would have told you was flawless, I also have this major attribute of being brainy! So how can I fail?

I really do have a high IQ—brains to you—and here I quote from a school report: *Jessica will always be capable of achieving whatever she sets out to achieve in life.* So there you are—no problem.

However I would now like to add, that I will not be complacent about my being a lady detective, for I have been sat down and advised what my life as a PI might be like, so I'm under no allusions of it being grand, especially after I'd been thoroughly brain-washed, finger-wagged, and lectured at by Stewart, for he told me, that being a PI was going to be one rough, tough, dare'y, scary, exciting, and boring, mind-boggling, and soul-searching a job as there'd ever be.

He'd also told me 'There will always be more down's than up's, more low's than high's, and many more bad-times than good-times.'

Yet after all that, I still hoped that being a PI would be a fulfilling and enjoyable occupation—regardless of Stewart's unglamorous portrayal of the job. Of that I can only hope.

*   *   *

Now I must tell you if I may, that going back in time to when I'd been a little girl of eleven, and having read stories about an old lady and a Belgium detective, who as fictional characters had solved all manner of crimes, I'd then realized I wanted to be like them when I grew up.

In fact my life from the first moment of my liking both characters, and during the years it had taken me to grow up to be a woman, seemed to have been put on hold, as it were,

❖ 3 ❖

The reason, was my wanting to be a Private Investigator had remained.

"Get away with you," I hear you saying "are you telling me that in all that time of your growing up, you had never wanted to be anything else but a private sleuth?"

So ok, I'll admit there had been various times during my growing up years when I'd forgotten. Well not exactly forgotten, let's say the thought had been put onto a back-burner in my mind until it had been the right time for it to have been brought to the fore again.

Maybe the cause of my temporary loss of faith had perhaps been due to my having developed curves in all the right places, and had for a while, fancied myself as being a top fashion model, or a famous actress—which I might so easily have been, had I really set my heart on it, for I did have my chances.

However I can assure you, that I had in all honesty, never really forgotten my childhood dream during all that time, and once I'd gotten over my day-dreaming of being either a famous actress, or a model, my mind had again reverted to what I'd always wanted to be, a PI.

So now at the ripe old age of twenty-two, I'm about to make that dream come true, and be a reality, far-fetched as it once seemed.

I suppose having read and re-read every one of Agatha Christie's books, I'd always wanted to be like those fictional characters, my idols, and had wished to copy, and hopefully emulate them as a great solver of crimes.

In fact, I'd been totally amazed that whenever they'd been called upon to use their considerable 'sleuth' brains to solve a murder, or mystery, how different both Poirot and Miss Marple' methods of detecting were, and it was that which had given me all the inspiration that I'd ever needed to be a PI.

Poirot, had to me, always portrayed the prim and proper Belgium ex-private detective of some repute, who was known for using his famous 'little grey cells'. These he used to call his brain, 'to solve zee crime, is it not so?'

THE LADY DETECTIVE

What surprised me most about them, was that regardless of any other activities they might have been involved with at the time of their being asked 'to help', they had always been able to say . . . *'Well of course I will help'* . . . . and then had quickly gone about solving whatever the crime they'd needed to solve.

It was also amusing, the amount of crimes they'd been asked to solve that had even baffled the best detectives in the jolly old police force—in the novels that is! Yet these two did solve them!

The obvious similarity between the two; and their biggest asset you may say, was their brilliance in deducing in double quick time who the criminal, or criminals were. Miss Marple even had a particular knack of solving some crimes whilst sitting at home in her armchair, enjoying one of the many cups of Earl Grey tea she loved to drink. In Poirot' case, it was whilst he was nibbling upon pieces of his favourite delicacy, namely Belgium chocolate, with zee little finger of one hand pointing towards the sky.

Whatever the crime, it never seemed to have made any difference for those two. In fact, having been given the same clues as those presented to the police detectives, they'd still been able to deduce who the criminal(s) were before the police. The how-factor of how they'd done that, solving a crime so quickly, was to remain a mystery to me for a very long time.

On a number of occasions, to solve a crime, they had both needed the help of the Police forensic department which in the main the police were obliged to allow, for they had grudgingly respected the investigators fortitude and brilliance, and to also gratefully respect their unique powers of deduction and detecting, having themselves been too often, bewildered, bemused, or befuddled by the crime.

I had always thought that for them to solve any crime, it must have been similar to someone wanting to complete a difficult crossword puzzle.

For them, the clues of a crime were something to seriously think about. And as a difficult question, the answers were similar to their having to put down an answer to a question, or clue to the crime, neatly in the blank spaces provided, and similar to a crossword, for them to fill in all the blank spaces to complete all the clues in order to solve the crime. It was all about that dear sweet old lady, or that fussy man, piecing together all the clues, much like they had been asked to complete a crossword, and by filling in the right answers, that would then be enough to have had the thief, the blackmailer, or at times the jolly old murderer, arrested and locked up for the crime.

And now after many years of waiting, it was soon to be my turn to have a go at being a crime-solver. Though I thought it would be a bit fanciful had I been sitting down drinking a cup of earl grey tea, or eating chocolates, when I did it!

Frivolity aside, I'd try at least to copy them in their philosophy regarding the criminal, for they stated that it was no-matter to them who or whatever the type of criminal that had crossed their path, that once they had found out who was the criminal was, they would, regardless of who they were, be dealt with accordingly just like any criminal. And so I had secretly hoped, that I would prove myself to be a capable woman private investigator, and do what a woman PI must do, which was to do 'da businesses', as they say.

Of course I hadn't known it then, that I was to be baptized into the business of 'solving zee crime', very much sooner than I had envisaged, or expected, having been put in a very compromising position where I would need to find an answer to a very personal problem, in order for me to avoid being hung up by the neck on the gallows—for murder.

So dare I say it, my actually hoping that I would one-day be as good as my childhood heroes in my being ultra-perceptive to any situation, I hadn't been perceptive enough to have seen my own problem coming, so I now wondered what hope would there now be for me to have ever been as good as them!

One can only hope, for such things, can't one?

CHAPTER 2

So I had become a sleuth, eventually, because prior to that, whilst I'd been studying Law, it had always seemed strange to me why they, the Government, had needed to show us common mortals what an incompetent lot the majority of today's politicians were. Moreover, they would not have been wrong on that score either!

So hand on heart, having studied Law for eighteen months, I can honestly say that I had become a thoroughly disillusioned young lady. In fact I had quit law, for there is nothing more annoying for a law student, or any student for that matter, than to have a bunch of fools constantly changing or amending the rules of the subject that you are studying—thereby making the life of the student more difficult. And having a fool for a Home Secretary certainly hadn't helped.

I suppose it had finally dawned on me, that our Members for Parliament would as MP's, have spent most of their time either debating, arguing whether to add a word there, or take a word out here, or even to completely alter the law altogether, or scrap it. Then they would spend more time making new laws . . . to again change in time.

So having to put up with that, I'd asked myself a question of who would benefit the most from these law changes, and having answered '*It certainly isn't you*', I'd quit being a law student—having had enough.

So why do politicians need to always be doing that? Answer: because they would always need to plug up the many loopholes in the laws that they had themselves created; and which the cleverest of lawyers chose to exploit at will.

Do you know, I've known Lawyers and Barristers who belong to my father's circle of friends, who've done precisely that for years, exploiting at will what politicians would call 'Improved laws', because that is exactly what clever lawyers do unfortunately for the MP's, they mercilessly exploit the law-system.

Unfortunately, this exploiting is done not so much to benefit the public, but to earn the extortionate fees they collect from a client, for winning, and even losing a case. Which when thinking on it, I suppose is not a lot different from our lovely politicians always taking advantage of us, the gullible public, over one thing or another.

So to repeat, having finally reached that stage in the proceedings—lawyer's jargon you see—when I couldn't face another day, let alone several more years of having to learn a load of mumbo-jumbo legal clap-trap about English laws that were constantly having their goal posts moved for one reason or another by our 'beloved' politicians, that had been enough reason for me to have quit Law school altogether.

Incidentally my reason to quit, was not because some of you people might have thought I'd taken a blow on the head, or something similar, to not want to complete my studies and getting a degree in law, having already spent eighteen months studying the blasted subject.

Another reason, among many, of my not wanting to be a lawyer, was because I had really begun to hate those endless late nights, and days, having to always study for one exam or another, and so had finally given up, done with studying, and then rented an office to be a PI.

CHAPTER 3

N ow where was I before I began waffling? Oh yes, I remember I was about to tell about what had finally made up my mind up to be a Private Investigator, well the first thing I had done after quitting law school, was to rent an office to work from.

Now this might come as a big surprise for most of you, when I tell you that I'd set up an office in one of my father's building, and in a somewhat seedier part of the city.

After that, I had James, who was a friend and lawyer, and a decent chap as well, to have written into the contract, a further two year continuance option, so that had I wanted to continue as a PI after one year, that added clause would then allow me to stay in my office for a further two years, and who knows, maybe two or three years might not be enough. Was this wishful thinking!

Incidentally, James was in love with me when we were younger. It all helps as they say.

In fact I had rented a very large open plan office in one of my father's buildings; now when I say it was open plan, what I meant was, it was one massive room, having four high walls and not much else in between, except junk, which I had speedily removed.

So now, what if I were to tell you that on Monday morning, which was in a few days time, that was to be the day when I opened up for business. That was to be a day that

❧ 9 ❧

was supposed to be the day of all days for me, when I would finally kick-start my new career, and was hugely important to me, then you might then understand why at this time it was so worrying for me. More of that later.

Looking back to how it had all begun was when I had finally decided that now would be the right time for me to become a Private Investigator, was whilst I'd been spending a convivial evening with some of my closest friends, and been discussing politics, more like joking about it really.

That sudden realization had been after we'd been discussing crime and punishment, and the changes each of us would like to make to our Law system if we could, when I had childishly, though joking, had said:

'Governments are constantly amending the laws of the land, particularly criminal laws, take my word for it. So maybe a way forward, would be to scrap all the laws that are causing us, the public, the most problems to understand, and again introduce them back again . . . with a proviso that they should now all be in a simpler form!'

By way of expanding my joke, Stewart had added. 'Actually that might not be such a dumb idea, and then make the punishment fit the crime, or is it make the crime fit the punishment? And perhaps at the same time, we can also abolish the stupidity of prisoners being given time taken off their sentence for good behaviour.'

Jenny said. 'Ah ha, you mean that once a criminal has been send down, they should then not be allowed to get up again?'

'Well it's always been my opinion that because of their good behaviour, criminals should never get out of prison any earlier than their sentence. And why is that you ask? Answer: Because they should have been on good-behaviour, prior to their being sent to prison, that's why.' Added Lynda, who'd always been my best friend from way back to when we were in diapers—well almost.

Bruce chuckled. 'Now that idea would definitely keep the criminals off the streets, although it will also keep the

THE LADY DETECTIVE

prisons all full as well, and that will be more expensive than letting them out, un-fortunately, hence the good-behaviour bit!'

'Ok, though I think its stupid, I also think prisoners appealing to have their sentence squashed or reduced, should be stopped, because all that should have been sorted out at the Court trial—unless they're saying that the Court is an ass, which it often is, or they have come across some very important evidence that has come to light, which wasn't presented at the trial.' Lynda suggested looking at Bruce,(he was a barrister) by way of making a slight dig—adding 'So whose fault is that?'

Bruce laughed 'Are you perhaps suggesting that we should now do away with . . . da-da, all defence lawyers?'

Stewart said enthusiastically. 'Well I concur to not let criminals out willy-nilly for good behaviour, for that would certainly keep the nasty criminals off the streets for a while longer, wouldn't it? Although my being a policeman, you would expect me to have said that I suppose!'

Then Lynda said thoughtfully. 'I suppose if criminals weren't allowed to have a defence lawyer at their side during their trial, it would be almost like asking a murderer if he was one, and when he replied no he wasn't, then treat him as if he was anyway. If you see what I mean?'

Jenny laughed. 'No we don't. Yet I suppose that is exactly what we do anyway, with our Do you plead Guilty or Not Guilty, palaver isn't it? Which is in itself all very matter of fact, don't you think?'

Lynda added. 'Almost like asking your neighbour, was the hedge any higher or lower than it should have been, and when they didn't know, you chopping it down anyway kind of question.'

The sort of silly talk would continue for as long as we were enjoying the banter, and there had been many, many times, just like this, when my friends and I would all chat merrily away whilst sitting around in a bar, a restaurant, or at each other's places, just talking utter rubbish for a few

❖ 11 ❖

hours, whilst attempting to ridicule everything, the news, the system, law, politics, and politicians.

Although to be fair to ourselves, all of our discussions were only meant to be silly, be fun, a laugh, although sometimes they could get semi-serious. However it had always been politics and politicians, who we found to be particularly good value, for they'd always supplied us with something 'fresh' to say about them to have a jolly good laugh about, cos they were jolly good entertainment.

For example, when we took great delight in discussing the various scandals in the political world, and particularly we liked to talk about parliament members (MP's) love affairs. Or in Stewart's words not mine—'The amount of cock-ups that all political party members had made over the years!' And considering the words *Party Members,* they'd have been the correct words to have used as well!

'The crazy thing about so many MP's,' Lynda now said, 'is that they are so bloody self-opinionated. And because they are so full of themselves, they often fail to realise what a great source of entertainment they really are for us, and the public.' She continued, 'not that it bothers them too much anyway, cos it's highly possible that one or two of the little darlings are too thick-skinned to even know when they're being so dam foolish, or to even notice when we're laughing at them. Why's that you ask? Because their inflated egos won't allow them to see it otherwise!'

Our lovely Lynda should know all about that, for we all remember her dating the Minister for Foreign Affairs—not abroad but here in England. How silly is that?

'Now we all know the man was a brainless buffoon,' said Jenny 'and we also know that had he been put him in charge of handing out six pencils to six people, he would still have needed to use his fingers to be sure he hadn't made a mistake!'

'We also know it's idiots like that, especially in the Cabinet, who have cost this country dear in so many ways! So my answer to anyone who says they are good value for

THE LADY DETECTIVE

the money they receive, then I would say, no they are bloody definitely not! Although I hasten to add, that is only my opinion of course.'

'Oh common Jen,' Bruce said with a presence snort, 'are you seriously telling us that had our beloved politicians been able to charge an entertainment fee for all the belly laughs they often give us, then you wouldn't have thought that was good value for money?'

'Well I suppose put that way, I'd have to admit they might then be worth it, particularly had it meant that we, the public, were to be only charged for the entertainment they gave us, instead of our having to pay them extortionate wages for their non-existent brain-power, then yes I'd go for that, because they are certainly hard to beat for entertainment value, even when comparing them to professional comedians on the stage or screen, that's for sure!' She giggled.

'Now, now, ladies, now you all know for them to give up politics altogether for entertainment money would be silly, because all but a handful of them would as comedians, earn enough to continue living in the style that they are accustomed to—if you understand my meaning!' Stewart said with a wink to us all.

Of course we'd all laughed, knowing Stew had been referring, with those words, to a number of recent scandals involving politicians. Then they had hit the fan full on over back-handers, tax fiddling, and false expense claims.

Shortly afterwards, our having had a good night discussing about everything and nothing, we had called it a night at 1 am in the morning, and had all headed off to our respective homes and beds.

It was then, in bed, I thought of becoming a Private Investigator, and put right any number of crimes or injustices against our fellow man. Now that would be something worthwhile doing in my life.

So from that moment on, I'd thought of nothing else than being a sleuth, and quitting law school had been first on my agenda, then renting an office.

⁕ 13 ⁕

CHAPTER 4

However some weeks after that event, this has still remained untold to my father and mother.

Of course fearing trouble ahead, I had tried to tell my parents on a couple of occasions what I'd done, and to give them the reason why I no longer wanted to be a lawyer—yet every time I'd been about to say something, something happened, and so for one reason or another, I had not said anything at all.

However tonight I was determined to tell them, having been given an ideal situation to rectify that 'small problem', yet knowing it'll be difficult whichever way I went about it. Truth is, my father, who was normally such a dear, could just as equally be such an awkward pain in the arse so-in-so when he had the mind to be. Still I will need to tell them what I have been getting up to without their knowing for the past weeks, if only for my own peace of mind.

Knowing that my father loved parties, I could but hope that daddy will be in one of his ever so jolly moods—which often tended to be an embarrassment to my mother. Reason: he would quite often act rather foolishly on such occasions, especially in the company of people he knew, friends and relatives, and would 'go over the top', as mummy liked to call it.

So this evening, being my mother's 45th birthday, it was fortunate for me, knowing daddy would again be liberally

❖ 14 ❖

refreshing himself with many glasses of quality wine at the meal table, and then for 'afters', drink large measures of cognac, Remy Martin being his favourite, and give me an opportunity to say something.

Of course you could almost 100% guarantee, that at some-time after the meal, he'd repeat the same old words that our family, friends, had heard him say them so many times before, and knew by heart, so would as a chorus, be then seen mouthing the words he was saying. Being:

'Ladies and Gentlemen, might I say that this lovely, lovely brandy, which as you all know, is only meant to wash-down what has for me been a most enjoyable and excellent meal, so now I say we give a loud three cheers for the jolly old chef, and of course the host,' which in this instance had been my mother, and the meal beautifully cooked by Gladys and her kitchen staff. So when he had got everyone to hip, hip hooray, a number of times, it was no wonder that my mother would call it as being 'over the top'.

After his going 'over the top', much to Mummy's annoyance and embarrassment, that would be the favourite for me to talk to them both—I thought. Well as luck would have it, after he'd gotten himself another large glass of brandy after his small speech, I'd quietly pulled daddy and mummy aside, and told them my secret, and all that had happened during the previous weeks.

Then taking my father's quietness to be a good sign, for not once had he interrupted me while he puffed away on an enormous cigar, having known he wasn't the best of listener's unless he really wanted to be, I'd felt almost justified over what I had needed to tell them—for a moment.

My father, who'd at first just sat back in his chair looking at me, then at my mother, who was actually looking slightly amused, had finally drawn in a deep breath, and blasted out: 'I sincerely hope you are having a laugh young lady?'

He then paused, before he again repeated the same words, though this time they'd been said in a much quieter, more threatening tone, until finally he added 'And if you're not, then . . .'

It was then most fortunate, and timely, that the live dance band. had at that moment, started up with another tune, and the volume hadn't allowed anyone, besides mother and me, to have heard his angry words, before she'd then given him the evil eye. And daddy not wishing to spoil her birthday party, thank goodness, had said no more on the subject, and instead had partaken of another large brandy, probably to make up for the sobering effect that my revelation must have given to his nervous system! Not that my dear father, had ever needed a reason to drink his favourite tipple to boost up to his alcohol level . . . or of course to temporally forget all about me, and what I had said to him.

CHAPTER 5

The day following my mother's birthday party, I had telephoned her to apologise, and then enquire how my father was. She'd then told me what daddy's mood had been like after all the guests had gone home, saying he had tried 'manfully' she put it, 'to get over the enormous shock of it all." Although she did laugh when she said 'Your father had resigned himself by the morning, to the 'enormity of the situation'—his words darling, due probably to my having spent many hours during the night, calming him down.'

Poor love. I owed her big time for doing that for me, especially with it being her birthday party!

She then told me that daddy had now appeared to have become more intrigued about the whole business of my becoming a Private Investigator, and had by the morning, even tried to have had a wager with her on my outcome, by giving her a choice of two options of whether a) "whether his daughter had the makings of being one totally pathetic, totally useless, and utterly dysfunctional sleuth; or b) whether she would have the where-with-all to make a resourceful, totally resolute, great busy-body detective." And she told me 'he had laughed when I had of course declined them both, although the arrangement (meaning odds) your father had offered me, was very generous indeed. Then she told me, 'that he could probably be found now at his club, taking wagers on one or the other.'

❦ 17 ❦

Regardless of knowing now of his better mood, it was still my intention to keep well away from him for a day or so, for my father could at times, change from being a highly cultured human being, into a rather loud, even volatile person—though rarely have I seen this happen, thank goodness!

I also had another good reason to have kept out of his way, for I hadn't wanted him to know anything about the business premises I'd taken on; or for him to have wanted to ask me any awkward questions as to where I going to work the detective agency from, before it had become absolutely necessary to truthfully answer that I had had the audacity to rent an office in one of his own buildings.

My main worry, besides my adding insult to injury, would be to have my father exploding into extremes of anger, and giving me an almighty verbal blow-out on hearing of what I had done behind his back, possibly resulted in his having a minor stroke! Heaven forbid.

Quite understandably, he might have yelled and shouted, and then bashed on any table or flat surface within his reach, and yet that would have been quite un-surprisingly, so unlike my mother's reaction or attitude to the situation, for she'd always found time to listen to my problems, and would have tried to understand the reasons why I had in this instance, wanted to become a sleuth, and then had rented one of my father's offices.

My mother might have smiled, and said something on the lines of "You were quite right to follow what your heart has told you, dear." At least she might have done had I had the courage to have told her or my father, where my new offices were going to be. Though little did I suspect at this time, that I would have needed to tell my parents about that situation, much sooner than I had ever anticipated!

CHAPTER 6

Prior to my wanting to be a private investigator, I had been studying law. So now, looking back to why I had 'foolishly' quit Law school, well at least some of you would think that, I need to tell you now hand on heart, that besides my studying that blasted subject for the past eighteen months, and becoming a thoroughly disillusioned person, I can honestly say that I hadn't realised I was also fast becoming a 'dull chick'; because that's what studying law does to a person.

In fact when I told Stewart, my best male friend, weeks earlier, that I was going to quit my studies, he said. 'Is it because of the laws always being changed that you go on about?'

I'd replied. 'Well not just that. Another reason was that I didn't fancy being known as a modern day Dracula!'

Having put on a stupid effected voice, he questioned. 'Do explain yourself dear lady, do?'

'Well let's say, it would have been embarrassing for me to have obtained money by over-charging a client.' I explained.

'Meaning?'

'Meaning, that lawyers can within certain boundaries, drain from their hapless client or victim, all of their hard earned money, until they have nothing left in their kitty to pay the lawyer for their services. (Legal Aid not being in existence then of course) And that lack of empathy by lawyers really makes me so mad. Surely you remember my previously talking on the subject?'

Stewart held up his hands. 'Yes I remember! Although for now, let's dispense with the Hyde Park corner tittle-tattle shall we, and you tell me if that was the only reason why you wanted to quit?'

Then I told him that I'd already spent enough of my life swatting for one exam or another, and I didn't want to do it anymore. I also said that kind of life would have been soul destroying for me—and totally boring. Adding 'If you don't believe me, you only have to look at the miserable faces of any Barrister, Solicitor, or Judge, to know what I am saying is true!'

Laughing, he asked. 'Are you saying you quit law because you hadn't wished for anyone to see you looking miserable in your job?'

I gave him a face, and continued. 'Well that's enough reason, isn't it? And I wanted to have a great deal more out of life than having my head stuck in some law-book for the rest of my existence. What I want is excitement and adventure in my life; and I want to be out in the fresh-air having fun, and enjoying myself, not being stuck in an office/courtroom!' I paused for a second, then added. 'And more importantly, I want to do something worthwhile in my life, and that doesn't include my having a day after day boring inside job. And yes I also don't want to be known as someone who doesn't know how to smile—ok? So are those enough reasons for you?'

'Oh dear, I'm afraid to ask, is there anything else you don't like?' Stewart asked, knowing that by his being annoying, he was trying my patience when he continued. 'Oh you poor, poor thing, then I suppose you don't know that millions of people all over the world don't get a chance to often smile at work, do you? So you having a, 'Now look at me folks, I'm in a not smiling job,' really doesn't seem a very good reason at all for you to have quit, does it?'

❀ 20 ❀

THE LADY DETECTIVE

'Surely you don't blame me if I didn't want to finish up looking like that miserable lot? Ah, Bruce (A friend) excluded of course.'

'Correct you are old thing—I wouldn't blame you!'

'You know Stew, I really was starting to wonder if any of them really had wanted to ever smile again, once they'd become a Judge or a lawyer. Do you know, even when I saw them being paid big bucks for what some might have said had been for surprisingly little work, they could still barely raise a thank you on receiving the payment, let alone giving a smile.'

'I suppose now you've mentioned it dear old thing, for anyone to receive lots of dosh in this life, especially if it were to make someone as morbid as you are, is really not worth looking forward to, is it?.' He facetiously replied, then laughed, making me want to punch his arm.

'Well studying, tends to make one just a little morbid and ever so slightly dull, as some of our friends may have told you I'd become.' I said defensively.

Stewart had gasped—pretended to be shocked, then said. 'What was that? You . . . morbid, and dull! I can't believe my ears. Never! Never! Never! No Jess, I cannot see how any of our friends could have ever thought that about you.' I'd been about to thank him for that, before he'd with a wry smile, continued to be sarcastic, by adding. 'I suppose now with your always banging on about politicians, and you not wanting to be a lawyer, the world's environment issues, that would I suppose qualify you for being slightly dull, and morbid. And yes, now thinking of it, I could add, even slightly boring.' He then smiled before adding. 'And there's me thinking that you were only being your normal lovable self . . . !'

He left the rest unsaid once he'd begun to defend himself from my none too playful punches, before I feigned with a left, and then had punched him fairly hard on his left arm with my right. Ouch!

So now before you ask, maybe it would be best to quickly point out to all those who might have been concerned at

❦ 21 ❦

the speed of my calling it a day on a decent career, to say it was not because I had always wanted to be a lawyer for goodness sake, it was a daddy thing. In fact all I had done was to comply with his wishes, and being a dutiful and loving daughter, I did. Humph, where did that come from?

Incidentally, my going to law school had not been because I'd also needed a job, or had even needed to earn money, because I am in my own right, extremely rich, all thanks to my grand-father leaving me a fortune in his will.

CHAPTER 7

Having told you what I'd always hoped to become; a great deal of thanks must go to my dear grandfather for gifting me money, and lots of it, which allowed me to have been able to lavishly set up my Private Investigator business—making swish offices and so forth, without having any concerns as to the cost.

So now, because of him, the lack of money was never going to be an issue, for as you can gather, I am already seriously, seriously, rich, and that must go entirely to my beloved multi-rich oil billionaire grandfather, who'd seen to it that his one and only grand-daughter, being me, would be adequately taken care of, money wise, both before and after his death. So this obviously meant to have set up this business in the lavish way that I had, would have been impossible without the money my grand-father had bequeathed to me.

I admit that even now I did miss the lovable old codger, a lot, and I still have a little weep at odd moments when remembering him, even though it has now been a little over six years since his demise.

So being rich, that part of being a PI had been all too easy for me to do, and it wouldn't have been too difficult for anyone to have worked out that I had a few bob stashed away, had they known I owned a beautiful cottage that was surrounded by eighteen acres of beautifully isolated woodland, approximately ten miles from the city centre.

I'd even had my own wide stream running through the bottom of the garden, which I'd often wade into, or even swim in, on hot sunny days. This meant that I hardly ever used the inside-heated pool that I had especially built, using it mostly in the winter months.

Perhaps it might have been because you'd seen me driving around the town in the latest open-top model of a famous sports car manufacturer, whose name I cannot of course possibly divulge, for we can't have any jealousy here can we? Or maybe you could tell that I had a few bob to my name because of the clothes I wore; which were mostly very chi' high fashion. Which meant I'd be normally wearing the very latest in fashionable clothes for women—which of course were very expensive to buy more often than not, believe me!

So having money, and lots of it, my only problem as a PI would have been as far as I could see, to have had an injury. For in terms of this business, besides it obviously being a bad break, sorry, no pun intended, it would have normally meant my taking out various insurances to safe-guard the possibility of loss of earnings, should anything happen to me!

However, having money, this had meant I hadn't needed to concern myself with having an insurance policy for any injury sustained whilst I was doing my job! Though I do realise that even with my having lots of the green-stuff, money, that wouldn't have been of the slightest use to me had my injury been so serious that I was . . . dead! Sorry, just joking!

So unlike other PI's, I would never need to put money aside for a rainy day—even as a precaution. Besides, quickly moving on, I've always had this odd's-on feeling that I'll always be the one who'll get all the good luck, all the good breaks that were going, if you understand my gist. And as silly as this sounds, I'd always fancied my chances to have had much more luck than any of those flat-footed detective guys, private or not, and that would include any female detectives of course, or other private Investigators, who were soon to be my opposition.

THE LADY DETECTIVE

Although, with this being the early '70's, there weren't going to be too many of them in my line of business to have concerned myself about anyway.

However, with our social structure changing so quickly, some would say for the worst, my reasoning has lead me into thinking that being a woman Investigator at this time, might have been an ideal occupation for someone with a heart for adventure, which I had. I'd also pre-supposed that most women in general, will have been more inclined to divulge all matters of the heart, or similar, to another woman than a man.

They might have, for want of a better word, preferred to have had a woman detective, who would surely be more understanding, more sympathetic to their thoughts, than any strange unshaven man, when looking into their spouses, boy-friends infidelities, with other women. Why? Because most men would have probably, thought 'Oh good luck to you old chap,' then acted out as if they had been doing something about it! Cheating the client in other words!

I'd also felt that many crimes, situations, would have needed to be solved, to my advantage of course, by using my gut-wrenching good looks; my never-ending charm; my in-exhaustible and bubbly good humour. Plus of course my being exceedingly clever, wealthy, and my having a considerably high self-opinion of myself might help. Ah!

Besides, I really did have this 'odds on positive feeling', as I've said, that being a female with all the above, would help me to get any of the answers I had needed to solve any ticklish situation, or crime.

Also I believed that women had many more men problems, or things related, than a man would have, and so would offer me many more varied case opportunities coming from my own sex, than I would ever imagine being offered by the stubble chins, bless them!

❈ 25 ❈

Chapter 8

Ok, so now onto my favourite subject, which of course is, tada—me. So now I'll need to tell you that I am a very beautiful young woman, and a Lady of the realm ta-boot.

I'm five foot eleven inches tall, and have a glorious size fourteen hour glass figure. I have luxurious thick raven blue-black hair that falls over my lovely shaped shoulders, and have what is known as, a peaches and cream complexion, which would make me I believe what our friends from across the pond, would call 'a living doll'.

At least that's what my so many admirers would have said about me. Added to that, I have the deepest cobalt blue eyes above the whitest cutest even teeth that you could ever hope to see smiling at you. In short, besides my being a 'living doll', I've also been gifted with a brain, and a clever brain at that, so although it may seem unfair to many other women who don't have my attributes, it is fair to say, that it's said that every woman has at least one thing about them that is beautiful.

I'll also need to tell you that I'm regarded, by some, as being a thoroughly spoilt child. Of course, having been born into a family that has over a five-hundred year old history going back to Cromwell; and being mega-rich might have something to do with it, cos that would have meant of course, that I had parents who were always prepared to have given me anything that I wished for . . . within reason.

Also I am fortunate to be the only child of a doting handsome father, whose also a dynamic businessman, and alcoholic; and a mother of high breeding, who is both clever, and the most exquisitely beautiful of women.

Ok, so I'll admit, my life has up to this moment been one of an almost sugary kind of existence, as you may have gathered, it being an extremely pleasant voyage on a calm and tranquil sea. In other-words you might have said I'd had a laid back existence; a life of which I had no reason at all to complain about. It also meant, I also had no worries to concern myself about in my life.

*   *   *

My story up to now is that when at sixteen, I had finished Senior school with an armful of GCE's, and other certificates, and thought I'd be going on to University, but daddy and mummy had other ideas, and told me that I would instead be going onto two of the best Finishing schools for young ladies in Europe, there to finish my studies. Which I suppose hadn't really surprised me, so I had of course, gracefully accepted the idea of being taught all the social graces at these two schools in Europe.

'You will be taught,' my mother told me, 'grace, poise, and social manners.' You know, how to eat properly at the dining table, to push the soup away from you, and which spoon to use; how not to sit; how to correctly get in or out of a car; and walk correctly, that kind of thing. to converse, and I had even been shown how to curtsy correctly should I have ever been presented to the young Queen—which in fact I have been—five times.

My mother had also thought that by my going abroad to a Finishing school, would have been a grand opportunity for me to improve upon the foreign languages that I already spoke fairly fluently, along with a smattering of other languages thrown in for good measure. In short, mummy had strongly emphasized in front of my father, and me of course, that her daughter would be taught everything there was to know on how to be a Lady.

'And you will become that Lady,' had all my father to say on the subject.

So it had been their wish for me to become a young lady of breeding, and the darling daughter of one of the best known, handsomest looking, and certainly the richest couple in the country.

And so by my nineteenth birthday, I'd been taught at two of the finest Finishing schools in the world for young ladies, who had made me into a more cultured young lady.

Besides my having been schooled in the social graces of how a sophisticated young lady of good breeding should act in public, having been taught everything my parents had ever wished me to be, both schools had also taught me to become more of an outdoor girl than I'd previously been.

My mountaineering and horse-riding skills had improved, and I had certainly become a better skier. I'd also been shown different ways on how I could best defend myself, by whatever means, against horrible brutal people who might have wanted to physically abuse me. In fact, I'd been taught by experts in all of these subjects, the best in their field they said, although perhaps the school should have at the same, taught me how to defend myself against experts in the art of love; for one of these experts of the great outdoors, was to be my very first lover, who would coach me on how to become an expert in this part-time activity, an activity I might add, that considering it hadn't been part of the school's curriculum, would become a very enjoyable leisure pastime!

I must admit, that this part of my learning process at one school where I was to have only learnt how to become a young lady, I'd enjoyed very much indeed, and can honestly say that I had never missed one single lesson!

THE LADY DETECTIVE

It was also to be my first experience of being in love; and my first and only taste of feeling heartbreak, though I've now gotten over that part of my life, for it did happen a long time ago, in fact four years ago. Ah!

Of course, from an early age, I have always loved most outdoor sports, with archery and skiing, being my personal favourites. In fact I've always been an extremely fine athlete, as many of you might have known, had you been regularly acquainted with the tabloids.

Yet it had been in archery, shooting, and ski-decathlon that I excelled at, and always achieved my best results. So I'd been chosen, on merit, to represent my Country, at junior level, in both of these sporting activities, and having won Gold Medals at the last World Junior Olympics, and Winter Games in both sports, have twice stood on the winner's rostrum. I'm also my country's current Senior National Champion in archery.

So winning medals, combined with my good-looks, meant I'd been photographed a lot, so naturally fame had followed, so now I have a reasonable following of fans, most of whom are men, obviously!

CHAPTER 9

So there you have it folks, not only am I a top bird, have top brains, and have top preservation skills, besides my having these major attributes, I would also bet anyone of you, that on my physical appearance alone, which I have already described to you, that alone would have got me through many more closed doors, and have gotten me many more yes's than no's to my questions, than any amount of questioning those delightful lesser mortals with their stubble chins, and nicotine fingers, would have ever got, with or without their using brute force instead of their brains!

Besides I've always felt that I'd make a great success at being a detective, and besides all the above, I am also physically handy were I to be backed into a tight corner, and I'm loaded.

Oh to clarify 'being loaded', that doesn't mean that I go around carrying a gun with bullets in it, you understand, for that would be really silly, as we all know, that even for police officers, as much as for me, or anyone else for that matter, we cannot have a gun on our person without having a fire arms certificate, which strangely enough, I also have.

What I mean by being loaded, is that I have money, and were I to be involved in any fisticuffs, then I am fairly handy in various forms of self-defence, judo and so forth, though it has not been previously mentioned, and I am particularly

❖ 30 ❖

THE LADY DETECTIVE

knowledgeable in handling certain lethal weapons; a bow and arrow or cross-bow for example, and I knew how to use them.

However, being knowledgeable with weapons, combined with all of my other assets, will become, you must agree, important to my being a successful Private Investigator—yes?

Of course another big-plus to my probable success, was to have access to lots and lots of top-notch places, celebrity bashes, golf clubs, fashion shows, and so forth, and have access to most well-known, top-drawer, professional contacts—that would at least be able to advise me on the practicalities of any subject that I may have needed advice on.

Of course, most of these contacts were friends and business acquaintances of mummy's or my father, and were numerous of course, Well those people combined with a smattering of my own, who are far less numerous of course, would be jolly useful had I wished to appear more knowledgeable to my client than I actually was on many subjects.

In fact, my having gleaned useful information from these contacts, this knowledge could then have been passed on to any grateful client, and I would have almost certainly suggested to them that they should consider that knowledge, or information, as sound advice.

Well people don't mind paying for sound advice, or a good service, do they?

And to top that, I'd also two aces hidden up my sleeve, who would at a moment's notice, be induced into leaning their considerable weight and expertise into whatever I had needed them to lean on.

One you might say was a high flyer in the business world, and the other happens to be a Detective Chief Inspector in the Metropolitan Police Crime squad.

One ace is my father, and the other is Stewart, my best man friend.

My father was probably best known for being the richest man in Great Britain, and less known as a businessman,

❧ 31 ❧

although having been left a considerable fortune by his father, my grandfather, he had in his own right, enlarged that fortune ever further.

And then there was Stewart, whose parents had lands bordering on my own parents lands. Now he would, I'd been led to believe, soon be put in charge of a newly created 'National Drugs Squad', the NDS, though I'm not supposed to have known that, yet! All hush, hush, you see!

What I mean is; we all know how useful it is to have access to an ace in any game of chance don't we? It's very important, don't you agree?

CHAPTER 10

Of course the past few weeks had been really very difficult for me; what with my quitting Law school to become a Private Investigator, and my needing to tell my parents about my wanting to be one. There'd also been my concern over renting a room in a building owned by my father, without telling him, and then making many alterations to what are now my new offices.

Added to which, there'd been my antics in the hallway, when I had been thinking far too much about the 'Roads of life', when I should have really been thinking only about things that wouldn't have concerned me quite as much—my impulsive nature being one of them.

So ok, in the hallway, I'd been thinking about pulling out from what I had really only wanted to do in my life. And my doing that with only days to go, had made me wonder if I was getting cold feet, although it had been my mind telling me to call the whole thing off, and forget that whole 'stupid' idea, whereas 'the roads of life' hadn't bothered me before, so why then? Now that was the problem.

Strangely, I hadn't once thought to be concerned about my own safety, in the physical sense, in that time, though losing my life whilst doing a job would be tragic enough. Truth was, I'd thought danger, or the possibility of it, as part and parcel of what being a PI was all about. Well it was, wasn't it?

It wasn't even Stewart telling me a week before—and he should know—'there are a lot of rotten scummy people out there on the streets, or hiding behind closed doors, and many of them you would never have even classed as being human,' that you'd have thought, been enough of a reason to pull out of what I'd always wanted to be since a young girl, I mean that was crazy. He had even further told me, 'because you'd have thought some of them were going under the disguise of being a human, when they acted more like sub-humans.'

Stewart obviously had scant respect for these so called members in our society, and it showed. So having been told by Stewart, the policeman, and Bruce, the Barrister, who were both my friends, that there was another level of society, another form of low-life that had also existed 'out there', whose lives consisted only of their being involved in drugs, booze, blackmail, prostitution and killings, and all manner of other vices and crimes, which would for them be classed 'as a normal way of life', much like eating and breathing is classed as being normal for you or me

And then to make me think about the possible dangers, Stewart had told me with a sigh. 'And these are the people who you will need to be involved with, unfortunately, if you are to do snooping for a living.'

Bruce and he had also advised me that I could always rely on these people to tell you a good yarn, meaning a complete and total fabrication of the truth, saying they were excellent at telling lies. 'Penniysm' my friend Lynda called it, after one girl in our class at school, who'd always be telling tales, and making up story's to get herself noticed, or to get people to talk to her, yet hadn't cared in the slightest what problems her tales and lies, had at various times created.

Another factor to be aware of Stewart was to tell me. 'Was that I should try to never be affected by the overall seediness of these other people's lives,' which he assured me, 'will be inevitable'. He told me that I must always have a 'strong and positive attitude, be strong minded,' particularly when listening to their sob stories, his knowing I could be a bit of a softy when

THE LADY DETECTIVE

it came to hearing tales of woe, broken romances, or similar, like so many women, and men are.

In fact, you only need to ask mother, or any of my friends, if I don't sometimes have a small weepy moment when I'm watching a sloppy movie, or listening to something similar.

So ok, whilst I'm sleuthing on behalf of a client, it would seem obvious for me, not to get caught up in any tales of woe, wouldn't it? Because as Stew had said: 'You must always be on your guard against their sob stories, and try to never be hood-winked by these people, and stand firm.' So now I'll keep telling myself—*If that's what it takes, then I am the one who'll take it.* Ha-ha!

I've now also told myself, countless times, that I am going to be a no-nonsense totally solid type of PI. And I also visualized on top of that, being immovable, not easily swayed, well maybe sometimes, when I'd made up my mind about something or other!

I had also visualized myself as being one of those rough and tough Investigators if needs be, who would be seen not to give a tinkers cuss for anyone that tried any of the 3C's out of me. My meaning, Concern; Compassion; and Compromise, and more importantly, I'd also need to always tell myself that I was only a small part of a whole, the whole being the result of a job well done that I was being paid to do, because that was what being a PI was all about.

Of course I'd promised Stewart, and myself, many, many times, that during the course of any investigation, I would never allow myself to become emotionally, or personally involved with any of the downsides of the business; to ever be affected by people, or their sob stories, which Stew had said 'would be considerable, and above the Richter scale.'

Importantly, I would take everything in my stride, whilst doing 'da business'—no matter what I'd be getting myself into!

And now with only a few hours to go from now, I'd known that I'd soon be doing private investigation work, that unfortunately would mean my meeting up with these unsavoury types that my friends had warned me about.

CHAPTER 11

FRIDAY NIGHT

O f course that hallway episode had all become clear, when the man had turned around to me to say. 'After I've had a cuppa, and eaten my sandwiches, I'll press on and finish the job,' before he'd sat back with his back against the wall.

At that, he'd taken out of a dirty canvas khaki coloured shoulder bag, and a dark green thermos flask, from which, he began pouring black tea into a black plastic cup.

I'd looked un-reservedly with open admiration upon my new office door, and the half-finished sign, imagining it to be the mother of all doors, and thinking how could anyone on entering it, not believe they'd not been introducing themselves into the exciting world, and complexities of the criminal mind, and the solving there-of.

I would have thought that any potential client having opened that lovely glass-panelled door, having immediately seen my tastefully decorated offices, would have on stepping into my world, the world of crime, been in awe, and have instinctively known that whatever their problem had been on the hallway side of the door, would on this side of the door, have no longer been a problem.

At least I hoped that would be the case for the dozens of new clients who had entered through that door, having problems for me to solve, before leaving, having had their problem solved, sorted, cleared up, been kicked into touch for good, who would be a happy, satisfied client, and would be for ever thanking me. Or am I dreaming again?

Where was I? Oh yes. Having now gotten over all my doubts, panic attacks, and moments of previously feeling, 'Oh, I can't do this', I now found I had a small lump in my throat, and my eyes had suddenly become hot and moist, obviously having another one of those stupid emotions I have yet to tell you that had given me problems earlier!

The tears I knew could be wiped away with a quick movement of my hand, whereas, when this little man had finished with his 'arty writing' stuff, I knew that would mean I was just that little bit closer to my opening up for business on Monday morning, and then it'll be just little old me, versus the big nasty world of crime.

At least I now knew it was certainly those nasty reasons I'd had previously in the hallway, which had left with experiencing some kind of nauseous feeling, and left me feeling slightly weak, and having a foul taste in my mouth.

My mind had been playing tricks, which had now been put to rest, when the little man had later lain down his paint brushes before him, and sighing loudly, stretched out an arm to point to my name scripted on the glass panelled door that he'd been so splendidly painting on.

The red and gold letters that had stood out bold and clear, were stating my name, and what I was going to be. Now he said. 'All that remains for me to do now, is to add your phone number below your profession, and then it's finished.'

*   *   *

Now having told you that, it might be as good a time to inform you all, that should you ever be thinking of walking through that lovely door of mine, and into the Heart and Soul of what will from Monday be my new business; then that very expensive door you'd have entered, for those who could afford to pay, my services would not come cheap!

Well after a pleasant moment of day-dreaming—let's get back to the here and now shall we, cos when the man with baggy overalls had then brought me back to my senses by saying: 'Well that's that then Miss Felliosi. It's all done. What do you think?'

To be honest, as he sat back on his haunches, I'd been looking at his handy work, and I looked, and looked, until suddenly I realized that I'd been standing behind the man with my mouth open. Now shutting it with a smacking sound, whilst still looking at the work the balding man had been referring to. I saw it said

JESS FELLIOSI
PRIVATE INVESTIGATOR
'Your problem is my problem'

and seeing my name in lights, as it were, I'd been overcome with another emotion, and had to hastily brush away the tears that fell gently onto my cheeks, and then down onto the head of the little man below me.

'Brilliant' was all I could think to say. 'Absolutely brilliant'

He smiled, and I smiled, then he smiled again, and when he stood up, I gave him a big hug, whilst gently patting him on his back. That had of course then given the little man, an excuse to give me a hug back, and as he'd snuggled in, he'd added sympathetic words of 'Ah, come on love, don't cry now, my work isn't that good you know!'

Him saying that had made me smile; and he must have been equally pleased with what I was doing, for he just hung in there with his head on my chest like he was a large overall'd lap-dog—or something!

THE LADY DETECTIVE

I suppose my other reason for crying, was that I really was relieved that another item could be ticked of the 'to do' list that I had been working from. Or was it because I really had been working so very hard over the previous three weeks or so, you know, organizing, ordering each and every item that would be needed to begin my business, even down to what metal door handles were going to be put on—which were brass, so although I felt physically drained, one might have said I was relieved, having known another job had been completed.

I suppose ticking anything off the list, would now to my beleaguered senses, come as a sense of relief. In fact, every twenty-four hours had had its up's and down's, high's and low's, and to be honest with you, getting everything finished in such a short space of time was always going to be a nightmare to accomplish.

Of course I now knew I had bought my little trauma onto myself, by allowing myself only twenty-four days in which to get the whole job done and dusted, when I suppose would have in normal circumstances, been much wiser to have taken many more days than I'd allowed myself. So not too clever, one might have said.

So it was no wonder that I was feeling tired, exhausted, and dare I say it, emotionally drained. I suppose I'd been too impatient for it to have all been finished with as quickly as possible, so that I could get on with starting my new business. Though it might have also been, not to give myself any more time than was necessary to reflect over what I was soon to become, and then to possibly change my mind.

Now as I paid off Joe, the sign-writing man, and noted from the way he'd been looking at me, I could have sworn he'd been expecting me to have given him another hug, after thanking him again for his good work! Of course, that delight he didn't get on this occasion—and to be perfectly honest with you, it really was something that I thought I wasn't capable of giving at this moment!

❀ 39 ❀

So I'd thought, enough was enough . . . for now, for tomorrow I knew would be another very busy day, both for myself and the workman, who would now be putting the final touches to the very fine work they'd already done to the 'big' room, which was, dare I say it, now looking grand, marvellous, and was completely different from the room I'd inherited some three and a bit weeks before.

So now with the workman having left over an hour before to go home, which would now include the little sign-writer man, I knew it was time to finish work for the day, and lock up, and yet I had to think out what my agenda was going to be for the rest of the evening, so thought to myself:

"It'll be one long hot soak in the tub for you young lady, with the distinct possibility of you sharing your bath-time with one very large glass of something that does you good stood on the table beside the bath. Then afterwards, you'll make yourself a bite to eat, maybe a cheese omelette, and then it'll be off to bed with you."

But before leaving, I'd again, possibly for the tenth time that day, caste an approving eye over all the work that had been done by the other workman, and now seeing the sign writers work, had felt an urge of gratitude to them all for what they had accomplished in making a drab, dingy open space, that had a grotty wooden door for its entrance, into two delightful offices, and a reception, and now had a door with sign-writing on it that told people about me, my new profession, and with everything looking so beautiful, I could have cried with pleasure.

Wearily I double-locked my office door, and treble-locked the hallway door after me, and made my way to the old fashioned metal-framed lift, and having pulled back the metal sliding door, had wearily entered, to then make the slow descent to the ground floor.

Then saying goodnight to the old man sat in the office behind the reception desk, I headed to my car, parked in a reserved space, and in slightly more than twenty minutes of driving, I'd arrived home.

CHAPTER 12

Going back to before I'd actually had the new office door for 'da business', what had happened was that I'd been standing in the hallway, behind the little man, and on an old red stained carpet that ran in front of my new office, which had in turn overlaid an equally tatty plain grey linoleum, and on them, I had been doing some very strange movements—which fortunately no-one had seen me doing, which was just as well really, because had anyone been standing close-by, without their knowing the circumstances, and then seen what I'd been doing, they might have been forgiven to thinking why had a tall, young, statuesque, and very beautiful young woman was having what we mortals would call, *an attack of nerves*.

I know that most people might have thought, had they been observing me having an 'attack of nerves', which in their opinion, had been nothing more than their being embarrassed with seeing me having my 'attack of nerves', would probably have just shrugged their shoulders, meaning that whatever I was doing, was to them of no significance whatsoever, even had they been willing to listen to what I had to say to explain why—had I known.

Of course I also knew there'd be some people, whilst still not knowing what reason, or reasons there might have been to have upset a beautiful young lady, would have spoken of my attack of nerves to others, as something to have been

❖ 41 ❖

laughed about, or worse—which shows that people could not only be callous, but also cruel in the eyes of all churchgoers.

Of course, we all know there are people amongst us,: the gossip mongers of this world, who my father called 'Marchers', where problems such as I was undoubtedly having, would have been a sufficiently good reason for these busy-body members of our so-called caring society, to have then spread vicious-tongued false rumours amongst their so-called 'friends'.

These 'friend's' would then see to it, that whatever they'd been told, would then be spread even further among like-minded people, meaning, that would have done that, just to stir up further trouble for their 'victim'.

These people, besides being gossips, would also not have been adverse to spreading lies and malicious stories behind the backs of their unsuspecting 'victims', which meant the victims secrets that had been told them in good-faith to others. Although it is also true, that most of these scheming souls, and there are many of them, will hide behind their own un-happiness, inefficiencies, and problems, just to cause other people problems, and will do whatever else their diseased, warped, and perverted minds enjoyed to do, against the likes of say, this young woman, being me of course!

Daddy had referred to these people as 'Marchers', because the Marchbinds, being their correct name, had been a notorious family who lived in the 19th century, and by using their enormous wealth, had cultivated as many so called 'friends' as possible around them. This they had done, in order that they might pass on any information that they had expertly wheedled out from any 'innocents', meaning their innermost thoughts and secrets, so that they might later cruelly amuse themselves, by talking about them, and then passing on these secrets to others of their kind.

For example the problems I'd been having, combined with the antics I'd displayed, would have immediately made these 'Marchers' into summoning other like people to their lavish mansion, to no doubt have wine and tit-bits to eat, or receive small gifts to keep them sweet, just so as to have one of their tut-tut meetings, in order that they might all agree that comments such as 'She was suffering from an attack of nerves' could have been talked about further, and then been either beefed up, and made more vitreous, or not.

The end result would have been whether this bit of news, or situation, had enough meat on the bone for it to have been interesting enough for them to continue maliciously gossip about; or for it be sent to somewhere in their cobwebby minds of unused trivia; at least until another occasion arose, when it might again, be 'aired', with greater effect.

So much for the compassion of some humans, eh!

The 'Marchers', or Marchbinds, had been a cruel vindictive brainless lot—evil most would have said, and what was worse, there'd been eight in the family who had all spent a good deal of their lives causing, or at least disrupting, the life's of others with their deceitful ways, often resulting with dire consequences for their 'victims' because of their vicious tongues.

They'd continued, my father had told me, with all that nastiness, right up to when they'd eventually been found out for what they were, misfits to society, and their 'victims' had in turn, wanted revenge, and turned nasty on them, by organising other men and women who also been a 'victims', to curse them, and one by one, the 'victims' who the Marshers had loved to talk, or gossip about, had vowed to get rid of the 'Marchers' in one way or another—meaning most painfully and very unpleasantly in every instance.

So whatever my fate might have been in their hands with my having 'an attack of nerves' I wouldn't know, except to say I might have been quietly concerned at that moment in time in that ornate high-ceiling hallway that had scuffed white-painted walls, had I known that some people like the Marchers, might have made a great deal more out of my making strange body movements than was intended!

Perhaps I should not have refrained for so long to tell you that in the hallway, I appeared to have been hopping about; some might have called it skipping, when for want of a better word, it was actually skip-hopping; which meant I'd been continuously moving from side to side, from one leg to the other, and then forwards and backwards on my heels as if I'd been a rocking horse in a hopping sort of way!

On this subject I shall say little more, except to say that it was blatantly obvious to anyone with half-a-brain, that apart from my skip-hopping shenanigans, it appeared I was distressed about something or other.

In other words, no-one could not have imagined why anyone should have wanted to carry on the way I did, without something being wrong! Because by no stretch of the imagination could it have been classed as normal behaviour.

In fact, those awkward movements would I imagine, remind a person of what they would often see when visiting fair-grounds, rugby matches and so forth, for they weren't too dissimilar to when we humans do when we are made to wait impatiently for it to be our turn to go into one of those new outside cubicles that has Lads & Lassies painted on its sliding bolt doors.

Did I just mention the word normal? Well that word could have been open to all sorts of interpretations; for these days we all know that abnormal behaviour is widely accepted as being normal by many, don't we?

So regardless of whatever is classed as normal these days, this might have still been an understatement had the finger been pointed at me. Reason being, I'd been continuously flicking my thick luxuriant braided hair away from my lovely face, with quick flicking movements of my head, as if attempting to swat a fly off a custard tart.

I had also been continually licking my full sensuous red lips at the same time! So had you observed any of these strange actions, you'd have obviously thought of them as being highly suspect, especially having seen they had been repeated far too often for them to have been classed as normal.

Being clearly agitated, my father's lovable old Negro housekeeper from Alabama would have said:

'Heh girl, dem signs you is giving out, are mighty big on de nervy scale, isn't they? Yes sir ma'am, they are as big as nervy as anything I've ever seen in my whole life.'

Of course 'dem signs', still wouldn't have given anyone any real clue as to what had really been causing me to have these emotions. Emotions which you felt only members of my family, or close friends, might have known what had been going on in this pretty head of mine; having known my large Sophie Loren blue eyes, had rarely shown anyone anything that was troubling me.

Ah ha, I heard you say. 'So in normal circumstances the people who know you, might have thought, looking upon your determined face; that at any other time you might not have been susceptible to this or any other type of emotion, and have dealt with this, or any other problem, without any fuss or bother at all. And by that, I mean it would have definitely been kicked straight into my mental-waste-bin, having been regarded as far too trivial to have ever been bothered about.'

In suppose in normal circumstances this may have been true, however there are also times, unfortunately, when even for such a determined young lady as myself, having an emotion such as this, could be one too many. In other words, I should have tried not to have been overly concerned over what some people might have thought this emotion had been about.

What I mean is, that I have heard that the word 'Worry' would have been a particular favourite for people to have used, cos people do worry about their not paying un-paid bills and so forth. I'd also heard that word was especially used when people have been concerned about their wives or husbands infidelities, or their kids playing truant, or been anxious over someone's health, or their own, etcetera, etcetera, ad infinitum.

Actually, my own 'worry', had been in retrospect, very unfair not to have been a touch more thoughtful or kinder towards me. What I mean is, it could have at least had the

ROBERT H FELLOWS

balls to confront me on one of my better days, say on one of my—'oh that's far too trivial to be bothered about'—days. Instead of which, it had arrived completely un-announced, and totally un-expected, whilst I'd been stood in this grubby-looking hallway overlooking a small man's shoulder doing something nice to my office door.

And then had you observed my hair-swishing, lip-biting, and skip-hopping, you might have felt that even this emotion was now vulnerable, having thought this 'worry', could very soon be replaced by, oh, surely not, no please don't say . . .' Panic!

CHAPTER 13

Strange thing was that I had vaguely known I was having a bad time of it in the hallway, and remembered my problem had started with seeing my name being scripted onto a new thick shatter-proof glass panelled door that was directly in front of me.

It must have been the horrible realization that I had needed to decide on making that all important decision in my life, other than which car to buy, dress, or the house maybe, as I had never needed to take any unnecessary risks that I hadn't wanted to before.

However risk-taking was by its very nature, my nature. It was taking those un-necessary risks, or facing the unknown that I liked, for that had always given me what I called 'an adrenalin rush' whenever I got myself involved with anything that smacked of being risky with possible consequences; all small time of course.

Sometime later, I'd freely admit to a few close friends, that I had felt almost compelled to stand and watch whatever a man was doing, during those emotional and fraught moments, as I had watched him paint my name on to the new door. I'd say: 'It was like I'd been put in a trance, and been held very tightly by two very strong hands, and being forced to look at whatever the man was doing,' I told them, 'and my antics, for want of a better word, had started then when I thought that this man had been the cause of putting

❦ 47 ❦

me into a trance like state, and then induced me into doing that shoe shuffle movement that I'd been doing, in what you might call 'a state of limbo'.

So it had been whilst I'd been in that state of limbo, that the roads and other thoughts had all been racing through my mind whilst I'd been stood behind the man, my having wondered how on earth could this man have ever known what letters to paint on my door. And more disturbing, how had he even known what my new career was going to be, or my name, when no-one else, other than Stewart and Lynda had known?

And then I had wondered if perhaps something much more sinister was involved? For example, I'd wondered why a little man in dirty red paint covered overalls, who was clutching a pallet in his left hand, and two different paint brushes, should have always been continually dip, dip, dipping these brushes from a paint pot to a pallet, with the brush going up and down, up and down, before quickly transferring the brush with paint onto my new glass panelled door if it wasn't?

Maybe all that dip, dip, dipping, and all that upping and downing, had been to frighten me, I'd been thinking, and making beautiful letters was his way, his method, of trying to hypnotize me, otherwise why on earth should he have wanted to be doing that, if that wasn't it?

So now depending on whether you're interested in my state of mind or not, then suffice to say that weird feeling was as if I'd been deliberately and quietly drawn further and further into a lion's den, just like I had read in the bible that Daniel had been. I had imagined that we'd both known that we had very little time to work out how to escape from our 'problem', having known if we didn't think of something, and quickly, then that would meant . . . what . . . my being eaten by hungry lions, and my end!

All of this, and other things, had been going around in my head whilst I'd been stood in the hallway, which I now find difficult to explain, except it was possible that all these weird things going around in my head had meant I'd been unstable, off my head, sort of brain-washed, been in that hypnotic state of limbo during the time I'd been watching him continuously repeating the same motion, again and again.

Having had that problem to get over, and other things, I had also realized after having a horrible tight-feeling in my stomach, it was imperative for me to get all of these nasty emotions, feelings, back under-control.

To my credit, because I had been trying so desperately to do precisely that, and because it had been such a mental struggle, that might have been the reason that had caused me to have made those curious body movements, which surely must have put older people in mind of the bad old days in America, had they seen it.

*   *   *

The story goes that during the Depression years in the good old US of A, my soft-shoe shuffle swaying movement would have reminded them of what people may have seen many, many, times on dance floors all over America, had they lived there. Couples who'd been so anxious to earn a 'dollar or two' for food, being poor, they would have shuffled around a dance floor for hour upon hour, sometimes for days at a time, in front of paying jeering audiences, just to earn the 'winner takes all' money prize!

The 'audience' would have seen all of these couples who had needed to keep standing to win the prize whilst they danced, would have become so desperately tired, they'd have needed to hold on to each other, just to stop themselves from falling to the ground, and then been disqualified, leaving the others to continue on, still shuffling aimlessly around the floor to the sounds of big band music, or even to Dixie to often speed them and their tiredness up, so they'd had needed to desperately hold on to their partner, and each other, to have finally stood a chance to be last man standing and to obtain the prize.

People can be so cruel to each other—for sport or otherwise!

CHAPTER 14

O f course that prize wasn't the reason why I'd been constantly transferring my weight from one very shapely leg onto the other, and then had repeated the same movement over and over again, so it had appeared as if I too had been paying my own special tribute to those bygone dancers, and had also needed to overcome my gremlins to take the winners prize!

Looking at it another way, the problem I'd had in the hallway, hypothetically speaking, had been my mind being parked in a scruffy looking lay-by on one of those new wide dual carriage-ways that were suddenly beginning to appear everywhere in our countryside, and I'd been staring up at a large multi-road sign that may have suggested to anyone that to have driven on any of those roads, they'd have then be taken to wonderful exciting places; to unknown adventures, and yet sub-consciously knowing that any of those roads could have also take me to places that were fraught with danger.

So even in my trance-like state, I'd not been so naïve to not know that from time to time I would have to travel on what might have looked to be a safe-road, might yet turn out to be a very dangerous road indeed.

Again hypothetically speaking, I'd needed to do as Winston Churchill might have done when telling the troops what should be done before going into battle. Which was to stand up straight; be square shouldered, be prepared, and most of all, to have looked the enemy straight in the eye, and then have faced all of the dangers that were going to be thrown at them with guts, with determination; and with enough bull dog tenacity to become a hero.

And the same would now apply to me if I were to go ahead with being a new PI as a profession.

Of course I had also thought that I might need to at some time, turn onto some bum-numbing bouncy road, which could be called 'High Risk', or 'Am I just being plain Stupid road', which had stunning landscapes, fancy restaurants, combined with deceit. Or be made to face up to any amount of traumas and problems having taken another kind of up and down roads, that would ultimately finish up as being a dead-end road, going no-where.

So I must have been mulling over whether I'd actually wanted to take any of those roads in the hallway, having told myself that any one of those roads could lead to my downfall, and should have, as a warning, really be named 'Danger ahead' or 'Highly Dangerous' road.

Not knowing of my hallway dramatics, I had of course also been wondering whether I should go on living the easier life by choosing one of the much safer C-roads that would have also been more pleasing to the eye, and then put off any thought of being a PI altogether, even knowing they would have been a completely safe and unexciting road to continue my life on.

So in the hallway, the facts were whether I should, or should not, get involved with something that would have not have been preferable to continuing on with the easy-life that I'd known for the past twenty two years, or should face up to, forced myself even, into wanting any amount of traumas and obstacles, even danger, and to take any of the potentially more dangerous roads that could be the life of a PI.

So now, had you not already guessed it, was why my time in the hallway had been so difficult for me; for there'd been so many emotions, so many weird imaginings to control, and I had so many concerns to become unconcerned about, whilst stood in the hallway going through that state of limbo nothingness, as each one of them had been flowing around and around in my head.

I had in the hallway, been deciding, here and now, whether I wanted to have a life at doing something which I'd always wanted to do for a large slice of my life, being a sleuth, or not.

CHAPTER 15

Days later, I'd admit to Stewart, that the little man did make me feel nervous about myself. I told him that whilst I'd been observing the little man completed every letter, I'd been thinking to myself, maybe it was possible that this little man had been able to read my thoughts, and emotions! After all, he was putting my name on the glass panel!

I told him 'then what he'd scripted, had brought home to me the seriousness of what I was getting myself into, and that had been a huge emotional barrier I had needed to climb through, to have to then make that an all-important yes or no decision.'

That 'important decision' had been I'd told him, much more important than my deciding which glass panelled door I will buy, having spent a long time on selecting, to tell everyone what my choice of career was going to be.

I told him that because of my fears, and seeing my name being put on the door, I'd nearly given up on my dream, which would have been un-thinkable, and it was only because I'd always felt somehow committed to becoming a Private Investigator, that had pulled me through that bad time, and now that horrible experience will hopefully, have given me more inner strength and belief in myself.

THE LADY DETECTIVE

*　　*　　*

Later, in bed, having again realized what was due to happen on Monday might also have been one of the reasons for what had happened to me in the hallway.

During the past weeks, having wondered many, many, times, had my life been all about preparing me for Monday onwards, that might have been the reason for my becoming over-excited, knowing what was soon to happen in my life.

I suppose now, having looked back to when as a little girl of eleven years old, I had made a decision, a futuristic decision, as to what that little girl had most wanted to do when she had grown up to be a big girl, and now that little girl has become a big girl, you better believe it, and knowing I was now about to make that childish dream become a reality, this must have seemed like I had been given a brand new toy to play with—though never a doll—and having this brand new toy, (meaning the business) in my grasp, had made me feel like I was that silly little girl again.

So maybe, in the hallway, with my mind working over-time, it was all due to my being far to over-excited, and just a little frightened what the future would now be for me, had I been completely honest with myself, and not some mumbo-jumbo stuff about roads or magic.

*　　*　　*

Whilst I'd been lying in my bed, I'd also reflected back on my life that had up to tonight, been sprinkled with just a little adventure, a little excitement, and certainly no worries. So I really had no good reason to being extremely apprehensive.

Thinking back on the scripting man and his scalp, might now send me to sleep, thinking less of the little man as being a sort of Anti-Christ, when in fact he was just a harmless looking, plump faced, balding man, who even had combed down long wisps of his hair in such a way as to attempt anyone discovering the sparser areas of his shiny scalp.

However it was now this man's scalp that I found most interesting—which I'll now tell you about.

So do you know, that by looking down on a person's scalp, let's say your partner; your best friend; or boss, that a fact that many of you may, or may not be aware of, was that you can actually learn more about that person by looking at their scalp from above, than you could ever hope to learn of them just by studying their faces, eyes, or reading their hands!

For example, my having previously described the little man as being plump-faced, I could by looking down at his scalp, now see that his two face cheeks were wider than his forehead. And what was as interesting, he'd also had two very large pointed ears, very much like those of a pixie, both of which he'd also attempting to cover over with long strands of his hair.

Then at the back of his long-pointed skull, there was an area that is very much overlooked, and that is commonly known to be a double crown, which you can always tell, cos around that region of his head, the hairs stand up straight and true, which I doubt even a skilled barber who knew a thing or two about what he was doing, would have been unable to have helped the little man control!

So the result of my quick observation was that I now knew the man to be a vain man—because of his trying to cover over his pointy ears and bald patch with long strands of brown, going on white, hair. And then with his having a double-crown, and having wider cheeks than his fore-head, that had also told me that he was lucky in life. Yet I knew both could also possible mean that he was a deep thinking man, an introverted man, even though he was outwardly jovial.

As for his pointy skull and ears, well that could only mean one thing; that in some small way, his by-gone relations had obviously been related to the pixie family. So once again, he'll be known as a lucky person!

So now had you asked me how was it possible for me to have obtained all that knowledge just by looking at a person's scalp, rather than directly at his face or his hands, then I will have to admit . . . you don't, cos I'm joking, and thought it would be better to tell you this than my counting sheep!

So for now, I will bid you all goodnight, sleep well, and I'll see you all again bright and early tomorrow morning! Good-night!

CHAPTER 16

I suppose now would be as good a time as any, to tell you that the little man had not scripted my full name, which is Lady Jessica Constance Anna-Bella Felliosi. Anyway this Jessica is twenty two years of age, unmarried, and is going to be a sleuth . . . a Private Investigator—no less!

Goodness me, that all sounds as if I was introducing myself to Hughie Green, who was a TV presenter on one of my favourite programs, Opportunity Knocks, and A Star is Born.

Looking back for a moment on why some of you may have thought I had so 'foolishly' quit Law, well I need to tell you that it hadn't been because I had been lagging behind the others in class, or because it was due to my probable getting the proverbial push, because it was nothing like that. In fact, not once during the eighteen months I'd been studying law, had I not come out best of my class when it came to taking tests, or exams.

In other words, I really had been way ahead of all the other 'would be' lawyers when it came down to what is commonly known as the 'brains box department'.

So there you are, I'd always been the brightest star in a dull-night-sky you might say; so my resigning, quitting, giving up, was not because I'd been dumber than the others, it really was because I had needed to change my life style, and wanting to put extra pace into it.

THE LADY DETECTIVE

In fact for some time now, I'd wanted this, for I really had begun to regard my life as being very droll indeed, as being so far, a stroll in the park, and now what I wanted, needed, was to become a crime buster of criminals, a Private Investigator extraordinaire, a solver of dastardly crimes, and that meant to spice up my life, my not wanting to be a defence lawyer. I no longer wanted to keep criminals out of jail, or get them released, or have known when they'd pleaded Not Guilty, to have suspected they'd been guilty as hell, for I now wanted to put all criminals into jail, and no longer be a lawyer of any description.

If the truth was known, I never had wanted my name to have ever been associated with my having got some sleazebag of a client released from custody, let off the hook, exonerated, for a crime they had committed, on a pretence that I was only—hold it—*competently doing my job.*

In fact my thoughts on that are, that any lawyer who defends a prisoner on a Not Guilty plea, having known they were a complete sleazebag when he suggested for his client to plead 'not guilty', knowing they would re-offend again, and again, until they were caught . . . again, having got them released from charges, or from prison on a crummy technical fault, he would himself be a detriment, and even be a danger to the society in general, for all lawyers should feel obligated to getting all sleazebags locked up, and remain in prison, and if they didn't, they should themselves be prosecuted and locked away for 'being a menace' to the society. My opinion obviously!

❖ 59 ❖

CHAPTER 17

FRIENDS

My friends and I would often speak of politicians who had no more idea of running the country, than their passing a 11+ exam even with their having needed a white collar worker to advise them on their spelling. Although it appears that all are quick-witted enough to exploit, and hold out their hands, like some poor urchin in one of Dickens' novels, for anything that was free.

Which will of course include, 'extra' expenses, entertainment, travel, and so forth, which is strikingly similar to lawyers, who may even charge you for a staple—if used!

Well this night, my friends and I had all been sat around Stewart's town apartment, having settled back with a glass of something that does you good, having already shared and eaten three extra-large pizza's, and two extra-large side salads, that Bruce and Jenny had collected from Donatella's, a recently opened Italian takeaway.

'I must admit I like that idea, Jess,' Jenny had said to me, 'you saying that a life sentence should be just as it says, nothing more or less.' She enthused. 'Yes I like that idea a

❖ 60 ❖

lot!' And smiling, she started to clap her hands gently at the finger tips, a mannerism she'd always had from way back to a child, whenever she was pleased with herself, or something.

Bruce sighed loudly. 'You sound as if you would have liked to have given them a touch more than a life sentence if you could have . . . you hard embittered women you!'

'My motto, darling, is, let's keeps things simple! Besides, serving the sentence they've been given in court, will tell everyone exactly what we can all expect if any of us don't keep inside the Law. Don't you think?' Jenny asked.

Bruce nodded; 'I suppose simple changes like that would give our creaking penal system some needed uniformity, for even the sentencing is all over the place!

Hearing that, Lynda was suddenly struck with another thought from the another night's chatting. 'Jess, do you remember saying that if all laws went back to its original form, now if there'd been no more defence lawyers, or appealing against a jail sentence, then the beauty of that idea would mean it will be pay-back time for all overcharging Barristers and lawyers, would it not, because now we'd have no use for them, therefore they wouldn't then be able to charge us extortionate fees any more—would they?' We both giggled whilst looking at Bruce' face to see if he had taken offence

No worries, he was smiling as he said, 'I do believe you are implying, that from then on, we lawyers will not then be able to make small fortunes from you lot any more, eh?'

'Well I suppose you will have your so called 'lost causes' to fall back on, eh darling,' Jenny suggested, 'which you have mentioned is costing the tax payer loads of dosh?'

Bruce laughed 'Oh yes, now that's another case of our screwing up the legal system which is costing the tax payer loads of money!'

We knew, that he knew, that he was a jolly good Barrister. Brilliant I've heard, who made an extremely good living on lost causes, meaning people's rights, by his pulling apart the laws to help put-on-upon people, particularly immigrants have a fair hearing.

Now he added. 'Surely you're not saying that we poor Lawyers can no longer get some gullible Home Secretary to again change a Law of the land willy-nilly, just to please us are you?' He then pretended to sulk. 'If so, I'd say that's a bit steep, don't you think?'

With a sweep of her hand, and then pointing around the room at us all, Jenny continued. 'That's right pal. We're all advocating a-did-you or did-you-not system.'

Bruce then nodded, before saying. 'Ok, so if I have heard you correctly, you are advocating we have a system that has no defence lawyers, no more appeals, or reprieves for a prisoner, and no more time off for good behaviour . . . oh, and you are also suggesting that a life sentence is to be a life sentence.'

He paused, and making his bottom lip quiver, he continued. 'Although all that is completely daft, I do agree that standardizing sentences, would mean huge savings to the Tax payer, but unfortunately it would also mean much poorer Barristers. Boo ho.'

Once we'd all finished with making statements like: 'Don't you worry Bruce, we'll all chip in a quid or two for you'—Stewart, who in the real world, was a Detective Chief Inspector, having known the most about real crime and criminals, then added. 'Well ladies, it'll certainly make my job a lot easier with a system like that!'

Jenny Withers nee Dingle, who in reality was the loving proud wife of Bruce, winked at me, and not looking towards her husband said. 'As you say Jess, it'll certainly put paid to some Barristers from getting fat fee's to defend cases . . . who shall remain anonymous, that are . . . shall we say, 'iffy' to start with, particularly with cases involving religion, or other debatable issues, such as manner of dress, immigration and so forth.' Smiling she added. 'Did you know there are Barristers who make a jolly good living from those less fortunate than us?'

Bruce laughed good-humouredly at his wife, knowing all the while his wife had been referring to him, as we all

THE LADY DETECTIVE

did, because among other things, Bruce did make a highly lucrative living in defending the rights of the immigrant in all of its various shapes and forms. He now presence growled.

'Is that so, Mrs whoever you are? Well madam, let me inform you that this very handsome and offended Barrister, has always said that our Divorce laws need to be downgraded somewhat in its complexity; and if by doing so, that'll make it much easier for a man to get a divorce against highly disillusioned wives, then I'm all for it!' He grinned. 'Now as a down-trodden husband, and a tax payer, I think that idea will certainly save the husband, and the tax-payer, a lot of money, would it not?'

'Touché darling' his wife had said with a side-glance smile towards her husband.

Jenny asked, looking around her. 'Ok, call me thick, call me stupid, but can someone please tell me what this Community Service thingy is all about that they are thinking of introducing for the criminals, because I for one, wouldn't want to see anyone walking around with a stamp on their head, doing the C service!' She looked at each of us before saying. 'I mean it'll be like seeing someone going around the streets wearing a chain and collar around their neck, like in those American movies? Alternatively, it'll look horrid if the law got them wearing a bright yellow C-shirt or jacket to tell us, the good people, that they are bad un's amongst us.'

She did like to have 'a go'—at times, did our Jen, although she had a point, because the 'dippy ones' had also been discussing confining criminals in their own home, and having the small offenders, working in the community—for no wages—as a punishment.

'Ah as you asked us to call you thick and stupid, Jenny,' Bruce chuckled, 'I will say this, thick and stupid, you won't ever see them wearing a C—shirt or C-jacket, because the Court, probably with the Government's approval, will have thought it might embarrass the little darlings if they were made to wear anything that would say they were . . . criminals. Civil rights and all that palaver, you know!'

❉ 63 ❉

Stewart had then moaned as if to say, that should never be.

*   *   *

Then to change the subject I said: 'So what's with this European Common Market thingy that the politicians are considering we join? Because, with France, Germany and Italy already in it, if we do join up, I'll give it no more than five years before you'll hear rumbles of total disharmony setting in.' Smiling I then added. 'And I further predict that in the longer term, say fifty years or less, that this agreement will all fall apart in the end, it having been all a complete waste of time, and money.'

'And of course the money that it's supposed to cost us to join is enormous, so I hear.' Lynda added.

'Millions upon millions I've heard,' Bruce added, 'plus it'll cost us a further fortune each year just to pay the wages and expenses of our having the new English-European MP's, who a friend has told me, are to be filled by the useless, or discarded English politicians. And I heard, they will also have much higher expenses allowance than their English counterparts, and because they'll be living away from home, they'll be able to demand higher wages of course.'

'Oh poor dear's, I suppose that means that they may have to learn a foreign language?' said his wife, bowing her head in mock humility, and smiled wickedly.

Stewart with a snort retorted. 'They'll have interpreters doing that I would think. Although you have forgotten to add, that as well as their higher wages, I hear they may have to build for them luxury living quarters, houses, villas or whatever else thrown in, and all of this is to be paid for by us, the gullible English public.'

'So how many will be needed as Euro MP's?' enquired Lynda.

'A hundred I've heard,' said Bruce 'could be less.'

'Heaven knows, I can't see any sense to it me-self.'
Stewart exclaimed. 'I suppose we could always get rid of
some of them over here, after all we've still got our County
and District councils to make a mess of things, and they tend
to always override anything the MP's say anyway!'

'Well I'm sure that European lawyers, and I intend to
be one, will be getting similar opportunities to justify their
existence,' Bruce added with a grin. 'And they'll probably
be getting even more money than our over-the-top charging
Barristers or lawyers get over here when it happens.'

Draining his glass of malt whisky, Stewart quickly
added. 'More importantly, you must not forget that if our
English politicians weren't able to make, or amend our laws
quite so easily any more, that could effectively put paid to
at least halve the MP's, don't you think? After all, voting in
the Commons on this or that, is all that half of them ever do
anyway—if you get my gist?'

After a few nods of agreement from around the room,
Lynda had with a chuckle said. 'Now that would be a pleasing
thought, particularly if those among them were first to go
who hadn't had one sensible idea. since their being voted
in as a Member of Parliament. So yes, let's get rid of all the
dry-wood MP's, and if we can do that, then Euro MP's would
certainly get my vote!'

'And mine' giggled Lynda

Stewart added. 'So if we got rid of say four of the six-
hundred and fifty so called English MP's, because they had
made little or no contribution to the Country's affairs that
would make any difference, that will in terms of money, be a
real saving had we less MP's, meaning astronomical savings.
And then the Country might then get a better Government
than we have been getting, with less Party conflictions!'

'Trouble with our MP's, is that having been voted in by
a load of people who haven't a clue about who, or what, they
are voting for; just as long as it's for the same party that their
parents, grand-parents, have always voted for, they wouldn't
mind having less MP's, having probably forgotten a month or

so after the election, whether it had been a man, or a woman, they'd voted for anyway,' teased Lynda.

'Nasty!' I said looking at her. 'Talking of which, and going slightly off the point; it's also my opinion that most lawyers must have criminal tendencies in their overall make-up! Present company excluded of course; because how on earth can they possibly present their extortionate charges to a client for services rendered, without showing any apparent signs of embarrassment, or humility? Surely that must mean they have a con-man attitude, or have no feelings at all for their fellow man, or woman, other than wanting their money!'

'Hear, hear,' Bruce said clapping his hands, who for a man in his early thirties, was already a known and highly respected Barrister. 'I for one, will always agree they always need something for their services, money, and so I will apologise right now for the silver cutlery I'm going to steal to-night for any advice I may have given tonight, and call it attendance money, shall we?' We all laughed, having thought his words amusing.

'It's certainly true there is an art in keeping a straight face when needed, and the similarities between lawyers, politicians, and criminals, are both alarming, and somewhat frightening to see. And as strange as this may seem, the criminal, and the politician, also act and look very similar when they are being interviewed, or when confronted with evidence to disprove what they had said. And I should know, being that I'm face to face with different kinds of criminals on a day-to-day basis, as you are Bruce,' said Stewart smiling at Bruce, 'even before you're going to court!' He then smiled and gave my leg a squeeze.

'Oh, very funny old man, very funny!' Bruce mumbled, 'but unfortunately also very true of course!'

We'd all laughed again; the wine making the mood of the evening, extremely convivial and pleasantly warming.

*　　*　　*

THE LADY DETECTIVE

I'd had similar discussions with my father, who would often rant on about anything to do with politics, or law, and probably women and religion as well with his cronies at the club.

Take the Police for instance; now don't go funny and say you don't want them! Well their problem will always be our oh so clever politicians, who wanting to win votes, and keep in with the crowd, being us, must be always seen to be doing, especially on voting days. So what do they do? They gave us promises to bring down crime statistics, and then give the poor old 'Rozzers' more work to cope with than was necessary by voting in new laws.

They'd even known that the rozzers already had, with scant praise I might add, and being under-manned as they were, had valiantly tried to clean up the streets after they'd been dirtied by all the low-life' in our society, who'd then been treated, for humanitarian reasons, as if they'd been the wronged person who had faced charges in any courtroom!

My father, bless his cotton socks, could be often heard snarling in his study, saying to the TV 'Why don't the 'dippy ones', meaning the politicians, 'bring back some of the old ways, eh? That'll sort the buggers out.' He meant the criminals.

A man of few words was my father when he wanted to be—though he'd been known to 'have had a go', meaning a face to face confrontation with the 'dippy ones' on TV programs or elsewhere, even when he'd not had a few stiff brandies down his throat.

I have also heard him occasionally say, perhaps it was the same when he was at his club with his pals, when they'd been discussing; debating; arguing, about how nice it'll be to change the punishment system back to the old days; for he'd then be particularly crude, and be heard to say 'Stuff the buggers', meaning do away with the worst re-offending criminals of course, and add, 'that'll be less mouths to feed!'

Do you know, there have been times when he'd be peacefully sitting, listening to the radio or TV news, when

❦ 67 ❦

he'd suddenly stand up and start to rave, either at me, or anyone else, in his strong cultured voice about the, 'Bloody stupid laws allowing another low-life to be released from prison on a technicality.'

He'd then look at me and grin, his lovely eyes showing that marvellous mischievous twinkle that I've always loved, before he added. 'Probably they got the bugger off because they hadn't allowed him, or her, to cut their toe-nails, or go for a wee or something just as ruddy stupid.'

He said he wouldn't have any problem with our country sharing any penal colonies with other countries, say in Alaska, or the North or South Pole, or even the Gobi desert, especially for those criminals who'd been 'bang out of order' for murder and other serious crimes against their fellow man, or even criminals who couldn't, or didn't, want to be cured of their criminal tendencies.'

He said he'd like to above all, bring back the death-sentence for murderers, though not for crimes of passion. Dismemberment of the part which had been offended against, was also something that I knew was of special interest to him. Why? Because he'd told me 'The bible tells us an eye for an eye, so if a low-life wants to deliberately break someone's leg, or take someone's eye out, then the same should be done back to them.'

He'd laugh and add. 'Christianity isn't all-about believing in the good things we wish to hear from the Bible, it's also about our believing and doing the bad things it says we should do as well!' Then he'd added. 'Anyway if that was done, that'll make the blighters think the next time they want to harm someone, cos then the next time they're caught, they'd have known what their punishment would be, and so might never again consider to want to do anything bad like that . . . unless they're completely mental!'

My Father had also some strong views on general crime, mostly old fashioned of course! Like the time when he told me he'd like to re-introduce the use of stocks and the birch to the criminals,' and growled 'and start tougher sentencing again,

THE LADY DETECTIVE

particularly if our wishy-washy governments and the 'dippy ones' are always insisting on not imprisoning the buggers, or now wanting to stop the death sentence.'

He thought it might also be an idea to give out the names and addresses of the offender, just to embarrass them, and make sure everyone knew the crime they had committed. And when I said that could be totally unfair, he'd said. 'Not so sweetheart, because his family, the wife, the mother, or other members of the family, would have always known, or have had a fair inkling of what their old man, or sweet kids were up to, and had chosen to ignore, or do nothing about it.'

I'd said. 'So I suppose just for a bit of a fun, you would also like to go back in time, and show up the criminal in front of the public, by having people jeer at them in the stocks, probably under floodlights. In fact you would make it like an outing, and have it probably organised, say twice-weekly, at all soccer grounds, where you'd have sellers selling rotten fruit and eggs, and charge an admission fee!'

'Nothing wrong with that, or enterprise,' he said.

'You were definitely born into the wrong century father,' I told him, the Roman arena is for you,' but secretly I'd thought that I couldn't really find fault with some of his 'Modern days, means modern ideas'.

CHAPTER 18

MY OFFICE

Oh now for my reason for not setting up shop in a posh area, in a classier more up-market area of London. It was because I'd thought I'd prefer the down to earth vibrancy of this side of town to where I lived, that most of you would have thought of as not being conducive to attracting the more monied type of client, which it certainly had been.

Never-the-less, the area I had chosen, the West-end, was in fact famous going back for many centuries, and dare I say it, was infamous for its crime, not un-similar to the East-end, was better known for its night clubs, and for having numerous down-the-stairs bars, where strip joints had suddenly become so fashionable, that one local pub fairly close to my office—that will not be used by me I might add—had joined in the girly fun. Strictly to please their clientele of course!

The area also had its normal smatterings of sweet and paper shops, one or two normal corner shops, and a greengrocer. It had also two very dubious betting shops. There were also a new Indian, Chinese, and Turkish take-away, as they now call them.

THE LADY DETECTIVE

There were also two wet-fish shops, four butchers, that included one halal, and approximately one hundred yards away from my offices, there was a medium-sized shop that was calling itself a 'Super-Shop', that had stocked it seemed, almost everything and anything, including their own TV dinners, would you believe?

The shop also boasted under its roof, a meat and a fish counter, and had a fine range of vegetables and exotic fruits on display. It was only a convenience store, yet the idea I thought of having a range of goods in one shop, could catch on.

Bookshops, record shops, gift shops, and shoe-shops abounded, and with it being in the early seventies, everyone still hadn't got out of the habit, or skill, of not knitting their own jumpers and pull-overs, socks. So separate wool and ribbon shops still survived, but it was now becoming more fashionable to buy clothes off the peg, and they would soon be no more.

This was now then the coming age for fridges and freezers to be owned by the masses, that would do away with pantry's; so now shops and manufactures, could provide a better range of food, not only for the hot summer English months—hot being my little joke of course!—but also for the cold winter months.

This was also the time when people had starting to travel abroad on what they would later call Freddie Laker type sky-train 'bucket holidays'. This was to be the beginning of the airline and travel companies offering cheaper travel. I was also a time for more outrageous styles of music, and dress as started by Mary Quant with her shorter mini-skirts in the Sixties, also unheard of foreign car names, and then of course there was Harold Wilson and Edward Heath.

On a more sombre note, the sixties and seventies was also a time for the Cuban crisis, abolition of Capital punishment, and relaxing the laws on homosexuality, and our applying to join the new Common Market, soon to have different names like the European Economic Society—and then there was the Profumo affair.

It was an era for crap awful properties, or old houses being sold off cheaply. Derelict areas, particularly around London Docks, which had been previously bombed during the war, or were run down, were now high on the list of properties to buy for a new kind of entrepreneur, the con, and increased crime, all due to the Wilson Government backing, the 'entrepreneur' would buy up at 'knock down' prices, streets of houses, and then would as the phrase goes, literally 'knock 'em all down, and build them all up again'.

The game was, that in order to make a fortune from owning houses, the entrepreneur, would either hold on to them, and then when the time was right, sell them on years later for a way above buying price, or buy up the old houses, do them up a bit, and rent them out to the new wave of Commonwealth immigrants who were being allowed into the Country, mostly Caribbean, or other poor people, and packing them sometimes four or five or more to a room.

I have even heard of men doing night shift work, having bed rights during the day time . . . and visa-versa for the day workers at night. Unbelievable! Anyway Councils in their wisdom, that's a joke, had removed people from age old communities, and instead had put them into what was supposedly good quality high rise flats, some rising to even sixteen or more floors that had a lift which would for most of the time not be working, thus making, the older person, a prisoner in their own flat, and not knowing anyone. And they called that Progress!

Unfortunately, when the 'old' families who had lived in an area for generations who were now moved on by un-thoughtful Councils, worse still had been they'd forever been separated from each other which gave rise to the 'council estate's, and that in turn gave birth to more crime, whereas these extra criminals who'd have previously been living and be known in communities where everyone had known each other in their own 'manor', would have previously been

THE LADY DETECTIVE

sorted and controlled all its occupants without the Rozzers, policeman, being involved.

I personally know a little about these so called new-style entrepreneurs, because nearly all the Estate agencies, as they called them in this and other areas, had been under different names, mostly owned by my father, who it was said, had done it to 'make a killing'—if you know what that meant!

And finally, this was an area that had many, many, small businesses, mine being one of them of course; and having checked thru the local papers, and the new business telephone directory called Yellow Pages, it had seemed that I will be the only woman Private Investigator, in all of this bustling, lively, and very overcrowded neighbourhood, so with that in mind, it could only bode good things for me, couldn't it? If they could afford me! Joking!

Several weeks before I'd opened for business, Lynda, who you know now as my closest friend, had asked, 'Had it been a coincidence for you to have chosen an office in a building owned by your father', and 'did he in fact know you had taken one?'

The answer to that was yes and no. Yes, it wasn't a coincidence, as I'd always known who the office building belonged to. And no, because had my father known at the time that I had quit Law, and then taken an office in one of his buildings, he might have throttled me!

*　　*　　*

There were any number of different businesses in my business premises, and a varied lot they were too.

They ranged from one jolly old accountant man, to an import and an export business, a rug seller, both strangely enough on the same floor as myself; and various sales offices for various products, stuffy solicitors and accountants, and one very talkative new style travel agent—although the

❀ 73 ❀

offices on the ground and first floors, were stock brokers, assurance and insurance companies.

My own office was situated on the fifth floor, the top floor, which I'd particularly chosen, because of it having one large room. This room could be reached by using the stairs, all ninety-one of them—or you could use an old fashioned ornate metal cage lift that had sliding gate doors on two sides. So depending on which side of the building your office was on, front or back, you could get into the lift on one side, and get out the opposite side by using the opposite sliding gate. All very quant, and quite bizarre!

On my floor, known as 5A, which was at the back of the building, I shared the floor with six other businesses, with my offices being on the end furthest away from the lift. The floor layout, after getting out of the lift, was like an old fashioned T without the centre. There were three offices facing the lift, and two separate men's and women's amenities. Then making it a semi-courtyard shape, there'd been two more offices on either side of the hallway with a centre wall that separated us from them, being floor area B, which had the same layout as we had on A, making the two floor areas, A & B, into a square shape.

All the offices would total fifty-nine in all. Fourteen on each of the top four levels. Then add the three offices on the ground floor, and a further two amenity rooms, making the rest of the ground floor being the reception area and hallway, with an entrance of a revolving door, plus a door on each side of it.

The building itself had style and good looks, and having been built in the late 20's, had been lucky to have escaped being bombed in the second world war, so was now one of the grandest and most stylish office buildings in all the West-end, either owned by my father or not, and was up until now, one of the largest.

In fact my office were in this large spacious building, over eighty-fifty feet in length, and those on the sides and front of the building, only sixty feet. So you see the building was designed the way it was, to give it a strong feeling of space, which showed with its wide hallways, and large marble reception area, and yet it still retained a certain quietness in its style and thick walls.

A rule was that all offices were supposed to be locked up at night. Yet for further security, this grand five-floor building was kept safe at night by a sprightly old night-porter! Some hopes! Particularly now we are in an era where violence was now happening all over London!

CHAPTER 19

SUNDAY

Having had a really hot shower to liven me up; eaten two slices of toast, with chunky thick marmalade; and drunk two cups of strong tea, made all the stronger by using a two-cup James Aimer tea-bag; I was now ready to leave the warmth of my home. I wanted to arrive at my office, nice and early, and with it being early Sunday morning and before 8.30 am, I'd then drove through almost car-less streets.

Oh gosh, did I just think 'my office'? You know it was even good thinking of it.

Unfortunately, the day had turned out to be nasty, cold, and cheerless as an overnight stay would have been, had I been stuck in a tent sheltering from a snow blizzard on the North Pole. This had been slightly warmed by my being immediately greeted by the workmen with their cheery 'Good morning Jess's.'

The men had been chatting to each other whilst waiting for me to arrive, on how the Gunners or the Hammers, and Spurs, who were names of three top London soccer clubs

❧ 76 ❧

would you believe, had won or lost in yesterday's football games.

I had separately returned their greetings as I unlocked my new office door, having by now known all the workman by their Christian names, whilst knowing they'd now be fairly keen to get on with whatever jobs they'd had to get on with that day, to complete the work they'd been taken on to do. Then they had all complimented me on the door, whilst I was unlocking the door, by saying 'How great it looked with my name on it.'

Still partly frozen from by my experience with the weather, less than a half-hour before, the first thing I'd done after closing the door, was to switch on the heating that I'd had installed.

My mentioning the weather, truth was, from the moment I'd closed the front door on my warm and very cosy bungalow, and then stepped out into the open air, I had immediately been confronted with a cold blast of wind that would have had enough chill factor in it to have made a polar bear shudder.

Although not being satisfied with that, the cold wind had then proceeded to burrow right into and under my thick tweed overcoat, thru my thick sweater and underclothes, and finally, and without my permission I might add, had the audacity to burrow itself then even further into my warm flesh.

In seconds my poor old legs had been partly frozen by ye old Jack Frost wind, and having had all the blood vessels attacked so ferociously by the cold wind, I'd then given a real life like demonstration of how to walk like Frankenstein's monster, with my legs doing an exact copy of the monsters own stiff jerky leg movements, whilst I'd battled head-down and directly into a strong head wind to get to my car.

In fact, no-one could have not failed to have noticed as I struggle-walked, and not have imagined that Scott, the explorer, would not have walked something similar when he'd been on his way to conquering the North Pole; which in my case, was not so vastly different with my trying to get as quickly as possible to the cold-comfort of my car, having dreaded my being completely frozen to death before I got there!

So as the day approached midday, having now three hours later, spent the best part of the morning trying to warm myself up by drinking hot soups, and chocolate, from the vending machine, and refusing offers of 'cuddles' from the workman, I could now to be seen busily tarting and titivating up the offices, and generally making myself useful.

I'd hung up paintings, cleaned & polished dusty furniture, alphabetically arranged empty files into two new dark green four-draw filing cabinets, sharpened pencils, and it almost goes without saying, had made loads of non-vended tea for the workman.

When they'd at last at around 14.00 to 14.30 pm, begun to put the final, final finishing touches to their work of making this old office into these smart new offices, I had to admit that they really did look like they were the finished article, by being great looking.

The reception area and the two offices, having been timber built, were extremely pleasing to the eye, and having been wood stained, they looked friendly and warm—aided by the fact that I'd chosen to have clean looking cream-walls on which to hang the eight paintings I'd bought.

And finally, I'd put bits and pieces of brass here and there, and to stand on and enhance perfectly laid great-looking rusty-coloured Wilton pile carpet, was some great looking leather furniture, which had set everything off nicely.

So even though I was the only person whose opinion mattered on anything around here, I did think my offices were now looking exactly as I'd wanted them to look, for it now suited my style and taste, so I was pleased.

CHAPTER 20

I must admit that it had all been very much of a rush to complete everything just as planned on time—being by today of course.

I also planned to have, and then ordered, a new state of the ark, wooden panelled small telephone switchboard, two new Dictaphones, and these had been installed by a BT man, who would soon got everything working to perfection.

Also delivered was the Wilton pile carpet's for the three separate offices; office furniture and stationary. Also delivered, had been three, four drawer filing cabinets; some pictures for the walls, and so on. I'd even arranged to have local advertising and mailing leaflets done and sent out locally; and of course there had been the task of employing a sign writer, who you now know fully about, and of course—a secretary.

From day one, I'd been in the middle of all the mayhem that had been going on around me, when it seemed that everywhere you looked, had either been torn down, torn up, put in, moved, rubbed down, or painted.

I'd had electrical wires going everywhere to contend with, or trip over; and endless amounts of dust always in my throat and eyes from floorboards being rubbed down, wood being sawn, and etcetera.

And as there'd been a great deal of drilling and wood cutting, banging, on or knocking out over the course of the

❦ 79 ❦

twenty-four days. And there'd been the workman constantly moving back and forth, in and out of these offices during those weeks, carrying whatever tools, parts, or materials they'd needed to be brought in to finish the job—and I had to also put up with a fair amount of noise each day. And there'd also been various goods I ordered during that time that I needed, to be taken in and signed for, until gradually one job after another had been completed.

And now, just as I'd requested, after occasionally reviewing the style, and layout of my new offices, all this was now to my liking.

I had to also deal with a number of complaints from people in other offices, who'd not taken too kindly to the noise, but fortunately it had been men who had come to complain, and been sent away quite happy, having been made to see reason by my profusely apologising, and smiling at them.

CHAPTER 21

The new switchboard I'd installed the previous Friday, would at least make me feel, from Monday onwards, that I had some form of contact with the outside world, should no-one have cared to walk thru my brand new office door. Hoping that would not happen of course.

I had placed the switchboard cabinet, alongside a desk that I had especially built in a similar wood that would match the other items of furniture in the new reception area, and it did look very smart and proud looking as it now stood in its own wood stained cabinet.

Bert Trimmings—my lovely carpet man, had over the previous week, been an absolute darling with his returning a total of four times to complete his work, his having to wait until each area had been cleared before carpeting. Meaning, after the skirting boards were painted or the woodwork completed, or after the area had been finally cleared of the other workmen's tools and tables. He needed them to do this, so that he could lay down what was a very expensive, hardwearing carpet. He'd also been generally helpful to me, by doing an odd job here and there.

The carpet was first laid in my office, as befitting a proud new owner you might say. It had also been the first to be completed by the workmen. Bert had afterwards, made further visits to finish off in the other office, and reception

❧ 81 ❧

area, into which I'd installed the latest table-top free hot-drinks vending machine, called 'Mr Beverages'.

Duncan, the electrician, had also been very kind to me with his frequent visits; which I'd noticed, had become more frequent with the advent of Pasha arriving on the scene!

I know I shouldn't go on about it, but I really couldn't believe the transformation that a bunch of workman could have made to a once very drab office, and I'd needed to often pinch myself that it wasn't just a dream, and all of this, was very, very, real.

I suppose with my having had all the old woodwork ripped out and replaced with new, and then having that either varnished or painted, so now having had its final touch up, and gleaming brightly, it did look great.

I'd had the walls tastefully covered by an expensive and heavily embossed patterned wallpaper; that with the new leather furniture, had given the rooms a feeling of relaxation and repose, which Lynda would soon have definitely vouched for, seeing as she would soon be seen 'reposing' on the sofa.

The thick pile Wilton carpet that I'd chosen, was a cheerful rusty-red mixed with dashes of cream, so that combined with the walls, and brownish comfortable leather seating, would certainly help potential clients to relax before they started to relate to me what they had wanted me to do for them. At least I hoped it would. Although for some people, maybe posh, might also appear to be too much for them to take in, so they'd have taken one look, and put their cheque books back into their bag, or pocket again, after saying to themselves: "I can't afford to employ these people" and have walked right out again!

Pasha however, had endorsed my opinion that to have light-cream walls 'to offset the colouring of the carpet', also made the reception area warm, bright, and inviting.

In my own office, I'd added brass ornaments, and in all the rooms put up a number of tasteful landscape paintings, and even a flowerpot in the reception, with flowers, making the whole vision bright and cheerful. At least Lynda and

THE LADY DETECTIVE

Pasha would say they liked it, and that was important to know, even though as I'd previously said, it was only my opinion that mattered; but getting favourable comments like that, was still good.

Obviously, I'd been optimistic that this was going to be a very busy little office, and even had two telephone lines put in, and what's more, I had needed to beg BT to give me two decent telephone numbers; and then given, finally, West End—WE9990 and WE9991.

Now wasn't I the lucky one to have obtained such good telephone numbers you are no doubt thinking? Answer, not at all, for there is nothing lucky about having to give a bribe, a back-hander, in order to get what you want, or to even get a job done in time, if you get my drift. However I had in this instance, got what I wanted, without bribing anyone. Just a lot of hassle, and smiles!

That thought had made me wonder if I would need to, perhaps many times over, in order to get the results I needed, to bribe people. I thought that perhaps, I would need to sometimes do this had I wished to have a successful business! I suppose this really is about the time we live in, unfortunately.

◆ 83 ◆

CHAPTER 22

As I might have mentioned, in those few weeks, I'd also had to find the time to interview a dozen or more women applicants who'd answered my 'ad' for a post as 'Secretary Receptionist wanted, for an exciting new company', knowing that I would definitely be requiring the services of a bright; youngish; nice-looking woman for the job. And hoped I would find someone to fit the description!

The woman, who I hoped for, would be in charge of running the office, need to attend the reception desk, and be involved in all manner of other things. She'd need to be super-efficient, above average intelligence, and capable of running the front office reception in a tip-top manner, without being told by me what to do, or how to do it. As if I would have known what running an office would mean?

Also she would have to, when it was required, double up as my private secretary, so will be requiring adequate shorthand and typing skills. Mind you, I did have my doubts of ever finding a girl like that, maybe it would be someone half as efficient in all I required of them.

When I had interviewed all the applicants, It turned out that four of them had been young girls, one of them being as young as seventeen, who wouldn't have had any, or very little experience of anything in life, let alone her having made an excellent secretary, with good typing and short-hand skills, or for her to have known how to run an office on her own.

❦ 84 ❦

THE LADY DETECTIVE

So we will forget about those young applicants shall we? Even though all these applicants had un-fortunately, been a source of much amusement to a delighted bunch of workman, and much discomfort and blushes for all the ladies.

Three other applicants also hadn't any work-experience at all in Office Management. 'I can learn' they said, but had never stood a snowballs chance in hell of getting the job. Moreover, not one of them had shown me any character, or sense of humour.

Another four ladies had also looked so dowdy looking in their dress sense; they had never stood any chance of getting the job, either. In fact, one of the women had even smelt highly of body odour. Not nice.

In fact, there had also been one girl who had been so slow in thought, that I even had plenty of time to get myself up from my desk, make myself a cup of tea, and been had just about to return to my seat, when she began to answer the question I had put to her before getting up to make the drink! Crazy Huh!

There had also been one poor soul, who had such a bad lisp, that it sounded like gas had been escaping from her mouth. And there had been another, who I thought could have been a man in disguise!

So all in all, a really poor lot for my purposes, and what had made it even worse, was that having spent the best part of two days interviewing all these ladies, I still hadn't so far any hope of finding that suitable girl.

In fact, I had really begun to believe that the workman had been right with their thinking that I had put on these interviews only as some sort of a 'thank you' to show my appreciation for all the hard work they'd been putting in, even though I had been quick enough to tell them that these interviews were not for their benefit and amusement.

Yet I'd never been too sure whether they had really believed me or not, for here I might add, and without my knowledge at the time I might add, being told later, that nearly all of the applicants had been embarrassed by the workman

❀ 85 ❀

when they'd been waiting their turn to be interviewed by me, and that included the one who I would have sworn could have been a man!

I was to hear that nearly all of them having had to endure the workman's flighty comments, and wolfish looks, and would eventually walk out of these offices muttering various oaths at the workmen, who had laughed even more.

It appeared that most of the woman had in the reception area, gone through that kind of treatment similar to passing through the gauntlet, both before coming into my office, or on leaving it, or both, and had almost run out of the reception area and into the hallway if only to escape from the workers, and any further comments, except for this one girl, who had strangely enough been the thirteenth applicant, who I heard had given the men as good as she got, with a little bit more besides.

Whatever it was she'd said to them, I never did get to find out, but she seemed to have impressed them enough to have shut them up. Also, I could have sworn that I'd seen two of the workman, named Jeff and John, actually turning away from her looking red-faced and sheepish when I'd come out to greet her, because of her having obviously said something to them, cos they had then certainly seemed to be in a big hurry to get back to their work again. At least it had seemed that way to me.

So if I was to tell you, that I had chosen to employ this cheeky, bright, red-headed beautiful girl, as my new Receptionist Secretary, I doubt if that hadn't been much of a surprise to you. Also, what if I was to tell you that this young woman had brains in abundance, which was as far as I was concerned, of course a bonus!

Her full name was Patience, who I was soon to call Pasha; because she had later told me that she preferred Pasha to Patience, and with my also preferring my own abbreviated name, Jess, I knew what she meant!

CHAPTER 23

Pasha in fact was twenty-two years of age, 'going on twenty three,' she had told me, and was 'a very single lady at this moment in time', before she added, 'cos it's very hard these days to find a man with any substance in his bones,' meaning someone who was willing to work hard, and was go ahead'ish, which I'd not found not at all difficult to believe, knowing the people I knew.

Her academic credentials had also glowingly told me that she was not only a brainy University graduate with a degree in Philosophy, but also had a diploma in Secretarial studies: 'Just in case philosophy doesn't do me any good,' she'd said.

Besides her academic qualifications, Pasha was also the kind of character who you'd enjoy having around you, as she would almost definitely add much needed vitality, glamour, youth, and fun to the office . . . besides me of course.

Jeff and John, the two workmen who'd been put in their place by Pasha, had regardless, thought that she would—'definitely be the right one for the job.'—'A blooming' winner that one is,' one had said, and I for one would not have disagreed with them, cos I had also thought she was 'a blooming' winner'.

In fact, from the moment she had joined the business, all the workmen had immediately begun to fall over themselves, in attempting to do whatever she asked of them to do. So quickly realising this, I'd spoken to her about her getting the workman to do with the offices, what I had wanted to be done, which she had, and that had also been another big bonus for me, and time saving.

Following her interview, Pasha had started work the day after, which was on the Wednesday of this week before my grand opening. Then over the days that followed, had made us all see how much fun she really was, for not only did she have a wicked sense of humour, which could send myself and the men into spluttering, coughing, choking caricatures, she also proved herself to be a very clever mimic, so much so, sometimes I needed to hold onto my sides, less they should split, or became a laughing wreck.

With Pasha quite capable of changing her voice, posh voice included, or accent, at a drop of a hat, someone had suggested "that should we ever have an irate phone-caller on the line, she could make believe them into their thinking they'd been passed over to a more senior person." The thought being the caller might also have thought I also employed many staff.

Good point, although I fancied I could have done the same, to a lesser degree of course, had I needed that to happen. More fanciful thinking me thinks—eh!

CHAPTER 24

The reason why I had now returned to the hallway was my knowing it had still required a little more loving care & attention, even knowing that cleaners who being employed on a daily basis by the management of the building, to keep the hallways, stairs, and lifts clean and tidy, this also included some paying offices; though you would never have believed that they'd actually done anything, because the hallway seemed to look so filthy.

These daily cleaners were obviously of the attitude of saying to themselves: "I'll clean only what I can see needs cleaning, but as for the rest, well they can bloody forget about it." Hard work it would seem, was not for them, or me; so I'd arranged to have my own women cleaners to clean my offices, and my part of the hallway, so was just checking.

Of course, employing cleaners had been the easier part in setting up this business, for I had over the previous four weeks, employed electricians, decorators, carpenters—each one of them having come highly recommended by my friends, as good workers.

They had, with my ideas and planning, then done an excellent job on totally revamping, and restyling, what had been a shabby looking large room into two separate very plush offices. They had also added a smart and modern looking reception area in which to greet potential clients, who were going to walk through my new office door—I hoped.

❦ 89 ❦

From day one, there had actually been sometimes of up to eight different workmen, either coming or going, and all doing their bit.

First, there had been an office clearance firm, who had on my instructions completely cleared the room. They had pulled up filthy old carpets, broken up cobwebby built in cupboards, broken desks, chairs, skirting boards, and would have even ripped up the heavily stained wooden floor boards had I asked them, which I hadn't, and having now been rubbed down, and re-stained, was looking fabulous outside of the new carpet that I had laid.

Then once the large room had been cleaned of all obstructions; an electrician named Duncan, who Bruce had recommended, had come to do a complete re-wiring job, as well as his putting in extra wall-sockets, fancy light-fittings, and so on, had also promised to call in during the weeks, just to see if there might have also been any extra jobs that had needed doing; such as the jobs that I hadn't thought of at the beginning, alarms being one of them.

'I will do anything at all for you Miss Felliosi—anything.' He said with a wink! Another letch it would seem, but a good man and a jolly good worker! And he was still here even to-day, being the last day before all was finished.

CHAPTER 25

SUNDAY LUNCHTIME

And now returning to my office, having attended to this and that, I saw Lynda. Now she and I had been to the same kindergarten as children when we'd been three or four years of age, and she and I had afterwards always remained the 'bestest of chums'. In fact she was my 'bestest chum in the whole world'.

The reason why she was here, was that today she had promised to 'help me', and true to form, she'd turned up at 12.30 pm, when she had said she would arrive here at midday, twelve o'clock.

At first, she had swished into my new offices, and greeted me with an 'Oh I'm so tired after last night darling, truly I am!', and then had promptly sat on the sofa, and done nothing more!

Story is, that she had phoned me yesterday morning, and had then most graciously offered to help. She offered her services by saying: 'I will help you in any way I can, darling!' Then added, 'I will of course give you, my best friend, a hand by putting my own unique finishing touches to whatever work you've done so far!'

❦ 91 ❦

And instead of her 'helping me', or even asking what she might do to help, the little dear had within a minute of her arrival, immediately headed to my eight-foot new office sofa, and then lain down in one of her favoured positions, which was 'One of repose' as she liked to call it, and which I called 'her lazy cow pose'.

And so far I was right, as she had so far, it being now past 2.30 pm, had for the past two hours or so, stayed that way, bar her going to the toilet.

And as far as her showing me her 'own unique finishing touches', which had also gone completely un-noticed by me, or anybody else, our Lynda had done nothing at all to help.

However by her spreading her delightful form most elegantly on my new office sofa, as was her habit, the little love, had of course greatly distracted the workmen, although if truth was out, I suppose I really hadn't expected her to have done anything different from what her normal self would always do.

It was nevertheless good having her here, if only to hear whatever opinion she had on everything and anything we were doing, which was, coming from her, would always be a laugh, and be an added bonus to the proceedings you might say!

CHAPTER 26

Having placed one of a matching pair of sofas in my office, and the other had been placed in the reception area, along with three of eight matching armchairs. Three more armchairs were in the other office, and the remaining two in here with me, in my office.

The reason for my saying Lynda's opinion being a laugh, was for as far back as I can remember, any opinion coming from her on decor, dress sense, sensible shopping, etcetera, had always been shockingly wrong—hence my saying it was 'always a laugh!'

In other words, had Lynda been left to her own choices, and had it not been for friends or people helping, her house would now have looked a delightful colourful expensive mess—as would her choice of clothes.

Truth is, that Lynda had always needed to be advised, normally by me, because she really didn't have a clue about the furniture, colours, or even what clothes she ought, or ought not to buy that would have suited her. She would have even needed to be advised on what décor would be best to match the furniture she wanted to buy.

However to-day she did look lovely, even though she had at various times since her arrival, moaned about her aching head, inflicted last night she told me, 'from excessive drinking at the 'Rankers Club'.

❦ 93 ❦

Shall we also say she did 'look' the part of a wealthy individual, who had spent the better part of the last two hours in her 'repose' position, and who had not, I hasten to add, been helping me, before she had told me why 'she was so tired'.

'It's all because I've had an almost zero amount of sleep last night, darling, and that is all due to the rowdy lot that Brian brought back to my place. Thespians, you can keep them all!' She continued. 'He is working, as you probably know, at the famous Apollo Theatre, doing Theatre Management would you believe? Although he has told me, 'It's just for a laugh.'

Why it was 'just for a laugh', was because we both knew Brian, and as we both knew that would be true, for he did never need to work, being never short of money, so knew the job could only have meant one thing—it being an excuse for him to get closely acquainted with all of the lovely chorus girls that danced there.

Oh, and Brian had also been a member of our kindergarten crowd, and was a dear friend to us both.

So if you haven't already surmised it for yourself, then I must now tell you, that if our lovely Lynda could ever find an excuse to show anyone how lazy she was, she would, for this was regarded as normal by all of her closest friends, but to others, who hadn't known her since she was a child, like myself, they'd have thought of her, as most people did, as being brought up to be a very lazy and terribly spoilt person, or brat if you prefer. Much like myself, I suppose, and most of the people I hang out with.

So true to form, and certainly out of habit, she had allowed herself to have sunken even further back into the softness of the sofa, before saying.

'After last night's shenanigans, you must know . . . darling, why I am now so totally and absolutely exhausted, for had you been out with Brian and little me last night, you'd have known why I am now feeling so totally and utterly shattered.'

THE LADY DETECTIVE

It was certainly true that Lynda did give out those vibes, signals, to those people who didn't know her, and would also give them the impression of her not being a 'doing' sort of person—which she certainly wasn't.

Now I said with a pretence glare. 'Well . . . darling, I suppose if you can't find anything useful to do, then the least you can do is tastefully be sprawled out on the sofa, darling.'

'Not sprawled out Jess,' she replied, 'one must be in a state of tasteful repose.'

She then adjusted herself into a slightly more comfortable position on the sofa, and with an enormous sigh had continued. 'How on earth you can possibly keep up your torturous work-rate beats me. I mean, my just watching you walking back and forth at such a pace, is really so tiring . . . darling!'

'And I will continue to walk back and forth until the work is completed . . . darling!' I said with a smile.

She ignored me, and in an exhausted pretence voice had continued. 'How on earth you are able to keep this pace up throughout every morning and afternoon, and for all of three weeks, really astounds me! It really does!'

She then looked at me, and had with another sigh, then asked. 'So how do you do it Jess? I mean this is so very much like hard work, just watching all your comings and goings, and really is so very tiring on the eyes.'

The two workmen who'd been touching up the paintwork in the room, having heard her say this, had begun to laugh at her feeble rhetoric, and when I'd also laughed, this had been followed seconds later by Lynda laughing, so in moments, all four of us were having what you call, a jolly good belly laugh, and had all felt the better for it.

❧ 95 ❧

Chapter 27

A few moments now to tell you about our lovely Lynda, for she had ever since she was a child, our jovial, lovely Lynda, had always enjoyed her own kind of play-acting, which had always demanded people's attention. Although she'd always known that I was one of a few people who would more or less know when she was play-acting.

And now as if to emphasis this point of her being an actress, there were times even for me, when it would have been difficult to have known; for she could be so deceptively affective. Not this time though!

Now the actress gave a soft moan, and had then spread herself further along the sofa, and in a much feebler voice had said in what I believe to have been a Scot's accent—though it would have been hard to tell for certain, as it had been so bad.

She said: 'Would you mind getting me a wee drinky darling? Cos ye do know without having had a wee drop of something that does ye good, that I couldn't possibly attempt to do anymore hard work, having already worked so hard!'

Not believing my ears at her audacity, I'd nearly choked on hearing that, and the drama queen still hadn't finished, for she went on. 'So a wee dram will do very nicely lassie, and I'd be so grateful if ye oblige me, wouldn't mind doing that small thing, Jess.'

THE LADY DETECTIVE

She'd then in her normal voice, continued. 'Although with my mentioning Lassie, don't they say that the hair of the dog does the trick when you're feeling down?' She grinned 'After all, its lunch time-ish, isn't it?'

Now totally speechless, even knowing she was play-acting, I gestured towards the new oak drinks cabinet, 'Help yourself ye poor ol' thing.'

Of course I had known the drinks cabinet was well stocked with a good selection of alcoholic beverages for her to choose from, together with the latest model of an ice cabinet, that I had bought only yesterday. I'd known immediately as soon as the words had come tumbling out of my mouth of 'Help yourself ye poor old' thing', that it would have been a totally unproductive thing to have said, and duly waited for a reply from Lynda, which had been immediate.

By flapping her hand around like she was a distressed chicken on its back looking up at a sparrow hawk, she moaned. 'Oh common Jessica, you know I am far, far, too tired, to even attempt the smallest of chores. So please be an absolute sweetheart, and pour little me out a large drinky. I mean you do know, don't you darling, that I couldn't possibly do that for myself—I'm too tired!' Adding a pleasant—'Plea . . . se'

She'd then, as if to emphasise how very tired and weak she was, brushed the back of her left hand over her forehead as if wiping away imaginary perspiration, before she had with her right hand, taken from her cigarette case an gold ended Sobranie cigarette. Once she'd lit one up, and sucked in a lungful of smoke, then said in a lovely firm voice that sounded more like her normal down to earth self.

'Dam it Jess, I've just remembered that I've got a dam boring board meeting to go to this afternoon. On a Sunday would you believe?' She let out another long sigh. 'It's supposed to be something about my buying into, or my buying out another company. Something like that, though what the difference is, beats me!'

Just to look at Lynda as she was now, and to hear her talk like that, you could immediately understand why so

❦ 97 ❦

many business people had underrated her so often, and been totally fooled by her seemingly lazy couldn't care-less attitude that she would often portray.

However, our lovely Lynda was certainly not the lazy simpleton that she often made herself out to be. Far from it, though she did quite often play the slightly dim-witted, could not care-less, and oh so bored character that had become her spiders web, and because she played all the deadly parts so beautifully with perfection, her 'victims' would have been lured un-surprisingly into that web.

Of course they'd only have themselves to blame for her, as she would call it, 'kicking them into touch', after having been sucker punched out of business existence, or at least been relieved of something that was important to them, and having gambled and lost, had left our lovely Lynda, as always, in the centre of the stage, and in complete control.

Lynda had, when required to, continued to play both of those characters over the years with absolute perfection from a young age. Meaning she'd always been more than capable of playing the part of a beautiful girl who was slightly dim-witted and lazy, to being a smart cookie, and getting what she wanted, when she wanted.

She'd once told me. 'That under this dim-witted act, I'm a very smart cookie indeed—almost a witch.' Which was true, for underneath that façade was a very shrewd, very tough young woman, to do business with!

However in this instance, she knew that I knew her well enough not to be fooled by her play-acting—it being 'her style'.

CHAPTER 28

Four years before, Lynda had told me she intended to start a business on her nineteenth birthday, and so it had not come as a big surprise to me when during in the following three years, she'd already become known in the Communication systems business, as being a shrewd business woman.

Facts are, if she were to continue to make the same progress that she's made so far in three years, she'll become a respected person both nationally and internationally—as would her Company.

In short, her being totally dedicated; hard-working; shrewd; and clever, and by using her inventiveness and acting abilities, she will achieve an exalted status in her own business world, and her acting skills would have certainly played a large part in her becoming known as, 'A young woman going places.'

In fact I was also proud of her, and pleased for myself, for I'd been one of two people to have invested money into her company once she told me her original idea. So now I own a fair slice of her company, 30% to be exact, and with her mother as Chairman having 17%, and owning a chartered accountancy business that was extremely useful; that had left Lynda as Managing Director, and nobody's fool, holding the other 53% of the company's wealth, that would on the death of her mother, increase to 70%, there being a clause in the agreement, that if that should happen, then she'd inherit her mother's shares.

Ok, now having obliged her, by pouring out for her a large port and lemon, and handing it to her, together with a look that said "So you little madam, what did your last servant die of eh, exhaustion?' she had in turn, given me a little smile, and a small nod of thanks, I'd then left her to go out to the hallway, still elegantly posed in her favourite position on the sofa, now reading the latest Tattler magazine.

In the hallway, I stood in front of my new fancy office door, looking back into my new fancy offices, and began to grin, for you could say that I was pleased as Punch, chuffed to death, at what I saw.

It had been my intention to again polish the new brass door handles—and that would have also included my polishing my great looking sign-written door; for the second time that day. Instead I'd done neither, for I needed to go back into the office for a duster and tin of polish from the cleaning cupboard, having forgotten to take them out with me, probably because of my mind being temporarily all over the place—with excitement.

However, I'd been again proud to see my new door would tell everyone, who bothered to look at it, what my name and new occupation was going to be, with it saying: Jess Felliosi—Private Investigator.

CHAPTER 29

In fact I was still smiling with that inward pleasure that often comes from within yourself when you are happy, and had barely heard the old lift's ornamental metal sliding doors being opened and slid closed again from down below.

What had then followed was a whirling sound as the motors started up, followed by many squeaks and strange noises as the lift was finally sent on its way, towards its destination and barely heard the lift squeaking its way up to the 5th floor. It had then come to a stop at my floor, and there'd been a pinging sound, and more strange noises, almost as if the lift was saying it was satisfied that it had finally managed to reach its destination.

Then there had been one or two small screeching sounds as the sliding iron-gate facing towards this hallway was opened, which I'd heard and had alerted me, and I saw a man emerging into the hallway, a big man, a man who I could see was stood well over six foot tall, and was mighty big with it.

Though what had surprised me the most, was he was wearing clothes that looked as if they could have been worn by American mobsters during the Prohibition era all those years ago, being somewhere in the 1920's and 30's—when men like Al Capone, Bugs Moran, and Masseria, might have worn clothes similar to what this man was wearing.

❧ 101 ❧

In fact, this man could have been with his clothing, a reincarnated version of that Al Capone character had I not known better, having read somewhere that Al had been a small man in height, and was definitely dead, so this man could definitely not have been him, could he?

However because he did look like he was the complete article by looking the part, from his head to his shoes, this man could definitely have been any one of those bygone gangsters.

First off, he wore a floppy large brimmed hat that I believe was called a Homburg, or a Fedora, or something similar, which was roguishly tilted over his eyes. He then had on a long, fur-collared brown overcoat that covered his large frame almost to its entirety, with it nearly touching the floor. Then on his white shirt, that had a starched collar attached to it, he wore a wrap-around silk cravat. And to complete the spectacle, he sported a large clasp on the cravat, a bird of prey, an eagle maybe, with diamonds in place of the eyes. And on his large feet, I noticed he was wearing highly polished, brown tassel Italian styled shoes over ochre coloured socks.

This man did look extremely smart, dapper my father might have said, and I'd have to admit that no-one could have ever told him that he wasn't a sharp dresser, even though the man and his clothes had perhaps looked just a little too garish for my own taste. Never-the-less, the man and his clothes, had made me smile.

After stepping out from the lift and into the hallway, the man had at first stood looking to his left, and then to his right, before finally seeing little old me with a yellow duster in my hand, and then had turned towards me, and taking long leisurely slow steps as he approached me, I saw that his head had been pointing down to the floor, and sort of angled on its side.

Of course he might been eyeing up the linoleum, or the carpet, having noted the poor state of both; however it would have been a fair bet that from under the wide brim of that large hat, he'd only been looking at me.

THE LADY DETECTIVE

However, I could be sure, as I could only see the bottom half of his face, because of the wide brim of his hat, from his mouth to his chin to be exact, which as he approached me, had been enough for me to have seen he was smiling. Then having reached me, he'd stopped, which gave me another chance to re-estimate his height with his standing closer, so as he stood in front of me, I thought he'd be about 6'4" inches tall, rather than the measly six foot I had first assumed he was.

'Hi there,' he said, and then had touched the brim of his hat, and stood there all heavy and big looking, before finally he'd spoken again in a singy-songy voice, with an accent that sounded like he might have been American or Canadian, though I couldn't be sure which.

He was saying. 'Now I don't suppose you know of, or heard of the whereabouts of a well-known Rug company called Rugs and Tings, being around these parts, do you?'

Now it just so happened, that particular enquiry had not posed any problem at all for me, for I'd previously spent a little time memorizing most of the office-users in this building, and particularly those on this floor, having thought it would be best to know who my neighbours were, cos my thoughts had been, that you never know when you might have need of a firm that sells kitchen utensils, or even rugs and tings; so the answer to his request had been an easy one for me to answer, having known the name of the office on my floor.

I heard myself saying in my sweetest voice, obviously to impress, and also with a slight US of A twang, who the heck was I kidding with the accent, had said 'Now that's not a problem sir, it's just down the hallway, and it'll be one of the two offices around that corner.' I pointed towards the far end of the hallway.

He looked in the direction I'd pointed, and then slowly back towards me, and though I couldn't see his eyes, I'd known he was looking over my body contours in a nice sort of lecherous way, when he quietly spoke again.

❧ 103 ❧

'Well done to you young lady, and I'd say, whoever you are, you certainly do have good observation skills, which I assume you'll need in your job.' He pointed at my sign as I preened myself at his kind remark.

Then suddenly still facing my new sign, he'd surprised me by saying. 'I would definitely have to say that if you are part of that new management, then you would have certainly passed your observation exam with flying colours as far as I am concerned.' And continued 'So well done young lady, and carry on the good work.'

He sounded as if he might have been some military big wig inspecting a parade of soldiers, even though he still looked like he was a gangster.

Standing tall, he then nodded, and thumbing towards the top of the hallway, had said good-humouredly, with my still not being able to see his face. 'Incidentally young lady, it might come as an agreeable surprise, if I were to tell you that I also work down there.' He pointed up the hall again, and grinned at his having deceived me.

Not to be fooled I replied nonchalantly. 'I knew that.'

'How come?'

'Well because when you looked at the sign, you had said, 'part of that new management', which obviously meant having known it was new, that you've been here before. Am I right?'

'Touché young lady, now that's good, that's very good indeed. Though I might point out to you, that a new sign doesn't necessarily mean that someone new has arrived on the scene, cos it could have been renewed? And maybe a sign doesn't necessarily always say what they mean! However in this instance, you're right, and I'm sorry about my deceiving you. It was just my silly way of testing how good you were, or weren't. So no offence meant.'

'And no offence taken I'm sure,' I replied, 'Mr . . .' He had instead of giving me an answer, just smiled from under the large brim of his hat, when he said. 'And do you know what, young lady? One day I just might call upon you, let's say for some friendly advice.' He paused for a moment, then added. 'You know I really do hope that one day, I might personally be allowed to return a favour or two to you!'

He made to continue down the hallway, whilst I was mulling over what he must have been thinking about, before he said 'It'll also my personal wish that I'll see a great deal more of you in the very near future . . . now with you're being so close to me!'

Although his innuendoes now sounded slightly more lecherous than before, I gave him a nice No 7 smile. Now why do you think I did that, my giving him that top of the pile smiles? Careful, Jessica my girl.

And now he seemed to have been smiling at his own words, which had left me blushing at the audacity of this exciting man's remarks, even though as previously mentioned, I still hadn't been able to see his eyes, that hadn't stopped me from knowing that he'd still been looking with long approving glances, over my body. So for that I couldn't blame him I suppose, for that sight must have appeared to him, being he was a nice kind of letch, to have been sheer female perfection!

He then touched his down-turned long brim of his whatever you might call it, and turned in the direction of Rugs and Tings, before sauntering off down the hallway with slow long strides. And then as if he had known I would still be watching him, given me a small wave of his hand from around his head, before finally disappearing around the corner.

CHAPTER 30

Suddenly the hallway seemed to be a lot lighter, and felt less friendly than it had been a few moments before, and then going back into the office, I told Lynda all about the tall mysterious stranger I'd met in the hallway.

Then twenty-five or so minutes later, Lynda had, bless, eased herself off of the sofa, saying. 'Do you know . . . darling, that having had a little rest, I think I can now manage to do a little more work, although please try to understand that I really don't wish to exhaust myself any more than I already have, meaning I don't wish to overdo it.'

"What!" I thought, "chance would be a fine thing." And had instead said 'Is there any little chance of that ever happening . . . darling?" And then saw that she'd risen from the sofa, yet when she'd taken only one step, then surprise, surprise, she suddenly stopped as if stung by a wasp, and putting her hand up to her mouth, was saying in mock surprise:

'Oh no, of course I can't help you, can I? Do you remember my telling you that I had a meeting at five o'clock? You do remember my saying that, don't you? Well darling,' she said looking at her watch, 'because it's now so late, I won't have enough time to go home and change my clothes were I to get too messy with dust and things . . . would I darling?'

She'd then smacked the arm of the sofa in mock rage, and looking lazily into the distance had with a pretence groan, said: 'Dam and blast Jess, it's such a shame, and I was so enjoying myself being here, helping you out.' Then she'd sighed heavily again, whilst at the same time looking at my smiling face, having known full well that I knew that she'd again been up to her old tricks.

And now having said that, our Lynda had again sat down on the sofa, and said in a slightly bored voice. 'You know Jess, it's dammed hard work having to always make important decisions,' she yawned and stretched, 'and the thought makes me so dam tired even to think of it.'

'You poor old thing, perhaps you should now consider resting awhile longer,' I commiserated, 'and maybe take a small nap. Or perhaps you might like another refreshing drink to help refresh your aching limbs. Would you like that?'

Looking up, she smiled. 'No need to get nasty Jessica, it doesn't become you! However as you have now mentioned it, I will take you up on your offer, and cos the last one was delicious, I will partake of another large port and lemon please. Thank you . . . darling.'

After I'd poured her out another drink, and handed it to her, we'd both smiled at each other, enjoying the game she was playing, and after nodding all was well with me, had left her to go back into the hallway, having seen I needn't have been too overly concerned with her 'problem', because by the time I'd left the room, she'd once again reclined herself gracefully back into the sofa, and now sipping her drink, was now flipping through the pages of last month's Vogue magazine.

CHAPTER 31

Having now come back into my office, some minutes later, and having suggested we should toast my new business, we three girls had been drinking bubbly after Lynda had said it 'Would undoubtedly become a very successful business', and Pasha had endorsed that by saying; 'You took the words right out of my mouth,' and then we'd all raised our glasses and toasted 'to the business,' and 'to me'.

Pasha, had after looking into her second glass of bubbly, and giggling like a young school girl, said: 'These bubbles really do get right up your nose, don't they?' Adding, 'which could also be said about one of my neighbours,' and then concluded with, 'This is really lovely.'

To quickly explain why Pasha had come into work on Saturday and Sunday, was because 'I had nothing planned to do,' she told me, 'and thought I might be more useful here, if you could find me something to do.'

And now as there was nothing for her or me to do, she had for the next fifteen-minutes or so, told a hilarious story about one of her neighbours, who she regarded 'as being a bit weird to say the least, because,' she told us, 'they don't like birds, bees, bushes, butterflies, bud-leigh trees, bonfires, blue bells, or even Ben, who is my father. In fact, those people don't like anything that starts with a b.b.b . . . B,' she presence stuttered, 'except to say bloody this or bloody that.'

❦ 108 ❦

Lynda and I had laughed nearly as much at her turn of phrase, as the stories she told, also it was then that I knew that Pasha and I would get on famously. I just knew it!

So with the time being almost five minutes before 4 pm, and knowing all of the goodies for my 'Thank you' party had been delivered and laid out on a trestle table that stood outside in the hallway, with the food covered over by a white table-cloth, I knew we were ready to celebrate.

My little 'thank you party' had of course been, as you might imagine, welcome news to the ears of the workman, and they'd all heartedly agreed that they wouldn't be adverse to their receiving a little bit of pampering—particularly, you thought, had it been by either Patience . . . sorry, Pasha, I'll get it right soon, or myself!

Now the reason I'd had the table put in the hallway, was that I'd forbidden anyone from smoking, drinking, or eating inside the new offices, and this was only a precaution for my not wanting to have had my new carpets messed up with spilt beer, or even worse, to have had food squashed underfoot and into the thick pile of the new carpet; or to have had cigarette burn marks on the new woodwork. Made sense to me!

Another reason, was my not wishing to find any holes in the carpet from carelessly stamped on fag ends, not because the workman would have intentionally done that you understand—it was because I didn't want to give the workman any opportunity to ruin what they had worked so hard to accomplish, to then spoil a good job done, and I wasn't going to have them anywhere near the office area, and that was that.

Besides they didn't seem to mind one tiny bit at my requesting them to stay out in the hallway, for as far as they were concerned it made no difference to them where they'd stood, as long as they'd had a glass of something in their hands.

Besides that, being on the 5th floor, and on a Sunday, there wouldn't have been anyone we could have disturbed, or annoyed with our little party being out in the hallway, except my Al Capone friend, was there?

One hour before, my phone had brrr-brrring, and having answered it, found it to be the catering company I had employed, to say that they'd be arriving around 3.30pm this afternoon—which was perfect, having been previously told by everybody: 'We should have it all sorted by 4.00 pm, Jess,' meaning they'd have removed all their tools and gear—and tidied themselves up.

I'd had delivered a cask of bitter, and a crate of Light Ale, and Bitter, which the caterers had set up on one end of the table, with the food on the opposite end, alongside the bottled booze.

Facts were, that in one of my dizzier silly moments, I'd put forward a suggestion to them that if they completed all their work, to my satisfaction, by Sunday afternoon, which is today; then I would lay on a few beers for them, and maybe for good measure, a bit of food, rolls, crisps and stuff. That had been on Tuesday of this week if I remember correctly, just after I'd interviewed Pasha for a job. So maybe there was something in that, who knows?

Surprisingly, the final two days had in themselves been less eventful, and been nothing more than my supplying tea, tidying up, and testing the equipment, making the hours for us girls, difficult, for we both couldn't wait for it to be Monday—the day when my doors would finally be open for business.

"Monday, Monday, it's good for me" so sang Mamas and Papas—at least I hoped so!

So now at 4.00 pm, I'd known that all the hard work that I'd asked to be done over the last three and a half weeks, had finally been completed, and now I could relax and begin to enjoy the surroundings they had provided for me. Also, now I could at last put behind me all of the anguish that this place had put me through, and just enjoy.

And so I had taken out a bottle of bubbly, for us three girls, from the cooler box, to treat us all to a glass of champagne.

Chapter 32

At 3.55 pm, one of the two cleaning ladies called Agnes, had said, waving a yellow duster at me. 'Doris and me are all done, Jess.' I'd previously seen that the two ladies had done a lovely job, for now all the woodwork in each room had been waxed clean and smelt fresh. I would later employ Agnes as my permanent cleaner.

'I'm also finished' said Dave, the carpenter man. 'Me to', said Duncan, the electrician. 'Oh and we're all done, Jess,' called out the other workers in unison.

Having now asked Pasha and Lynda, 'Would either of you like anything to eat?' Lynda had, with a big effort, got up from her new friend, the sofa, and mumbled something, before saying: 'Oh I am so sorry darling, I've got this five o'clock meeting, as you know?' She looked at her watch, 'And now with it being twenty-past-four, I really should get my butt into gear'.

She had then turned to Pasha, saying. 'Besides I couldn't have done an awful lot more than I had, could I?' I laughed, and she gave me a glare before saying to Pasha. 'It's been so good to have met you Pasha, and please look after the old gal,' pointing to me, 'for she really is very important to me you know?' Then finally she had turned to me, and giving me a big hug said, 'and I'll see you tonight sweetie, ok?' Then had again swished out of the office just as she had on her arrival, and into the hallway.

❖ 111 ❖

I followed, telling her how grateful I was that she had popped in, and thanking her 'for her lively and scintillating company over the past few hours,' before adding facetiously with a smile. 'And a big thank you, for all the hard work, and enormous amount you accomplished in such a short time, for it has really has made such a world of difference to the new place!'

Then grinning good-humouredly at her, added 'You are truly amazing!'

In return, she'd given me one of her slightly wacky smiles, saying. 'Yes of course it was amazing darling, and I too have enjoyed immensely doing it all for you!'

Then giving me one of those smiles that said—*"you are my darling friend, taking the proverbial p-i-s-s"*, had never-the-less kissed me on both cheeks, turned, and said cheerio as she walked past the men who were still in the reception, and then wiggled her hips, and then had given me a wave over her shoulder as she walked towards the lift, without looking back to me, before saying 'See you to-night.'

Now that's two back-waves in one afternoon, it was obviously catching! I thought, before it had then been at that precise moment, whilst she'd been sashaying her way down the hallway that the tall man with the brown fur-collared long coat had walked past my office without saying a word, and had continued directly towards the lift. He had then on reaching it, stood directly behind Lynda, and I noticed that he had also said nothing at all to her! Strange!

I saw he was still wearing the same large wide-brimmed hat as before, although just a little straighter on his head, and slightly less roguishly. He was also wearing the same shoulder-to-ankle length overcoat he'd worn earlier, although this time he had the collar up, as if he was cold, and that had covered his shirt and cravat, as well as the lower side of his face even more than previously.

However, there seemed to be a slight difference between this man and the man I had spoken to earlier, besides the fact, that this 'unhappy' chappie was not at all like the

THE LADY DETECTIVE

same chatty smiling type I had previously met, his whole demeanour had also appeared to be different—unless it was my imagination, or he'd been putting on an act of course, cos now *this* man had been mumbling to himself as if he'd had a bad day at the office.

Unless my judgment had been affected by the fact that he had passed me by, without any kind of acknowledgement whatsoever that he knew me!

I mean, because the man had not even given me so much as a glance for me to have had a chance to offer him a drink, had he wished it, because he'd passed me by so quickly, and had ignored me standing here, and had been all the time he'd been walking towards the lift, been mumbling to himself—I had thought that was very strange indeed!

Perhaps the workman had with their loud laughter, made too much noise, and upset him? Although he didn't have to be so ruddy bad-mannered about it, did he, regardless of our being the cause of his bad attitude? And there had been something else that I couldn't put my finger on, that had bothered me about the man that made him appear *different*!

I hadn't known what that was, until later, when I remembered he'd been wearing black ordinary lace-up shoes when he left, which had now struck me as being very interesting, strange, and even puzzling. So why would the man not continue to wear the same brown tassel shoes I'd seen him wearing earlier? Now that was a puzzle that I failed to understand.

In the meantime, above the worker's voices, I faintly heard the squeaking and moaning of the steel lift as it made its way very slowly down to the ground floor, having Lynda and this 'unhappy' man as its passengers, and him as her companion.

CHAPTER 33

I t really had been my own intention to have had only one or two drinks with the workman and the cleaners, just as a gesture of saying thanks.

The reason for this being, that I was due to meet up with a group of friends that night, that would again include Lynda, at a popular restaurant in Bayswater, where I would then be wined, dined, and danced; and all that had been arranged and would be paid for by Stewart as his special treat to me, in celebration of the new business.

Now Pasha in particular, and myself to a lesser extent, had continued to entertain the workman for the next hour or so—not literally you understand, for there'd be no song or dance act from me on this occasion, though Pasha, you felt, would have been game to have done both. You also knew that the men would have liked to have had her sing or dance for them, yet as long as there had been plenty of drink and food for them to enjoy, they were happy!

At approximately half past five pm, they'd all finally left to go home, and all men had all uttered words of undying devotion before disappearing from sight, having had their pockets filled with the cash money they had earned. They'd said such things as:

"Now don't you forget to call us any-time, day or night, if you ever need anything done, ok luv!" And, "You're a bloody good sort you are Mrs, so I'll tell you what, the next time me

THE LADY DETECTIVE

or me mates 'ave a need for a bloody good lady detective, than you'll be the first one we'll come to. Straight up, and ere's me hand on it."

One man had actually said: 'If ever you need a help out, me or me mates can help,' he whispered, 'cos were all a bit handy, if you know what I mean.' And winking said, 'you know by doing a spot of private-eye, eye, work,' he sniggered, and with some more wink-winking added, 'we'll all be pleased to help you out, no problem.' Another said. 'I won't forget you ladies, ever, for as long as I live . . . straight up.' Which was more than he was, having downed many beers down his throat!

'Ah, who knows,' I said to Pasha when they'd all left, 'they do say that miracles can happen even in the most surprising places,' I smiled, 'though it goes without saying, that with their pockets full of crispy five pound notes, and their tummy's full of free beer and food, they would be feeling cheerful enough to have wished me all the luck in the world for the future, wouldn't they?'

She then laughed before saying. 'Men eh—I mean nearly all of them are like that when its booze that's doing the talking—free or not.' And then un-smiling, added 'cos when they've had a few, and brahms list, pickled, that will either mean that they'll have nice things to say to you, or they'll smack you about. Goes with the territory, you might say!' I said nothing!

CHAPTER 34

Minutes later, having told Pasha she should take home with her any of the food or booze she wanted, that was still left on the table, we'd said our good-night's.

Now left on my own, I'd sat quietly on my new sofa, with another glass of champagne in my hand, my second, and had for a further ten minutes or so, just stared out of the tall office window watching the last moments of a flam-red sky slowly becoming dark blue.

As I watched, I had seen the sky becoming a darker grey-black as the blacker night clouds had slowly began to surround and then muscle their way into the lighter daytime sky. It was as if they were making sure that daytime had known that for another twelve hours or so, it's time was over for now, and much like a publican ringing out last orders, before finally closing down the pub for the night, so it was with the daytime making its way to somewhere else, allowing for the night-time darkness to happen.

I had then mused on the thought that this would occur again, and again, until the end of time.

My watching the sky-changes; had got me thinking about the changes the man with the floppy hat and the fur-rimed coat had made. For it had surprised me, how the man had become two different characters, and in such a short space of time. First he'd been the likeable chatty jovial character,

❖ 116 ❖

THE LADY DETECTIVE

a Mr. Happy you might say, and then had altered into a very un-likeable, bad-tempered so in so, a regular Mr Grumpy you might say.

Also the man had earlier that afternoon, impressed me with his boldness, and being a likeable letch, yet this second character, hadn't given me or Lynda a second look. Weird!

So alright, maybe it was because I was still annoyed that Mr. Happy hadn't had the good manners to have said goodnight, which in my book could be classed as gross bad manners, and I admit, had come as a big surprise. Or maybe it was because I'd been peeved that he hadn't bothered to have wanted to say goodnight to me? I mean how could he have done that—to me?

Ok, so as the man hadn't wanted to say anything more to me, even had it been only to say 'good night', why hadn't he been at least civil enough to have said something to Lynda, like 'good-evening?' For it appeared he had said nothing at all to her at the lift, which considering how the man was an obvious flirt, and she being so attractive, I admit I found strange!

I was convincing myself that none of these things had bothered me particularly, and I suppose even his bad attitude when he left the building, could be allowed for, considering how chatty and ever so slightly lecherous he'd been earlier this day. No, what was now bothering me much more, was why would the man have left the building wearing those horrible lace-up black shoes, and been wondering why he hadn't been wearing those very nice brown tassel shoe's I saw he'd worn earlier! It was that which was really bugging me—as they say!

So now thinking logically, what would have been the explanation for his doing that? Why should any man have wanted to change his shoes? Maybe the answer had been the man had suffered from having smelly feet, and being offensive, had needed a change of shoes.

Ok, so he obviously had a spare pair of shoes that he kept in his office, although it also seemed more logical, I'd have

❄ 117 ❄

thought, to have changes of socks, besides it being wiser and far more convenient, wouldn't it? I mean socks weigh a lot less, and he could have kept as many pairs of them in his office desk as he wanted, had he a real problem with his feet. Though I suppose a spare pair of shoes could just as easily have been left as well, though heavier to take home.

Anyway, regarding his bad attitude, that might have been the cause, or perhaps it was nothing more than the poor man having had a lousy day at the office, and liked to change shoes! After all, I knew my father has rotten days in the office, and I would imagine many of his business friends imagine had; and there were also times when even I had them, so why not that big Lomax having one? I smiled wickedly when I thought that perhaps one of his clients had upset him, by telling him he had smelly feet. Well it could have been that simple, couldn't it?

On reflection, having mentioned his clients, no-one had passed by my office, either today or yesterday from those offices. In-fact, other than the workmen, Lynda, and Pasha, and the cleaners, I'd not seen one strange face walking either to or away from the offices all week, although it wasn't as if I had been waiting around in the hallway all day long just for that to happen you understand; for I had been far too busy doing what I'd been doing inside my own offices to have concerned myself about anyone else during that time. Although I suppose it could have happened!

Even so, for the man's attitude to have been so bad, it must have been one very angry customer, and it could have been an irate client on the phone.

Ah well, no point dwelling on this any longer was there, for I'd already spent far too much time wondering who he was, or wasn't, for one day. So I'll now finish my drink, lock up the office; go home; have a lovely hot bath; and then get ready for tonight's celebration.

*   *   *

However before I do, I need to ask you readers for your advice. Because this man and his shoes has really now become one of those 'What if' moments for me, and nagging doubts were arising.

Reason being, it has now become an issue for me to go, before I went home, and find out whether my new neighbour in Rugs and Tings, was, or wasn't, the same person who had twice passed me by in the hallway that day. Maybe the first guy had lent him his hat and coat?

The problem was, and we have all had these moments, when in our lives we are left wandering—what if? And yet at the same time as knowing that I really should forget all about my wondering, and go home, what if I had done this, instead of doing that? What if, instead of my doing nothing at all, I had done something, or wondered would things have turned out any different if I had done something, anything at all different to what I did.

So now, it was not so much knowing whether I should go home or not, unfortunately, it was my wondering whether Mr Nice guy might still have been working in his office. And then my problem was, if he was, what then?

I mean readers, what possible excuse or reason could I possibly give the man for banging on his door? I mean 'Hi there, it's only me, and I've come to say goodnight' would have sounded plausible to you? Or might he have thought that I had been flirting with him? You know; giving him the gentle come-on now, ask-me-out kind of approach. As if I would! Trust me. I would not!

Ok, now allow me to ask another question. Would you think that anyone, even an outrageous full of fun person like he was, would have ever believed me saying something like that, without thinking I was flirty? And might he misconstrue that as being just a little too up front, too bold, or even thought it was a little crazy, especially knowing I would have normally left the building by going out in the opposite direction!

Now wearily lifting myself up from my lovely new leather chair, I'd begun to pace around the office talking to myself: saying words like: *"He who dares wins"*, and *"Should I stay, or should I go now"*, until hearing negative voices in my head saying.

"Oh common Jess, don't you dare go down to the hall, it is absolutely none of your business whether he is, or isn't, the same man." And then my positive voice saying: *"Well are you, or are you not, going to be that bright new brave PI on the block, and get your sweet butt down there and find out for sure?"* Then it asked. *"So Jess, are you that person?"*

"Of course she is scared", said my inner negative voice, *'so maybe after all, she is not that all defeating, brand new dynamic all conquering professional nosey parker Investigator she makes out she wants to be."*

"So young lady, are you my new all-conquering private investigator?" my positive voice saying, *"Are you brave enough to now make this your business, or not?"*

"Or is it possible you are scared? Because if you are, don't you dare go and investigate." Said my inner negative voice.

Well having heard both sides of whether to go or not to pay the big man a visit; my positive voice was now telling that I should go for my own sanity, after all, he told me, he could only tell me to "get lost" couldn't he?

So finally, I made up my mind to have a look-see, wondering if it was my way of being macho—not that I'll always want to poke my nose into other people's affairs, you understand, well not unless I was being paid to do it. However, just like any good PI would do when intrigued, I will now go up to his office.

Actually it might be my women's curiosity telling me that I needed to see for myself if it had been the same man, and being a woman, I will regard this as nothing more than a woman's curiosity.

What do you mean, 'Oh yes!' As if you didn't believe me. So common readers, give me a little backing here, because my wandering down the hallway to do what I had to do, could

❋ 120 ❋

in part be put down to my being a new PI, and partly to my being a woman, it's that simple! Right?

So there you have it folks, it's my being a woman that gives me the right to poke my lovely nose into anybody's affairs, and not because I have a nosey-parker licence.

Of course my license does mean that as a fully qualified bono-fide Private Investigator, I have the right to suss out anyone I wished to suss out, should I ever need to suss them out—which I do now. Besides, what's the harm in my wanting to do a little snooping, having a little look-see? No harm at all—is there? Although here's the rub, not all snooping is legitimate, and some of you are thinking that I could get into loads of trouble if I did.

Never mind, because now I have already made up my mind to be a nosey-parker; and really should go and have a look-see, a gander, which my father would have said was being a nosy-parker, and that combined with a woman's curiosity, could potentially be a lethal combination.

Which I suppose that was one of the reasons for my wanting to be a professional investigator, and also to be paid for the privilege, which many of you may have pointed out, would be every woman's dream.

In fact, because I'd at last decided to go and pay my neighbour a visit, it would be a decision that I'd later come to regret—more of that later. Now I know that many readers would have also arrived at the same decision as I've now made, had you been in my place, and not said 'That's all Folks', as if you'd witnessed the end of another Looney cartoon.

Besides, I couldn't at the time, see how I can get into loads of trouble by doing this. Famous last words you might say, cos it would get me into a lot of trouble!

Or let me put it another way. Had I been playing chess, what I'm about to do, would not only have been thought of as a bad move, it'll have almost certainly, seen me walking straight into being check-mated—as you'll now read in the following pages.

CHAPTER 35

Having finally resolved what I was going to do. I'd got myself into an active snooping mode, and then proceeded to double-lock my office door, followed by treble-locking the hallway door 'Best be safe than sorry', my grandmother would always say.

I'd then noted that the caterers had already collected and cleared away all the leftovers from their trellis table, and had even left all unopened bottles of beer and spirits by the side of my office door. "Nice of them," I thought, "and honest."

Unlocking the hallway door, I'd put the un-opened bottles back inside the office, wondering why the Caterers hadn't bothered to come in to say goodnight, before I'd again treble-locked the hallway door.

In fact I had failed to grasp the logic of why the caterers hadn't, except to think that this might be a new kind of 'fing' to do. Perhaps saying 'goodnight' for people around here was taboo! If so I had not heard of it, or maybe I hadn't heard anyone knocking on the door!

*　　*　　*

CHAPTER 36

And now I was heading down the hallway towards 'Rugs and Tings', and then having turned the far corner, had seen ten feet or so further down this part of the corridor, an office door saying 'Byways Ltd—Import-Export Agent', and noted they had their office lights on!

Approximately twenty-five feet or so further down this part of the hallway that was out of sight from the main hallway, there was this red and white sign sticking out into the hallway like it was promoting itself to be an old fashioned barber shop, and on it read 'Rugs and Tings—Import Sales Agent', noting there were no lights on in this office!

Now outside this door, I had knocked, and received no answer, not that I had really been expecting for there to have been an answer, having already seen the man who was supposed to be working here, leaving the building over an hour before. There weren't any signs of life in the office either, it was too quiet.

Now most people would have given up at this point, and have turned around and headed straight back towards the lift, and then have gone home. However, that person was not me, besides you know the expression 'You'll never know until you try' didn't mean what I was about to do, could justify my being completely stupid?

I knocked again, this time a little louder than before, and still no answer, and then I tried turning the doorknob, and surprise, surprise, the door was unlocked, so intrigued why that should be, I'd already began to push open the door saying 'Hello, is there anyone here?' And immediately thought, "how silly was that, my saying 'hello is anyone there?" as if someone would be sitting in the darkness just waiting me to open their office door so that they could say 'Oh please do come in, I'm sorry, there's only me, will I do?' Stupid! Stupid! Stupid!

With my hand fumbling along the wall to where I pre-supposed a light switch should have been, I eventually found it at least three foot along the wall, and switching it on, I began to look around.

The first thing that had been very noticeable was that the air reeked with a stale smell of a strong tobacco. Then I noted there were ashtrays provided for the smoker to put his ash or cigarette stub into on either side of the mantle-piece above an old fire-place, which considering there were signs of 'Please no Smoking' on the walls, I thought was strange.

Also noticeable, was the smell of sweat, or body odour, yet I could have sworn the man I'd met in the hallway hadn't ponged. Not that I'd been close enough to him to have noticed. Anyway, these smells mixed together as a cocktail was not, as you might imagine, very nice at all!

Question was: why was there ashtrays in here for a non-smoking man? Also, why should anyone have forgotten to lock their office up after them? Or to put it another way, why should anyone have wanted to leave their office door unlocked?

I won't spend time telling you all I saw in this office; so just allow me to only say it was void of anything that you might have thought of as pleasing to the eye. In fact I thought that as an office, it had looked far too dowdy—much too plain looking to have been an office, for surprisingly, it was almost bare of any decent office furniture at all.

And another thing, the telephone wasn't working, because I'd tested it to see. Un-plugged maybe; or the bill not being paid! Again very strange!

THE LADY DETECTIVE

The office itself, had also given off a feeling that felt as if the presence of the big man being still in here with me; and had I been into the paranormal, it might have further induced a feeling that the big man had perhaps not left the building after all! So having seen enough of this office, which in my mind I'd re-named Dooms-Ville, I left, making sure to turn off the lights, and close the office door quietly behind me.

Then setting off down the hallway, and passing on the way 'Byways Ltd', the office next door, I for no other reason other than my being nosy, had knocked on the door, and had received a no-no answer.

However with the lights being on, perhaps there'd been someone working in there, and had not wanted to answer my knocking, I'd knocked once more, and had slowly pulled down the door-handle to enter, though this time, I'd not been surprised to find it locked, and not having received an answer, had left shaking my head in bewilderment, finding it strange.

Setting off for home, I saw how different the hallway and my office door had looked when approached from this direction. It further amused me to think, when looking at my office door. *'Now that is a smart office-door'*. In fact I might have said to any person walking alongside me to the lift, *'Also I hear they are very nice people working there you know!'* Stupid huh?

Stopping, to again admire the little man's handy-work; remembering how he painted one beautifully scripted letter after another onto the new glass-panelled door, having known that each letter would be followed by another, and another, until finally all these beautifully scripted letters, would end up forming words, and those words when finished, would have told anyone who cared to look upon them, what my name and chosen profession was going to be, for they said: Jess Felliosi—Private Investigator. A sleuth no less!

❧ 125 ❧

I smiled, now knowing there'd been nothing sinister about his painting those letters of my name on the door, which had at the time deeply concerned me.

I looked at my watch, and saw the time was 5.55 pm, and having had enough excitement for one day, I was now looking forward to going home, having a nice hot bath, and then I would leisurely doll myself up, before setting off to celebrate tomorrow's opening of *my* new business with my friends.

CHAPTER 37

THAT EVENING

Two and a half hours later, you would have found me sat around a very large cigar-shaped table that had been suitably arranged by the owner Eduardo Ghoulardi for my friends, who'd placed three four-seating tables together to create one long table perfectly suitable for twelve people to sit and eat around.

We'd just finished what had for me been an excellent meal, and were all sitting back to have had an Espresso coffee, made by a Gaggia coffee machine, that had steamed and hissed its way thru the operation of making for some of us, a frothy espresso coffee served with some very tasty Belgium chocolate wafer peppermints that I like to nibble on.

Although others had preferred to miss the coffee and nibbles, Stewart being one of them, who'd preferred to have had a Martell brandy instead. And for those who preferred to smoke, slim panatela cigars were on offer, which Lynda definitely would be having, because I knew she liked the long slim ones. It was her style!

For this celebration dinner party, Stewart had invited ten close friends, although there'd been only four of us, as yet, who weren't married. They were, Lynda and Tim, who for the past two years had been Lynda's occasional partner, then me and Stewart.

Jenny and Bruce, who you know, had been married for two years; Katie and Donald, for only one year—whilst Elizabeth and Julian, were soon to be married, and living in sin. And all the ladies had been old school chums.

As for Stewart and jolly old me, well it has been said by some that we would eventually get married, although for it to have been such a big thing for some people, I could never quite understand! Of course were it not me who they had been talking about, I would certainly have been among the first to have endorsed anything the chatter-boxes had been saying about me.

Why endorsed? Well it might have been because we were so well suited in so many ways. He was 6'3" inches tall, and I'm 5'11" in my stocking feet. He was dark and handsome, and I am dark and very beautiful. He is a good athlete, and I am better than good, I'm exceptionally good. He is extremely clever, and I am that plus. He's very gifted in all manner of things, languages *not* being one of them, and is very funny— at times, and I am all of those, and perhaps a little more. He is not at all conceited, and I am terribly!

So you see, apart from one or two matters that are of no concern of yours, and being we are both so talented in so many ways, and he being not so unlike me, or me being not so unlike him, well! Another factor was that I knew he loved me, or he'd said he did, although with his laid back attitude to life, you might never have known it. Also, it would seem that he didn't want to commit to those kind of feelings too often, yet when he did, he was an extremely passionate man, so I was never quite sure of him at all in that department.

Part of his intrigue was I suppose, his being such a macho man, for he'd prefer to keep me guessing, as I would with him. Childish really when you think of it!

THE LADY DETECTIVE

Another point was, we are neighbours, with his father owning all the land next to ours, which had meant, despite his having had many other girl-friends, and my having had one or two boy-friends—to date, we would after spending a small time away from each other, then have always drifted back to each other over the years. Ah!

In fact, since we'd become old enough to begin dating, which in my case was fourteen, and he being sixteen, we'd drifted back together a total of four times. This time being the longest time yet, totalling fifteen months, was why even our friends and families, had quietly begun to whisper of a white wedding, and were counting out the months of how long we would last out. They were also beginning to call us—'the nearly weds'—behind our backs. Some hopes!

Of course we'd both known of these rumblings, yet both of us could not, or did not, wish to understand what all the fuss was about, even though we'd laughingly discussed the subject of marriage in the past two months, when I told him 'that they', meaning our friends, 'really didn't know us as well as they think they do, do they?'

Stewart it must be said was actually deeply committed to his job, and I for one, thought it only right that it should be, especially having been told by one of his senior officers, a Chief Superintendent Knowles, some months before, that he was regarded as a brilliant officer. Then he had tapped his nose before saying. "It's also rumoured, that he's already been earmarked to soon be eating from the top table."

So we'd both agreed to give marriage not a further thought, though I did think at the time, it might be nice to be just a little bit married!

*   *   *

So there you have it. I've now cleared up that little matter of matrimony between us, and hopefully squashed any rumours of our getting wed, because we're both not interested at all in all that matrimonial sloppy stuff, as I've told you. So now can we now get on with matters to hand, if that is ok with you!

I'm sorry if all that sounded just a little bit bitchy, because I wouldn't know any more than you folks do, and please don't ask me why that is! I mean why I am just a little touchy on that subject. Although now looking at the man in question over the rim of my glass, all of that had flooded back to me, making me realise how very dear he was to me, so I had leant over and kissed him.

Chapter 38

I was also grateful to him for helping me come to terms with the fact that I've now become a Private Investigator, because that might not have happened had it not been for his help in getting me my PI license. He had helped pave the way in my overcome the many problems that I'd been confronted with over the past weeks, and been brilliant.

It was also mostly due to him, and his having friends in all the right places as they say, that I'd finally received my 'Private Dick' license to be almost unique for a woman to be.

Of course, becoming a PI, had been made all the more difficult by not involving my parents, or any friends of my parents, or to even involve my own friends, besides Lynda, during the time it took to set up the business. Reason being my new 'adventure' was to be all very hush, hush, and have no doubt come as a big, big, surprise to them all, as it had certainly been to my parents, you could say that again! So having had this tall, very handsome man, who was sitting beside me, looking extremely debonair in his evening-suit, had been a Godsend.

Stewart had been wonderful. In fact, just by being there at my side through 'thick and thin', even when daddy or anyone else might have put obstacles in my way, he had among all men since my quitting Law school, always been there to back me up to the hilt and acted as a rock to help me overcome any objections they or I had.

❦ 131 ❦

In fact, there'd been people who'd quite deliberately tried to stop me getting a license. People, who had wanted me to fail, who'd tried to shatter my lifelong dream, and now those people I will always, long-term, quietly remember.

I suppose my having a background and a social status that was verging on being known almost as a super-star by some, had in part added to the difficulties that I'd needed to overcome to be a PI.

Besides of course, my being a very beautiful; healthy; young; and very rich young lady, which I am!

CHAPTER 39

Stewart having probably guessed my thoughts, for he had then suddenly stretched out a large elegant hand to take hold of mine, saying softly.

'Jess, I know it's been a worrying time for you over the past few weeks, and I can only say, if it helps, for you not to worry ok, for up to now, all of your worries will have been in all honesty, nothing like as bad as they are going to be . . . in the future, when you start work!'

The sod! I tried to punch him for being horrible, and saw he'd been grinning as he defended himself from another playful punch, by putting up his hands to, so I'd kicked his ankle instead. Ouch!

Then he had looked at me with such a serious face, he'd got me slightly worried, before he continued. 'Jess, you must think of any worries you have had, as being the beginning of many, many, more that are bound to follow, because there are going to be much harder days, weeks, months, even years ahead of you to worry about, if you really want to be the most successful Private Investigator that has ever walked this planet.

He smiled another one of his cheeky smiles, before adding. 'Although I have no doubts at all, that you will become top dog—or should I say, top cat in the business.'

He then stood up, and tapping gently on his glass with a spoon, looked directly at me whilst saying with a slightly raised

❦ 133 ❦

voice: 'Ladies and gentleman, a toast to Jess. Here's looking at you Jess, and to say that all of us here have no doubt at all in our minds, that you will be highly successful in your new career.' He paused whilst they sipped their drinks, and then added. 'And now Jess, if you were to look around you, you'll see looking at the slightly inebriated red-faces of your friends, that should you ever need anyone of us to help you become the most beautiful; the sexiest; the cleverest; and soon to be the most successful private 'eye' in the World—ah sorry, England if you like, well at least London, or shall we say in this room—you can always count on us to help.'

He paused whilst waiting for the slight applause to settle before looking down at me and saying. 'Anyway Jess, we are always here to obey and be your willing subjects, regardless of whatever Lynda has had to say about your foul-mouthed horrible moods that you are often in. So ladies and gentleman, I will ask you to be all upstanding, and raise your glasses to Jess, and toast her success for the future by saying those immortal words of a rugby song after me:

'She should be publicly pissed on, she should be publicly shot, and then put in a public urinal, there to bloody well rot, rot, rot.'

Which they all did, and then as Stewart had requested, they three cheered me as they'd all stood with their arms outstretched, pointing their glasses towards me.

Of course, our Lynda had afterwards been the first to add. 'So besides our having to put up with her tantrums, Stewart, I suppose you will now be wanting for us all to kiss her feet next? Yuck!'

My friends had laughed, though I'd failed to understand what Lynda had been talking about! Tantrums . . . what tantrums?

Of course I did realize that Stewart, when he'd suggested that my friends would always do anything 'to help' me', really had been speaking for himself, although they probably would have helped, and/or kissed my feet for fun!

So with his having given me the loveliest moment of the evening, for that toast and those words had been especially important for me to have heard coming from him, I'd again lent over the table and kissed him.

Stewart had pretended to be shocked at my kissing him, and was saying, 'Unhand me madam. What is this show of sentiment may I ask?' And then with a dirty grin, added. 'You are, umm, not getting amorous with me are you young lady?'

I smiled, pouted my lips, and winked!

It had then been that my drink fuddled brain had suddenly twigged on to what Lynda had said about my tantrums, and Stew saying about my being foul-mouthed etcetera, for it had only been, as you might have guessed— them winding me up with fibs said in fun! The sods!

CHAPTER 40

It must have been an hour later, around 11 pm, when I'd felt the evening was beginning to lose its enjoy-en-joy . . . ability, both mentally and physically, for my mind and body had arrived at that stage when everything you do or say, begins to slowly go downhill! I had now reached that point, when even a most enjoyable and wonderful evening could quite easily be spoilt because of all the booze I had drunk.

I also knew, that it wouldn't be long before all the happy and fun moments of the evening, could be ruined by what my Mother would call her 'feeling a bit ticky moment.' Well my friends, I'd now reached that 'bit ticky moment', and known it was time to go home before I made a fool of myself, my having felt just a little more than being 'a bit drunk', cos I knew I felt totally inebriated, sloshed, and was fast becoming Miss Slurrsville.

I'd had a most enjoyable evening, for everything about this dinner party; my friends; the restaurant's atmosphere; the lovely food had all been as splendid as I could ever have wished.

The food, as I said, was superb, and I'd eaten fresh and crisply fried whitebait, with fresh lemon and homemade brown bread. This had been closely followed by my having a huge lobster to eat, that had been cooked and presented most beautifully to me on a very large square plate that had

❖ 136 ❖

THE LADY DETECTIVE

been barely big enough to cover its huge claws. This had been served with a hollandaise sauce you would die for, and a coleslaw side-salad with all the trimmings. And I had drunk many glasses of wine.

Nevertheless, I should have known better than to allow my tiredness to have got the better of me! My fault I suppose, for I did have far too many glasses of an excellent Merlot, in order to wash down my enormous meal, having always known that having too many of them, I would only finish-up being totally embarrassed.

I also admit, I'd even asked for a doggie bag, so that I could take home the huge claw that I'd been unable to eat, there being far too much lobster for one sitting.

And having now reached that time when I should have gone home, having had a wonderful evening, I'd for no reason whatsoever, except of my being reminded by Lynda, of her "kissing my feet" had blurted out to Stewart what I had said next. So I will blame her for reminding me of that man and his blasted shoes, his smelly feet, whatever, and my now needing to now tell Stewart all about it. So I had after pulling at his sleeve, had in a slurred and raised voice, said.

'Stewart, I've got this big problem that I need to talk to you about!'

CHAPTER 41

Lynda told me days later on a girlie night out, that everyone around the table had then immediately stopped whatever it was they'd been doing—talking, eating, and so forth, and had all suddenly looked at me with new interest as I proceeded to drunkenly tell Stewart what I needed to say, being completely unaware of the curiosity I'd stirred up among them.

With slurring words I said. 'Stew, I really do have a problem! And it's a very strange sort of problem. In fact I would go as far . . . go so far as to say Stew, that it was what you might call odd. Yes, that's what it was, it was odd! And do you know what me old pal Stew, it might have even been odder than odd . . . honest Injun!'

I was told I had then pulled at his sleeve again, and said: 'Do you know what, you might even call it . . . now what's the word, oh I know—odd-strange, yes that's the word for it old boy—odd-strange. Now how strange is that—eh Stew?'

Lynda told me that everyone had by now gone quite quiet, their being all ears you might say, whilst trying to understand what I'd been attempting to say to Stewart, whilst heavily slurring the words.

Though I hadn't up to then, noticed my friends had been listening to me, perhaps because I'd been bibulating all evening long, getting pie-eyed; getting sloshed, as most people now call it, so because I was feeling slightly more than

❀ 138 ❀

ticky, I found myself mentioning that strange man with the brown tasselled shoes who I'd met in the hallway!

I suppose I'd thought that I couldn't put off for one moment longer, my telling him what I suppose I had wanted to say to him all evening. I suppose it had needed to be said, if for no other reason that I could think of, than it should be said before I had totally forgot what it was I wanted to say.

So having said what I had just said, lovely Stewart gave me a large grin, then raised his hand as if trying to tell anyone who wasn't listening, to now keep quiet, and said: 'Jess, I really have no idea what it is you are telling me. I mean what is this something being odd-strange, or whatever it was you said?'

'Never mind, s'not important' I replied, prodding the table with a fork.

'Come on Jess, out with it. What isn't important? And who or what is this odd-strange?'

Linda was to tell me that I had at this point, looked around the table, and said "What's up?" to every-one, and had then repeated "what's up", before saying, 'Oops and double oops, now you've definitely let the bag out of the cat, haven't you? So now there will be no point upsetting the applecart before the fire would there, by my not telling you?' I slurred, and then had continued on with the story of whatever odd-strange was all about.

Apparently I'd then told everyone, in my own inebriated way, all about the tall man with the big floppy hat, and the fur-collared coat. Telling them, how he had puzzled me, by saying.

'When the man had earlier come to work wearing brown shoes with a tassel on them, he'd later, when he left work, been seen wearing black shoes with laces in them. Now I don't mind telling you Stew me old fruit, that I find that very strange indeed. Even odd-strange, as you call it.'

Then it had seemed, my slurred words and erratic hand-movements, had given my friends cause for amusement, judging by their amused faces. However not to be deterred, because I really hadn't known much about what I was saying, let alone my wondering whatever was it they'd found so amusing, or been the cause for such jollity, so I'd continued talking.

Lynda had told me I'd then asked Stewart. 'Could you—would you plisse exp l . . . tell me Stew, why this . . . in the morning, early, this . . . this Mr Nice Guy, who was oh so nice and friendly, had later turned out to be a big, bad-mannered, and oh so very unfriendly Mr Grumpy guy. Per . . . perhap'sh you can explain that eh Mr Detective?'

I can vaguely remember I'd been stabbing at his chest with my finger at the time, and then had looked up to his face, my head having been previously somewhere near the table, and that was when I noticed that poor old Stewart had been crying, and not realising why that was, I had taken hold of his hand and told him: 'Oh don't upset yourself Stew-art, it's only a man's smelly shoes I'm talking about!'

I'd then noticed that it was not only Stewart who'd been crying, and had large tears now running down his face, it was every-one of my friends. And what's more, I'd seen some had even been busily wiping away the tears from their cheeks with their napkin, and some were flapping their hands, and holding their stomachs.

You know readers, I hadn't realised up to that moment, how sentimental my friends were. I mean it's only times like that when you realise how touched one can be over your friend's concern over whatever words I had said.

That sentiment was again born out when I had told them all. 'You really are all so kind you know over my being concerned about this man's smelly shoes, and you being so unbelievably sentimental, does make me sad.' And then they had all started to cry all over again. I mean you can't help loving your friends, can you?

Lynda had then told me I had continued by saying in a slurred voice. 'And there is another thing, Stew-art', whilst I'd been wagging a hand, or was it a finger, at him—or of course

THE LADY DETECTIVE

it could have been both a finger and a hand at once, for all I remembered! So to continue:

'And another thing; would you believe me if I told you that one of the offices—up there—was to . . . totally closed up, err locked up I mean, and the lights were on, and the other one, the other office, was totally un-locked, and had no . . . sorry, didn't have any lights on, to see anything, you see! So detective, what do you make of that, eh me old Stewing-pot? How do you work that one out eh, one office having its lights on, and the other not having its lights on? Cos you know what Stew, I've not been able to shed any light on any of it, yet, even if it was an odd-strange!

Or the other thing . . . again a puzzle; why one office was locked, and the other unlocked, eh? Because for the life of me, I can . . . cannot fathom that one out either. It doesn't turn my key—haha.'

All of this I had said, Lynda told me, whilst all the time slurring my words.

Although I do remember that my friends had again been trying to hide their crying from me, by putting their napkins up to their faces, for no reason that I could understand, and were either nodding or shaking their heads, though it really had been comforting to have seen their concern! And at that point, I also remember having noted that my dear, dear, friend Linda, had also been crying, poor old thing, for I could tell, because some of her mascara gently running down her face.

I had also seen she'd been desperately trying to cover over her embarrassment, by biting on her napkin, and when she'd interrupted me, I remembered her saying what she said in a matter of fact voice to fool me, however with all that love, it could never fool me, and that's a fact, because I'd already seen her dabbing tears from her eyes when she said.

'Everything that Jess has said about the man in the hallway, I can confirm, because that poor man, what did you call him? Ah yes, Mr Grumpy, well he must have been completely out of sorts, because, even though he'd been

❦ 141 ❦

sharing a lift with a most gorgeous of woman; me being that woman of course, that man had still completely ignored me.'

She paused taking in breath. 'So the question you must ask yourselves is, is how could a normal full-blooded sane man have possibly ignored a living doll like myself, particularly with his being in such a confined romantic space as a lift with my good-self?'

My friends had laughed, when she had added. 'And even then, with his having such an apparition of beauty right before his eyes . . . that still hadn't helped Mr Grumpy change his grumpy attitude. And what's more, he had still remained that unfriendly Mr Grumpy, right up to the time we had both finished our ride together down to the lobby, and after he'd left the lift, and we'd made our way towards the main door, he hadn't said a word to me.' She pretended to sulk 'Now that was both insulting, and demeaning!'

I'd with the rest of us, applauded Lynda's story by banging on the table with a spoon in my hand, whilst looking past her ear, trying to focus on her face, to say. 'So old Mr Grumpy was in other words, a total jerk with a capital G. Eh?'

Then I'd been told by Ghoulish, the manager, or whatever his name was, 'to keep it down,' which I'd thought at the time, he was referring to the food I'd eaten, because I'd wondered *"How on earth does he know that I'm feeling queasy?"*

So I'd then whispered to Stewart, saying: 'I cannot for the life of me understand why everybody—even those people on the other tables, are so unhappy,' for I had seen some of them looking at me wiping tears from their eyes, and asked. 'Surely they can't be all unhappy, can they? Ah, perhaps it's a wake they're having; or it's what someone might have said to them.' And then I'd waggled a finger towards Ghoulash saying, 'probably it was Ghoulish telling them they've now got to do the washing-up after showing them the bill.'

Then Stewart said something about telling him a little more about my problem, which had quickly been endorsed by our friends, and others in the restaurant whose table was close enough to ours to hear what I said. Even Ghoulish,

Goulash, or whatever his name was, had smiled, and nodded his head saying "further noise was fine with him."

Some, with Lynda being one of them, were actually smiling after I had slurring said. 'Well I will in that case, continue with my Mr Grumpy and Mr Happy story', and received some light clapping.

'So St . . . Stewart, back to this shoe-business thingy . . . cos I really cannot understand any part of it; though perhaps I could understand it better, if someone had told me the poor man was suffering from horrible, horrible, sweaty, fishy smelling feet, or something just as bad. I mean, had I known that the poor, poor man, had actually been suffering from foot rot, or something similar, you know it would have been ok by me. I mean, had he wanted to have talked to me about it, the smell I mean, I could have told him it was ok. I'd have understood. Honest! Instead of which, the bloody man just rushes off ssh . . . saying nothing at all to me!'

I paused, and then having taken in a deep breath, moaned. 'Do you know Stew, some people have no manners, no manners at all, and I will tell him that the next time I see him you mark my words.'

I had then become exhausted, and shut up. Lynda was to later tell me, though for the next ten minutes or so, smelly-feet jokes had suddenly become the only topic of conversation, and entertainment, around our jolly table, so much so, all of my previous concerns about their tears had quickly been replaced by feet jokes, and the man in the hallway, temporary forgotten by my friends.

Of course I was happy with them being happy, for I now hoped they'd done enough crying for one evening!

Then I heard Stewart telling everyone that he was about to take me home, and a cheer had gone up, followed by more clapping. Then I'd seen some of my friends were actually doing silly dancing on the small dance floor, whilst others were drinking and chatting. Now drinking, or dancing, even chatting, were not now, obviously, for me, particularly dancing, for I could hardly stand up anyway, which I assume must have been because I'd been so, so, tired!

*   *   *

Days later, Lynda had told me that my friends hadn't been crying as I thought, they'd been laughing at me so much over what I had said about the man, that had brought tears to their eyes, and not because of their being sentimental, as I thought. Friends eh, don't you love them!

CHAPTER 42

Stewart had finally got me home by taxi, and having arrived back home at my lovely old cottage in the early hours of Monday morning; had told him that I was far too tired to ask him in for a nightcap. I'd then thanked him, by sort of kissing him goodnight, and had headed off down the path to my front door, always thanking him for a lovely evening.

He later told me that in watching me walk to the front door had been in his words, "one of the highlights of the evening". "a cracker".

He told me I'd walked in a side to side movement, which he said "resembled a crab", and with a small chuckle, said "and a drunk one at that".

I suppose he'd meant that I'd been swaying from side to side on the pathway, which if true, then it must have been a small miracle that I had even got to my front door!

I do remember on reaching the door, my awkwardly half-turning back towards the pathway, and blowing kisses back towards where I thought he'd be standing, and saying as if he'd been a casual friend. 'It was a great night Stew-art, thanks for everything—we must do it again sometime.'

I had then thought my saying thanks again, and blowing kisses, had been too late for Stewart to have heard anyway, for I'd noticed the rear lights of the taxi lighting up a clear cold morning, as it drove off.

❋ 145 ❋

Stewart was to also embarrassingly tell me, that I had at the door begun mumbling over and over again. "It was a great night Stew'" whilst I'd been with difficulty, trying to find the two door key-holes with my fingers. He told me, I'd then the problem of inserting the keys into either lock, having already spent what had seemed to have been 'at least five frustrating minutes fumbling around in my bag looking for the keys.'

When finally I had unlocked the door after another angry five minutes of fumbling about, it was only after I had heard him chuckling, and having slowly turned around in case I fell down, that I saw him Stewart standing a few feet behind me, with both hands on his hips, having obviously been amused while watching all my fumbling.

I do remember telling him he was 'a sod', and that 'I really hadn't needed to have bothered with all that fumbling around, had he been a gentleman?'

'True. Very true,' he said, 'although you not knowing I was here, did add enormously to the immense enjoyment I had of watching you making a fool of yourself.'

He had after taking the keys off me, lecherously added. 'Still I'm glad you thought it was a great night, so now perhaps I can now make it seem even better!' After that, believe me, the rest of the night was just a blur!

PART 2

CHAPTER 43

MONDAY MORNING

When I woke-up at 7 o'clock in the morning, and whilst attempting to climb out of my warm double bed, had on looking down on myself, saw that I was only wearing my matching silk-laced light turquoise coloured bra and panties, and felt a horrible mess!

Then suddenly, to add to my woes I'd had a gift wrapped blinding headache to accompany my feeling a horrible mess. Both of which I would have gladly swapped for anything!

Now I'm sure that each one of you will have had such a feeling at some time in your life, be it after a wedding reception, a birthday, a divorce, a wake, or any number of reasons to make it an excuse for having a knee's up, and to get well and truly bibulated, plastered, drunk!

Unfortunately, along with our having had a great or pleasant evening, most of us will then have to suffer the aftermath, the fall-out, of our having enjoyed ourselves! And it isn't fair you saying that I bought all of this on myself, because I already know that, but there is no need to laugh at me as well, for having had a good time last night, was there?

However what I can tell you that might make those cynical bar-stewards among you even happier, was that it sometimes takes me a long time, many hours, sometimes a day, to feel normal again, and that is principally why I don't do that kind of partying too often. Besides, I have always found it a problem following on from a 'good night out'. I suppose my problems would appear to be the part of the course for all night revellers, who'd in general, been only trying to enjoy themselves, and life, and unfortunately, having this kind of headache to wake up to, was the price we had to pay because of it! Well in this instance it did!

I suppose having such a headache; generally known as 'a blinder', you can imagine that it cannot have been for me at all nice to have one, especially with my having one on this day of all days. Besides, everything seems loud during the following morning, and often throughout the day. Banging doors, cars hooting, high-pitched laughter, screams, dogs barking, even sounds like now whilst I am eating my toast, had always seemed to grate on my already shattered nerves, which is now very painful and hurting. Need I say more?

My celebrating the opening of the business had now meant I would be starting my special day with a massive hangover for company, besides my feeling like death warmed up. Not nice, not nice at all! Why? Because this had not been in the plan of things I had for today, because this day was supposed to have been, or should be, the pearl of all days, a living jewel in my life—so for me to have even allowed last night to have been a blast, and to have drunk so much that I would now be suffering as much as I was, had been nothing short of madness. Well in most people's eyes it was—and probably childish ta'boot! And yet unbeknown to me, worse was still in store, for I would soon be confronted with a more horrible scenario, one which would give me an even bigger kind of headache. Which meant that my special day, would from here on in, can get only worse, much, much worse! Although the one I now had was enough for the time being, thank you very much!

CHAPTER 44

Still that aside, and back to the here and now for one or two moments, for it had seemed that Stewart must have put me to bed, and had then departed before I woke up, though he had left a note saying:

"Now you have a lovely day . . . sexy, and good luck." Then had added, with many exclamation marks "Blimey Jess, I really did enjoy myself thoroughly last night, ha-ha," and had underlined the thoroughly and the ha-ha.

Surely, that hadn't meant he had taken advantage of my 'condition', had he? No not that; for the man was far too much of a gentleman to have stooped to such a low level. Besides, I was still wearing my underwear, so he couldn't have—could he? Ah the sod!

Moments later, I'd pensively thought that it had been such a pity that Stewart hadn't thought to have taken my headache with him, when he'd left me, then left me with my only having 'a lovely day' instead.

It seemed that men never have any consideration for a woman's feelings when we women needed them to have! Perhaps the women readers among you will know that I am right, won't you?

Now as you all know, to-day is to be my first working business day; and here I am partly dressed, needing more sleep, and feeling worse as every minute goes by.

❈ 151 ❈

'Dam and blast my over-indulgences. Never again, ever, ever, ever again,' I scolded myself softly.

In the meantime I knew that I had to eat some food to soak up the alcohol in my body—though the big question was *"could I face cooking anything?"* And then I'd heard my inner voice saying *"Oh come on Jess, be a brave girl now"*.

Yet at this moment, I had begun to wonder what other problems would fate bring me on this, my special day, for surely nothing could be any worse than my having the mother of all head-banging headaches, could there? Unfortunately I was soon to find out, that there were!

I'd then spent a leisurely half-hour slowly preparing, and then eating some bran, toast and honey, and even made myself fresh orange-juice, and ground coffee. Although when it came to eating, I had to adopt the same method as I'd used when preparing the breakfast, which was to do things slowly, not that I had much alternative, because to hear my jaw and teeth moving together over the toast, or bran, when that horrible crunching, chewing, grating sound hit my brain, was almost unbearable.

That alone to help continue the process of sobering up, had got me guzzling what seemed like gallons of black coffee. I'd then tried to forgot about the 'slow leisurely' part of eating the breakfast, and instead had tried to eat normally, and take any pain as a form of punishment. After all, if I were to become a tough unsentimental private Investigator, then I would need to overcome such adversities, right? Right!

Having somehow survived the breakfast, I then had to overcome the pain of the shower water beating on my head. It had felt and sounded as if I'd been at a rehearsal for Carmen, and having that song 'Beat out that rhythm on a drum' continuously belted onto my head, as the water had pounded on it, having been accompanied so many times by the many ooh's and ah's that had been uttered by me in pain.

That copious amount of water from a 'great height' onto the soreness, had felt like it had been beaten into pulp, because it.

THE LADY DETECTIVE

Having eventually dressed myself in a smart two-piece grey suit, with a matching cream blouse, that I bought for the occasion, and having my hair tied back, and very little make-up, and wearing only pearl earrings, I had finally taken a long look at myself in a full length mirror, and wow!

Believe me my friends, regardless of how I felt in my head, I still looked great, even if I say so myself. So now I was sort of ready for work, at least from my neck down, and did look ready to take on whatever the day was going to bring me. Or so, I thought!

Do you ever find it strange that as soon as you start to think good thoughts, you always know, that you had thought of them too soon! I do.

I mean, having thought that I looked good, and how I was now ready to meet the day head on, I had then picked up my smart brown leather case, which had again got me thinking about those brown tassel shoes! Stop it, stop it now!

I should have instead perhaps been considering the state of my head, and not have allowed myself for one biddy moment, to think about the weather interfering with my day, because if I were to tell you that it was bad, that would have been an under-statement. I mean, having looked out of the window, you really have no idea how bad it was actually was.

So what if I was to tell you just for starters, that the skies were now actually chucking down hail stones the size of a baby's fist, and in bucket loads, would you believe me?

I had thought as I watched them slamming into the earth, how strange that to-day of all days, those guys up there in the watery heavens had gotten themselves bored, and having already got everyone down here soaked to the skin, had suddenly thought to get rid of some of the left-over ice that had been meant for somewhere else—the North pole maybe, and wanting to get rid of it before they'd all gone home, and then filled massive size bucket's with massive sized hail stones from the ice lying about, just to chuck down at us in bucketful's. Weid eh!

❦ 153 ❦

So there you have it, now you all know why we often say—'bucket loads of rain, hail'—although this had not just been 'bucket-loads', but bucket-loads of treble-size hail stones.

Now that I really mind ice cold rain, or even treble-size hail stones, I can live with that, under cover of course, but having to be bombarded with goose-eggs and endure icy cold winds out in the open—never!

Worse of all, with it being that time in the year when unusually icy cold strong winds would often come straight down from the North Pole, these winds are as fresh and cold as a fish lying on a fish slab full of ice, which meant that a wind of that kind would send an icy chill throughout your body, and gnaw into your bones, no-matter how warmly dressed you are! The stupidity of that thought had strangely amused me.

And now un-fortunately, I had another problem with my car being parked and sat in the driveway and not in the garage only yards away, twenty tops, from my cottage. So now I'd needed to make a quick dash for it, and then climb quickly inside to get out of the cold wind. Easy you'd think, yet that had proved harder than easier to be done.

I mean you may ask yourselves why, why had the weather been trying to make the most important day in my life, besides my having already a blinding headache—just a little bit more miserable. You answer me that?

Ok, so now I was stood just inside my partly open front door, and ready to make a dash for it, knowing that many others at this time, would also be doing the same, whilst they'd also been thinking about these icy cold conditions, and all hating it, before they had to also make their own dash to their own car.

Anyway, now steeling myself to make that explosive twenty yard dash, having decided that now would be the right time, I'd opened fully the front door, and faced the elements, and had after hurriedly locking the door, hurled myself across the open space to where my car was parked, and on reaching it, had then spent precious icy-cold seconds

THE LADY DETECTIVE

flapping around the door trying to see the key-hole through the driving rain.

Eventually I'd got it open, and threw myself into the car seat gasping very unladylike. *'I can't bloody believe this sodding weather.'*

Now taking in deep breaths, I'd slowly gathered myself together, before I'd turned on the heater, and the radio, half-expecting to hear the weather man say, *'this day would be mostly be dry with scattered showers* before I began to shiver most violently with feeling the cold and heard him say. *'and some warm sunshine.'*

However nothing was going to deter me from having my wonderful day, and even as I felt icy water creeping down my back, and looking towards the grey heavens that was now chucking down enough water to re-float Noah's Ark, I had felt a warm glow somewhere inside me.

I'd even warm thoughts for all the other cold suffering humans, having actually heard the newsman telling what was in store for me/them that day, which would be their own headache of sorts! The news-reader had then told us all there was to be a train-strike from ten o'clock on such an such date. And had then added would you believe this?

"It is also thought that ground-staff at the airports would be also coming out in sympathy from midday of that day." And to make things worse, the newsman had then added, 'Also it is rumoured that all public transport buses would also go on strike, if their own money demands weren't met!' And then thought—fools!

Can you believe those guys? And as for the airport, and then the public transport staff coming out in sympathy, my derriere, for even a child of three could have told you it was just another ploy, knowing that when it was their turn to put in for more wages, or go on strike, they too would get substantial backing from the other transport unions; which was just another instance of how these selfish, mindless, bar-stewards were, having intended to frustrate, upset and

❦ 155 ❦

annoy their fellow humans, for no other reason than their own greed—what else!

My dad would have said, 'they'd all known the terms of employment when they took the job, and the wages they'd get, so if they weren't satisfied with them, why take the job on in the first place?'

I might have also added. 'You may also have noticed that the unions do not strike during school-term, do they? Reason being, not to incur the wife's anger, or a heavy frying pan bounced around on his head.

And if that was not enough of a reason not to strike, when the wife had insisted her days 'were not to be messed up' with having to look after a load of screaming kids hanging around, and not going off to school, you'ld have thought she'd have then told him to not even consider it, cos strikers received no wages, which also meant no money for food, or to afford a baby-sitter on her only night out, and instead had to be grateful for having her hubby hanging around all day, doing and earning nothing!

So there you have it, so another quick kick in the where it was always painful for the long suffering travelling passengers. No wonder that more and more people are now saving up for a car—or so I have heard.

CHAPTER 45

At 08.49 am, I'd hoped to have put on a grand entrance, as I'd fully intended for a few minutes, to introduce myself to everyone and anyone either entering or leaving the building and tell them that I was now working with my own business on the 5th floor. 'What do you do?' they'll ask me. 'Oh I'm a Private Investigator' I'll reply. Because who knows, I might even get one or two jobs by doing that. 'Some hopes' my grandmother was fond of saying, we'll see.

Of course I'd also hoped for a lovely sunny day as well, and hadn't got that, and here I was about to make the second lightening dash of the morning, having parked my car in a car park, and in a pre-paid reserved space, a little less than 50 yards away.

Having dashed from there to have quickly got out of the wind and rain, I had on reaching the building's entrance, spent one full minute struggling to return my umbrella from inside out, after it had been blown 'out' by a gust of icy cold wind.

I'd then been greeted by another kind of chill factor, in the form of a big burly policeman, who'd been laughing his socks off at my being blown about in the cold wind, standing inside the double-door entrance, before I'd finally fiddled and got my inside-out umbrella back into place to get in the door.

❈ 157 ❈

Now having stepped inside the door entrance, I'd then been abruptly stopped from entering any further, not because of my umbrella, but by a dark blue arm with a large chubby hand that lay across my shoulder.

'And what is your business here, miss?' He stared at me in a kind of 'just watch it mate' hard looking way, and then had kind of growled 'Do you work here?' In probably his nicest sounding voice, even though to me it had still sounded like he was running his tonsils across gravel paper.

I turned to him, and politely in my sweetest voice had facetiously told him. 'I do have the honour and privilege to work here in this building Constable.'

I swear to him above, that this character had in all the time I'd been standing there, with his beady eyes staring out from his flabby face, had not for one second stopped looking over my torso, particularly at my breasts. His eyes you could see were trying to burrow under my coat, when he'd continued in a slightly more deferential tone of voice, to say.

'And what floor would that be on then, Miss?' in a tone almost as if was saying: *Now see here, I'm not one to be taken in by your beauty. I'm a man whose head is not easily turned, ok?'*

He'd also said the 'Miss', like he'd been told as a boy by his Granny, or maybe his mummy, that anyone who was as lovely as I am, must surely be always a Miss, and was one of those dangerous species to beware of.

I told him 'The 5th floor.'

'Oh the 5th floor you say. Well, well, do you now!' He said, and then had made me almost jump out of my high denier stockings when he'd shouted almost in my ear across to another police officer who'd been standing beside the metal lift.

'Bobby, this young lady says she works on the 5th floor.'

At the lift, I saw this burly police officer, he had called 'Bobby', standing by one of its sliding doors, and then the first copper added 'So you might want to accompany her up—to it!' he said with a smirk.

THE LADY DETECTIVE

'Bobby' I thought was an unfortunate name to have had, with him being a Peeler, a policeman; and wondered how much both of them had known about Robert Peel, then had thought 'perhaps nothing' having thought this particular policeman called 'Bobby', had looked slightly stupid, as I saw he had been nonchalantly watching both of us up to this moment.

So now having met the other burly one, I had that guy's mate, now smiling a sort of lopsided grin, similar to all those grins that I had already seen so many times in my life, that I could have even placed a bet on it happening.

So now I had a pudding-faced policeman called Bobby to contend with, as if I didn't have enough of a headache for one day!

Now the creep had started off the conversation by saying after I had walked over to him. 'Now don't you mind Dave, Miss,' having given a glance over towards the first creep, 'he is just a big old softy really.'

You could have fooled me. I mean the man was creepy. In-fact they both were! Because now he had been watching me with an open mouth that hung somewhere below his huge stomach, say by his boots, and saw his eyes had kept wondering all about my torso! What is it with some men?

I swore under my breath *I'd bash this fat creep in his baby farm if he doesn't let up!* And puzzled by what was happening, I asked.

'Perhaps you can tell me what this is all about Constable? Why all these precautions?'

'Ah! Well there's been a spot of bother . . . here . . . last night, Miss.' He shrugged in a 'do-I-really-care' kind of manner, his eyes having finally taken over from where his mate's had left off.

'Well I had already guessed it'll be something like that Constable, though you might not care to believe it!' And gave him a look that said *'Do you really think I'm as stupid as you look'*—not that he noticed, and instead asked. 'So what sort of bother are you referring to, Constable?'

❧ 159 ❧

He was still looking down towards my bosoms, making me thankful that I had been dressed in a thick coat and not a bathing-costume—or less, and after shaking his head, had continued in a doleful manner. 'The dead body sort of bother miss.' And continued with his staring!

Seeing he wasn't in a chatty mood, I'd then followed the fat 'blue-bottle' into the lift, and stood silently to the right of him, before we both had proceeded up to the 5th floor in 'ye old metal cage', this being one of those old metal lifts where you could see through the metal framing, so even before we'd arrived at the 5th floor, I'd known there'd been quite a number of people stood in hallway, cos that is the advantage of travelling in the 'ye old metal cage' not being modern I suppose!

Having arrived at its destination, the old lift had given out its customary ping, and on exiting, I'd been quickly surrounded by another two uniformed policeman, who'd then tried to keep the half-a-dozen reporters who'd been in the hallway away from me, for they'd suddenly all rushed up to me, and besides rudely bustling me, had been asking stupid questions.

It seemed as if they'd been all talking nineteen to the dozen; asking me what I knew about the dead man, who he was, and was he perhaps a boyfriend, or my husband, and many other equally stupid questions on those lines, which considering I hadn't a clue who it was they had been referring to, was totally stupid!

Whilst all of this had been going on, bulbs had been flashing in my face, and the reporters, plus the cameramen, were now becoming more confrontational, and scary.

I do know at the time, I had begun shaking my head at them in total bewilderment, before saying: 'Look, I haven't got the faintest idea what this is about, but I will suggest, that if you don't back off right now, then one of you will get hurt.' And they did back off, slightly.

Then a further half-minute had gone by before a very tall, extremely overweight gentleman, dressed in an ill-fitting sombre looking grey stained suit, which had seen better days, as had his scruffy blue-striped shirt with the collar on one side sticking up in the air, who called out loudly as he pushed his way through the reporters and photographers. 'Now come on you lot, give her a bloody chance will you. Move away—now.' And they all did, at once.

Then the big man had after a quick word with a slightly older looking plain clothes policeman, who I later know as DC. Williams, who'd then had a word with this Bobby character, who'd then had a word with another Constable, had both gestured threateningly to the reporters to move to both sides of the hallway, or else, and let me through, they did.

CHAPTER 46

This grossly overweight man had then taken hold of my arm, I let him, and pulled me not too gently up the almost empty hall, and as we both walked behind Williams, had released my arm and turned towards me saying, 'Sorry about that Miss. I'm Detective Sergeant Stokes, local CID'.

He'd paused, and rolling his wet-looking eyes at me, had begun to lick his fat sloppy looking lips as if he had just finished a mouthful of something enjoyable.

Now my basic instincts were telling me that I didn't like this man any more than I had liked his fat colleagues; the two policemen who I'd previously met. However there was something quite repugnant about this man, besides his grossness, and when I had to shake his limp hand, I had shuddered with revulsion.

'Right, so who might you be then, Miss?' He demanded in what seemed to me to be either in a Devon or Cornish accent, 'and what is the purpose of your visit here, might I ask?'

Do you know what really annoys me about policeman? Is there saying Miss? Why is it, nearly all of them had assumed you were a Miss when they address you? It's always Miss this, or Miss that. Now why do you think that is? I mean do I look too young to be married?

Alright, as I was wearing gloves because of the cold, he certainly hadn't been able to observe my wearing any

❖ 162 ❖

THE LADY DETECTIVE

rings to call me Mrs. Perhaps they can all tell us single girls because we look happier and have less worry lines on our faces than most wives normally do! Although I have a feeling, that there'd be some policeman who'd have said Miss to their Grandma.

'Well Sergeant *Stokes,*' I said emphasising his surname. 'I happen to work here,' I replied in my most casual manner.

'Oh do you now! And what office would that be then, Miss? It wouldn't by any chance be Byways Ltd, or perhaps Rugs and Tings, would it Miss?' There he goes again with the Miss!

'Neither one of those . . . Sergeant,' I answered haughtily.

The fat man appeared to have suddenly become disappointed, perhaps I hadn't said the words loud enough for him to have heard, so I repeated. 'I don't work at either of those places Sergeant; I work for a Private Investigation Agency.'

He seemed to suddenly go into a deep thought before saying. 'Oh right Miss . . . good . . . well that's alright then.' He then scratched at his chins before asking. 'And what is it you do there then?' He said puffing out his cheeks in a peculiar way, 'some sort of receptionist, are we?'

The cheeky blighter, now his saying that had made me dislike him even more than I had before . . . In fact, I now loathed the man!

'That's perfectly amazing Sergeant! So how did you know I'm *some sort of receptionist, are we*' kind of girl?' I replied facetiously, now beginning to lose my cool, then abruptly said. 'Now it's your turn to answer my questions if you will.'

He'd nodded quickly, so I'd notice his chins flapping up and down like a flag in high wind, before I continued. 'So perhaps you can now tell me why all of these questions? And what is this rumpus all about?' I asked.

He just stood there, his huge stomach overlapping his belted trousers, and breathing heavily, and when he again nodded, I'd again been intrigued by all his chins wobbling when he said. 'Oh, I can only tell you that we've found a body in one of the offices, and I can't tell you which one.'

ROBERT H FELLOWS

'Ah, oh dear,' I said all knowingly, 'so who is this dead person? Now I can only hazard a guess that he, or she, was found in either Byways Ltd, or Rugs and Tings. Am I right?

He stared at me then said, 'All will be revealed in time Miss, all in good time.'

'It was because you sort of said it was one of those two, didn't you Sergeant, by you asking if I worked at either one of them? And now I would hazard a further guess to say that the body was actually found in Byways Ltd. Am I right?'

'And how do you figure that?' He asked as he lent over towards me, so that now I could smell his cheap after-shave, or was it his body odour? Well, whatever it was, it smelt gross, just like the fat Sergeant was.

'Because you asked if I worked at Byways Ltd, before Rugs and Tings. So am I right?'

He ignored me, which confirmed my suspicions, before he said. 'What about our going to your workplace for a little chat, just to see how much you really do know about those two offices, and who works there,' he growled 'if that'll be convenient with your Guvnor, that is?'

'Oh that won't be a problem. Private Investigators can be most amiable creatures—at times.'

CHAPTER 47

I 'd needed to brush past him, just, to make my way up to the further ten yards to my office, and had heard his clump-clumping footsteps as he struggled to keep up with my faster pace, until I'd reached my new office door, and then stood proudly looking at it.

Stokes had now also taken a long look at my new sign, and shook his head in puzzlement—before saying. 'Nice door. Very nice,' as he stood looking at it, 'though I've never heard of this Jess Felliosi fella before,' he'd grunted, before absent-mindedly starting to scratch, or was he fondling, his crutch.

Even though the man had totally disgusted me, I'd nevertheless been distracted by this spectacle, and because of it, had spent an extra few seconds fumbling around in my new briefcase feeling for the office keys.

Truth was, I almost never carried a handbag, even though I'd brought with me a new briefcase, and now thought it'll be far more convenient just to have deep-fitting pockets added to a suit, or a jacket whilst doing this job, and will now never again continue to use a briefcase.

Finding the keys, I'd opened the office door as wide as I could just to let the fat man inside, and as he passed me, I'd again smelt that awful whiff of after-shave, or stale body-odour, that had assailed my senses like a nightmare. In other words, this man smelt terrible, and would be high on

❧ 165 ❧

my list of people who I did not want to be near without an oxygen mask!

Obviously I wasn't too happy about that, particularly as he'd been the first stranger to have entered my new domain, and I'd suddenly hoped that his smell and presence, wasn't a sign of what was to come!

'Jeez,' he said when he'd looked around my new offices, 'if being a Private Investigator gets you all of this,' he waved his massive arm around in a circle, 'then I'm definitely on the wrong side of this business.'

I smiled quietly to myself, inwardly thanking him for his remarks as he was nodding his approval, and I'd even smiled when he said. 'Whoever this Jess guy is, he must be doing pretty well for himself by the looks of this place.' He looked to Williams, who'd nodded his agreement.

I left him to ponder on his thoughts for a few moments more over what he'd said, though I had been secretly pleased as punch about his pleasant reaction on seeing my offices, and thought, *"well if it pleases this clown, then as sure as dogs are dogs, it's going to please all the non-clowns that'll hopefully be following him into here."*

'Would you or your colleague, like a Coffee or tea?' I asked, after I'd switched on the 'Mr Beverages' vendor, looking at Williams who'd nodded. 'Ok, black or white?'

'Coffee black, no sugar, thank you,' said Williams. Then I said 'Mr. Stokes before you ask your questions . . . would you like a drink?'

He looked sharply at me. 'It's Sergeant Stokes or just plain Sergeant. And yes, a cup of tea would be just fine Miss, and will go down very nicely, thank you. No sugar though,' he said looking a little sheepish and down at his stomach, then at Williams and myself, 'reason being, my good wife is now insisting that I should try to lose some weight. What do you think?'

Without bothering to look at him I said. 'You know Sergeant, most women do have this uncanny knack of being right when it comes to knowing about that type of problem!

THE LADY DETECTIVE

But you'd know that of course?' He'd nodded, and had then looked at Williams who was smiling quietly to himself.

Stokes then awkwardly shifted his huge bulk in my new leather armchair to make himself more comfortable, and each time he moved, the armchair had started to give out groaning sounds, whilst he considered what I'd just said about his weight being insulting or not, so I added.

'So to answer your question Sergeant, you do most certainly need to lose weight. In fact I would say you need to lose a lot of weight . . . for your own good . . . health-wise that is,' and handing him his tea said, 'and no sugar it is.'

He'd finally whispered. 'Right you are Miss. So that's ok then. I mean she . . . the missus, must be right then.' He paused to think for a moment longer, then gave the faintest of smiles before saying. 'So to change the subject, shall we get on to something that is at this moment, *also* very big on my agenda?'

Surely not! Surely this gross man didn't have a sense of humour, did he? He didn't look the sort.

He continued. 'So tell me what you know about those two offices up there?' He asked looking down at his notes, 'umm, Byways Ltd, and Rugs and Tings?'

Sitting back in my own office chair I replied. 'What can I say that will help you, Sergeant? For I know nothing at all about either of the offices . . . really nothing at all. In fact until yesterday, I hadn't known anyone who'd even worked there until I met this all hat and long coat American type man!'

I paused looking at his face, then asked. 'So tell me Sergeant, was it Byways Ltd where the dead body was found? It was wasn't it?'

He eyed me, and growled. 'Oh that's very good that is. Got that one in quick didn't you Miss? So now to answer your question, yes it was the office. In fact a very dead person was found there, as is, who may have died there sometime during the week-end, so the doc thinks.'

'Though we'll know better once we get the lab report back later on to-morrow,' added Williams pleasantly.

❖ 167 ❖

Stokes stared at Williams as if to say now don't say too much feller, before saying. 'Now are you sure you've never met anyone else from up there before yesterday—it being Sunday?'

'No not until yesterday, as I've said.' Then I'd had a thought, so added. 'Surely the dead man couldn't have been that man I'd met yesterday morning in the hallway could it? No, that couldn't be, because neither he, or anyone else had for that matter, been in either of those offices when I'd paid them both a visit last night.'

I knew then that I should have said no more, instead I had added 'Also Sergeant Stokes, I was here all of yesterday from before 9 am up to 6 pm'ish last night, and I'd seen no-one besides the man I met early yesterday afternoon in the hallway, as I've said.

CHAPTER 48

Suddenly sitting more upright than before, so again the poor chair had groaned its anguish with Stokes' sudden heavy movement, and unlikely as it would ever seem, Sergeant Stokes had certainly become slightly more alert, and said. 'Is this perhaps one of your riddles? How did you know there wasn't anyone in the offices at 6 o'clock—pm?'

Ignoring him I continued. 'And if it had been this man who was now dead, which it can't be, that would now narrow down the time of the poor man's death not to have been around two 'til 6 pm. However as I said, it couldn't have been him, because I saw him leaving not long after four o'clock in the afternoon, that is.' I said with a smile.

'Did this man give you his name?'

'No he didn't, although I can assure you he was the only person who I saw from up there.

'And that's all you can say about the day, is it Miss?'

'And as I've said, I do know there was no-one in either of those offices when I left here about 6 pm. 'Because I had already knocked on both doors about that time, as I was curious about the tall man from Rugs and Tings. And had seen the light was on in Byways, but not the other one!'

Oh dear, what have I said, so best explain. I then told Stokes all that had happened the previous day when I'd visited the offices—and about the time I'd spent with the man I'd met in the hallway. I then told him how he had got me wondering why his attitude had changed so much from being a Mr Nice guy, to being a Mr Grumpy guy, and how I had personally thought that he'd not been the same man that I'd seen entering, as the one I'd seen leaving—and he had a shoe problem!

You could see that he was now about to ask me a question about my having mentioned the 'shoe problem', which was still puzzling me, as I watched his chins wobbling furiously when the fat man was nodding his head. 'And what shoe mystery would that be Miss? You mentioned this man had a shoe problem?'

'Not exactly what you might call a shoe problem Sergeant Stokes, more like he appeared to have had more than one pair of shoes in his office.'

'Oh I see, the man had more than one pair of shoes in his office, is that right!' The now baffled Sergeant asked Williams. 'So how many pairs of shoes did you find in the dead man's office Williams?'

Looking at his notes Williams said, 'None at all.'

I'd then explained to both detectives about the man having worn two different pairs of shoes that afternoon, and Williams replied. 'A brown and a black pair you say!'

'Ah, you find that interesting do you Williams?'

'Could be Serge, could be.'

I asked. 'Which coloured shoes were found on the body then, Sergeant?'

'That's classified for the moment Miss. Sorry.' He told me.

'Right, so now whose body was it that you found in Byways offices? Because that was where you said the body had been found, wasn't it Sergeant?'

'If you don't mind Miss, I'm supposed to be asking the questions.'

He looked sternly at me. 'Well I suppose there's no harm in telling you that the night porter found a man in Byways Ltd. He says he was going about doing his nightly inspection, when he noticed that the office lights were still on in Byways

THE LADY DETECTIVE

Ltd, just as you said you'd seen them, and just as you've said, he'd got no answer when he knocked on the door, so had opened it with the intention of turning the lights off, by using his own spare key from the set of keys that he always keeps in his office downstairs.' He puffed out his cheeks, and giving an almighty sigh continued. 'It was then he said he found the dead man lying on the floor. Ok, now you know pretty much as I do Miss.'

I thought for a moment before saying. 'You may be right, though you may consider the man that I saw in the hallway, had said he worked at Rugs and Tings, and had not mentioned Byways Ltd at any time.'

'So you say Miss. So you say.'

'Well you also said the night porter had found a dead man in Byways Ltd; well Sergeant, that man I've never met. So I suppose the next thing you'll be asking me to do, will be to look at the dead man, just to ascertain whether he was, or was not, the same man that I saw, although his face I never saw. Am I right?'

'Spot on Miss,' said Williams with a smile, and a glare from Stokes.

'Yes that's alright, we might as well get this over and done with now you've mentioned it,' Stokes said, and then added. 'Will that be alright with your boss when he gets in?'

'Oh there be no worries on that score Sergeant, *he* won't say anything!' I smiled.

Stokes had then with an accompanying grunt which had sounded like something painful, as he literally had pushed himself up from the chair, had after he'd lifted his large frame, then moaned. 'Both you and my Missus, could be dam right you know! I do need to lose some weight!'

'Yes you certainly should, Sergeant, and lots of it!' And then I'd seen Williams putting a hand up to his face to hide a smile. 'However to answer your question if it's ok to leave this office, well it's not very convenient for me at this moment, but should you give me, say thirty minutes or so, then the other receptionist girl will be arriving, and then I can oblige you.'

❖ 171 ❖

'Right, that's fine by me, cos I can in the meantime, see to it that everything will be ok for you to view the body down at the morgue. So I'll call back in twenty-five minutes or so.'

He'd then left, taking his smell with him, not meaning Williams of course!

CHAPTER 49

Fortunately, or perhaps unfortunately for me, Pasha had arrived early for work, obviously keen to make a good impression with this being her first official full working day for me.

When she walked through the door, her nose had wrinkled, and I had needed to quickly explain whilst I'd been opening the windows wide, that 'a fat Police Sergeant has been in here, who either had BO, or had a bad after-shave.'

I'd then quickly told her all that had happened along the hallway, at Byways Ltd, and surprise, surprise, she had already managed to find that out from 'Bobby' at the door.

Then I told her that I had now to view the dead body to see if it had been the man I saw yesterday, and asked. 'Can you cope ok if I left you to take charge of the fort for an hour or so?' Meaning for her to take down any enquires, phone messages etcetera, whilst I went off with the fat man to the mortuary!

Her answering 'that it'll be a doddle,' gave me the impression that for me to have asked and given her simple instructions like that, might have sounded to her as if I'd thought she might have been slightly dim-witted or something, and should have known that I'd never need to be ever concerned.

She said. 'My, my, I've only been working here for less than five minutes, and already my boss is telling me she needs

❈ 173 ❈

to identify a dead corpse, and now finds herself involved with a murder enquiry.' She laughed 'Now who would have ever guessed that this job could have ever been this exciting . . . and so soon?' She then shook her head and giggled, and said 'whatever next eh, Miss Felliosi, whatever next?'

Of course, not knowing she had tempted fate, she would again be saying those words a few hours later!

*   *   *

Now un-smiling, she had you might say been putting on a brave face, before I'd left the office with fatso Stokes, having had a sample of fatso's delightful odour when he returned. Although at least it seemed I had left her looking reasonably happy with life.

No so for myself—for her words 'Whatever next', had kept repeating themselves over and over again in my mind during the time I'd been driven to the mortuary in a police car, for this was to have been a double first for me, with my viewing a dead body, and being in a police car.

The journey to the morgue had given me a little time to mull over what had happened so far to me in the first hour of my being a new PI, and I'd pondered over what time in this day I would finally be allowed to actually make myself available to start in my own new business.

I'd been saying to myself. *"Surely it wouldn't be asking too much if I was to ask the fat man to speed things up a little, so that I could at least spend some time in my new office on my first morning!"*

Some hopes, as 'Whatever next' you will see would soon be ringing true.

After I'd arrived at the morticians, I had been kept waiting for over an hour to view the body, having had for company, empty wooden caskets, a few wooden chairs, and a small wooden table that had funeral magazines on it to look at. However the worst part of these proceedings was my having to listen to eerie back-ground music that had meant, I could only assume, to have been a calming effect on the bereaved. I'd personally thought it would give anyone the proverbial creeps. Well it did me!

Finally sixty-nine minutes after arriving, I'd been shown into a cold white-tiled room that had a body of a man lying on his back, on a metal slab. I was then being told by a very tall skinny person with whiskers, and wearing a long green butchers apron that already had several splashes of red on it, 'that unfortunately the long delay had been my cleaning up the body to make it more presentable for your viewing.'

'Great, thank you!' I said sarcastically.

Moments later I realised I'd thanked him too soon, for in the time it took him to present the dead man *In a favourable way,* he hadn't in the end done a good enough job as far as I was concerned, for I'd still failed to recognise the man, had he even been a man, because his face had been so badly damaged, smashed in more like, that it was unrecognisable.

I probably could have also have guaranteed, that anyone, including his own mother, would have been unlikely to have known who he was just by looking at him, so it certainly had been out of the question for me to have known who he was the man I saw. Gross!

In fact, I thought after leaving that cold morbid room, that viewing the dead man had been a complete waste of my time. However I did that morning, give the skinny undertaker man another job to do whilst he'd been listening to his classical music, which wouldn't I thought, be anything like as messy as cutting up a body, or be as upsetting as having to view your first dead body whose face had been so totally battered as to be unrecognisable, that I had as my parting contribution, needed to vomit on the skinny undertaker's clean tiled floor.

After that awful experience, and still feeling slightly nauseous, I'd been taken back to the Police Station canteen, and there, would you believe, had been offered a fried breakfast, which I had of course naturally refused, but did accept a cup of black coffee that had tasted more like a gorilla's armpit.

After that, I'd been sat down and interviewed in another tiled room, and been asked to once again repeat my statement once more on everything I'd witnessed and done from Sunday morning to last night, and especially everything to do with Byways Ltd—and that had even included the viewing of the dead body that I'd previously seen.

In the statement, I did repeat that I'd never actually saw the face of the man on Sunday, either on his coming or on his leaving the hallway, which I said, was due to the man having a hat with a wide brim that he'd worn, which had covered the upper part of his face.'

I had also repeated all I'd previously said to Stokes that morning, about it being my opinion, that the man who I saw leaving the building, might not be the same man as I saw entering the hallway, even though the corpse I'd seen on the slab that morning, had not looked too dissimilar to the man's physique who I saw leaving the building, and a lot like the guy who I'd previously met. So I could only assume, because of his stature, he was either Mr Nice guy or Mr Grumpy. I had then signed my statement.

Stokes having read that little lot, would now be totally confused; especially with my concluding my not being at all sure who it had been on the slab, having said *how could anyone be sure that it was even a man with his face being so badly disfigured! Although I suppose I could say all that was disconcerting!"*

I had also strongly stated, 'that for me to have viewed that body had been extremely disconcerting for two reasons. One) being obviously how the poor man had looked, and two) my having to wait around for such a long time whilst he'd been cleaned up, and made more presentable. And then added a third, which having to listen to eerie music for an hour, which was a joke.

And when I'd finally come to realise that it had been less than a day, less than 24 hours, when I'd spoken to the

THE LADY DETECTIVE

big amiable man, and had even enjoyed those few moments of his company; and now the poor man was dead, that could have been four, which made me feel a lot worse than one and two or three.

Finally I told Stokes 'that I'd also had responsibilities', and 'had spent enough time helping the Police, and would like to go back to my office, to work hopefully!'

Stokes had then offered to have me taken to my offices, although there'd been more than a hint of sarcasm in his voice when he said. 'Or perhaps you'll now prefer for me to have you taken back to your home instead . . . as you are that disconcerted.'

Sod him! I knew now even more why I really could get to dislike that horrible, fat, insensitive detective, even more than I already did.

So I had snapped back. 'You might like to try and get your domineering wife to take a look at a dead person sometime, especially one whose had their face smashed up like a squashed tomato, and then I suggest you ask her, Sergeant, if she had liked that any more than I did, especially were it to have been the very first corpse she had ever seen.'

Do you know, I do believe he'd understood that! Though I do believe as I had been walking away from him, I fancied I had heard a few titters of laughter coming from the other policeman, when I hissed back at him.

'And another thing, Sergeant, even though the taxes on my wages will certainly be helping towards paying your wages, who do you think will be paying my wages whilst I'm spending time trying to help you? Well it certainly wouldn't be you, would it Sergeant? So I suggest that you become a little more civil to the people who *are* trying to help the police . . . if civil is a word you know!'

When finally I'd been taken back to the sanctuary of my own offices, the time had been after 1 pm, having spent all that morning being around that overweight, obnoxious, smelly detective Sergeant, who I'd hoped had been left with just a little more than a bruised ego after I'd left the Police Station.

❦ 177 ❦

I smiled, as he undoubtedly would now be having a huge problem in solving the murder, almost equal to his having his own equally large problem of reducing his size to please his wife. Haha.

I saw him now either mulling over one or the other, though with it being lunchtime, I bet he'd have immediately gone to the Police canteen to stuff his fat face with greasy food, and in-between mouthfuls of jam doughnut, black pudding, or some such food, would be reflecting on everything I had written in my statement, as well as my having to answer verbally, all of the stupid questions that he'd asked me.

CHAPTER 50

As I was coming out of these childish thoughts, I'd noticed the driver of the police car who was taking me back to my offices, had been driving very slowly, which I thought was strange for any police driver to be that cautious, until I caught him looking into his rear view mirror—at me, which he must have been doing probably for most of the time he'd been driving.

I'd then immediately realised that I'd again been lumbered with another fat 'creep' as I hastily re-arranged my skirt, and pulling it right down over my knees. Then I had done up the top two buttons of my cream blouse, and buttoned up my suit jacket.

Now I'd known this fat creep had spent most of the time he'd been driving me back to my office looking at who knows what in his rear view mirror, I saw that the horrible man had smiled!

Then I thought that this man might have actually been related to those other two 'stout gentlemen' who I'd met that morning, and was another one of those who belonged to the overweight brigade of policeman fatties.

By why were there so many in the Metro, I asked myself? Perhaps the Police Force now had a new policy that I didn't know about, which was to actually fatten them up like they were Japanese Sumo wrestlers, then to show them off as a new police symbol of their having a comfortable job to

❦ 179 ❦

recruit others! Or were they now been employing a certain percentage of gross dirty-minded men as coppers, to help solve them solve all the sex related crimes?

Anyway, I swear by my No 16 denier stockings, that this man had not stopped doing the ogling bit for the rest of the journey, regardless if he'd known I'd caught him being a letch. And even now, after we'd arrived back at my offices, when I was walking away from him and up to the building steps, I still sensed he hadn't stopped his staring at whatever he enjoyed staring at!

Well that's some men for you, and I can assure you, I had only given him a 'thank you' type smile when we'd first met, which I can again assure you, is nothing like my 'come on baby light my fire' kind of smile.

Now had he seen that smile, and the look that went with it, he would have definitely found that disconcerting, the sick sod!

CHAPTER 51

MONDAY AFTERNOON

An hour and a half later, I was still slightly annoyed with the man, having completed marking up some new A to Z files for both the four draw cabinets, when Pasha had knocked on my door, saying. 'Sergeant Stokes would like to have a few words with you.'

What possibly could this fat slob want now with me I wondered? And thinking it couldn't be too serious, I had with a half-smile said jokingly. 'Ok Pasha let him in, however first open up my window, will you please?'

As soon as Stokes had waddled into my office, I saw on his face that he was far from being a happy man, supposing that might have been a normal face, for he hadn't been at all happy when I'd first met him, or about the murder, or even during the time I'd been at the mortuary, or even at the Police Station, and he definitely wasn't a happy bunny right now.

Abruptly without a greeting he said: 'We need to talk Miss,' and when I nodded, and then asked him if he would like a cup of tea, he then had also nodded.

'Pasha, would you mind getting Mr Stokes a cup of tea please? And um, no sugar, for the Sergeant's been told by his

❀ 181 ❀

wife that he has to try to lose some weight . . . and sugar is as you know . . . fattening.'

Had Stokes known I'd been making fun of him, he'd chosen to ignore my jibe, and had said. 'Look Miss, I'll come straight to the point.'

I'd grimaced at his calling me Miss again, yet smiled as he sat facing me, whilst holding heavily onto the arms of the armchair, which had again groaned it's protests of having to carry someone with his enormous weight as he maneuvered his oversized body from side to side.

He was saying. 'Do you remember you telling me that you didn't know anyone in those two offices up the hallway, other than your having had a brief chat with the man from Rugs and Tings. Do you remember saying that?' I nodded that I did, and began wondering where all of these questions were leading up to.

He went on. 'Yet you also said in your statement, that later you did that night, after you had seen him leave the building, and because you weren't sure it was him, had gone down the hallway just to make sure, after you had closed up shop for the night, Is that right?' Again I nodded.

He paused, and with a look that looked very much like a smirk, added 'All because you wanted to say goodnight to the man. Correct?' Again I nodded. 'So now I'm wondering why you would have wanted to have done that, Miss?'

I gave him a look as if to say "Now you say Miss just one more time buster, and I'll bust you on the nose."

He'd continued sarcastically. 'Surely that might have been thought by some people, as being a bit unusual wouldn't you say? Although I thought it might have been love at first sight kind of thing. Or maybe, had been kind of cheap, considering you previously told me you didn't know the man from Adam . . . don't you think Miss?'

Angrily I'd sprung out of my chair, and slapped him hard across the left cheek for calling me cheap, and once more across the right cheek, for calling me Miss again.

THE LADY DETECTIVE

'Now, now' he said rubbing his cheeks, 'there's no need for that violence was there?'

'And there was also no need for your sordid cheap implications either, Sergeant! That could be classed as defamation of character, and you'll be lucky if I don't report you.'

Having been taken aback by his stupid wild assumption, and sordid mind, I should have then also given him a further full broadside of my tongue, as I had promised myself for the past few hours to do the next time I saw him, especially having now thought his remarks had been extremely insulting, and shown a lack of respect for a well brought-up girl, when Pasha had knocked on my door to give Stokes his cup of tea.

'Thank you. Do you see this,' he said, showing her fat cheeks with my finger imprints clearly showing. And then had for no reason I could think of, it had then occurred to me that our fat obnoxious Sergeant obviously liked his 'loves' to be curvy, for his eyes had continued to look over her with a look that said it all, lust, sex, want, having obviously forgotten for that moment, why his stupid assumption had gotten him the slap.

Clapping my hands together, had brought him back from his lusty revelries, and nearly made him spill his tea, when I said. 'Love at first sight did you say Sergeant,' looking at Pasha, 'now don't be so silly, there is no such thing.' And yet I thought our fat obnoxious Sergeant did now obviously believe in 'it', by the way he had continued to ogle Pasha.

Continuing the conversation in a soft threatening voice, so I'd almost spat the words at him. 'Sergeant Stokes, to get back to the point, you might say that by my making a gesture of that sort, would not have been so dissimilar to you going to your new next door neighbour to say hello, and maybe taking them a gift of some sort to cement the neighbourly relationship, as mine would have been by going up the hallway to the man. Not that you would understand small niceties like that, would you Sergeant?'

❧ 183 ❧

Then thinking I would definitely smash him up if did say anything derogatory, it was fortunate that he didn't.

Instead he'd ignored my sarcasm, and growled. 'For some reason, instinct some might call it, I don't think you are telling me the truth Miss Felliosi. You see, your finger-prints were not only found on the Rugs and Things door handle, they were also found in the man's office, and even on the telephone amongst other places. And not only that, Miss Felliosi, your finger-prints were also found on the door handle of Byways Ltd, the office of the deceased, meaning where the body was found!'

Then deliberately plumbing up his voice he said. 'Now was that also your being frightfully friendly was it?'

I spoke back to him in the same way, with an added cold tone in my voice after taking in what he had said. 'Sergeant Stokes, you may recall I have already spent a great deal of my day telling you everything I know? And now because you can think of nothing else that you can do to find the killer, you thought once again to come here and waste even more of my valuable time, which I might add, is time that I can hardly charge you for, is it?'

Having said that, I gave him time to ponder over what I was going to say next, before I'd then added. 'So might I suggest a quicker method to answer your questions, would be for you to now go back to your Station, and then read my statement . . . thoroughly this time, Sergeant!'

I'd been surprised when he chose to ignore what I said, by his saying. 'And so having found your dabs on the door-handle of Byways Ltd, my next question is obviously not surprising. Which is, why should you have also wanted to try to break into Byways Ltd, having already broken into Rugs and Tings?'

I gasped, for I thought both the point and his question were valid enough, and as I hadn't mentioned my having a look around Rugs and Tings in my statement, I would now need to think of an equally valid answer why I did, and as I couldn't, I'd said light-heartedly.

THE LADY DETECTIVE

'Oh Sergeant, facts please, its Rugs and Tings, not Things as you said,' not meaning to be sarcastic, and had at the same time smiled, and feigning concern, I'd in turn questioned. 'Surely you're not thinking that it was I who killed the man . . . are you?' He sort of nodded. 'Really, are you seriously thinking that I had something to do with savagely murdering the man, and thinking that I might need a lawyer? Well are you?'

And when he'd again nodded, I hissed. 'You can't be serious?'

'Not at all Miss Felliosi, because the man had been lying on the floor very dead, at around the time you say you tried the door, according to the pathologist! So I would like you to tell me what it was you wanted from the dead man's office that had made you so determined to get into Rugs and Things . . . Tings, and Byways Ltd?'

'I have already told you, twice, why I went up there.'

Ignoring me 'And then there's you saying you hadn't known anything about the owners, except to have spoken a few words to the man you call Mr Happy, and then wanting to break into this and another complete stranger's offices. Strange action wouldn't you say?'

He glared at me, and growled: 'So bow I'll repeat. Don't you think that was a very strange action for a young lady of your standing to do, particularly when you hadn't any valid reason to have done it?'

'Look,' I said, now feeling very uncertain of myself at this moment, 'I've already told you why.'

He paused weighing up in his mind what was to be his next question. 'Oh yes, so you have, and assuming you are as innocent as you say you are, you say you knocked on a man's office door that you had never met before, being Byways, and that was after rummaging around the office of a man who you'd just met, that strikes me as kind of weird wouldn't you say? I mean whatever made you want to do that to people who you say you didn't know?'

'It's all in my statement Sergeant.' I said unconvincingly.

✦ 185 ✦

'And then you say you had unlawfully entered into the office of Rugs and Tings, having found the door was open. So again, what on earth was so important to have made you want to have a jolly good nose around, after putting on the office lights first?'

'I was being curious, with it being open.'

He looked hard at me. 'So you were being curious was it? So what made you want to use the phone? Common less lies please!'

He'd stopped talking, and instead had continued to look at me with a curious sort of delight in his eyes. Then he'd continued in a gruff voice. 'Ok, so having done that, why then should you have especially wanted to be in that office in the first place, when no-one was home? Curious wouldn't you say? And surely not something that a normal person would have done—was it? So yes, you could say you might be in need of a lawyer.'

He'd then taken out from his breast jacket pocket, another old cigar-butt, and without asking my permission if he could smoke in my office, had lit up, giving Pasha and myself a strong whiff of the cheap foul smelling cigar smoke, which did for a moment, of course help cover over his strong body odour. Small blessings don't they say?

I then snapped at him. 'You can do whatever you want if you are that way inclined, Sergeant, however I must ask you to first put out that foul smelling weed out in my office.' And this was before he'd even had time to have one puff of that foul weed he'd held in his large spongy hand. Then I said. 'Now if you please.'

He seemed surprised that I had allowed him to smoke; and probably at the strength and tone in my voice, and was now looking around and asked for an ashtray, to which I glibly told him that 'I hadn't one,' and Pasha had just shrugged when he looked at her.

Not knowing exactly what he should do, Stokes had spent a few moments just sitting in his armchair, holding onto a cigar that he had no further use for, at least not in my office he hadn't; before making an extreme effort to rise from out of

THE LADY DETECTIVE

his chair, had then excused himself, and I assume had then headed to the men's communal toilets situated further down the hallway, into which, I can again only assume, he'd flicked the lit part of the cigar into the urinal, and then probably pocketed the remainder of the cigar stub back into his pocket, before returning again to my office.

My office, don't you still love the sound of that?

In the meantime, Pasha had whilst he'd been doing that, asked me 'if I was alright?' and 'was there anything she could do for me?' and had on my saying 'no thank you', disappeared from sight saying, 'that man is what you might call a nasty piece of work, and for whatever reason, he must have deserved the slap you gave him.' Smiling she'd finally added 'besides the man's so smelly.'

It was good to see she had noticed the slap-mark, and that had inwardly made me feel a lot better within myself, especially with her having made me laugh with what she'd said about his being smelly, especially after she had hurried out of my office, and then came back seconds later, with one of those new air-sprays that gave out a nice odour of roses; and once she had given the room a liberal dosing of it, had thought for a second to open the windows before my saying. 'No, it'll be too cold.'

I quickly told her what Stokes had said to me to get the slap, and had said 'Even though he's a fool, he could if he wished too, cause me a load of trouble just for the sake of it,' and she'd nodded.

Stokes re-appeared minutes later, apologised, and had again sat down, still looking slightly sheepish, red faced, and sweating.

When I say he had sat down, I really meant he had in fact dropped himself down into the armchair like he'd been a sack of potatoes, which again gave licence for the poor chair, judging by the anguished sounds it made, to once again appeal to anyone for help.

That anguish I thought I knew better than anyone else at this moment, just by my having to sit opposite this obnoxious man, for he was not, as they say, a pretty sight!

❦ 187 ❦

CHAPTER 52

N ow he continued with a slightly less hostile manner than previously, when he said. 'Now where was I? Oh yes, I remember. So to repeat myself, don't you think it strange you doing any of those things, just because you had wished to say goodnight to a man that you didn't even know!'

I kept silent, knowing he hadn't this time, said it as an insult.

He continued. 'So come on now Miss Felliosi, surely you are not asking me as a grown man, to believe that was the truth—are you?'

Now he was sounding like a Barrister winding up a murder trial, and was positively beaming with self-satisfaction when he added.

'You see, I think I know why you went to say goodnight to him,' he paused, 'it was because you had already known him. In fact I think you knew him very well; and probably because he had tried it on in his office, and with you having none of it, had turned nasty, and then you had somehow banged him over the head many, many times, with something that was very heavy, having killed him in self-defence. That's the answer isn't it?

Of course forensics have pointed out to me that the heavy object still hasn't been found. Although to establish who or

⚜ 188 ⚜

THE LADY DETECTIVE

what it might have been,' he pointed at me, 'you can be sure that we will find out what it is, even if you don't tell me!'

He then sat back even further into the chair, again making it squeal its displeasure before he continued: 'Now I know you are more than capable of killing someone, because I have read-up about your skills in how to handle yourself. Plus you have a temper.'

He rubbed his cheek, and then tried to ease himself further back into the chair, creating a few extra squeaks of the chair, before looking at Pasha and asking her. 'What do you think Pasha, would you believe her story?'

Pasha had shaken her head, being amazed at his asking her that question, before saying. 'What I think detective; is neither here or there! However, if you really think that Miss Felliosi was the murderer, then I'd have to say that you are one sick detective, detective.'

She had then laughed at him whilst shaking her head—and he sort of smiled.

'And I'll endorse that,' I added 'which means we both think your synopsis of this murder is a load of cods-wallop, Mein Feurer Sergeant Stokes . . . !'

Now looking angry and flushed looking, he'd ignored both of our remarks, by saying: 'I was about to say—that not for one moment do I really think that is what happened.'

"Ah" I thought, the man is winding me up, before he added. 'I mean the seduction bit! No, I think maybe it was over something else, but what that something else is . . . is baffling!'

Again he paused, and sort of smiled, although it was kind of hard to gauge whether it had been a smile or not, because his mouth was doing so much moving about with our reaction to his weird logic, and being obviously pleased with himself, now said flippantly ' . . . because your strange actions on Sunday night, was not at all the sort of action that most ladies, particularly well-bred young ladies, like yourself shall we say, would normally have never done on their own accord.

❖ 189 ❖

So Miss Felliosi, I must say that problem does need sorting out in my mind, because I'd have thought that anyone from as decent a background as yours, would never have been doing such things! So that's now my problem you see. So what did you really go down there for, eh? I mean it really wasn't just to see him was it?'

Having again understood the logic of his argument, being a logical summarisation of what any normal girl would not have done had they been ever been put in the same situation as I'd been? However you might have also said I was not a normal girl, and had again attempted to make light of a situation that was darkening by the minute.

'Oops' I said half-heartedly, and with a fake smile answered: 'What can I say to that detective, except to say it's a fair cop, and you've got me bang to rights.' I fluttered my eyelashes, 'I should have known I could never have fooled you Serge, cos you are so clever!'

When I tuned to Pasha, and smiled, I saw she wasn't looking too happy at what I'd said, or when I'd offered my wrists up to the fat Sergeant.

Pasha had in fact known, as I should have, that to have joked about anything like that with this fat obnoxious man, could be a big mistake, and I should have known that Stokes being the man he was, would not have appreciated my dry sense of humour. In fact the fat man would never have been amused, because he was the kind of man who'd not appreciate any humour, unless it was on his terms, even I'd thought at the time, what I'd said, had been amusing.

Having known he'd been in a bad temper from the moment he'd walked into my office, I was now wondering if I had said too much in front of this serious minded oaf of a Sergeant, thinking, how in heck was I to have known that his wife had probably told him that lunchtime, that he was the fattest, ugliest, and most repugnant man she'd ever known in her life.

Joking aside, I did think it might have been a big mistake, saying and doing what I did, and should have known better—and I'm not joking!

CHAPTER 53

Well whatever it was that had previously upset him, my joking around had only added to his foul mood, for now the man had face that was livid red, and eyes that appeared more venomous than ever.

Now I was concerned. I mean you could say his eyes had been blacker than a cobra's eye, and had I cared to have looked even closer at him, I might have even spied two horns growing from his forehead.

Now he hissed a warning:. 'Miss Felliosi, unless you can come up with more satisfactory answers, and make less stupid remarks to my questions than you've already done, you will find yourself in seriously trouble. Do I make myself clear?'

I then gave him back a look that might have scared a more vulnerable person, even had the person had horns on his forehead, yet he'd again totally ignored me when he said by saying. 'And you can cut-out that fooling around, because I'm not in the mood for it . . . do you hear?' He glared at me making it one each in stares.

Having finished with his veiled threat, he almost absent mindedly, reached into his jacket pocket, and pulled out another old cigar-butt, and again without asking my permission, had lit it, and begun puffing on it with obvious enjoyment on his fat sweaty face, daring me to say something.

❦ 191 ❦

This time, for some unknown reason to me, funk probably, I'd not raised any verbal objection to his smoking, or on anything else for that matter, for I'd been kind of stunned by his offensive attitude, and sitting back in my office chair, was wondering how I'd got myself into such a mess . . . and how to deal with him.

"Dear, oh dear, oh dear, you poor thing," my inner voice was saying, so readers what can I say? Except to try at least to calm him down, and said. 'Sergeant Stokes, I apologise for my frivolity, and joking about!'

Pasha then interceded by saying sweetly. 'Oh Sergeant Stokes knows that Miss Felliosi,' whilst looking at Stokes, 'he knows you're on edge, because of your having to visit the morgue this morning, don't you Sergeant? And now you not believing she was telling the truth, after her making a statement, that's upset her. You can understand that can't you?'

She continued to smile sweetly at him. 'I mean even for a man with your experience, you must know that it isn't every day that someone has needed to go through all she has in one day. It's highly stressful!'

I had thought to add, that with 'one thing or another', besides that screamer of a headache I had for the best part of the morning, and now because of him, I'd got myself another—but didn't. Instead with seeing the fat Sergeant's face suddenly lighten up with her being nice towards him, I'd seen an opportunity to quickly add.

'Pasha's right Sergeant, this has all been extremely stressful for me, thanks to you and the dead man, it really hasn't been a very enjoyable day.'

I continued in a low voice. 'Also I'd had a late night last night, so I'm very tired, Sergeant.

Stokes was smiling at me, and saying. 'Oh it's not you being tired that's a problem, it's you not telling me everything I need to know, and lying.'

'I have truly told you everything that I knew about the man; from the time I first saw him coming out of the lift,

THE LADY DETECTIVE

and his asking me to direct him to Rugs and Tings, right up to his walking out again.' I paused looking at his blank face and thought *"Gosh this man is certainly hard work to talk to, so sod him!"* Then looking at his sweaty, chubby, impassive face thought. *'Why was explaining anything to this lump of lard so hard work? I'll even bet his wife thinks exactly the same as I do."*

I then said. 'Ok, to repeat myself—once again, I thought the man leaving the building, was probably not the same man I'd met, even though the man had been dressed the same. Ok?'

'So what man would that be who was dressed the same?'

'What do you mean?'

'Well was it the man you saw arriving whose face you couldn't see because of the hat, or was it the man who left, whose face you also hadn't been able to see because of the hat?' Then he added sarcastically. 'So what else didn't you see that you haven't told me about?'

Blast the man and his blinkered thinking, and had angrily replied, being equally stupid. 'If I recall, Sergeant, as it's only been three times that I've told you, I admit I had been intrigued by the man, and had thought to go and check for myself whether the man leaving the building, had been the same man I saw coming into the hall. And yes again, I did go and see for myself if it was that man. Now is that perfectly clear to you, or not?'

And after he'd said nothing, I added. 'Now they do say that curiosity killed the cat Sergeant, and they also say that curiosity is second nature to us women, as you undoubtedly know with you having a wife, so please allow me a little leeway here.'

I then asked myself, *'had I talked too much,'* because I did read somewhere, that when someone talks too much, or too quickly, it was a clear give-away for someone wanting to cover their tracks. In fact my breathing had been getting a little ragged both from the anger and the frustration building up inside me,' and Pasha, bless, having noticed, had been

❦ 193 ❦

quick to fetch a glass of water for me, and whilst I'd been gratefully drinking some of it, thought it wise *not* to say anything more. Though with seeing Stokes again shaking his head, and me being such a blithering fool, I'd not heeded my own advice, and instead had said angrily.

'Ok, what's not to believe? I've already told you many, many times that I hadn't seen another living sole all that day, or the previous day, besides my workman and Pasha of course. So I would now suggest that you trot off, and ask the workman if needs be, or even ask at the reception desk if they'd seen anyone on those days. In fact Sergeant, why don't you go off and do anything else, except annoying me.'

Oops, now he is looking annoyed—again, what a dumb-head I was to have said that! However Stokes had replied. 'Is that all you have to say, for me to go and ask the workman? Well is it?'

Stupidly I'd then said. 'To repeat what I've been continually telling you, I'd only gone up there to satisfy my curiosity, to check him out! Surely even you can understand *that*, can't you?'

'No I can't, Miss Felliosi, even though some of your story might sound very plausible to a lesser detective than myself, your statement has not convinced me at all. In fact if that's all you have to tell me, then I'll say this to you, that I think your story all sounds a bit too thin on reality, and more on fairy tale.'

Pasha gave him a smile: 'Oh common Serge, I'm a big believer in fairy tales, and it sounds alright to me, even if it sounds a little comical.' She gave him a big smile 'Oh I hope you don't mind me saying that Sergeant, that's only me giving you my opinion, if that's ok?'

He'd then nodded, before sickingly saying. 'Oh, not at all Pasha, not at all; every person is entitled to their own opinion; and no-one's opinion is better than yours, if I may say so?' He continued to look at her as a big cat would have looked after eating a tasty impala, and after shaking his head to make his chins wobble like a lump of jelly, and said. 'Everyone's

THE LADY DETECTIVE

entitled to have their own few words on any subject. Free speech they call it. Besides, I really do appreciate anything coming from you that will help me.' Yuck, I felt sick! He looked at his watch, and surprised me that he hadn't added 'love' on the end of what he'd now said. 'Now seeing as it's late, hadn't you best be getting off home for your tea Pasha?'

She again smiled at him, and he had lovingly returned one back to her, all sloppy like. So double yuck! She said. 'Now that is a kind thought Sergeant, however I have one or two things more to do,' giving me a look, 'so best that I stay on for a little while longer—if that's all right with you?'

I looked at my watch, it was 5.36 pm.

CHAPTER 54

aving seen how Pasha had been getting on so well with the blob, who'd suddenly started to act like one overgrown school boy towards her; with his manner visibly softening whilst he spoke to her, I really should have cashed in on the lightened atmosphere, and said something like: "W*ell like you say Sergeant, maybe it's time we all went home, don't you think?*

Instead of which, I realized afterwards, I suppose I really should have known better when to keep my mouth shut, and will be needing to have a few hundred lessons on how to be more tactful with someone like Stokes, instead of mouthing off at everything I'd been thinking, had said.

'Heaven knows why you choose to continue not believing what I say Sergeant, because I can only repeat for your sweet little pinkie ears only, for what is it, the third or fourth time by mouth, and one written statement, so now would you please remember what I say this time—ok?

I saw Pasha wince at my words, yet ignoring the warning, I'd obstinately continued to repeat what I previously told him about the door being unlocked at the Rugs place, and next door having their office lights on, and no-one answering my knocking, and how I found the door locked, so that was how my fingerprints happened to get on the door handle.

I'd then paused to look at his grave face for a moment, before flippantly adding. 'So tell me Sergeant, where in my

THE LADY DETECTIVE

statement was it so difficult for you to understand to perhaps help you? I mean all your colleagues had found it simple enough, so why not you?'

I felt I should have added *'everyone else but you, you fat oaf'*, but refrained from doing so, which was fortunate, because now looking back now on what I'd already said, would give me nightmares in the weeks ahead. I mean I should probably learn to be more subservient, which was not in my nature, unfortunately.

However I did afterwards realize that I should in the future, learn how to be a little more humble, and refrain from speaking my mind, even if I was, as now, totally bored with this man's stupidity, and everything to do with the ruddy murder, as I really couldn't think of anything more to say to this horrible man. I suppose all my feelings, and particularly my dislike for him, must have shown in my manner and tone of voice, and those of you who know me, knowing I don't suffer fools gladly, it must have shown in my face.

Though I might have normally walked away from this situation, with my having obviously lost my patience, with having to explain my small involvement with the dead man, again and again, and because I couldn't, it was perfectly feasible that I should have had a few choice words to say in the ear of Stokes, which unfortunately had been the case.

Pasha had tried to lighten up what had now become a bad situation, because of my impatience with him, and she'd actually succeeded in pacifying the big blob for a moment, before I blew it. Blast! I know I should have taken her lead, and spoken to him with more deference, because had I done so, it might have been for my own good. 'Humble pie' or 'Button it' should become my motto in the future!

However, with the man being an idiot, my having to eat humble-pie, and biting my tongue when it warranted it, would be difficult, and not in my nature. Though acting like a spoilt brat I suppose was. Now being annoyed, because the fool hadn't believed me, I was thinking::

❖ 197 ❖

'It wasn't because he'd found out that I'd been graded as one of the best all-time liars on the liar charts, had he, or even that I lied?, so when I'd again looked at his smug, sanctimonious face, and noted his satisfaction, as if he'd been given a tasty suckling pig for his supper, as he puffed on his cigar, which was stinking out the office with its cheapness; added to which his now profusely sweating smelly-self, had also added to our discomfort, I'd had enough after seeing Pasha hinting her dislike for the smell, by opening wide, as a hint, the already partly open window, which had let in more cold air onto his back. Then seeing as he had continued to puff away, and saw part of the lit end of the cigar had fallen off on to the floor, to then burn a small hole in my new carpet, that had finally been the last straw, it being to me like a red rag is to a bull, and had angrily stood up with fists clenched, and then stepped menacingly up to him pointing all the while at the burn mark in the carpet, saying. 'You will pay for that, you sad pathetic, gross, bad-mannered horrible sloth of a man. You will also put out that horrible smelly cigar right now, and I want you to leave this office.'

He looked slightly taken aback at my outburst as I continued to glare at him, and when he didn't reply, angrily added. 'You were asked not to smoke in here, Sergeant, and yet you ignored me, and now you have ruined this . . . this brand new carpet.'

I continued to not being nice. 'I will also have bet, with you being a wimp, that had your wife told you not to smoke, you wouldn't have ignored her, would you, cos you'd have been too scared to! So now you can get out of my office, and take that horrible smelly cigar with you.'

CHAPTER 55

Stokes then lightly blushed in his embarrassment, and looking directly at Pasha, had said: 'Well that is as it is Miss Felliosi, however I can't see an ashtray to put out this cigar in; and as for my paying for any damage, well everyone knows that we coppers are paid notoriously low wages to ever be able to afford a carpet like this, would be out of the question.' He paused 'However, I will say most sincerely that I do apologize for my appalling bad behaviour.' And then acting all casual said 'So now can we get on?'

I saw there had been no real apology in either his voice, or manner, and saw from his face that he had only been mouthing the words and growled, 'Your apology is not accepted', as I walked out to the reception area to pick up a saucer from inside the beverage cupboard, had on returning, thrust it into his fat chubby hand, hissing thru clenched teeth at the same time, 'now use this, and get out'.

After he'd put the remainder of the cigar into the saucer, having struggled to get out of the chair after doing my bidding, his face had become even more scarlet when he'd placed the saucer on my desk, and I said 'Not there,' and pointing to a side-table by the door, 'over there.'

After taking the saucer to the side-table, he still hadn't left as I'd wanted him to, and had instead turned to Pasha saying. 'I'm only going on the facts as I see them Pasha, and you can't get away from facts can you? And one big fact,

❦ 199 ❦

is that Miss Felliosi' fingerprints were on both office door handles, and another fact was, her fingerprints were the only ones we found on various other items inside the room, other than the dead man's.' He gave a half smile. 'Strange don't you think, for someone who was only saying goodnight to a person she hadn't known?'

Then he sort of smiled, before adding. 'And of course there is the small matter of one murdered man, and her finger prints all over that poor man's office door handle, could mean she'd put them there when she had hurriedly locked it up again, after doing him in, couldn't she?' He almost looked at her as if he was asking for her forgiveness. 'So Pasha, you can now see my position in all this, can't you?'

'But surely, that'll not be enough conclusive evidence to prove that she did it, Sergeant?' I heard Pasha say, and he did for a moment seem to be considering what to reply, because he'd began to rub his chin, or I should have said, chins, before I'd then had a funny feeling that I'd now been put on a ski slope by this fat Sergeant, let's say St Anton's in Austria, and that my future was now going to be just a tad too slippy-sliddy for me to handle without my falling over.

So I said. 'It doesn't of course explain why the man I'd seen, was found in the wrong office, does it? Of course knowing how difficult these murders are for you to crack, I honestly hope that you aren't asking me to make something up to please you—are you Sergeant?'

Oh! Oh! Oops and double Oops. Now I've gone and done it again! I mean how often does it take to instinctively know that as soon as you have said something, that whatever it was you had said, was the wrong thing to have said? And now, here I was once again saying the wrong thing. Fool!

I mean you get those feelings every now and again, don't you? So I thought I'd better say something tactful to back up Pasha, having heard her gasp, and had quickly tried to cover over the situation by saying: 'Though if it's any consolation to you, Sergeant, I am also inclined to agree with your thinking, for I too would have thought that whatever I'd previously said

❦ 200 ❦

THE LADY DETECTIVE

must have bordered on the stupid, and had it happened to any other woman . . . besides myself of course, I don't think I would have believed her either.'

Eat humble pie Jess, eat humble pie! Though now I had also wondered if saying what I had said might be taken as an admission to guilt. Oops!

I allowed him a few moments to bask in that half-baked compliment, before saying. 'However I am sure that you will solve the puzzle, and in doing so, will then know who the real murderer was—eh Sergeant?'

CHAPTER 56

I left him with his thoughts for a moment, before looking directly into his beady eyes to see whether or not he'd thought I was extracting the digit as they say, and noting there'd be no change in his facial expression, before he said.

'Miss Felliosi, I can assure you that you have no need to worry yourself about such details, and really should be concerning yourself more on what I am thinking.'

'Oh dear, with the dead man being in the wrong office, surely you are not suggesting, that after bashing in his head, had he been Mr Happy, I could have somehow carried a man of his size and build, from his office to the other office—are you?' He didn't answer.

'Sergeant, you do know this murder is probably as much a puzzle to me as it is to you at this moment, and I cannot get my head around understanding the puzzle of why the dead man was not in his own office, and I'm assuming, had I moved him, there'd have been bloodstains on the hall carpet and in the offices? Now don't you find that most puzzling?

In fact Sergeant, would it not have been difficult, even for you, to have picked up such a large man, having slung him over your shoulder, and then dumped the poor man into the office next door, after being over your shoulder, not to leave any blood stains on the office floor, having first to open it?'

And still not finished all I had to say yet, being I was on a roll, I'd paused, and gulping in air, continued. 'Now

❦ 202 ❦

THE LADY DETECTIVE

this is where it gets interesting:, for having unlocked the door with this heavy man still slung over my shoulder, and of course, not dripping blood all over the place after having had his head bashed in so much that his face had been totally unrecognizable, I'd then calmly locked up that office again, and walked out the building, being very careful to have left my finger-prints on the door, and the office lights still on, for my victim to be found all the quicker. Does that make sense to you?'

He grunted, and I saw he was again beginning to lose his composure, and with Pasha now shaking her head as a warning to say no more, I said. 'Ok, so now after that puzzling train of events which you have no answer for, cos you think all that was premeditated, here's another one for you. How do you suggest I got that office key from, eh, the one I placed the big man in?'

I gave him a smile that was not a smile, you know, the kind of smile that most politicians have been coached to give, both before and after they'd spoken to us as idiots on something we all knew to have been a pack of lies, or a total fabrication. In fact I now had a new word for it— POLIGRIN—meaning the false smile of a politician.

Yes I would have definitely have given a Poligrin smile on this occasion, for that've been the appropriate smile to have given him on my smile chart, for that would have been the worst smile to have given him, other than my No1 or No2 smile, which would have been my version of a pure hate smile; which I'd never felt in my life, fortunately for the fat man, as I'd never had a reason to have given it to anyone—yet!

Although watching him, I was perfectly sure, that had the fat Sergeant been given half a chance to act out his thoughts, and been able to have got away with doing the deed, would have at that moment given me a hate smile, or even strangled me, considering the mood he was in. Instead, he had balled up his fists, and through closed teeth, had hissed loudly like some kind of demon on sighting their prey.

❀ 203 ❀

ROBERT H FELLOWS

Then readers, had you been here and seen with your own eyes, and heard with your own ears, what the fat man had to say, you may still have never believed in a month of Sundays what had happened next. I didn't. For Fatso Stokes, had begun to wring his hands as if he had been Fagin in Oliver Twist, and with un-controlled glee, began saying: 'Well with you being my one and only suspect, unfortunately for you Miss Felliosi, I am now intending to do something about it.'

Ok, I suppose I'd again been wrong with saying what I did, but I couldn't stop myself. 'Is that so, Sergeant? Which I suppose probably means I am your prime suspect—does it not?'

'Oh yes Miss Felliosi,' he hissed again, 'you definitely are!'

'And you say I needn't worry myself about such details! Bit of an understatement wouldn't you say detective?'

'Miss Felliosi, I have now the unsavoury task (meaning pleasant task) of arresting you for the murder of one unknown man on . . . blah . . . blah . . . date.'

CHAPTER 57

MONDAY NIGHT: THE POLICE STATION

With my being arrested, that had ended, business wise, what had for me been a shocking business day. And as for my beginning to be a private investigator, well forget it, and would later call the day a 'so nearly day' because I hadn't been given a chance to have made it into anything like a normal working day, had I? For I'd only been involved from 9 am that morning in only helping the police to solve the horrible murder of an office neighbour . . . so maybe I should consider joining the Police Force (joke)

However, what was now so annoying for me, was that after having done my good Samaritan stuff, and without any compensation at all I might add, it had only been because of the facts I'd disclosed, that had got me arrested, and would now see me put in jail. I mean is that fair?

Ok, it was a fact that my amiable neighbour has been murdered, but why in heavens name should Stinky Stokes think I had done him in? Me, when I hadn't even known the man, and now it could be said I will never know him, knowing he was dead, especially after knowing his face was all messed up as it was.

I mean how was it possible because of that briefest of encounters, chat wise, to have said I had known your smashed in face, having only known the man for five minutes? Anyway, here I am being taken to jail, and being thought of as the prime suspect for his murder! Beggars belief, I would have said.

I mean you could have knocked me down with a feather, when the fat man had said he was arresting me for murder. I mean, that had been totally un-expected. In fact I had been sucker punched, and been put against the ropes. Now the fat-man had continued to tell me what he was proposing to do to me, without my really listening, let alone my taking in what he was saying, for I really had been too shocked. Although now I had woken up enough from my stupor to hear him say. 'So I must ask you now Miss Felliosi, to accompany me down to the Station for further questioning.' Probably meaning for me to help him solve who'd really done the murder!

I replied, with venom to say. 'Unsavoury you said! You say it's unsavoury! You do know, you fat oaf, with this being ridiculous nonsense, you really are making one big mistake you know.' Boy was I angry. I mean so would you have been had you been arrested for a murder that you didn't commit, and then said, whilst not looking at him. 'Can you believe the crass stupidity of the man, because I can't?'

Obviously I was very angry and upset, and had almost laughed at this point of how ridiculous all of this was, and instead had snarled at him. 'I repeat, you really have got this one all wrong you know? And right now, you oaf, you are making the biggest mistake of your fat life, which I suspect may well have cost you your job by this time next week, or next month, because of your stupidity!'

Until finally, with a little extra venom added. 'This is what most people would call a farce, Sergeant, fit for the stage, because at this moment in time I really do believe you haven't a clue as to who the real murderer is or might be,

THE LADY DETECTIVE

unfortunately, even not knowing what planet you are living on, you dumb-cluck!'

Pasha bless her, had certainly seemed as shocked as I'd been over his saying I'll be arrested, although not shown her surprise as much as mine must have done on her face of course. She'd then given me a brandy, a large one, and had ignored fatso! A cool girl, that one! Having had the drink, it had given me time to recover my senses, which I'd put to good use, by giving her a few hasty instructions of what she should do before closing-up the business for the night.

And so for the second time that day, having asked if she was ok if I left her in charge of the business, that had meant all hopes were now lost for this day at least, and maybe many other days, of my ever getting this business off the ground at this rate had it been left up to Stokes. And on a day that had been especially important to me, had seen Pasha spending more time in these offices than I had!

Later on I thought. "Poor Pasha, what a tale she'll have to tell her parents and friends that night. I mean were she to tell, she could say that on her first day of working for me, there'd been a murder a few doors down the hallway from where she worked; her new boss had been asked to identify a murdered man's body at the morgue; then had witnessed her new boss being arrested, and taken away to prison for murdering the same man whose body she'd been asked to identify, who she'd fervently said she hadn't committed. I mean who would have believed her saying all that?"

I mean it also seemed so unbelievable, that even for me I was finding it hard to believe as Pasha was, of my being arrested for murdering a man who I had only seen and met once, and that had only been for a few minutes. So even for me, that would have all sounded much too much like it had all been a fantasy story!

In fact with all of this now happening to me, it almost had seemed as if this had been purposely arranged, and I saw one nasty ogre pointing a long bony finger in my direction, and condemning me!

❀ 207 ❀

Still, tongue-in-cheek, I had at least known that my first day as a Private Investigator, had not been half as dull as I had expected it to have been! Not only that, what the fat oaf hadn't realised was that I had been deeply shocked to have heard he'd been murdered, and then had to view the murdered man, well that was hard. It's true, because that really had been the very first time that I'd ever seen a murdered person close up, or even a battered face murdered person, or had even seen a dead body in my life.

Also I'd never in my life been questioned by the police about any crime; and it was certainly the very first time that I'd been put on a murder charge, and be locked up in a police cell. So yes, you could say that the day had been an eventful one for me, couldn't you?

And then I realised that I would now have to explain to my parents, and Stewart, about this monumental balls-up, which beggar's belief, and face up to what they had to say, especially knowing of my father's fiery character. So best not think about it, I say!

Well at least a quick result had been achieved as far as Stokes was concerned—but not necessarily a correct one! And what I still hadn't realised, was that the day wasn't finished with me yet!

CHAPTER 58

So in a nut-shell, my first day as a Private Eye, had been one un-dull-non-earning day, hadn't it? Having helped the Police for approximately 80% of the day, that meant I'd spent all that time without earning one-penny before being arrested, and now, fantasy murders aside, I'd done nothing to warrant my getting such notoriety.

Having arrived once more at the Police Station, though not this time as an all-round-good-helping-citizen, but as a suspected murderer; I'd been again cautioned, given my rights, and then been charged with murder of one un-known individual. I'd then been allowed one phone call before the cross-examining had begun, so I chose my father, who having been told that I'd been arrested for murder, nearly had a blue fit over the phone, and had begun to shout down the line 'You have bloody been what?'

So I had quickly told him where I was, and had afterwards put down the phone whilst he was still ranting away on the other end, and then been silently walked to the 'interrogation' room to await the thunder and lightning that would accompany my father when he arrived at the Police Station, with a solicitor.

The Police, having now been informed that my father was Francis (Frankie) Felliosi by the time he'd stormed into the Police station, and had been pre-warned. And having been accompanied by our family lawyer, had

❖ 209 ❖

In the meantime, shortly after I'd been charged, and before their interviewing me, daddy had at 8.45 pm, stormed into the police-station, and immediately demanded to know why his daughter had been arrested, and who the fool was who'd authorised my arrest. He'd then been heard to demand the appearance of Stokes, after being told he'd been the arresting officer who had charged me with the murder.

When he'd been told the arresting officer, having been told Stokes, was now off-duty he said. 'Well that man must be some sad stupid tosser,' and other similar words. And when he demanded to know on what grounds was his daughter arrested, and having been told, he'd again growled angrily.

'I suppose the tosser is now sat at home all warm and snug in front of a fire, whilst my daughter is now freezing her bottom off in one of your cold cells, and all because of this sad demented idiot not being up to the job.'

Then he added. 'Maybe I should have a quiet word in Commander Wilsons' ear, and have this Stokes feller moved on to fairy-land. Either that, or the demented idiot, strongly needs a pointy boot up his back-side, for it would seem the man doesn't have a clue about the job he's being paid to do.' He'd continued.

'Perhaps I will recommend to Commander Wilson, who I know very well, a friend you might say; that he should either fire Stokes from his job, or should at least be given an rollicking and then demote him to the stations toilet attendant, cos it's obvious this man is a fool.'

Not one to mince words was my father, particularly when defending me.

Daddy had afterwards been told politely after asking if it was possible for him to, on the telephone, have a few words with the Sergeant 'who doesn't have a clue about the difference between a criminal and his mouth, which should, in my opinion, be permanently closed,' had been told "No it wasn't", and had also been told "No, it wasn't possible to see him," after asking for the address of the detective.

THE LADY DETECTIVE

The Duty Sergeant had then warned my father, "That he ought to think long and hard about finding out where Stokes lived, so he could pay him a visit, and could get into serious trouble, so needed to think very carefully as to his conduct."

The duty Sergeant did however mention that he knew how my father must feel, having had "a teenage daughter of my own." Bloody cheek, I'm twenty-two years old, but he meant no harm.

Daddy had then been shown to a room where he could wait until after I'd been questioned!

CHAPTER 59

The dingy room where I was sat with two detectives and my dad's lawyer, was freezing, and having been previously ushered into this dingy room to await my lawyer, I saw there'd been bars on the window, and the plain table and four chairs in its centre, had all been bolted down my side.

I had then been interviewed by two detectives, one being a tall young Welshman going by the name of Jones, surprise, and the other I recalled as Williams, who was not Welsh, and had looked just as kindly as I'd seen him to be that morning.

The detectives had of course again asked me to repeat, for the benefit of the tape, what I had already stated that morning in my statement, of what I knew about the dead man, and again this afternoon had told that fat obnoxious Sergeant Stokes twice. So boring!

Whilst I'd made out the statement, repeating all I had previously said, whilst they had all been patiently sat listening, it gave me the impression that nothing had been told to these two detectives, in any conversation I had with Stokes, and so it would appear that team-work was non-existent these days! Oops steady.

They had in particular, wanted to know the reason why I'd been looking around the dead man's office, and touching things of a man that I didn't know. Here we go again!

❖ 212 ❖

THE LADY DETECTIVE

I did my best, without losing my patience, to tell them, before I told them why I had slapped Stokes' face, and had called him some nasty names, and that had made the detectives laugh, and my lawyer shake his head.

I'd again been asked, 'why did you go looking for a man you didn't know,' and 'why should you have wanted to have done a 'walk about' in another person's office that you hadn't been invited into?'

Dad's lawyer, now my lawyer, I had known all my life as Bert, Albert Harold Beavers was his full name, who had said hopefully 'You don't know for sure if my client hadn't been asked into the office.'

'Well if that was a fact,' said detective Jones, 'then you'll also be saying your client had known him well enough that she could; when your client has already told us that she didn't know him—besides the five minutes chat. So which is it? True or not true?'

Bert and I had looked to each other, and I had uttered 'I wasn't asked.'

After that I told Williams, Jones, 'this will definitely be the last time I'll talk about the week-end, and the events, because I am tired of repeating the same answers to the same pointless questions, and I will from here on, give you only a "No comment" to any further questions you ask that has previously been asked.'

I then told them, 'so you can get lost up your own trouser leg if you think about asking me anymore about Sunday and my meeting the man, because I have told you, the police, so many times, that by now you would have thought you'd have known my story off by heart!'

I then thought before they had finished questioning me; it was time to have a little fun at the expense of these two very nice detective Constables, so I leant back in my chair, and began to posture myself in such a way that I knew would definitely excite the pants off both of these men, let alone Bert, although daddy would have had a fit, had he observed me!

❋ 213 ❋

What I had done was to take my suit-jacket off, saying 'It's a little hot in here', and had then slowly stretched myself to show off my superb contours that were adequately displayed so beautifully inside a sheer silk cream-blouse, that had left little to the imagination. After that, I'd done a little more posturing, by pushing back my hair, double-handed, again leaving the little darlin's smitten by my beauty, and hour-glass figure.

In the meantime, Bert, who had now also been having trouble with his keeping a professional attitude to the proceedings, and wiping a handkerchief around his face and brow, more times than it takes to whip up an omelette, making the younger policeman, whose name was Jonathan, and the elder one, whose name was Frank, having little else to say to me after that, with Jones saying. 'All's done for now Miss Felliosi. In fact everything was more than satisfactory, thank you,' had quickly closed this interview, and then had smiled!

After that, the two policemen couldn't do enough for me, after my disgraceful posturing, making me wonder if they could be induced into letting me go home, which I doubted, but maybe worth a try, don't you think?

These little loves, meaning Jones and Williams, had afterwards when locked up, had never stopped offering me coffee and sandwiches, after my enraged father had left. In fact, had I accepted something each time they'd asked me 'was there anything I wanted', I would then have had enough goodies for me to have opened my very own Police canteen!

Though they had been very official and straight-faced, these two men had always remained perfect gentlemen to me at all times, both during and after the interview, which I thought was nice, and not at all like the dirty minded sods who I had met that morning, for they had talked respectfully to me, and never once had they needed to get annoyed, or shout at me, which again was very nice.

And then during the first few hours of my being locked up, before they went off duty, they had always been asking me if I needed anything; and was I warm enough, which I had been at the time, even though the cell was semi-warm, due to the white-tiled-walls.

They'd also asked me had I wanted to go to the ladies room, and though I rarely smoked, asked if I had enough cigarettes and things like that, which was also very sweet of them.

Although having said all that, I would honestly have to say, that had I been asked if I would have trusted myself with being left alone with either one of them in a cell overnight, especially the younger of the two, then my answer would have been an emphatic no!

CHAPTER 60

Bert, had I know asked for bail for me, and had been refused, being told that Sgt Stokes, the arresting officer, would not allow it until after the Court hearing the following day; due 'to the seriousness of the crime'.

'What utter rubbish!' Both Bert and my father had told him, as if they hadn't known that it may be difficult to obtain bail for me. And that had been that, as they say!

Following a fond goodnight to my father, and Bert; and having then to listen to their endearments of, 'chin up old gal', sort of thing, I had then been subjected to the most horrible night of my entire life!

For not only had I had a horrible, miserable, completely insane sleepless night, it had been freezing-cold during the early hours of the morning, and I spent most of the night shivering, just as my father and the detectives had said would happen—I never listen!

CHAPTER 61

Although I'd in part contributed to these circumstances I was in, due to my big mouthing Stokes, which was why I thought I was now here in these un-hospitable surroundings—I'd also had other problems that night.

One was due to the light above my bed; for this light had been switched on at all times throughout the night, and even though I'd politely asked for it to be turned off, or down, or dimmed, in the cell, I'd been told firmly—'That can't be done Miss Felliosi',—which meant that I had, along with the other prisoners, no choice but to spend the night staring at the none to cheerful, very white tiled walls, or at a bright uncovered light-bulb.

However my being cold, or looking at that stupid light bulb, had not been the worst part of my being locked up? Oh no, it had been my having to listen to a bunch of jabbering, screaming, brainless, shouting morons who had also been locked up in the other cells, and had for some unknown reason, preferred not to sleep, but to instead spend the whole night either screaming mindless abuse at each other, or at the Police, or even at people who were not even here—usually the wife had it been a man, or the husband, had it been a women—or the whole world.

In fact these brain-dead morons, had for no other stupid reason that I could think of, continued to shout their mouths off about anything and everything during the dark hours much to my chagrin!

Do you know there had been one dozy idiot, who had, it seemed, actually been having a slagging match with Micky Mouse and Pluto. He'd been arguing with them because of their not giving the other characters in their films a chance to act, because they'd always demanded all of the limelight, and had always been always over-acting. The blithering fool!

Then there'd been other brain-dead head cases, both men and women, who had preferred to go way over the top with their swearing. This crummy lot, obviously having had little or no knowledge of what was called the 'Queen's English', had instead created their own gibberish language to communicate to each other with.

Well good luck to them I say with their F's and C's etcetera, though maybe they should have all been put together someplace, meaning somewhere way out in the open, where they could all swear at each other for as long as they wanted—though not on this night, eh!

Un-surprisingly, there'd been some prisoners who had spent the night, off and on, shouting and screaming abuse at complete strangers in other cells, telling us all they were innocent of whatever crime, or crimes they'd been incarcerated, banged up for. And surprise, surprise, not committed!

All of these people, would no doubt be all going to Court with me the following morning, and had they been found guilty of their crime(s), would again incur the [dis]pleasure of Her Majesty's Prison. And that would again give them a further reason to vent their supposed innocence into the ears of whoever had, or hadn't, wanted to listen to them, who would no doubt in turn, get them to listen to their own ear-banging story about how they'd also been wrongly accused, and were also claiming their own innocence.

Thing was, this would no doubt have continued to be said in the real prison, until they'd been permanently not heard. Meaning of course, their release, their death, or been given the death sentence—which I've heard, will soon to be abolished!

However most of the prisoners who'll be accompanying me to Court, had, during the night, not given me any alternative but to have listened to their lurid and explicit conversation to who knows who prisoner, who might still not have known until the following morning, who had graced one of the other cells they'd been babbling on to. Weird huh!

Chapter 62

TUESDAY: COURT DAY

So the following morning, at 6.30 am, not having had a wink of sleep all-night because of that rowdy lot, I knew I had been well and truly introduced into the behind the walls world of the criminal, having been mixed with our un-savoury humanity who we all read about in our various daily newspapers.

This night spent with them, had certainly opened my big baby-blue eyes, and given me a greater insight of how sordid life would have been to have lived among some of these people, who we call human beings. And that thought, or opinion, had come after having spent only one night in the cells amongst them!

These human beings, or people, who I'd now some first-hand knowledge of, might be the people I probably meet, or associate with, from time to time, were I to ever become a successful sleuth, because Stewart had already pre-warned me that I would need to fraternise sometimes with the "prison fodder, as this was your job." That's if I'm released of course.

The thing was, I still thought that these people were not as debased, or as two-faced as many of our well-known monied people, who my father would mix with. My knowledge being, that many of these people were far more crooked, and far more capable in their quest for money, to do more harm in one day to their fellow human beings, and to the environment in general, than a life time of whatever this little lot who I spent the night with, could ever do in a life-time of petty crimes. And that's a fact.

Ok, so now back to what was going to happen to me on this cold Tuesday morning, having now had a sudden probable yet illogical thought that these rowdy morons who I'd had spent the night with, who'd also be going with me this morning to stand in front of the 'beak', that none would be charged with murder—I didn't think?

Unfortunately, that thought had stayed with me a lot longer than any other thought I had that morning. Although laughingly, that thought I admit, had also given me a feeling of upmanship, and my being in a different class to these petty criminals. Because my supposed crime, would had certainly been classed in a category way above those crimes committed by this ordinary bunch of criminals, who really shouldn't have been sharing the same space as I was in!

However by the time I had arrived at Court, it had by then also occurred to me, that I would definitely prefer to now change places with any one of them, before I had my 'big' moment before the 'beak'.

Why? Because after being sentenced, I might still not be feeling as smug as I'd been before the hearing, and about my being a different class of criminal, had I been thought of as being a murderess, cos that will mean I'd have been given a custodial sentence for life, or being given the noose—meaning my being hung up by the neck after the main trial. So maybe they had been the clever ones after all, with their having one month, or one year prison sentences! We shall see!

CHAPTER 63

Having experienced, and travelled in a sweaty highly offensive smelly body-odour vehicle—which I'd thought might have been Stokes—and actually was what the police called a 'meat wagon'. This large van, that had a number of small lockable cubicles in which to transfer a dozen or so prisoners from the Police Station to whatever Court their crime had warranted them to appear, to receive whatever sentence the Judge had deemed appropriate for whatever misdemeanour they had committed, against his, or her fellow man, which may have meant, that the same meat-wagon would also be returning some of them to now complete a proper jail sentence.

Having for the very first time in my life taken any journey to Court, it had also been the very first time that I'd even had to hold up in my right hand in the air, a bible (left had I been a one armed person) and to then plead guilty or not guilty.

In fact as I stood to be charged with murder in a dock, (where did that expression come from?) I hadn't seen any reason to my not pleading anything else but 'Not Guilty' of course, and so I did, and then been asked to sit down and face a rather austere Judge, who it was said, could have rivalled Judge Jeffries in his heyday for his 'liking' hangings!

On either side of me, and kind of perched on either shoulder, were two heavy-looking sorts, before I'd then had

❖ 222 ❖

THE LADY DETECTIVE

to listen to our fat friend Stinky Stokes, and Bert, my father's private lawyer, cutting and thrusting away at each other, to probably impress the judge, who actually appeared not very impressed at all being told whether I would or would not make a suitable applicant for bail or not, and was in fact looking away to somewhere else, before he'd finally set the date for the 'main' trial.

Stokes had then agreed not to oppose my bail. *"Now wasn't that decent of the fat man,"* I'd thought sarcastically thru tightly gritted teeth, before wondering why this very stern looking Judge had set my bail on my father's reconnaissance for the huge amount of £20,000 pounds; before it had become obvious that he'd known of my father, maybe personally, and not liking him, and knowing of his great wealth, had posted the bail according to his means! It was also equally as obvious, that the Judge was never a friend of my father either, nor could he ever expect to be—now.

I couldn't put it any simpler than to say that after the court hearing, and my release, I couldn't have been any happier.

Not so my father, for now we were out of earshot of anyone that mattered, he had by giving me, his favourite and only daughter, the biggest mouth lambasting that I'd ever had the misfortune in my life to hear coming from his mouth, had shown he was not at all happy. The last time this 'mouthing' had occurred, was when I'd been a child of eight, when I had been at the bottom of our garden, frog spawning, in the deep end of our large fish pond, and had slipped and nearly drowned. Now having said what he'd had to say, he was now holding me close, and continuously repeating—'You stupid, stupid girl, whatever were you thinking of?'

He'd obviously been very worried for me, and now shown he loved me.

CHAPTER 64

Fortunately, daddy had calmed down somewhat after we'd walked over to a large pub that was conveniently situated directly opposite the County Law Courts.

The pub was called 'The Chancer', and the chances were, humph, that whoever owned it, had made a very good living out of the people who'd been, or where about to go to Court. Especially for those who having been out on bail, this pub might well be the last chance to have a last one or two before being 'sent down' for a long time, as the expression goes. Or for people needing to drown their sorrows because their loved one had already been sentenced. Or even to celebrate their having been given some good news, like my Father and me, having been granted bail, or had escaped being sentenced to go to prison!

Having chosen the Lounge area, we'd sat on either side of a centre-leg round wooden table that had been literally covered with hundreds of cigarette burns; and even wobbled when you leant on it.

Poor daddy had then spent most of the first five minutes looking down at his second large brandy that he'd placed tantalisingly on the table in front of him, or had been looking towards the Court house through a window directly behind and to the left of me.

He was, as you might imagine, still very unhappy with me, and yet he was controlling his emotions admirably,

❀ 224 ❀

THE LADY DETECTIVE

although the tone in his voice, when he spoke, had become a mixture of both un-civilized and civilized, when he'd began to have a moan at me.

'The thing is,' he said, looking at me whilst holding an empty glass, 'why you should have bloody well ever wanted to get yourself involved in a mess like this in the first place, beats me,' he'd said, before leaving me to again order another two large drinks for himself, and then had on returning, continued to moan.

'I knew it, I bloody knew that something like this would happen as soon as you said you were going to be a Private Investigator, a snoop, a sleuth, for a living. I bloody knew it. You ask your Mother if I didn't say "that as soon as you got mixed up with the bloody criminal fraternity, you'd soon be in trouble". I bloody well knew that something would happen, and now it's happened. And what makes it worse, it ruddy well took you one day, one ruddy day, to do it. In fact it might have been even less than one day, for you to be suspected of being a ruddy murderess! Were you mad?'

He paused and quickly downed the first double brandy before saying, 'Bloody Norah Jessica, that has got to be some kind of record don't you think? And what the hell is mummy going to say when she hears about this I would hate to hazard a guess? She might have a ruddy stroke or something!'

Up to then I hadn't realized that daddy hadn't said anything about this to mummy. Oh dear!

Finally, having again stared down to his now empty second glass, he was now looking at me, and started to smile, for daddy could never be angry with me for long. And now with his stern face relaxed, he gave me a 'come here' gesture, and as I leant over the table, causing it to wobble, he gave me a big hug, and had whispered in my ear 'I love you kitten, and know you would never have knowingly have wanted to ever get yourself involved in anything like this . . . I know that.' I thought it best just to say, 'Thank you daddy.'

And as he and I were still bent over the table hugging and patting each other's back, was when I'd became aware of a group of young men standing at the bar looking our way, having no doubt been interested by this show of affection, and wondering what it was between a much older rich-looking guy, and a beautiful young girl.

I'd smiled over his shoulder, and gave them probably a No 5 smile, and a two handed upward palm sign, as if I was the Pope blessing his congregation, which to me had meant—'Oh come on guys, you know how it is'—sort of thing.

In return, they'd all smiled back at me, and were now all knowingly nodding their heads at me as if they'd fully understood what showing them the palms of my hand had really meant. In fact two of the men had actually raised their glasses to me, as if from this moment we'd fully understood each other, and now were great pals.

My father's good mood didn't last much longer than their nodding heads had; so a minute or so after I'd sat back down again, he'd once more been doing a little more pondering whilst looking into an empty glass, and had said to me. 'What's to be done, eh Jess, what's to be done?'

I shrugged, 'what's to be done? What do you mean daddy?'

He ignored me, 'More's the point, how in hell do we get you out of the mess that you have bloody well got yourself into eh. You answer me that?'

With one quick tilt back of his head, he'd drunk down what little of the brandy he thought was left, and tasting nothing, had twisted around in his chair, and spent a little time getting the attention of the barman, and when he did, he'd ordered, by pointing two fingers at his glass, and with the other giving him a two finger horizontal sign, and mouthed brandy.

Then he continued: 'Where was I? Oh yes. Because I'll tell you what my girl, this problem is not going to go away. It's not like you were taking a small stroll in the park and afterwards forgetting you've done it, you know? Ok, now the way I see it, we'll need to find who the real killer is to get you out of this mess. Reason: because even with such crap evidence that the police have against you, which is not only

THE LADY DETECTIVE

very weak, it's bordering on being insane crap; it could still get you put down, guilty as charged, because,' he took my hand, 'the police don't have to come up with anything more substantial than they have.'

He'd with-drew his hand and continued. 'I mean they have already given you a hard time over this haven't they? So ok, now you're a professional snoop, if you don't want to go to prison, then you had better do some snooping, and fast, because I would suggest you'll need to sort this lot out for yourself to get permanently released—with my help of course.'

He then sat back, lit a cigar, and blew smoke. This smoke I liked.

Then he enquired. 'Whoever this plonker was who arrested you, this Sergeant Stokes, well this man has got mud for a brain, because I tell you what my girl, he is really stepping in it right now, right up to his nose if he thinks he can throw that kind of muck at my little girl.'

I looked at his determined face hoping to see a smile at his use of those words, instead I saw only the anger that he was trying so hard to suppress.

'Daddy, you must promise to leave this man alone. This is a professional man, and this problem will be dealt with my way, and with no un-necessary violence I might add. Besides if something happened to him, the police will suspect you straight away, regardless if you were going about it to settle a score.'

He thought for a second or two, and nodded. 'Shame really, but you are right. Though that won't stop me from having a quiet word in the large ear of the Chief Constable about his stupidity, will it? I mean the Chief plays golf at my club you know, at least he does at this moment in time, but you know how things can change in this life, some would say very quickly, and I'm sure the Chief Constable would wish to remain a member of the club, don't you?' He laughed happy at this thought.

❖ 227 ❖

Following my father's mood, I continued in the same 'nothing you do bothers me' pretence type-character, just as that film actor James Cagney had done when playing the part of a 'tough hood' in a film, when to keep faith with his old pal the priest, and to convince the kids of the block that he wasn't as tough as he made out to be, he'd pretended to be a coward, and pretended to cry before he sat in the electric chair, and that was only to stop the kids who idolised him from becoming hoods like himself. Nice touch!

'Now see here Daddy, don't you dare worry about me,' I said all tough, 'Aren't you forgetting that this here girl is one foxy lady . . . and is without doubt going to be the best Private Investigator around.'

On hearing my phony American accent, he spluttered into one of the double brandies that had been bought over by one of the men at the bar, who I saw, when he returned to the bar, had smiled at me whilst raising his glass. He obviously fancied his chances I thought, yet I thanked him with a small smile.

My father was saying 'May I remind you young lady, that it was because of that dam stupid attitude of you being a foxy lady, that got you into this dam stupid mess in the first place.'

I said nothing, yet at the same time I had noticed that the chap who'd come over to the table and given daddy his drink, was now preening himself before his mates on his cleverness of bringing daddy's drink over to impress me, and then getting that smile, not knowing that was all he would ever get from me for his—waiter service!

'Daddy I'm sorry, I'll get rid of the foxy lady immediately!' Then trying to lighten up the situation, had taken his hand into mine, saying, 'there you are daddy, all gone.' He seemed unimpressed.

'Oh common daddy, you know I was being silly, and my saying that was only trying to make this situation seem a little lighter than it is—don't you?' I continued 'And I am so sorry for all the worry that I'll have caused you and mummy—honest.'

THE LADY DETECTIVE

I gave him a confident No6/7 smile, which I really hadn't felt like giving at this precise moment to be honest, still feeling the effects of spending last night in the cells, and being today in Court. I looked seriously at him and saying, 'Seriously daddy, I will promise you that I'll sort this out. And daddy, you mustn't forget that I am your daughter, and no pushover. Also I have the big man (meaning Stewart) on my side.'

Then I heard some laughter, and heard the guys at the bar saying after seeing me again taking hold of daddy's hand. 'So she's a dead cert eh Billy! You did say she was didn't you?'

Ignoring them, I was thinking with a little trepidation, as I sat across from him "You're right, it's not going to be easy to solve the murder," and then "yet if I don't solve it, that will mean I could look forward to spending many more cold nights in another one of those cold prison cells with its white-tiled walls, and having for company, a bright light on all night above my head." It didn't bare thinking about.

What's more, I certainly hadn't fancied having again to listen to the ravings of those idiotic prisoners, night after night, who'd still be claiming their innocence of whatever crime they 'hadn't committed'. I knew if I didn't come up with an answer, before my real trial for the murder of a man who in hardly knew, then I might also be head-banging my head on the tiled wall claiming my innocence, and probably be raving just as loudly as any of inmates in the prison.

Although, now thinking about it, because I really would have been innocent, that would have made matters only worse for me, because then my ravings may have probably been with a touch more hysteria and feeling to it than the others. So in one way or the other, I really did need to come up with a solution to resolve this potential nightmare.

CHAPTER 65

Half an hour later; having talked about this and that, mostly that; my father had suggested that maybe I should spend the next few days with mother and himself, and I'd refused, probably a little too hastily, by saying that I would now need my own space to be able to sort myself out! He'd finally agreed. Acquiesced you might say! Then had suggested that it was time for him to leave, as he'd work to do!

Once outside the pub, with no parking in the vicinity, Rupert, my daddy's long serving chauffer for over fifteen years, who'd been driving slowly around and around the block during the time we were having our little chat in The Chancer, not being permitted to park, had when he saw us both standing on the pavement outside the pub, pulled into the kerb-side. Daddy had at once requested for him to drop me off at my cottage, not bothering to ask me if that was what I'd wanted. Fortunately it had been.

Then on the way home, having now poured himself another large brandy from a decanter that he kept in a small bar in the car, he'd begun to slightly slur his words whilst having another little grumble at me. So by the time we'd arrived back at my cottage, his voice had become almost amusing; particularly the part where I'd needed to listen to his views on modern society in general.

❦ 230 ❦

THE LADY DETECTIVE

Arriving home, daddy had got out of the car, and opened his arms to me, and again gave me another very big hug, and had in a breathless boozy voice said. 'Now Jessica, you keep your chin up ol' girl, do you hear, cos between us, we'll grind the buggers down,' booze often made him maudlin.

Rupert, who'd been standing behind daddy winking, had then put up a thick thumb in the air enquiring soundlessly if I was really ok, that made everything seem so comical, that I'd found it hard to suppress my laughing out loud, and instead, gave a small nod of the head, and silently mouthed a silent yes.

Moments later, daddy had said 'well must be off now young thing . . . ah, to a meeting,' and Rupert had again gave me another knowledgeable wink, and quietly tap, tap, tapped the side of his nose.

It seemed to be catching on this winking business; first it had been Fred, then Bobby the copper, then the lads at the pub, and now Rupert was at it, and they might have all waved me a goodbye over their head no doubt, had they thought of it!

Of course both Rupert and I both knew, in this instance, what an 'important meeting' had meant. It meant my father going directly to his favourite club for a few more cognac's, whereby he would on meeting his chums, probably just to add some pathos to the situation, he'd no doubt have a boozy chat about the on-going problems of his strong minded, wayward daughter; and then would tell them, was at this moment in serious trouble, having been charged with killing someone.

I'd gave them both a sad-looking No5 smile, before I'd heard my father saying for Rupert to take him to the Regency club, having obviously already forgotten he'd told me he'd work to do!

Then I smiled when I saw that he'd back-waved a goodbye to me through the rear window, before I had in turn waved goodbye.

❧ 231 ❧

CHAPTER 66

TUESDAY NIGHT

Having entered the front door of my cottage, I'd stooped to pick up the morning mail from the mail box, and then had gone directly to the drinks cabinet in my lounge, and poured myself a very large vodka and tonic, and then gone into the kitchen for some ice. Strangely, this was something I wouldn't have done in front of my father!

Once accomplished, I then sat down on my sofa, drank the drink, then fell asleep. When I woke up, I'd then listened to any messages that may have been left on my new answerphone machine, and found five messages had been registered, including one from Pasha, who I'd totally forgotten about today, as I had very nearly forgotten about my new business, my mind being, as it were, on other things—as you know!

One of the messages had been from Susan Trumpshaw, an old school friend, to tell me that she was having a dinner party the following Sunday, and would I attend, and to please phone her with a yes or no.

Another had been from Lynda saying that on Sunday, she forgot to tell me that she had finalised a cracking good deal in business, and needed to talk to me about it. The third message had been from Bruce, my barrister friend, who'd asked *'What the hell's going on'*, and could he help, for he must have seen my name down at the Court Registrar, or was it by coincidence he'd asked that question? And finally there had been two messages from Stewart, not saying much.

I'd phoned the first three, and explained what had happened to me, until finally, a half-hour later it had been the turn of Pasha.

I must admit that having received a phone message from her, and hearing what she had to say, had made me wonder about my attitude, both towards myself and the business, then having heard Lynda cracking on about her 'fab deal', I realised I'd definitely need to get into my own mind-set, and be much more positive from here on in, especially, if it were at all possible, to try and sort out the 'big problem' which I intended to do something about. Easier said than done me-thinks, for then maybe, the business would be pushed a little more into the background.

Pasha last message had said 'that as it was nearly 5pm' and she would shortly be 'leaving the office for the day', and she told me she'd 'be going directly home if you want to talk to me.'

She had then gone on to tell me 'the whole day has been very quiet, with only one person phoning in that could be a potential customer, and that person would be coming into the office the following day, for a chat'

She had hoped all was well with me, and said as she hadn't heard from me after Monday night, she'd phoned around the Courts later that day, and been told the good news of my release. Then finally she'd said. 'I might try to phone you again later on.'

Realising that she'd been very concerned about me, I had spent another five minutes going thru my suit pockets to find the piece of paper on which I'd written her friend's home telephone number on, telling myself, that I would need to treat her to a telephone, and pay the bills.

Then I phoned her, and told her all was well with me, and telling her all about last night, and my being locked up. Finally I told her what had happened in court, and thanked her for her concern and message, and then rang off. Now there was only Stewart to phone—oh heck!

CHAPTER 67

Sitting on my sofa, with my legs tucked under me, and drink in hand, I'd then realised it was still only Tuesday evening, though it seemed as if a whole month had gone by since yesterday morning, and could hardly believe all that had happened to me over the past 30-odd hours or so, since I'd taken what I'd thought was to be my first momentous journey to my place of work, and the start of my new career.

With a wry smile, I can still remember the feeling of high expectations, and my relishing in the newness of it all. And now I knew my first day would be remembered for all the wrong reasons! And yet I'd still smiled, having now remembered the icy wind when I'd left home; and my then being confronted by the two police constables at the office building' entrance; the reception I'd received by the news people, and stopped smiling when I had finally remembered Smelly Stokes' interrogation.

Although what was also not nice, was my viewing the dead body, and all that had meant. Then finally, I'd thought of my being thought of as a murderess wench, arrested, locked up, having a hell of night, then my court hearing, drink with daddy, and finally here I was sat on my own.

Having thought all about that, I must admit, my thoughts had quite naturally, continued to include that fat useless sloth of a Police Sergeant, who I now disliked more intensely

❀ 235 ❀

than I ever did anyone else before in my life, and thinking as far as he was concerned, he could go and boil his head in a vat of tar before I would ever help him again.

Why? Because it was because of his foolhardy bungling, and attitude, was why I had then spent a night in a cold noisy jail with a bunch of screaming morons; and eating with a plastic spoon!

Also, let us not forget that my present situation was all down to his stupidity; and because of him, I'd had the added humiliation of having to go to Court for the first time; seen a dead body; been inside a police station; and then locked up in a police cell overnight. Also because of him, I had lost, or should I say had wasted, two whole working days, and all because of a look-alike Al Capone, Mr Nice guy getting himself murdered. Sorry, I had meant the poor, poor man. God rest his soul.

And now it would seem that his murder may have been committed whilst I'd been working and laughing in my own office! Dam, dam, dam, and blast, because I'd now had a sudden thought that with my being charged with murder, it may have warranted a mention in the newspapers, or on the news?

Then another thought had occurred to me, that whoever they were who had written or spoken about me, had better be very careful whatever they say or write, because daddy would definitely be looking for any hint or slur, had it concerned me or my reputation. And more importantly, had they done that, daddy would almost certainly sue that person who'd said it, and the paper for allowing it to be said.

I'd also wondered, besides my friends, who would be shocked at reading such horrible news, and then wondered if there'd be anyone out there who may have believed I was a killer anyway!

My friends might have actually thought of it as one big joke, knowing me, and even had they been told of the humiliation I had gone through over the past thirty-six hours, may have still thought it worthy of a mention on one of our discussion 'take the piss' nights! Some joke!

So what's now to be done, is for me to get moi out of this very awkward situation that I found myself in, otherwise it could mean the 'long stretch' for me, meaning my lovely neck lengthened in the gallows noose, and not the length of time I'd spend in prison.

Thing was, heaven help me, I could had I avoided the death sentence, it would at the very least mean I'd have to spend twenty years in some dark, smelly, drab, and dreary prison cell, forever protesting my innocence at the top of my voice. Ok I'm joking—I hope!

Now having thought of that, I'd hastily finished my drink. What I now needed was to have a good old-fashioned hot soak in my lovely round bath, and attempt to clean away all the grime and stench of last thirty-six hours from my body. Then I might eat something, or even read a book, and then afterwards, if I felt tired, have myself a full night's sleep. Knowing that lots of sleep was an immediate remedy, I wondered if I would be able to sleep at all, after considering all that I'd been put through both mentally and physically, yesterday and today.

I'd thought this whilst drinking down a strong cup of Plantation fresh ground coffee, before heading towards the bathroom, and there had turned on the gold plated taps to run a bath, before I'd liberally sprinkled lots of soothing Radox salts into the hot water, having known with so much going on in my mind, I would need to now relax . . .

Whilst I'd been laid back relaxing, and totally submerged in sweet smelling water with my long hair cascading all around me, I started to have really nice thoughts about Stewart. Oh dear, now my mind was telling me what I really needed was some comforting. when it suddenly came to mind that I should also have phoned him—not that we're in each other's pockets you understand, but it was polite to return a phone-call!

Blast! The man was going to give me hell. Probably almost as much as Daddy had, when I tell him all that had happened to me since we last met! Best not tell him tonight though, I'll now relax and telephone him tomorrow and tell him then. Besides, there's no sense in upsetting him at this time of night, is there?

Once again relaxing back in the water, I began thinking about him some more, and now with what I'd been feeling, it made sense for me to contact him tonight, and make any excuse that I needed to see and talk to him. I could perhaps say it was because he'd such a wonderful brain for solving difficult problems, that I had now needed for him to come up with a few bright ideas on how to solve both my particular problems!

Yet having thought about this one particular problem, I'd began to gently moan, and knew that I really could really do with Stewart spending some of his time concerning himself about *it*. Yes, I would need to talk to him tonight!

I suppose underneath it all, I'd needed him to offer me his large shoulder to cry on should I wish it, or for him to come up with a bright idea that would make me feel more relaxed with life than I was feeling at this moment.

Climbing out of the bath, I towelled myself down, and then had padded naked into my bedroom to the telephone placed on my bedside table. I glanced at the clock having now made up my mind, and saw it was only 6.29 pm. That's ok I thought, then I'll phone him at his work, and when a high pitched voice answered 'Metropolitan Police, how can I help you?' I asked for 'Chief Inspector Ross, please,' and then spent a minute telling her that I wished to talk to him on a personal matter—which it really was.

She'd then asked me in a sweet sickly manner 'And who shall I say is asking after him?' Then 'Can you tell me what it's regarding?'

'Jess, tell him Jess, and its private.' I thought *"As if I'd tell you what it's regarding you nosy receptionist you!"*

THE LADY DETECTIVE

After waiting for what had seemed like hours, yet had barely been a minute, the rich creamy voice of Stewart had finally spoken into the phone. 'Hello old thing, what gives? It isn't normally like you to phone me at work?'

'I wanted to know how you are. To return your phone calls, and ask if you are free tonight?'

'Well first off old thing, you're very lucky to have caught me still at my desk. Secondly, I was just about to leave, and go for a few jars with the lads. And thirdly, as you didn't answer both messages I made to your home yesterday and this morning, I wondered why?'

'Sorry Stewart, I'll explain later. In the meantime I've had this sudden idea you might like to buy a naked, wet, hot, and very simple thinking girl, one delicious Chinese takeaway, whilst she tells you why she spent all of last night in one of Her Majesty's jails.'

Having had a hot bath, I'd already changed my mind about making myself a small omelette with ham, tomato and chopped watercress, due to my thinking about 'things', so I'd not said anything more, as I couldn't think of anything more to say, though I wanted to make him feel concerned.

'What are you talking about Jess? Are you telling me you've been to jail, and now you're naked, wet, and . . . oh come on Jess you're not are you? And you are . . . you know, jesting with me!'

'No Stewart, I am not jesting with you about any of it, honest Injun! And I did spend the night in jail, having been booked in for B&B for the night, having supposedly murdered someone—as if!"

He laughed. 'Now I know you a lying. And now you would like me to get you a Chinese Take-away, after exciting the pants of me, then scaring me to death, am I right?'

'Stewart you are a love . . . and you are perfectly correct . . . on both counts.'

'Joking aside, you are calling me from your home, are you not?'

❖ 239 ❖

'Blast your cleverness. Once again you are perfectly correct,' wondering whether he'd thought I would be phoning him naked from a cell. Stupid thought.

'That's good! Now Jess, you stay exactly as you are, ok,'' he panted over the phone, 'and I'll be there with you in less time than it takes a thirsty man to drink a pint—ok? He obviously believed in my state of undress, I thought. 'Ok, and don't forget the spicy pork balls.'

'No worries on that account!' He said and rang off.

CHAPTER 68

Knowing I had no time to lose, I needed to dry myself off, empty the bath, and for comfort, put on a loose fitting baggy jumper with no bra, and slide myself into wafer thin tightly fitting pair of slacks that were tight enough to give any healthy male with half a brain; or any man, full brained or not, no allusions as to what hidden promises lay beneath these clothes; and Stewart, bless, had more than his share of brains!

So with just a touch of makeup, a little lipstick, and a squirt of perfume between the breasts, wrists, and behind the ears to add to the allure and complete my look!

Approximately thirty-five minutes after the phone call, the door-bell had rang its tune of 'Give us another one, just like the other one, give us another one do,' for me to answer, and I found Stewart at the door, holding onto a large brown carrier bag in one hand, and seeing me, had then put the other up to his open mouth in a mock expression of surprise.

I assumed the carrier bag held the Chinese food, and it certainly smelt as if it did, for us girls know about these things you know, and held out my hand to take it from him, saying 'Good evening Stewart, what's with the mouth?'

'Oh I was wondering what'll it be like to take a Chinese meal to a beautiful murderess, and now with you standing there, I know!'

❁ 241 ❁

'Flatterer! You are one funny man do you know that?'
And then as we made our way to the kitchen I said. 'It's true
what I said, I have been charged with murdering someone.'

'Bloody hell girl, first things first, come here and give
me a hug,' he said not believing me, and pulled me to him
one-handed, and kissed me with controlled passion, and then
pulling away, had gasped. 'Well if your pretending to have
murdered someone does this to me, you have now got my full
lusty permission to become a multi-murderess.'

'Seriously funny man, I really have been charged with
murdering a man who I don't know—unfortunately!'

And still he appeared to not believe me when he said.
'Oh, and because you go around bumping off people you don't
know, you thought it would be good idea for the condemned
person, being you, to have a Chinese meal as her last meal,
huh? Now,' he growled lustily, 'what happened to the wet,
naked, and hot lady that was part of the bargain you spoke
of, eh! More fantasy tales is it? Though I admit, I do still enjoy
looking at you as you are.'

'It's true what I'm saying. Honest.' And then kissed him
because he looked so adorable, and I told him so, and then told
him. 'Not to worry about that right now Stew, I have another
problem that needs your immediate attention!' 'We . . . ell I
suppose, as you look drop dead gorgeous in a zombie sort of
way, I could try to pay attention. But that, you already know,
don't you?'

'It's probably because I am so tired. I mean it really has
been a difficult two days . . . and the past few weeks have
not been plain sailing either—though that's another story.'

'Oh dearie me, come here.' He then hugged me to him,
and began to gently give my neck and ears little fluttering
kisses whilst saying. 'Blimey Jess, you must be the sexiest
bloody murderess ever. And you know what sweet-lips, I'm
here for you to do whatever you wish to command of me.'

Now that was just what I wanted to hear!

CHAPTER 69

Sometime later, having needed to warm up the Chinese meal in the oven, and having both devoured a very enjoyable meal, which by then I'd been ravenous for, I'd poured Stewart out a second beer, and had settled down next to him on the sofa to tell him everything that had happened to me since Monday morning.

At first he'd shook a finger at me in mock anger, and started to say things like, 'Oh yea', and 'Get away with you', but after telling him I was being serious, and he needed to listen to me—he'd listened quietly, with his mouth and eyes opening ever wider the closer it got to my spending a night in a horrible Station cell. Now looking positively angry on hearing Sgt Stokes hand in my imprisonment, he was now looking very concerned.

As I continued to babble on, he'd continued to just sit there listening, and not uttering a single word until I'd finished telling him all I had to say. He then asked me for a pen and paper, and quietly jotted down some notes on what I'd said. When he'd finished, and whilst we relaxed before a log fire with a glass of something that does you good in our hands, we'd then discussed the murder in earnest.

'Stewart, I really don't have any idea who the man is, and think it's all a bit weird, don't you?'

Nodding his head he then said. 'Though from what you told me, it's possible there could be a link between the two

❖ 243 ❖

offices, but what that is, I also haven't got the foggiest; though it's strange about one office being locked and the other being unlocked!

'I also thought that, and wondered if it might have something to do with one being an Import and Export Agency, and the other being an Import Sales & Business Consultant.'

And having thought a little more over what was previously said, I questioned. 'Are we perhaps suggesting that with them being next door neighbours, so to speak, that one office had not been getting on with the other guy, and then killed him? That seems a bit far-fetched don't you think?'

'Maybe it is, maybe it isn't!'

'And now with you agreeing with me, I suppose I should now try to find out who is renting those two offices—don't you think?'

He nodded. 'Exactly my thoughts young Jess. Exactly my thoughts'

'Well' I said looked at him smugly. 'I suppose I could get that answer pretty dam quick, because my father, bless, owns the building, and his office manager could give me those details.' I looked at Stewart's handsome face for some response. 'I mean it'll be something useful to be getting on with—don't you think?'

'Should you get those details, old thing, it would certainly be a step forward. In fact, you might say, I'll endorse that as a very useful idea.'

Suddenly feeling full of energy I'd said. 'Right then Stew, let's do it, and let's do it now. What do you say?' He looked at the fire, looked at me, then looked at his drink, gave a big sigh, and then nodded.

And without another word, we'd both made ready to go to my office, which he hadn't seen now it was finished, my knowing there'd be a night-caretaker who'd be left in charge of protecting the building for the night, who would give us those answers.

❦ 244 ❦

CHAPTER 70

TUESDAY: DETECTIVES WILLIAMS AND JONES

Earlier that day, the normally miserable looking Stokes was looking even more miserable when again he'd been sat in his make-shift office—the canteen, after he had attended the morning's court hearing, and had thereafter throughout the day, been berating himself, having known that he may have made one big, big mistake, in arresting the Felliosi girl, who he'd known had been granted bail before the real murder trial began, which had been set in nine weeks from now—and was strangely marked down on his forty-seventh birthday.

He also knew that in one way or another, he'd have to pay for his stupidity, and never more than from his own colleagues who were stood or sat about in the large room before him, who all knew his judgment of her, had been wrong, or too hasty. So now he could only look with a dumb expression on the faces at his colleagues, whilst wondering why he had arrested the girl anyway, for he'd known somehow, that all she had told

❦ 245 ❦

him about the murder, at least all that she had known, had probably been true.

He'd wondered if it might have been because of the sugar episode, when she had been laughing at him, or at least joking about him and his wife in front of Pasha. Or maybe it was because she'd made him look and feel such a fool over that blasted cigar? The thing was, he'd known at the time it had been a mistake to have stupidly lit it, especially having known she'd be annoyed. It was also stupid to have done something he would not normally have ever thought to have done, that was annoying!

Of course it might have been because she'd, just like the rest of those haughty-taughty women of her class, had always thought they were so bloody clever, and had looked on him as something beneath their feet. And now his wife, who had no doubt once loved him when he'd been slimish, was now always berating him about this or that, and all the time comparing him, his job, and the money he earned, to other people. Blasted woman!

So maybe it was his wife who'd been to blame for all this. Maybe it was his bloody wife putting him on a diet that had no meat in it, just bloody vegetables and salads that must be the logical answer, and reason, for all of his mood swings of late. Maybe, he hadn't been getting his normal high-protein food, or intake of carbohydrates, meaning a large amount of cakes and biscuits in his daily diet, which he'd regarded as normal food.

Now firmly resolved that his vegetable diet must have been the problem, he promised himself he'd now see to it that things would change when he got home that night, and had a few words with his wife . . . if she let him!

Strange thing was that Miss Felliosi, had, when they'd first met, been extremely decent to him, and had even offered him a cup of tea and biscuits. However from then on, he'd known that the things he'd said to taunt the girl into getting angry, had not been necessary, and was unforgivable. He wondered if his diet might have been clouded his judgement, and his anger and frustration within himself, been the reason why he'd arrested her, and made such a bloody fool of himself? In fact after he'd been to Court, he'd been grateful to have seen Miss Felliosi given bail.

And now he was exhausted, having hauled himself up two flights of stairs, because the lift had still been wet with new paint, before finally realising, that he hadn't an office to go to, because of the decorators now decorating his small office, and the Detective and Op's rooms, so had some minutes later, and completely out of breath, after traipsing through the complex building, with its many corridors, had now come back into the Canteen, and had sat himself again at the back of the canteen, and well away from Jones and Williams, who were looking at him in amusement, and he'd in return, glared back at them with a mouth now full of doughnut, having previously and angrily purchased a mug of tea, and the three doughnuts that he hadn't intended to have.

You would have thought, considering his love for food, and being sat in a corner of the police station canteen, it might have been one of the best places for Stokes to have ever been. It wasn't, and neither was his having to discuss about the Rugs and Tings murder with his team of detectives, because he was of course concerned about other ears listening!

So there you are then, wonders never cease, because no-one who saw him sitting there, couldn't have helped wondering if it may have anything to do with the canteen cooking, being as it was, tongue in cheek, a top-scorer for the brilliant cuisine that it always had on offer!

Surely that couldn't be it, even though the canteen cooking might have won awards for its fried up's of this or that, for it was a fact that all the main meals were always splendidly stacked with thick fatty chips, which might have certainly swayed someone like the fat Sergeant Stokes to have chosen the canteen to have done his thinking, work, whilst he'd been tucking into a large chip-butty, or similar.

Though strangely enough, this time it hadn't been for that reason that he was here. It was due to something far less exciting than the wonderful aroma and his having an English breakfast fry-up with chips. Although he could have been fish and chips, sausage egg and chips, steak and kidney pie and chips, or just chips, that may have persuaded him that the canteen had been the place to be!

His reason this time, was that the floor on which his office, the detective room, and the op's room were, was now out of bounds whilst the painters, decorators, electricians, carpenters, who'd been called in to brighten up the offices, got on with the job. So for the first time in eleven or more years, as a detective and Sergeant, he'd been kicked out those rooms.

It was even said, that the last time that the police station itself had last a lick of paint, or been cleaned up, was some eighteen years before!

Of course there would always be one or two people, Stokes being one of them, who'd have always preferred the darkness of nicotine stained ceilings and walls, the chipped wood-work, and the cracked frames of the old wooden filing cabinets, whose sides were now caving in under the weight of its contents, plus all the split and broken framed white case-boards around the grimy walls, in preference to it all being now replaced with new paint and new stuff.

And if that wasn't all, these people, being one or two of the old coppers who preferred the rooms looking worse than a junkies pit, would also hate to see old office furniture being replaced with new chairs and desks, because the old furniture had been tied together with string and tape, much like these old coppers being a dying breed of 'real' law.

Of course all the desks were marked and stained from endless amounts of spilt teas and coffee's, sweat, spittle, and graffiti doodling. besides their looking un-sightly, and there were some items, that were also a health hazard to everyone in general, particular to someone of Stokes' proportions, who it was said, had spent 80% of his time sitting on his arse anyway—not true of course, but close.

THE LADY DETECTIVE

*   *   *

Later that day he'd entered the canteen, and on seeing Jones and Williams on their break, had then come waddling up to the table saying, 'Ah!' pointing a finger at the two seated men, 'I thought I'd still find you two in here.' As if he hadn't known!

He'd then asked the two detectives 'how did you get on with the interviewing last night,' and both detectives replied, 'Fine,' and 'no problems.' Stokes had then said, 'No I mean was there any further problems?' He'd obviously heard whose daughter she was, had given a few problems over her being arrested, and his temper had been directed at him.

'Oh nothing for you to be concerned about Sergeant,' Jones said happily, knowing exactly what Stokes had been referring to, with Miss Felliosi' father created problems, and then had added, 'at least none that you will really want to hear about—though that's only my opinion of course! Sorry Serge!'

'Well Jones, that's extremely civil of you,' Stokes had replied, 'however I wouldn't have needed to have asked you, had I, if I had already looked into my crystal ball, and known that anything you said was not worth listening to.' He growled, 'So why don't I believe you?'

He now stood looking down at the tomato and chip on an otherwise empty plate, and then started to shake his head before saying. 'Hmm, bet your dinner was good.' Then he'd shaken his head saying. 'Nah, I can't have any of that, as much as I'm tempted, cos if the Missus were to find out, she'd kill me.'

He groaned, and licking his lips had again shaken his head once more before saying. 'Oh I also need to tell you that the latest news is no news at all, cos I've just been informed that forensic team haven't found anything more for us to work on . . . yet. In other words, no more clues other than the girl's fingerprints have been found. And they also say it's too soon for them to have got everything else sorted!'

❖ 249 ❖

He took a large puff of his cigar, and blew the smoke over Jones, and his plate; and Jones had stood and said aggressively 'Do you mind, that's our food you are blowing your foul smoke over Serge!' and had starting to flap his arms about him before sitting down again, prodding at the lone tomato and chip, before picking up his tea.

He then continued. 'Though I still cannot for the life of me, see where Miss Felliosi figures in all of this Serge. What would have been her motive? Now I know you must know what it was, Serge, after all you did arrest her,' he said sarcastically, still flapping his hands at some cigar smoke to keep it away from his face.

DS Stokes stood tall, all 6'3 inches of him, and twenty-odd stone, as he'd again dragged heavily on his cheap smelly cigar, similar to the one that had previously got him into a spot of bother at the girls office, and then had exhaled so much smoke from his mouth, someone would have thought he'd been competing against a steam engine for a most created smoke prize. Now he growled.

'That, detective constable Jones, is for the likes of me to know, and for the likes of you to get me some answers as to what the dead man was up to on the days before he was murdered, cos that may explain why she killed him. And I'd suggest, the sooner you do that, the better I and the Chief-Super, would like it. Ok?'

Williams smiled. 'So it seems to me, that you really have no motive, at least not one that you, or we, have yet found for her to have murdered the man!'

'Look you . . . ,' started Stokes, getting angry, and instead had continued after contemplating to say something nasty. ' . . . look, I want you both to get out there and find out anything you can about the dead man, ok? I want to know everything there is to know Brassy's background; his friends, businesses, wife's, mistresses, bank details, or even what toilet rolls or size underpants he wears. Just get me some answers, Ok?'

THE LADY DETECTIVE

Looking highly flushed, he had then looked towards the other detectives sitting nearby and hissed. 'And as for you lot, just do your job.'

Then pointing towards Williams and Jones; 'And you two, might find your jobs on the line, if you don't bloody well sort yourselves out, ok?'

He'd then walked off, with 'Bloody hell', and 'Blithering Idiots', floating angrily in the air behind him.

When he was out of sight, Jones and Williams had shook hands, for they both didn't like 'the hippo', as Jones un-affectionately liked to call the Sergeant, whilst the other detectives who'd overheard the conversation, were now laughing and smiling, knowing Jones and Williams had won that round against the bombastic Sergeant

They had again laughed, even though some people saw him as a lonely figure who'd always ben sat by himself in the corner of this large canteen, when detective Meadows, had mimicked Stokes' voice, by saying 'Right you lazy lot, don't just sit there, let's get to it, today if you please,' and that had been followed by another one of the group saying. 'Yes Sergeant . . . right away Sergeant! Three bags full Sergeant!'

CHAPTER 71

TUESDAY NIGHT: AT MY OFFICE

Thirty-five minutes later, Stewart and me, were both in the caretaker' office, asking him for the names of the people we were interested in, who rented the both offices. However Ben, the old caretaker, told us 'He wouldn't tell us, or even the police, what we wanted to know, without the permission of his Manager.' And then added 'Besides, with it being late, if I got him now, he'd skin me alive he would. Though I could leave him a note and ask him tomorrow, if that's ok with you?'

I told him 'it wasn't ok, and that it was important I knew that night.' And he looked more surprised when I said. 'And Ben, I'll give you a pound note if you give them to me, now, and maybe two pounds if I'm happy with the results!

'Sorry,' he replied, 'I could lose my job if my Manager ever found out'

It now seemed to me that the old man was digging in his heels, rightly so, so desperately I said. 'Ok Ben, what if I was to tell you that I'm the daughter of the man who owns this building, what would you say to that?'

❖ 252 ❖

THE LADY DETECTIVE

He looked at me with surprise in his eyes 'You telling me you're Mr Felliosi' daughter?' There was a little quiver of emotion in his voice when he looked closer at me and said. 'Blimey you could be as well!'

'I am Ben,' and admired how the old man had still stuck to his guns when he said. 'Well it's ok by me, but only if Mr Felliosi himself gives his permission. I'm sorry, it's my job that's on the line here if I got found out'

'I understand Ben. So if my father was now to personally speak to you, would that be ok, and would you recognise his voice?'

'Oh yes Miss, everyone knows Mr Frank's voice!' He'd have been right, for my father had many times been heard to talk on the radio, the news, and TV.

'Ok, that's good. So now, might I use your telephone?' He'd nodded his approval. 'Thank you.'

Looking at Stewart, I wondered if I was doing the right thing, for once I dialled the number of my father's club to ask for his permission to get the information I needed, he may then wonder if I'd had an office in the building. Though he must have surely been informed by someone, that a murder had occurred in this building, his building, although for various reasons known only to the police, it was possible for them not to have mentioned the address where the murder had taken place, or even the person's name.

Ah well, I thought, if he hadn't known it before, he'll certainly now put 2 and 2 together after this phone-call, when at last the phone was answered, and I'd asked to speak to my father, who I imagined was probably propped up against the bar, or sat in a comfortable leather chair, with all his 'boozing' mates around him.

Both Stewart and Ben had been watching me before my father had come on the phone saying breathlessly. 'For goodness sake Jessica, I've only left you at your home a few hours ago. Now what have you done?' Charming I thought.

'Daddy, I'm sorry to disturb your fun, but I'm in one of your office buildings, and urgently need to know the names of the people who are renting two of your offices. Now the caretaker, Ben, is saying that he will only give them to me, once he has the permission of the Manager, or yourself.'

I let him take in for a moment what I had said, and continued. 'Now this information is very important to me daddy, and it has to do with what I've been charged for, and my innocence.' Clever thinking, I thought.

'What offices are they?'

'The one's where the murder took place daddy.' I'd answered, with a 'Trust me Daddy'.

'Oh Jessica . . . Jessica . . . Jessica, I can't do that because you'll be interfering with the crime scene if you were to go into those offices—and the police will definitely not like that, will they?'

And with my fingers still crossed behind my back, answered. 'I just need the names daddy, that's all. So how can that possibly get me into trouble? I made no mention of going into the offices, before adding 'No keys you see.' I'd then un-crossed my fingers. 'Daddy I need the names. So what do you say, will you talk to Ben?'

I waited for a reply, and as he was obviously giving it some thought, pleaded 'Please daddy. I have Stewart with me, so I'll be perfectly safe.'

Then at last he said. 'Ok Jessica, I'll talk to the caretaker, but don't you dare do anything that would be deemed as being silly. I know you, so promise.'

With my fingers now tightly crossed again, I answered. 'Of course I won't, daddy,' then added, 'you're a good sport.'

Then turning to Ben I said, 'My father would like to have a word with you,' and passed the phone to the shaking hand of the old caretaker.

'Good evening Mr Felliosi, Sir' he said, almost touching his forelock. 'Yes I've got the names in my safe, Sir. Yes Sir, in a ledger. Yes sir, you just leave that with me. Yes, yes I'll do that with pleasure . . . and a very good night to you as well, sir. Thank you.'

THE LADY DETECTIVE

Beaming with pride he passed the phone back to me. 'Mr Felliosi wants to talk to you again Miss Felliosi.' And immediately I'd taken the phone, I'd needed to listen for a further minute to my father warning me not to get into any further trouble, and that he hadn't put me through the best finishing schools in Europe for me to behave like a miscreant rogue.'

He'd then mumbled something about my probably seeing him and mummy tomorrow for lunch, and not to get into any further trouble, as it would 'greatly upset your mother.'

'Of course I won't daddy! Yes that'll be fine, so maybe I'll see you tomorrow . . . I'll phone mummy in the morning. Yes, thank you.'

I'd been about to put the phone down, when I'd a further thought. 'Oh daddy, have you told mummy everything that's happened to me, yet? You haven't. Well might I suggest that you do so immediately, without fail tonight, before she finds out from someone else! Yes daddy, I love you too.'

I put the phone back into its cradle, and smiling said to Stewart. 'What's a miscreant rogue when it's at home?'

He shrugged, 'Not good Jess, not good at all.' So I shrugged.

'Right Ben,' I said turning to the old man, 'let's be having those names now, shall we?'

After spending the next few minutes looking for the names of the people we'd wanted, I'd been more than surprised to find that both offices had been rented out to the same person, a Mr Edward Brassy. And stranger still, both agreements had been signed for in different offices, and on the same date, by the same person. So being extra curious, I then noticed that both documents had been made out by one Solicitor, a Mr James Thomas, of Thomas and Beckett Solicitors. I made a note of both addresses, and their phone numbers.

Strange how those documents had now reminded me, that that on any agreement that my father had been asked to sign, had they been of importance, my father would always

❀ 255 ❀

insist that the solicitor should also sign the document, thereby acting almost as a Guarantor. My father had told me that he'd always do this, to get the solicitor to do their job more efficiently, and carefully, knowing that had they given my father wrong advise, that the said document having been authorised as true, and signed by them, it could also rebound on them.

So having got what we had come for, we'd both thanked Ben, and I slipped him two pounds for his troubles, and telling him that we were now going to do a little late work in my office. He seemed pleased with the money, although he said 'He'd have done it for free,' and 'you really shouldn't Miss, cos there's no need for that you know, cos me job pays well enough to get by.' However that hadn't stopped him from pocketing the money, even as he'd been telling us this!

Leaving Ben, we'd taken the lift up to the 5th floor, and let ourselves into my new office, where I'd proceeded to pour us both a much needed lemonade drink. Then Stewart had appraised the new drinks and ice cabinet, and afterwards the décor, before sitting in one of a new armchair which hadn't then made any of the strange noises it had made when Stokes had sat in it.

We'd been quietly sipping at our drinks, when he said. 'All this looks good, Jess,' moving his arm in a circular motion to mean the office, and then without saying a further word, we both remained deep in our own thoughts for a few minutes, until I'd made up my mind about what I'd needed to do, and getting up from my own armchair, had then sat on his lap, and taking hold of his hand, had broken the silence to ask sweetly.

'Stewart, I'm wondering if you would be so kind as to help me get into those two offices up the hallway. You see I need to see where it all happened . . . again.' And not waiting for a reply continued 'Cos you never know, we might find something to our advantage that might help me solve *my* problem, which in real terms, is the possibility of me getting my neck stretched on a rope.'

THE LADY DETECTIVE

'Now Jessica, you know I couldn't possibly do anything like that, don't you? It is a crime area you know? In fact it's more than that, it's Jessica's own murder crime area.' He then grinned. 'Besides with you being so clumsy, you might just muck up some vital evidence that could still be in there, especially if the lads are still looking for vital evidence of who may have done it, besides yourself of course.'

'Oh come on Stew,' I said playing with his ear, 'don't give me all that mumbo jumbo stuff, because you of all people should know what to do, or what not to do, to make sure we leave everything as it was, unsullied, untouched, virginal.' I purred in his ear.

Then with more concern in my voice, had added anxiously 'You do know that your police chums are trying to hang me out to dry—don't you? You do know, I'm the only suspect they've got—at least according to that fat horrible man Sergeant Stokes.' Now trying to copy Stokes voice 'So unless I can sort out this murder before the court trial, 'and now sounding more Cockney 'that grease-ball will ave sorted me out good and proper! So what da yer say?'

He said pensively. 'There might be a copper sitting at the door—you know?'

'Well we could at least looksee! Oh come on Stewart, you know l really do need your help if we are going to solve this ruddy murder together . . . don't you?' I twiddled his ear. 'You see with me being a murder suspect, and being the only one I might add, will mean, if you really wish to see me get off the hook, or is it out of the frame that you coppers say, then it's that simple.'

I paused looking into his grave blue eyes, and pouted sweetly, before putting my lips forward for him to kiss, though just for only a moment, before saying. 'Now surely, you wouldn't want little old' me strung up like a side of mutton and left to rot, would you lover? Or is it, cor blimey Miss, you'll say, what a waste of prime flesh?'

'Now stop it Jess, you know I wouldn't want that, though I could lose my job doing what you are asking me to do—if I were to ever be found out, don't you?' He then gave me one of his "What the hell smiles", and in return I gave him a whole lot better kiss, followed by a huge hug of gratitude.

'Blimey Jess, I suggest we get on with doing the deed before I go and lose all sense of reality.' He said gasping for air, pretending to slowly recover from my embrace. I then gave him another, and again he gasped 'Wow Jess, now that one was definitely one of your better smackeroos,' he meant kisses, and still panting, had made a pretence wipe of his fevered brow of perspiration, and then after a mischievous look at me, said 'after having that small sample, and wondering about the main course would be, how could I possibly not think of helping you?'

'You clown,' I replied laughing.

CHAPTER 72

RUGS AND TINGS

Minutes later, we'd left the warmth and security of my office, and headed down the hall towards the two offices. Then once Stew had sneaked a look around the corner to see if a Constable had been left on duty to protect the murder scene, we had rounded the corner after he'd waved me through like he'd been a goddam cavalry man on the hunt for 'Injuns', and I'd seen immediately on our left, was the office door of Byways Ltd, and some thirty feet or so, further down the hallway, the office door of Rugs and Tings.

Everything was deathly quiet, so much so that I could hear Stewart's breathing, and my own heart pounding. This was exciting times, for I'd never done anything quite like this before, not counting my snooping on Sunday of course, although this time it'll be a real break-in when we found both doors were locked!

Glancing down, I couldn't help noticing my feet, and thinking that two nights before, in this part of the hallway, my little nosy had caused me nothing but grief ever since— and here I was at it again, I must be mad! Although this time,

❖ 259 ❖

my feet would hopefully lead me on to a way of solving the problems they'd caused me first time around.

The hallway was, we saw, decorated with endless yellow/blue Police tapes that had been put up by the uniform or SOCO team, and that included both office doors, and had stupidly reminded me of Christmas.

As Stewart had pointed out, this end part of the hallway was a crime area, in fact, my murder crime area, and any unauthorised persons, like me and Stewart, were strictly not to be admitted into this area. In other words, these coloured tapes were a warning for us to keep completely away from here.

'Well partner it's up to you now, shall we stay or shall we go now?' I drawled—my meaning to get through this obstacle course, and go into either office. Then without any hesitation, we had both ignored the warning, and ducked under the tapes.

'Shucks ma'am' Stewart replied in as equally a bad American accent as mine had been. 'I'll see what I can do.'

And putting my hand up theatrically to my brow, and wringing my hands, I gave him a nod of the head, and I suspect a nervous smile, before saying. 'Just you remember darlin', you are doing this to save my life, as now I know you wouldn't want to see me . . . suffer most horribly would you?' I then gave a fake moan. 'Sir, as my very existence is now in your hands, you can do whatever you want with me, as I'll be forever in your debt.' Pretence sobs had followed.

He then looked at me before saying US of A'ish. 'Now shush now. And as I've done my biddy bit by getting us both this far un-harmed by any other goddam critter, I'll now suggest you remember not to touch anything, anything at all, without putting some gloves on.'

'Gloves?' I questioned.

'Which, I happen to have just here . . . in my back pocket.' He gave me a wink and handed me a pair, having known all the time that once I'd obtained the names of who the offices were rented to, I'd ask him to do a little bit of office-breaking for me as well, so had taken two pairs of gloves from out of his car's glove department. Crafty lovable soul!

'Right, here we go,' he said, and we continued past Byways Ltd down the extra yards until we'd both stood outside the office of Rugs and Tings.

'Now Jess, remember don't do hands if you can possibly help it!'

He'd then taken from his back pocket, a bunch of interesting looking keys, which I suspect were skeleton keys, and choosing one, had inserted it into the lock, then finding that hadn't worked, he followed that by another, and another, until finally on finding the correct one, he began fiddling it from side to side, and in less than fifteen seconds, we both found ourselves standing side by side inside Rugs and Tings office.

'You'd better give me a few lessons with that lot, partner,' I said pointing to the keys, 'or even better, you can perhaps get me a set—because you never know, I might have need of them in my new profession some day!'

'Now you are joking with me, Jess! You do know you could go to prison for having a set like these found on your person.'

'Nah impossible,' I said teasing him, 'besides if they're good enough for you; then they're good enough for me.' He shrugged as if it wouldn't happen.

The room we were stood in, looked similar to mine, before I'd made the changes, although smaller, and thought, taking my time to look around the room, had I been a potential buyer of rugs, I would have certainly not been at all impressed by what I saw in here. Stewart seemed to be having similar thoughts.

The furniture consisted of one large old sofa, with one arm rest broken and at an angle to the floor, three old captains wooden office chairs, that had seen better days, and all were facing in the same direction, towards an old-fashioned and ornate tiled fireplace, which had looked as if it had never actually been used for a decade or more. And on the floor, was a carpet that I would have described as being, a 'bit of tat', which was surprising when considering the dead man had supposedly sold rugs.

In the middle of the room there stood a leather-topped writing desk that also had seen better days. And standing to one side of the fireplace, in the farthest corner away from all this old stuff, was stood a newish looking drinks cabinet. 'Not out to wow his customers was he?' I suggested, more to myself than at Stewart, and walking over to the drop down lid cabinet, I'd opened it, and been surprised to find a number of full or half-full bottles of alcohol on display.

There'd been the old favourites, Scotch, Gin, Rum, Vodka, and bottles of Tia Maria, Pimms, Bacardi and similar, which having reminded me of my own new drinks cabinet, though slightly less stocked, I'd thought *"Great minds think alike"*

Stewart thought 'Perhaps this man was in the habit of getting potential customers drunk, before he proceeded to talk shop!' And as he had in fact said what I'd be thinking, I'd added.

'And I'll tell you something else Stew, from the look of those sorry looking display rugs,' pointing to where some rugs and carpets had been stacked for display, 'and from the state of this room, I'd have said he'd have needed to have got them as drunk as Lords to have even got a sale!'

Sitting down on one of the old wooden chairs, I said. 'Now here's an interesting thought, maybe he didn't need to impress his clients, maybe he'd already done the impressing somewhere else, so when he'd offered someone a drink, he hadn't needed to have been bothered about the décor!'

Even though the whole room did look totally unimpressive, I had been surprised by the tatty-looking rugs on display, more than the room itself, yet found the room, judging from the very poor quality of everything I saw around me, strangely interesting, so interesting that my thoughts had immediately thought if a deal had been already struck elsewhere, and all of this as being just a cover. Though for what, I asked myself?

THE LADY DETECTIVE

Stewart had now interrupted my thoughts by saying. 'I can't see it myself, it makes no sense at all to strike up a deal in more convivial surroundings, then to come back here, to this dump, to have a drink, so it had to be for another reason!'

'Of course he might have been an alcoholic.'

'What! And this was his "quiet time place", a place where he could get silently sloshed with nobody around to disturb him—his wife for instance!'

I laughed at the thought, before saying. 'Well I dread to think what a shrink may have to say about his client had he been asked to comment on this Mr Nice Guy, after seeing a newish drinks cabinet full of booze, and then compared that to the tattiness of the room.

'Well whatever the reason, this place really needs a big clean-up, a lot of TLC from what I'm seeing. Even those sash-blinds on those windows at the far end of the office are filthy.' Stewart added.

'Or having to view only those rooftops hasn't helped.' I said.

All that remained to mention in this room, was a dark-green metal four-draw filing cabinet, four dirty drinking cups, and the similar number of dirty glasses, two being left on the window sill with the remains of a very off bottle of milk stood alongside a Hobbs electric kettle.

This room, also hadn't any pens, paper, or brochures anywhere, and didn't have the feel of any Sales office/Show room that I'd ever seen, for there wasn't anything to view, besides tatty rugs, that had even suggested it had anything to do with Sales, even though there'd been an old looking Smith-Corona typewriter on one corner of the desk—it still seemed all wrong somehow!

I'd glanced towards Stewart, and saw he was feeling one of the rugs that had been stacked one on top of each other, and seeing his puzzled look, had said. 'I'm betting you're finding something not right about those, aren't you?'

❦ 263 ❦

He nodded. 'Well these rugs don't feel, or look like new rugs, do they?' I wandered over to him, and felt the rugs, and whispered.

'Thread bare might be a good word to use Stew. I mean they look almost washed out, don't you think?'

He then pointed to a rug three or four down the pile, 'Did you notice on the corner of that one, there's a small amount of powder?' he had as he'd been rubbing his fingers together, and had then taken a small white paper bag from his wallet saying, 'I'll take a sample.'

He then tasted that small sample, and smiled, had said 'I think this is heroine, Jess, or something similar, and if that's what this is, then me old fruit-drop, we could be onto something very big indeed, maybe even bigger even than your murder . . . ah, if I'm allowed to be so glib.'

It excited me to hear him talk that way; almost as excited as he'd been the week before when he was excitedly explaining to me 'That each person is in his own blood group, and now they're saying that from the blood, you can tell the DNA of a person, which is as unique as our fingerprints are to each other. So now, just by testing and verifying a person's blood, we'll in the future be able to know anyone's history, just as were now able to tell who a person was by their finger prints.'

Trying to make sense of what he'd just said, I mumbled. 'Well if that's so, I would have thought the detectives, or the forensic team, with that magic at their finger-tips, have wanted to take samples in here.' Then looking around the room, 'and then again, they might not want to have.'

I'd been looking over towards the fireplace, wondering when it was last lit, before saying. 'Your blood thing is probably very interesting to you, but what is now puzzling me, is what are these curious scuff marks in front of this old fashioned fireplace.'

I saw the marks must have been at least three to four feet long, and being parallel to each other. Intrigued, I bent down to take a closer look, then said 'When you have finished with whatever you are doing, would you come and tell me what

THE LADY DETECTIVE

you think might have made these marks on the carpet?' I pointed to them, and added 'because if you were to ask me, I'd say it looks like something has been pulled up to or away from the fireplace.'

Now standing next to me 'Now you do surprise me Holmes,' he grunted, 'probably pulling something up, a chair maybe,' and smiled. 'Best to take a sample I'd say.' And then had spent a minute or so, scratching samples off the brown mark, and putting them into another one of his little white bags. He'd then put it into his pocket with the samples he'd taken from the powdered rugs.

He'd then squeezed my arm, and said. 'Well spotted you. Anyway, I'll get that little sample checked out with the others.'

I said. 'It certainly looks like something's been dragged, yet those deeper ball-like marks, might also suggest the object was turned around!'

Having finished watching Stewart taking samples, I'd taken another look around the 'sales office', and felt my head shaking in total disbelief, for now I had noticed something that was going to be a problem for me to comprehend, and having spent moments thinking about it, blurted out.

'Stewart, now you may think this awfully silly of me, because there is something else puzzling me which I don't understand at this moment. And that is, why should a man, who obviously doesn't smoke, have signs stuck around the place saying 'Please No Smoking', then allow smoking to have taken place?' I pointed to two over-full ashtrays on the mantelpiece.

Stewart looked at both the signs and ashtrays with interest, and looking suitably impressed with my observation, nodded his head.

So I added. 'I mean you would have expected to have seen any ashtrays or cigarette butts in a room where a person doesn't smoke, would you?'

❖ 265 ❖

'No I wouldn't have thought so.' He then looked at me and enquired. 'Though I suppose you have an explanation for that, do you? He questioned.

'It's just that when I came in here last time, the first thing that struck me with those signs, and the smell in the room. And to answer your question—no I haven't an explanation, other than to say that maybe he'd been entertaining a client, an important client, and hadn't wanted to upset him by telling him/them, that they couldn't smoke in here!'

Stewart shrugged, thinking what I'd just said was perhaps a bit crazy. Now pointing to the cigarette stub in his hand he suggested. 'Well it must have been for a jolly good reason for any non-smoker to have allowed someone to smoke these foul smelling cigarettes in his office. I mean these are seriously strong, and smell foul.'

He put one of the cigarette butts under my nose 'Probably Turkish, Russian, or maybe a French cigarette, because all those counties like their stinky cigarettes you know!' Then taking another sniff at it, had bagged it as another sample, and put that into his pocket with the others.

Before finally turning our attention to the filing cabinet, and office-desk, we had for the next few minutes, both looked for any further clues that might have helped us solve the murder, or the puzzle of how Mr Nice guy was found in next door's office. Unfortunately, we also hadn't found anything to help us in cabinet or desk either. In fact Mr Nice guy hadn't any customer files, office files, or whatsoever files in the filing cabinet, it being empty. It had looked as if whatever had been in them, had been taken away, had there been anything!

I pondered for a moment if this may have happened, for there'd have been many opportunities over the past week to have done that, and not be seen. Though during the daytime it might have been difficult, as I or my tradesmen had always been about from dawn to dusk every day, so would have seen anything untoward, happening. Wouldn't we? Then I thought that's silly thinking, for the workman, or even me, wouldn't have thought it unusual for someone to walk out with an

THE LADY DETECTIVE

armful of files to the lift, thinking it have been business files, and none of our business!

'Ah ha, what have we got here?' Stewart said, pulling out a piece of paper that had been neatly tucked in between the draw runners at the very back of the desk. The paper had been folded very small, and could have easily been missed by the forensic team, or anyone. On the paper were written a series of numbers and letters, and as we tried to fathom out what they meant, I'd made a note of some of them, their being twenty-five or more in total. The numbers I made a note of were:

8000-64000 ZL; 4000-32000 AS; 4500-36000 RB; 3000-24000 BL; 3000-22000 GH;

'Could be significant,' Stewart said.

Of course he or I wouldn't have realised, while we'd both been looking down on it as it lay on the desk, just how crucial this little piece of paper would become in solving the motive for the murder.

'We'll attempt to try and solve their meaning at a later time', Stewart said, returning the paper to where he'd found it, after debating whether to white bag it.

Making sure we hadn't missed any other clues in the room, we'd spent a further few minutes sniffing about, when Stewart had said. 'Right Jess, let's get out of here, shall we? I don't think we'll find anything more in here of interest, though I am surprised the cops haven't been more thorough and taken away the milk bottle, cups, and booze bottles, cos they could have some interesting finger prints on each of them.'

CHAPTER 73

BYWAYS OFFICE

We left, again ducking under the police tapes hung outside the door, after Stewart had carefully locked the door after us.

For my part, I'd been elated with our having found the clues we'd found, and I'd also been very careful not to have moved anything from its original position, just as Stewart has instructed . . . though when we'd left Rugs and Tings office, I'd been intrigued when looking at two large prints on one wall of the office, thinking it could have been Turkey, or Afghanistan. Turkey was my bet, but thought it strange to have had these posters stuck up on the wall anyway— perhaps Mr Happy holidayed there!

Back again in the hallway, we'd again expressed our surprise that no-one had been assigned to guard the area, before I took hold of Stewart's hand, and giving it a little squeeze, had said 'Righto me bucko, let us finish this here assignment, by having a little gander at what Byways office has to offer. So what do you say—partner?'

Bending down over me, Stewart took me firmly by my shoulders, and looking into my big lovely blue's, saying firmly. 'You are young lady, trying to get us both crucified?'

Fluttering my long eyelashes at him I replied. 'Best be hung for a £pound than a penny I'd say, sir!'

Laughing lightly, he'd said. 'That apart, may I say that you are an impulsive, extremely gorgeous, hard taskmaster when you are fired up Miss Felliosi, and even a glutton for punishment? However I must remind you . . . ,' we both said the words in unison . . . 'you could get me fired if I got found out for what I'm now doing.' And we'd both laughed.

He now said. 'Seriously Jess, I could be hung out to dry by my superiors for helping you, don't you know?' He then gave me another one of his mischievous grins before saying. 'However I could always tell them that you had in fact, bewitched me. Or that I've always been a sucker for beautiful damsels in distress,' Then looking at me added thoughtfully, 'though in your case, I've made you an exception to my rule!'

I gave him what I thought was a very gentle punch on his arm, at the same time saying. 'Byways office, now if you pleeeease!'

He continued. 'Of course besides my losing my job; there's always office-breaking, tampering with the evidence, and whatever else they'd have in mind to throw at me.' He smiled. 'However it would be such a shame, wouldn't it, to have wasted this wonderful opportunity to unlawfully break into another office, seeing as we're here already?'

Punching the air, and pointed to Byways, 'So common then big man, let's you and me finish this, cos don't they say, better in than out?'

He gave a pretence moan, then said before stepping up to Byways Ltd door. 'And here's me thinking, how nice it would be for me to have lost one's job for the one you love, and willingly die with a smile on one's lips, for a particular beautiful lady in distress.'

Then as we'd both ducked under more yellow/blue police tape, he concluded. 'And the bottom line is that I'm not doing it for either of those reasons, I'm doing this for you.'

Laughing, I said—'You are such a horrible tease.'

Taking out the skeleton keys again from his pocket, he tried one or two, before inserting the correct one, saying. 'Now me Lady, the same rules apply about you not touching, ok?' I nodded. 'Right ye are then ye ol' taskmaster, let us go and see if there be anything in there that'll be of interest to I or thee.'

'Sounds good to me,' I said happily, liking the 'us' bit.

On entering the office, Stewart had immediately put on the lights, and I'd immediately noticed that the two dark-coloured blinds hung on two similar sash windows to those we'd seen next door, were drawn up. Then had at first glance, thought everything seemed to suggest that this office was a complete contrast to the one next door. For it had at least some order, neatness, and a few decent bits of furniture.

Though the room was sparsely furnished, it looked expensive, and the décor gave the impression that whoever sat in here, had money—and lots of it. Though I'd again had strangely felt there was something about it that shouted—I'm not an office. And as for the office itself, there'd been in the centre of the room, an expensive looking office-desk that had a centre-drawer, and a leather waste-bin had been to the left of the desk, on the floor. There'd been three matching comfortable chairs, strangely all facing again towards the fireplace. However, I couldn't help noticing that this office also had a strange musty smoky smell about it—strange!

There hadn't been a filing cabinet, or any shelving to take folders or books, which I'd again thought quite odd. Though there'd been an expensive looking sofa, and a dark patterned eastern looking carpet on the floor, Persian maybe, that must have cost a small fortune. And hung on light coloured wall papered walls, there'd been three poster landscape paintings.

And tucked into the corner of the room, was a small table, that had on it a kettle with four clean mugs; some dried

THE LADY DETECTIVE

brown sugar in a bowl next to a jar of coffee. And besides the table, stood a small fridge, whose contents included a un-opened bottle of bubbly, and the sickly remains of a chocolate cake; and nothing more. The owner had obviously enjoyed his creature comforts.

Checking through the desk drawers, we found them empty, whereas in the leather waste-paper bin, I found a number of shells that I'd recognised as pasticcio nutshells.

'You'd have thought the police would have taken away these, wouldn't you? I asked, showing Stewart the shells, the queried 'and what if there'd been any fingerprints on the champagne bottle in the fridge?'

'I agree it certainly doesn't look like they've really done anything in here at all does it? That's not to say they won't!' He looked unconvinced at what he'd said.

Attempting a joke, I pointed to the shells 'Maybe they'd all been shell shocked.'

'Not funny.'

Then thinking there hadn't seem to be anything more of interest to me in here, I had then noticed what again had looked to be more marks on the carpet by the fireplace. 'Lookie here Stew, we've got more of those strange looking scuff marks on this carpet, and they look strangely similar to those we found next door. Very strange me thinks—what do you say?'

'These do look more as if something has been dragged to or from the fireplace, don't they?'

'So maybe whatever caused these, must have also happened next door—yes?'

We both bent down to have a closer look at the marks, and then I noticed something out of the corner of my eye, at the back of the fire place—a cigarette stub. 'Well what have we got here?' I said as I moved up close to the fireplace, then found nearly a whole cigarette, and judging by its feel, it appeared to be fairly fresh. Also there'd been what I'd call, a roasted smell about it.

❧ 271 ❧

'I think this has a similar smell to those cigarette ends we found next door.' I said thoughtfully 'and if this does match the ones next door, what the heck is it doing in here?' Then looking more closely at it, I made out the letters GOU.

Stewart took the cigarette stub from me, smelt it, and said. 'Again good-thinking old thing, cos it certainly has a similar smell. However the question now arises, as you say, why would one of them be in here?'

'Plus why was this light left on? Also why was the body of Mr Happy found in here? These are all instances that are strange. So it's extremely important to know those answers. Also I'd particularly like to know if the shoes on the dead man, or his clothes, had fibres of this carpet on them.'

'Why do you think these fibres are important?"

'I have my reasons. Though, now we know that the two offices were being rented by the same man, this Brassy, who we are assuming is Mr Happy, so I would imagine he may have had his partner running this, or that, office.' I said pointed at the wall, 'so we need to know more about this Brassy person. In the meantime, the samples taken from both the offices, and in particular these floor marks, may hopefully help to come up with some interesting facts.'

He took another bag from out of his pocket, making me wonder how many he had tucked away on his person, and bending down, said. 'So old girl, you're suggesting whilst I'm at it, for me to take a sample of this brown mark for analysis—yes?'

'Yes . . . and what's with this old girl bit, eh? I'm not old, or haven't you been looking lately?' I wiggled my bottom at him suggestively, and we'd then stood grinning like children at each other, as if we'd been told we could mow play in a sweet factory—before I suggestively asked 'Well?'

He laughed, shrugged his shoulders, and looking warmly at me, had continued to look about the room in silence, for it had suddenly seemed the right thing to do, after what I'd said.

THE LADY DETECTIVE

Now looking down at the chalk outline that had been the final position of the dead body when it had been found, I'd been particularly interested to note that the head and body were pointing towards the fireplace, just as if he'd collapsed awkwardly whilst looking into the fireplace, then I said.

'I'll tell you what, Stewart me old war horse,' pointed to the chalk mark, 'there's also something about the positioning of the body that's bothering me.' I explained. 'Although I'm no expert, and because I saw the body at the morgue, I know he'd had his face smashed in, so I'm beginning to wonder how the murderer could have from behind the dead man, swung the murder instrument so often, and so hard, as to able to have done the damage that I saw, and yet there is no blood.'

I looked at him and added 'I mean there's no way that was possible after seeing the state of the man's face, and yet it says otherwise. What do you think?'

Stewart looked at me, then at the outline, pondered, then said. 'That was quite a mouthful, wasn't it detective? Or should I have said—you PI you—though the lack of blood is a very interesting point that needs seriously looking into.' He then pointed to the chalk mark, and to the fire-place. 'You can't possibly be thinking what I think you're thinking, are you Jessica?'

'What's that?'

'That the dead man was killed somewhere else, next door maybe, in his own office, and then was dumped into this one?'

I smiled, before saying. 'Well I didn't see any large blood stains to suggest that, but do think that maybe he was dragged through the fireplace from next door.'

'What! Now that's insane.' Then he became thoughtful, before he questioned. 'Ok, even allowing that to be true, how is that possible? Besides, what would have been the point of that, because whoever had this or that office, that would means that if it was our Mr Happy who was murdered, then his partner, whoever that is, would have pointed the finger of guilt towards himself . . . wouldn't he?'

❦ 273 ❦

I saw the logic to his words, before I said. 'Well there weren't any drag marks, or lots of blood in the hallway coming from next door that I saw, was there?' I the pointed to Rugs and Tings office, then back from the door to the dead man's outline.

'No there weren't,' he said, and added. 'So this might finally turn out to be a case of the murders elaborate scheming, to have turned out to have been all a bit of a drag, wouldn't you say?' He laughed, before defending himself in a hurry.

'Oh you funny, funny man . . . I don't think!

Then I said. 'Seriously, perhaps the killer didn't care if it was his office, or the other office that he killed Mr Happy in, for aren't you forgetting that both the offices were rented out to the same guy, this Mr Brassy, so being the partner, even if the police had thought he'd been Mr Happy's killer, he'd obviously known that there was no way he could be named, being just the guy from next door whose name wasn't even mentioned on any rental document, to have had a finger pointed at him—cos he doesn't exist—so far.'

Stewart looked like he was going to say something, and when he did, he said. 'You know, you might make a great PI yet you know!' He paused, looked at me, smiled, before saying 'So another puzzle huh? Now you're going to ask me, why had he even bothered moving the body in here?'

'That's right. Why did he? I mean the murderer had no fear of being found out, which meant he needn't have needed to move the body, had he? And another question for you Mr Smarty-pants, was why do you think the killer left the office lights on in here? Surely he hadn't wanted the body to have been found so quickly, did he? I mean that doesn't make any sense either, unless he really wasn't bothered, as we've said.'

'Murderers, or murders, seldom make any sense in the cold light of day, my dear, but as far as his not being bothered, well that might be true had he not locked up Byways Ltd after himself, had he not been bothered?'

'Maybe he panicked!'

'No I don't think so, for he wouldn't have locked this door, so that shows there'd been no-one around for him to have been concerned about, or to disturb him.'

'So are you suggesting that he was maybe the cool casual un-flappable type?' Then I gasped 'Speaking of casual— that could have been the killers first big mistake, for he hadn't known that I'd already spoken to the dead man, Mr Happy. Meaning had I not, it wouldn't now have given me an approximate time of when the murder had, or had not, been committed.'

'Of course, and with it being Sunday, he wouldn't have thought of that in a *month of Sundays*.' He smacked his forehead saying 'duh, silly me!'

Ignoring him, I had then thought of something else. 'Oh Lordie, Lordie, had his time of death been in the same time frame from when I first saw him, say up to the time when the man in the black shoes had departed, that'll mean I'm in the clear! Can't you see that? And I've witnesses who can vouch for me being around my offices all of that time.'

Stewart, now serious 'So you're saying that had the killing been in broad daylight during the time your Mr Happy brown shoes arrives at the offices, and the time your Mr Grumpy black shoes departs from the office, then it couldn't possibly be you . . . yes? Now if that's true, that would be very good news, but to prove the exact time of death in that small time frame will be difficult, though because it's a valid point, I'll check on it.'

I said excitedly, 'also had it not been for the light being left on that gave the game away, the killer wouldn't have expected the body to have been found so quickly, to help prove the time of death.' I smiled.

Stewart said. 'That's true. Though with the blinds being up, the murderer wouldn't have noticed them being on during that time he needed to rush away.' Stewart nodded thoughtfully, 'so that might mean the killer was there all the time before Mr Happy arrived. Well that's as good a theory as yours, if nothing else.' He smiled.

I nodded, and gave the light thing some thought. I'd thought about the day of the murder, weather-wise, and thought it couldn't have been on Friday or Saturday, cos there'd been enough bright sunlight on those days for the murderer not to have needed any lights on. Not so on Sunday, because I remembered, that had been a horrid, cold, miserable day.

I said. 'Although the murderer could have arrived when it had still been dark on any day, before the sun had shone into the room; and had switched the lights on to wait for Mr Happy, and having killed him, maybe hadn't noticed that the lights were still on, though not so on Sunday, being it was a horrible gloomy day!' Before saying after I'd thought for a moment. 'Of course he might have been planning to return to the room at a later time, a quieter time, say on Sunday for instance, to then dump it somewhere where it would never be found . . . a concrete grave for instance.'

'So who'd da ya 'tink he was lady, Al Capone?' Stewart drawled in his bad American accent. I smiled, then thought on how Mr Happy had been dressed, before thinking that would then make Mr Happy the killer, but kept that to myself as too fanciful.

CHAPTER 74

And now, because I was enjoying myself I'd then pointed at both offices, 'As they say Buster, they are two sides to every mystery. However which one holds the secret of the killing I ask myself?'

'Of course it's possible that the killer did come back to somehow remove the body, maybe out of the window, and maybe he'd known the body had been found by the caretaker, because he'd seen the plods outside the building—or he may have even chatted to them about what was going on. Now that might be worth following up, so when you go back to the station, best you find out the men who were on duty that day, and did they chat to someone who had smoked smelly cigarettes, or smelt of them.' (That had unfortunately, been another no-no)

He had then laughed. 'Ok, so having seen the cops, he knows there's no way he can now remove the body, which means his devious clever plan has gone ass over tit—as it were—a boo-boo!'

He smiled looking mischievously at me! And knowing that look, I hastily added. 'Well, I hadn't seen anyone strolling down the hallway on Saturday or the Sunday . . . or on reflection, Friday or Thursday, either. Not that I'd been on patrol in the hallway all of that time, you understand, but my hallway office door was open for most of that time, and my windows . . . work dust you see, and because of Stinky Stokes!

❦ 277 ❦

Never-the-less it'll be worth asking at reception if they'd seen someone carrying out large bags, or files, during the past week—or seen anything strange, besides you of course!' Stewart had then duh, duh'd me.

I continued. 'Besides, there's something decidedly fishy about Rugs and Tings being a Sales Office, and not appearing to be keen on presentation? I would have thought he'd have tarted it up! So why didn't he? I mean it looks as if he couldn't have been too bothered whatever the clients thought how it looked or not! Maybe they're using it as a front, eh?'

Stewart, who'd been still looking around the room with a practiced eye for any further clues that might have been missed, had not very enthusiastically replied. 'You've got an imaginative mind, I must say, and that dear Lady, might be a very good synopsis, however the question should now be, having known Brassy had rented both offices, how are the two offices linked? And as for the rest, for the time being at least, we'll leave the rest as being all theory, conjecture.

He continued 'Well, it would seem there is nothing else for us here, so let's depart encore, qui? Because my dear, I think it's time for us to jolly well allez-vous sont, mon cher ami,'as they jolly well say in dear old China-town.' As I've said, joking or not, French as a lingo, he was never any good at speaking it.

We then left the office after a final look around, and as we were heading towards my office I said, looking at my watch. 'It's five past ten, so maybe it's not too late to go to that little pub down the road, cos I could kill for something to eat; a sandwich or something.' I groaned, mimicking someone in pain, by holding my stomach. He sounded surprised. 'You are jesting me, you have just eaten every bit of that huge Chinese meal, and most of mine as well?' I pretence sulked, and now he said.

'Ok, so off to the pub we go, cos I can't have you withering away can I?' He gave a small laugh, 'anyway the sooner we're out of here, the better I'll like it, cos if I got found out,' we both said, 'I could lose my job you know.'

THE LADY DETECTIVE

I laughed, and followed him saying 'Scardy cat', and gave him a small kick up his backside. Turning around, he pretended to be frightened by pretence shaking his body, and giving me a frightened look, and said.

'And what makes you think it was a man who did the killing anyway? I mean, it could have so easily been a woman, say someone like you, you know, one of your sort, all masculine, tough looking, and totally effeminate!'

He'd then started to walk quickly away from me towards the lift, to escape my trying to repeat kick him on his backside, and leaving me mumbling 'Bloody cheek' when he got out of range. It was then I noticed him limping ever so slightly, and suddenly I'd had a flash back to Sunday afternoon, and remembered Mr Grumpy with the black shoes, also having a slight right sided limp as he passed me in the hallway, making his way to the lift!

'Why are you limping Stew?' Then thinking of Mr Happy's build, and why hadn't I noticed him limping before.

That made him stop, then slowly he had turned around, and looking very serious at me, had said. 'Probably because I'm always walking behind you old girl—and well worth it is, if I may say so.' He smiled. 'Truth is old thing, that yesterday I'd been sat on my bed all on my lonesome, trimming my toenails, and I'd used my own fingernails as a pair of scissors, if you know what that means,' I shuddered, 'well my big toe nail, had been so intent on having a go back at me on behalf of his smaller brothers and sisters, who I'd previously picked off, that pulling on this larger nail, I had this time pulled it back as far back as the quick, and it then inevitably bled, and now it's a bit sore.'

He smiled. 'Quite silly of me really, laziness I suppose, for I really should have used the nail scissors that I have in the bathroom. End of story. So why the sudden interest may I ask?'

'I'll tell you later, if it doesn't take you all night to limp to the pub' I giggled playfully.

❉ 279 ❉

On the way out, we'd stopped to say goodnight to Ben, and I asked him 'had he seen anyone moving out some stuff on any day last week before Sunday night?' He told me without hesitation, 'No—no-one at all.' I then asked him who had left the building that week-end that he'd known or hadn't known by sight, and to think on it, adding 'It's important for my father,' thinking that might get more of his attention after giving him a £pound for his 'pub' charity.

CHAPTER 75

After walking the two hundred yards to the little pub, Stewart having stopped off at a small confectionary shop to buy me a wagon wheel, which I favoured, saying with a grin 'Something to be getting on with . . . oh fat one.' We'd been warmly greeted by the little pubs landlord, for now we'd almost become a familiar sight to him, and his regulars, after half a dozen visits.

So now sat in a newish looking, very comfortable wing-backed cushioned chairs, and close to a welcoming wood fire in the smallish lounge bar, and having no-one else to worry about, we'd moved to only a few feet away from the open fire, which Stewart had given a prod with his boot to liven it up, and then ordering the drinks, asked the landlord if it had been ok for him to put another log on, and getting an ok, we'd on inspecting the menu board, and seeing there'd been two choices of snacks, Stewart had teased me by taking his time, before ordering two No1's.

Now with a warming fire, and a vodka and tonic in my hand, and definitely feeling more relaxed than at any time during the past hour or so, because even though it had been fun, 'Breaking and Entering' was still a crime. Yet as it was something that I'd never done before, the actual breaking and entering, had been a brand new experience for me, much more so than on Sunday night, and that had made me ponder whether it may become a normal part of my job, being a PI, then if so, tonight might not have been the last time I would be doing a little bit of B&E.

Stewart by taking a large mouthful of steak and kidney pie, followed by a very long glug of Strong's bitter, and judging by the ah sounds he gave, Stewart was obviously enjoying both.

Then he said. 'Oh you mentioned, back at the office, that my limping reminded you of something. So what was that about?

I'd been enjoying my own Pie, being ravenous, and had only partially heard the word 'Limping', but did recall my mentioning it.

'Limping? Oh yes, it was seeing you limping in the hallway that reminded me of Mr Grumpy having had a slight limp like yours, and on the same side as well. So seeing you limping had reminded me of him. It's strange how the mind can sometimes be triggered to recall various things or other happenings—don't you think?'

Stewart suddenly bent across the table and gave me a big sloppy kiss, smiled, and said: 'Now that old thing could be another important clue to solving this murder, what you have just said!' He was now saying, 'and I suggest that you tell that to your fat friend, Stinky Stokes, when you next get a chance.'

He drew in a deep breath. 'Also the fact that Brassy had rented both offices, although it's likely he's found that out already. Oh, and you ought to tell him that Brassy' solicitor had signed both lease documents as a character witness, and as a guarantor for any non-payment of rents on both offices.'

'I'll do that, even if it means doing his job for him after what he's done to me, the sod.' Then taking the final sip angrily of my drink, said 'though I'm wondering why different Solicitors addresses to sign separate forms, cod that's very strange!'

Having now finished my Steak and kidney pie, and placing the knife and fork just so, as taught at finishing school, I had picked up my empty glass, and wobbling it about at him, said, 'And I suppose there can't be many criminals

THE LADY DETECTIVE

going about London Town, having a right-sided limp; and smoking smelly foreign type cigarettes, whilst eating pasticcio nuts, can there?' Before I added, 'Also, it's such a shame about this glass being like it is you know? Why is that you ask? Then I'd say, 'well I think a glass always does look so sorry for itself when it's empty . . . don't you think?' from which Stewart then took the hint saying. 'You only have to ask you know. Where are your manners?'

After that, he'd gone to the bar, ordered, and returned with a fresh Gin & Tonic, for me, and a pint of bitter for him, saying 'Now does that make your glass feel any better?'

I nodded. 'Oh yes it does, and it says thank you.' I now took a sip, pointing a little finger in the air, alla Poirot.

And so for the next half-an-hour, until the pub had called time, we chatted about this and that—mostly that, not realising we had both completely forgotten to discuss the merits of a small piece of paper from which I had scribbled down numbers and letters.

CHAPTER 76

TUESDAY IN CANTEEN

Sat in the canteen before they had started their morning duty on the day following my arrest, both DC Jones and Williams had at first headed straight towards the canteen counter, with other detectives on their shift, had ordered their morning breakfast's, and were now sitting at a table at the back of the canteen, as far away as possible from Stokes, who was sat by himself looking like a Buddha.

Jones, who was a tall, slim, wavy-haired attractive young man who was now sat in front of Williams with his head bent over an old melamine table, looking down at a solitary tomato he'd left on an otherwise empty plate, and twiddling with his tea spoon. Now he had finished his meal, he felt like his father always liked to say when he had eaten too much, "stuffed to the gills".

It had been these two detectives who'd been given the task of interviewing the beautiful Jessica Felliosi on Monday night, and both men had thought afterwards, that it had been a big, big mistake by the Sergeant to have had her spending

❖ 284 ❖

the night in the cells, let alone to have arresting her for the murder of a man she said she hardly knew.

They'd both been to court on the Tuesday, and would hear that she had been allowed bail against an enormous amount of security money that had needed to be paid by her father, and were now discussing the arrest, which they both had thought had been in Jones' words 'a big stupid mistake', and other things related to the case, which they'd needed to solve.

Having previously collected their breakfasts after their order number had been called; they had been talking through mouthfuls of food about the murder. They hurried, before it got cold, and because they were due to clock on at 7.55 am.

Jones had ordered his normal early shift breakfast, which comprised of beans, two eggs, two sausages, two plum tomatoes, and three slices of toast, and when he could get them, mushrooms and black pudding. Williams made do with two slices of toast, marmalade, and a large mug of tea.

Now sitting contentedly back in his chair, having eaten his toast, and sipping his second strong mug of tea, Williams had sighed.

He was 53 years old, and having only a few months left to serve out his 30 years in the Police Force, he was looking forward to his retirement, a decorative clock, and his garden. And now all he'd wanted, had that been at all possible, with some saying the man was well past his prime, for those remaining months in the police force, to have been completely uneventful as was possible, until that day of his retirement.

His passion, as everyone would have told you, was his garden and roses, and he was looking forward to the day when this passion would not be interrupted by the DS Stokes' of this world being anywhere near the vicinity of where he'd been stood. Truth was, he couldn't stand the man or his vulgarities.

It had been rumoured that DC Frank Williams, had been a Detective Inspector in another Police Constabulary at an earlier stage in his career, and that he had over-stepped the line by using un-orthodox policing on something important, and afterwards been given an option of being transferred to the Metropolitan Police, rather than being sacked.

It was only a rumour of course, and his activity record since being in the Met, or at this Station, had not given any indication of his once being a high flyer at any-time in his career; for it seemed, all Frank had ever wanted was to have a simple uncomplicated life. Though Frank would have told you, had he been asked, that the past few months had been some of the best he'd known since his coming to this Station, having been made much more enjoyable by young Jones, his partner, who had uplifted his sagging spirits nearly as much as his tending to his large front and back gardens of his large house would have done.

He'd also been heard to say on a couple of occasions, "How he looked forward to the day when he saw the great Sergeant Stokes getting his up-pence" as he termed it.

Previously, Jones had lent forward to put another mouthful of toast and tomato into his mouth, and saying. 'There are far too many un-answered questions in this case for it to have definitely been Miss Felliosi.'

A few detectives who were sat around Williams and Jones had mumbled in a low voice, 'agreed', being aware that Stokes was in the canteen.

Continued Jones: 'One thing that really puzzles me, is why there'd been those cigarette-stubs we found in the dead man's office, when there were signs everywhere requesting people not to smoke? Also for what it's worth, they couldn't have been her fag ends either, cos we know the girl doesn't smoke . . . well at least she always refused our offer of fags didn't she, after she'd been banged up, and people like to smoke when stressed don't they Frank? Anyway, that's what I think.'

Stokes having crept up behind them all, then said: 'Oh that's very good Jones, very good indeed!' Then added sarcastically 'And of course, all you've said may be very true, so I can see now with you being such a bright observant chap

Jones, that I'll need to keep a closer eye on you, won't I? In fact Jones, your brains might be the missing link that this team needs!'

Stokes growled out the words, adding more sarcasm in his voice than was necessary, his beady grey eyes squinted as if he was getting used to the light as he glared at each of the men and women around him. He then sort of smiled, before adding.

'However, I do believe there was only one set of fresh finger prints we've found so far, being the girl's. Plus she did have a pretty ropy reason for her being in the dead man's office didn't she? So I suggest you back off having a moan if you think she didn't do it, and ruddy well come up with more reliable evidence, or answers, to prove that she didn't—ok?'

He looked at them, and smirking said. 'Common lads and lassies, now's your chance to be clever, just like Jones here. So either put out, or get out.'

Ignoring the man's sarcasm, Jones tried to explain. 'Sergeant, what I meant was, that it was strange that we found cigarette stubs in the dead man's office . . . and his body actually in his neighbour's office. So perhaps you can tell me why that was, Serge? Because we can't work that out either can we Frank?' Williams shook his head.

'No Jones, I can't explain any of that, yet,' Stokes growled.

Continued Jones, 'Ok then, perhaps you can now tell us all what weapon she used, cos there was no murder weapon found, and we need to know what this weapon was, besides how the victim was moved to the office next door, in order to prove the crime. Don't you think?'

'And we of course we will need a motive, Serge, unless you already know of one?' Williams continued, wanting the fat man to squirm in his own ineptitude and stupidity.

'Ah, I suppose your finding her finger-prints in the office, now makes her a cold blooded killer in your eyes now, eh Serge?' Jones snorted. 'So after she'd cold bloodedly murdered the man, why do you think she then went around the office wiping cleaning everybody else's fingerprints off everything, and then had thought "ah I know, I'll only leave my own dabs on bits and pieces to let the police know I've been in here?" Now that strikes me as being a bit weird. What do you think, Sergeant?'

'Maybe some would say, that person was stupid, eh Serge?' added Williams with a smile, 'however when you consider that she was reported to have been a bright spark at school, that also seems another strange one to fathom, eh Skip? But of course you would know all of these answers I suppose, after all, you were the arresting officer . . . for murder wasn't it?'

Stokes had again looking down at the table then ignored him, and shaking his head, had then angrily retorted. 'Williams, the Chief's now wanting a result on that hit and run case you are working on, so he wants a quick result, although heaven only knows what he'll do when he hears of this . . . this mess.' Before finally saying, 'Perhaps you should know, that when he does begin to jump up and down, and begins to breath heavily down the back of my neck like he was some bloody vampire on a blood crawl, then that will mean my two friends, that I'll be doing the same to you . . . got it?'

And breathing heavily now, he then walked off in a cloud of smoke to who knows where? Maybe home to his wife and another salad. Some hopes!

CHAPTER 77

True to my promise to Stewart, I did try to phone Sergeant Stokes to tell him the news, the following morning, only to be told the fat man wasn't in the building, and 'could anyone else help?'

I remembered Jones, the tall young policeman, and Williams, and asked if either were there. Jones was, and when he came to the phone I told him all that I had intended to say to Stokes, of how I remembered the man who'd left the building that Sunday afternoon, Mr Grumpy, had a slight limp, right side, and I also gave him the details of the Solicitor who'd witnessed both office agreements for Rugs and Tings and Byways Ltd, telling him about the two addresses. Oh! And someone called Brassy had signed both contracts, for both offices.

I told him, the solicitor had also acted as a Guarantor on both documents, and I'd even suggested that the solicitor might have been crooked; or perhaps the type of solicitor, who would always be ready to take a back-hander for anything bordering on the un-ethical, so must have had some sort of deal with Mr Brassy! Perhaps it may have been only a one off cash deal, and nothing more!

I didn't feel inclined to tell Jones about the other ideas or clues that Stewart and I had found, or discussed, even though they might have equally been as important, for I suspected to have done so, I would have landed my good-self into even deeper water with Stokes, and that probably could also be said for Stewart—and so I didn't.

And before you ask 'why not' tell him what you know or suspect, suffice to say that I didn't fancy getting into any more trouble, thank you very much, for I have already enough problems to sort out at this time, without creating any more for myself. So I will, for the present, remain stumm for at least a little while longer with what I know.'

Jones had thanked me in what I can only assume had been his normal cheerful manner; which thankfully, would have been so much better than the gruff insolent manner of his boss, fatty Stokes.

Jones did tell me, that he, meaning the police, were 'very grateful' for the information. This I could hear in his voice. And when he'd then added, 'All information is good information,' it had almost been as if he'd been drooling down the phone. Then said, 'My partner and me will get on to it straight away . . . and Miss Felliosi, might I say, you have done extremely well in finding all this out so quickly, so well done you!' High praise indeed!

*　　*　　*

I'd been having a late lunch at a little restaurant not far from the office, and about to eat the final mouthful of a deliciously creamy chocolate soufflé, when it had suddenly occurred to me what had been troubling me ever since I'd observed Stewart locking up both offices the previous evening.

For it had occurred to me, that the killer might not have needed to have had a key for the office of Byways Ltd. So now assuming that the killer had his own key for the door of Rugs and Tings, with the dead man's key not having been found, had the killer been the 'secret partner', I assumed as there wasn't any blood on any of the carpets, or in the hallway, and the killer had not dragged Mr Happy, from Rugs and

THE LADY DETECTIVE

Tings and then dumped him in Byways Ltd, that meant he must have used a secret entrance to have done it—a secret entrance which I must now find to prove my innocence.

Now thinking if that had been how it happened, then Mr Happy, the dead man, must have walked into his own office, next to the one where the killer had been waiting patiently, which would then explain the lights, and then the killer had then greeted him after coming thru the fireplace from Byways, had then seized an opportunity when his victim was facing away from him, say towards his own fireplace, and banged him on the head before the victim had time to turn around to see what was to happen to him.

Sounds good to me, though that still doesn't explain what those marks were doing on both office floor carpets.

Now guessing, the killer must have caught the body as it slumped backwards after bonking him on the head, then he'd afterwards smashed his face in, before dragging him through a secret door, or entrance, from Rugs and Tings back into Byways, and then made it appear that he'd been hit from behind whilst he'd been inside that office where he was found.

I took in a deep breath and thought. 'Then having forgotten to turn the light off in Byways, had then left by Rugs and Tings door, not bothering to lock it.

So maybe the man I'd seen leaving the building on Sunday afternoon—and I'm still guessing now, really had been the killer of Mr Happy, and had changed into his clothes, or had put them over his own, before leaving.

As I've been saying all along, the question now for me was to prove among other things, that he, the killer, had gotten from one office to the other, by using a secret entrance.

Oh this is getting me confused—I'll need to sleep on it.

*   *   *

At about 3pm, things had been going along nicely enough, when Stewart had phoned me to confirm that those cigarette butts we found in Rugs and Tings, had been identified as a French cigarette named Guilloise.

'Strong and smelly, and definitely French,' had been the forensic lady's report! And she has also written 'that they were supposedly a prerequisite for a person who might not have had any defining tastes!' What could that mean, as if I didn't know, cos it sounded like another Stokes, and his cheap smelling cigars!

Stewart told me, 'this cigarette can only be bought at a very limited number of tobacconists in the area, and I've already issued orders for uniform constables to check on all of these tobacconists.'

He said 'The DNA results on the cigarette butts will also be known before too long.' I then tried to interrupt him, and he told me he hadn't finished telling me what he wanted to say, so I apologised, and then he told me that 'forensics have however found traces of Cherry Blossom shoe polish on the samples I'd taken from before both fireplaces in each of the rooms,' and 'that on one sample, there'd been some fibre samples from both office carpets. And another strange thing was,' he said, 'that he was found wearing only his socks, and no shoes, and there weren't any shoes found at the murdered scene! Weird!'

After taking in a deep breath, he went on to say, 'Jess, I'm finding it difficult to believe how a scuff mark sample taken from one room, could have had similar fibres to another scuff mark sample taken from another.'

He admitted that it was all very confusing finding traces from both office carpets on one sock and not the other, and none from the hallway carpet,' and conceded 'that the body couldn't have been dragged for one office to the other,' as I'd previously suggested, 'so there must be a secret entrance, either a door, or through that old ornate fireplace must be the only obvious answer to how it could be accomplished, again as you said.' Then added 'Besides I knew it have been almost impossible, even for you, to have lifted on your shoulders a very big dead man from office1 to office2, without leaving any marks in the hallway—blood, or otherwise!'

'So you finally admit that a secret entrance would be the only way to have made it possible?' and when he said, 'Yes, you must be right,' I punched the air with joy.

I then suggested. 'What is now required, is for us to once again visit those offices, and find that switch, button, or whatever, to open that ruddy fireplace or door—yes?'

And when Stewart said that was ok by him, I blew him kisses over the phone and said excitedly. 'That will be brilliant Stewart, just brilliant. Everything it seems, is now coming together, don't you think?'

He said 'I'm glad you think so, although I'm not so sure yet, without finding the secret switch!' Though he had sounded almost as pleased as I was when I shouted down the phone line to him—'yes . . . yes . . . yes.'

I told him that I was also 'so pleased', with all the other news, which had also born out my theory of how the murder was done, though there were still some things I didn't understand—so maybe later.

When I put down the phone, I gave out another loud 'Yes', followed by 'Yippee', causing Pasha to put her head around my office door to see what all the excitement was about. So I told her most of what had happened, and then both of us had given another 'yippee'. Childish I know!

I told her she must now keep what I told her very hush, hush, before saying we should 'at least celebrate the good news by our having a small glass of something lively', and she'd told me she would abstain, saying 'not for the time being, thank you,' but 'would like to have one with you a little bit later on,' meaning at office closing time.

She had probably thought I was, am, too much of a boozer, and not wanted to be involved. She was right of course! And that had made me think that I had better start to control that side of my life a whole lot better than I had been doing so far.

Right, so where have I got to so far in solving this mystery murder? Well in my mind I had sort of proved that

Mr Happy must have been murdered in Rugs and Tings office, and that the killer had somehow moved his dead body into the office next door, Byways Ltd. The question now was, I kept on asking myself, where in the dickens was it most likely that a control switch might to have been; and even why the killer had wanted to move the body from one office to the other anyway!

Maybe the partner had been trying to cover up how he did it—if so, why? I thought maybe I could find the answer to the first and second part, but as for the third part, the reason why, I still didn't hadn't known an answer!

I was of course happy that my original thinking had been correct, and now knowing what I thought the answer had been, with the secret entrance, I now knew why the killer hadn't needed to risk being seen by any of the workman, with their continual going and comings to and from my office, him dragging a dead body down the hallway from R&T to Byways Ltd.

Besides the killer would have needed to be a man with steely nerves to have chanced that, even with knowing that workman can't see around corners. So now having shelved that original thought, having finally figured out that the secret opening was the only logical solution, I will now need to prove how it could be done—and that I had still to do with Stewart's help.

*   *   *

Having now thought how ridiculous Stokes had been to have thought of me as a man killer, I'd laughed, for had that been the case, I would have needed to have been an awfully strong woman, as Stewart said, to have even contemplated dragging such a big man down the hallway to Byways Ltd. Then I'd thought that perhaps the murdered man had been inside the office even before I'd knocked on the door on Sunday night, and remembering how I thought I'd felt his presence when I'd been in Rugs and Tings, when all the time he'd been lying dead by the fireplace. I shuddered.

I had thought afterwards to phone down to reception, and had spoken to Sidney, the daytime receptionist, and asked him the same questions as I'd asked Ben. 'Had he seen anyone leaving the building during last week, carrying large bags, or office files?' and received negative on that. And when I again asked 'Did he know everyone who'd entered, or left, during Sunday,' he'd said 'he hadn't seen anyone,' & 'it was my day off after 3 pm.'

Ten minutes later, I received a phone from Sydney saying. 'I had another look on those dates for people who'd put their name down in the book,' meaning the reception book, 'and there'd been no-one coming in or out for those offices, except a Lynda something or other, for you.'

So I asked him 'Do you remember the guy who came down to the reception at the same time as Lynda on Sunday?' This time he did remember, and said it was the 'guvnor' of Rugs and Tings.' However when I asked 'if he appeared to have been acting a bit strange,' he admitted that he hadn't really been paying too much attention to him at the time, but to the lady he'd been with, meaning Lynda, though he did afterwards wonder why his friend hadn't bothered to say good-bye, when he normally did!

So that idea had in the end become a big negative zilch, zero; as had that piece of paper with a list of any names on it, I'd had from Ben, which I'd forgotten, would eventually be another waste of time, after being investigated by the Police.

*　　*　　*

So having had enough positives and negatives for the day, it had been Pasha who'd firmly cemented my thoughts of their being a false fireplace, or door, into either of the offices.

Because she would later that afternoon, when we'd been having afternoon tea, and with it being quiet, we were having a chin wag about this and that, when she told me the story about her uncle who lived on one side of an old large house; when his half, 'had one day a chimney fire, and the sparks of the fire having fallen onto the carpet in his parlour,' as she called it, 'and of course that had happened when the old fool had been out of the room, didn't it? So then it had naturally caught fire, and completely gutted the room.'

She went on to tell me, 'that the fireplace surround, and the mantel piece, being all wooden, had of course been totally burnt away didn't it, and that had then revealed next doors fireplace, which had also been damaged.'

She explained. 'You see, it must have once been one of those big double-sided open fireplaces that warmed both rooms before one side of the house had been bricked up to separate them from next door.'

She told me. 'Anyway, my daft uncle, had afterwards, and ever since, because he'd been having chats to the daft bugger who lived next door,' her uncle called him, 'had both requested that the fire-place was to remain open when it came to being repaired, cos they wanted for their chats to continue. And to this day, it has remained like that—open!'

Hearing that, had made me happy, not only because of her story, but because I had definitely known the double fireplace could have definitely been the answer to the way the murder had accomplished hid gruesome task. Otherwise what other explanation could there be for why the scuff marks had been on either side, if it hadn't been his moving to or away from both the fireplaces, the body, or why the dead body had lain close to the secret fireplace entrance!

So if both the killer and the victim had known about this false fireplace, knew of the secret opening, wouldn't it now be logical to assume that the killer, could only have been Mr Happy' silent partner.

And just as difficult, how I was I to get Stokes to allow me into both of these offices to prove my theory without giving away the fact that I'd already broken into both offices before-hand . . . twice, for had he known what I'd previously

THE LADY DETECTIVE

got up to, he'd have almost certainly slung the book at me for 'Breaking and Entering', and anything else he had a mind to. Which I must admit might have been preferable, and a darn sight better than my being charged with murder.

I'd pondered long and hard, wondering how I could now prove my theory, whilst still keeping it a secret of my 'Breaking and Entering.'

Now needing someone to talk to, I'd then told Pasha my thoughts and she'd with a wink said. 'Well, didn't you tell me that you had come up with that idea about the fireplace, after your first and only time of going into Rugs and Tings? I do believe you had said that, didn't you?'

And when she smiled, I hugged her, it was so simple.

So it seems the answer to the whole mystery, wasn't such a stupid idea as I'd once thought. And for those scuff marks to have happened, now there'd been forensic evidence with the socks, it sort of proves that a switch or something had to be somewhere around the fireplace to have opened, or closed it.

And if that was the case, then logically the killer must have surprised his victim in Rugs and Tings, as opposed to being done in Byways with the victim lying face towards the fireplace, for it would have been almost impossible to have swung any murder weapon from the fireplace with such force on to the face of a surprised victim, to have been able to cause that much damage to the dead man's face.

So the murder had occurred in Rugs and Tings for there to have been enough room to swing the murder weapon with such force. So perhaps the victim had not been looking at the fireplace, and away to perhaps the drinks cabinet, to have logically swung the weapon. Then the mystery of how the murderer could have moved, dragged, carried, a dead man's body from one office into the other, and leave no blood marks in the hallway, was now solved. Also there hadn't been any scuff or blood marks/stains in the hallway, to further consolidate my theory, making the only answer to this puzzle, being the secret to the fireplace that I had now needed to solve.

I gave a small cheer, happy now that I thought I'd almost solved the mystery.

I'd then quickly phoned Stew, and told him my new plan; which he immediately approved; so had put my plan into action by immediately phoning Stokes, and asking him to visit my offices, and telling him I'd a proposition to put to him, that was to his benefit, and had then sat back to await the fireworks to begin!

CHAPTER 78

The 3rd morning following my being arrested, Jones and Williams had been called to Stokes' table that had five or six files on it, and to open the conversation, seeing a single jam doughnut, Jones had with a smile asked 'Aren't there any cream doughnuts, Serge?'

And seeing the look that Stokes had given back, Williams had added with a smile. 'No, I believe the Serge did say that all he ever wanted was answers, not cream doughnuts Jones'y!' He continued. 'Now as you hadn't previously mentioned that it was answers were all you needed, Serge, I can now see where we two have been going wrong.' He added facetiously. 'But now you've mentioned it, Serge, I can't believe how stupid we've both been until you mentioned it, eh Jones'y? I mean had any of us known that it was only answers you wanted, we'd have drunk many glasses of champagne by now, having cracked open many puzzling cases wide open. Wouldn't you say—Serge?'

Williams, and then Jones had given Stokes one of their very best smiles and still feigning stupidity, before Jones had continued by saying in a affected voice, and with as straight-a-face as he could manage without bursting into a giggling fit. 'I suppose now you've mentioned it, Serge, you could be onto a winner there, I mean who'd have thought it, eh Serge, you only needing answers!'

❧ 299 ❧

His partner added. 'On that point, I would without any reservation, indisputably agree with you Jones. I mean the thing is old chap, who'd have thought that in all this time we've been rushing about like headless chickens, the only logical answer to all of our problems would have been for us to have got, what was the word, oh yes, 'answers', to have solved them!'

'The thing is, Serge,' Jones added, 'you might now need to find some 'answers' to help you explain yourself to the Chief Super, as to why you arrested Miss Felliosi, eh Serge?'

'Of course the Serge may also be forgetting what Miss Felliosi' father has to say about his arresting his darling daughter being locked up without da-ra, any answers! And let's not forget the Chief Constable either, who I understand, Mr Felliosi knows personally,' added Jones. 'Now that outcome would be interesting, eh Sergeant, if you didn't have any answers?'

Stokes, whilst he'd been hearing what was being said, had been shaking his head in total disbelief, and rage, knowing he couldn't dispute why the two men were rigging him, even though he was barely containing himself from violence towards them, and so for now, he could only glare at them in dumb amazement at their total lack of respect, and fear of him.

He eventually replied. 'I would suggest that both wipe that smirk off your faces, and in double quick time Detective Constable Jones, Williams,' he growled, 'and before I do something I may regret, suggest the sooner you both get out there and get me some . . . answers, the better I will like it.'

'And so will the Chief Super—as you said.' added Williams innocently.

'And even the Chief Constable,' added Jones, 'especially if either of them are, like you say, breathing down your neck like some under-nourished vampire on a bloody night out— then better you than me!'

Seeing that Stokes was speechless, and trying very hard to keep a straight face, Williams had again seized this moment as another opportunity for getting his own back just a little bit more, had groaned. 'Ah well Jones'y, if the Sergeant here is expecting some answers from us pretty smartish, then I suggest we get to it, even if only to try and help him out of the mess that he's in.'

Williams stood back, now fully content having said what he'd said, for he had particularly enjoyed watching Stokes' obvious discomfort, as it had been particularly nice to get 'one back' on the obnoxious oaf, for all the ear-bashing he'd taken from him over the past eight years, since his being transferred to this Station.

Now he looked at Jones, and then at Stokes, and permitted himself the smallest of smiles on the outside, and one very big one inside, when he'd then enquired, having another dig at the open mouthed Sergeant deepening red-face of Stokes.

'Serge, before we go out to look for some, what was the word, ah answers, do you think it's possible that you might have been a little bit too hasty in arresting the Felliosi girl, cos we both think so, don't we Jones'y? Because if it was a mistake, we both sincerely hope for your own sake, that it's hopefully not too late to put things right, especially now you have bravely put your job on the line, as you have, in arresting the daughter of Mr God Almighty Frank Felliosi, particularly knowing that all hell will be set loose as soon as the Chief Constable finds out—if he hasn't by now. Oops!'

Stokes was now finding it extremely difficult to breath correctly, due to his trying to control his temper, before he pointed a fat finger at both of them saying. 'Look you two dummies, I'll see to it that both your necks are on the line— not mine, if you don't get out there and find me the answers I need!

Detective Frank Williams, had however ignored the barb tongue of the senior officer, Jones was saying. 'Now there's no point being a defeatist, is there Sergeant? Let's not let all our hopes dwindle in one set-back, eh?' Jones grinned.

And Williams, having taken a glance at Stokes who looked as if he was now about to explode his pent up venom at Jones, then said. 'This new generation of coppers eh Serge, they're so full of confidence . . . and cheek!'

After they had walked off, Williams had said. 'Bloody hell, that felt good, so now perhaps it'll be a good idea to check out Miss Felliosi's lead.'

'Now that's not a bad idea at all Frank. Good thinking. Yes we'll check out that angle first . . .' enthused Jones to his older colleague, although before that, we ought to check on what forensics might have to say they've found, don't you think, because we could do with a little help here, if for no other reason than to get that poor girl off of Stokes' hook!'

'I do believe you've taken a shine to her, haven't you Jones'y?'

'Well she is bloody lovely, isn't she? In fact I think she's bloody gorgeous,' replied Jones with some ardour.

*   *   *

LATER: 'Well, we can now tell you, Serge, that according to Customs & Excise, they hasn't been any record of any transactions between themselves and a Mr Brassy, the guy who Miss Felliosi gave us the lead on.' Williams said.

'Ah, I see! Then she and you are not so bloody clever then, are you?' Stokes said sarcastically, attempting to copy Jones' Welsh accent.

'If you say so, Serge, but no more on that, even though we had spent time finding out all we could about him.'

'Some hopes of your finding out anything by the sound of it.' Stokes chortled enjoying his joke.

Jones had in the meantime taken in a deep breath whilst thinking "Well I might as well hang myself now than later," and continued to explain his not finding anything on Brassy, and had then nodded his head at Williams, who had said nonchalantly. 'However, we did find out that Brassy also goes under another name, being Wainwrights.'

'Wainwrights?' questioned Stokes.

✦ 302 ✦

THE LADY DETECTIVE

'That's right. And it seems that this Wainwrights is a well-known criminal, because C & E, Interpol, and our files say he is.'

'And,' chipped in Williams, 'this Wainwrights is also reputed to be a womaniser according to the records, and has a liking for wine, drugs; and get this Serge, Turkish and French cigarettes. Now isn't that interesting?'

Stokes had then for some obscure reason, not shown he was pleased, but had reverted to a bad Mr Woo voice that he liked to put on when he thought he was being funny.

'Well honourable Detective Williams, for you it would all seem most interesting—however for this illustrious and great Sergeant, it conjures up a few honourable words to say. Ah so, yes, very good. So with me being an illustrious and clever Sergeant, and you being very lowly and not too bright detectives, I see this new knowledge as not being too significant, or likely to be of great use in getting our un-honourable girl killer off hook. Ok?'

Stokes seemed highly satisfied with his Doctor Woo accent, and had then said, in his attempt to dampen down any of the clever work done by both of these two detectives, for he had no intention of giving any praise at all to them, although he had been pleased to hear about Brassy' other name.

'What was that Sergeant? Did you say—it was good news, as it's likely to get the girl of the hook for killing a well-known crook?' Retorted Jones angrily.

'That's not exactly what I said Jones . . . .'

Jones angrily interrupted him ' . . . I mean do you honestly think that Miss Felliosi would have spent weeks of her time tarting up some tatty office, and spending loads of money on it, just to give herself a cover, an alibi, to kill someone like that? Do you honestly think she'd have done all that, when she could have just as easily, killed the man anytime, or anywhere, without needing to create an expensive embellishment?

❦ 303 ❦

Jones was really angry now, and it showed as he continued. 'And on top of that elaboration, or 'clever' plot?' then saying to herself after brutally killing him 'Oh, I'll now leave my fingerprints here and there so that I'll be caught, and at the same time, wipe away any other clues of who it was!'

He breathed in deeply and finished by saying. 'Now that would be stupid, would it not Sergeant, and Miss Felliosi doesn't appear to be stupid, does she?'

*   *   *

Sergeant Stokes did however, appear to be strangely unimpressed by his outburst, and even pretended not to have heard him, as he'd continued to suck heavily on his slim smelly cigar, that he'd bought very cheaply by the gross in Mexico, when he'd been on holiday with his missus. He'd even 'smuggled in' three gross of these foul cheap cigars into this country! Not an action of a law-abiding citizen, me-thinks!

At last he'd uttered. 'Look Jones, I suggest for now, you don't need to concern yourself with her at this moment, ok? Cos now I want you both to find out as much as you can about this Mr Brassy, hmm, Wainwrights. And Jones, don't for heaven's sake say the man is dead, because anyone of us could have worked that one out.'

No laughter came from anyone, over what Stokes had thought of as a joke, so slightly miffed, he continued. 'Look, I need to know everything there is to know about this man, his bank details, where he goes for his holidays, trips abroad, whether he's married, has a family, and while I'm asking, whose been checking to see who it was who'd rented the office next to Rugs and Things . . . Tings, this Byways, where he was found?'

'Tings is correct Serge, not Things, 'said Williams quickly, and smiled. He'd always been a passionate man in his likes and dislikes, and when it came to his disliking

THE LADY DETECTIVE

Stokes, he had now let this passion flow, just to see what would happen. Now he said facetiously 'Oh what a jolly good idea that is Skip, to check out who owns what office.

'I've all of the time many good ideas up here,' said Stokes, not tapping on his head, or rising to the bait, before adding, 'unlike the only one that comes out of your brain box each year, eh Williams!'

'Best not to rush into things I say . . . it tends to make you make mistakes, eh Serge!' Williams answered, repeating what Jones had previously said.'

Jones could see where this verbal fight was heading, and knew it would only end up badly for Frank, and interceded by saying 'It was Brassy who rented Byways—again on a tip by Miss Felliosi!'

Still glaring at Jones, Stokes had grunted after Williams had said 'Serge, have forensics still not come up with anything that might help us? Have they found any other finger-prints for instance, in the offices?'

'Forensics has told me they are still far too busy sorting out any evidence on two other murders committed last week. Thankfully not in our patch, cos with you lot as detectives, they'd have, as sure as you will always remain detectives, finish up on the unsolved list! But they did say it's too early to say, regarding any other evidence that might, or might not, have been found.'

He took another puff of his vile smelling cigar, and after blowing out a smoke ring. 'Though it would seem to me, she'll need to find a stronger motive than self-defence for what she's done. Don't you think?'

'Really Serge, now you do surprise me?' Williams said.

'You mean you really want us to find the real motive for why the *real killer* did him in, do you Serge?' said Jones. 'Because as I've said, I for one cannot see what possible reason a lovely woman like Miss Felliosi would have wanted to knock him off. Nothing fits into any of this, besides her being nosy, and of course her being around at the wrong time, cos her sort would never mix with the likes of him!'.

'That Jones, is for you to find out as they say . . . with a lot of help from me I might add, of course, the many facilities of the Metro Police Force.'

'Perfectly understood Sergeant,' said Jones smartly, making Stokes look at him suspiciously, and then said, directing his words to all the detectives seated about the canteen. 'Now as for the rest of lot, you get out of here, and get me some answers that I will like, the bosses will like, and these two will like, and try to upset this vampire that is now hanging around my neck—ok? Well get on with it!'

'Well I for one couldn't agree with you more Serge, that's what we need is answers, because without them, how, or why, this shocking murder was done, would be hard for us to solve!' Said Williams flippantly, trying very hard to keep a straight face, adding 'particularly now the Chief Constable must have heard of you accusing, arresting, and jailing, the wrong person for this murder!'

Detective Jones, then gave Stokes one of his best innocent looking smiles, then continued 'So regardless of you worrying whatever the consequence will be when the Chief Super has his say to you, I can only assume that if we don't find some answers, what Miss Felliosi' father will also have to say to you, knowing his one and only darling daughter has been imprisoned for no good reason that any of us can think of. Especially knowing the other night, he'd wanted to know who you are, and your address, which of course wasn't given to him . . .'

' . . . however I'd guess that this most important citizen will not be denied anything if he really wants to have words with you, eh Serge?' Williams said.

Stokes could again only glare at them both, his temper rising to boiling point at the audacity of what they had said, though he had been concerned over what they had both just said.

Williams saw that Stokes was about to lose his cool; much to the enjoyment of a half a dozen policeman who were grouped around, and were enjoying the discussion! He was, as everyone could see, really enjoying this moment of banter, as he continued to regard Stokes' obvious discomfort, because to see him squirming like this, was even better enjoyment than when he won an all-expenses paid free holiday to Butlin's Holiday Camp at Bognor, or heaven forbid, even a day of undisturbed pottering around his own garden.

For Williams, it was now all about getting one over on the man who had for the past eight years, tormented him mercilessly, and given him so much grief, for what? Now with only months to go before he retired, he'd permitted himself a little smile, having seen Stokes cursing him under his breath, when he'd then turned around and suddenly began to walk away, muttering loudly 'Bloody, bloody, bloody hell' to himself, leaving everyone who'd overheard the Williams, Jones and Stokes conversation, grinning at the expense of the disappearing bulk of Sgt Stokes.

PC Jonathan Jones, had however, been thinking he might have put his size 12's right into the 'I'm being sacked' category bin, by his talking to the Sergeant in the way he had, cos it was alright for Williams mouthing off, seeing as he'd only a couple months to go before he retired.

It had for him been like he'd been, with Williams, putting his big toe into the water to test the temperature, though he should have learnt by now, when to keep his thoughts to himself, particularly when a senior officer was involved, regardless of how intensely he disliked the self-opinionated fat oaf, and had known by mutual consent, they both disliked each other.

Chapter 79

THURDAY MORNING: all the detectives had again gathered early in their 'new office,' with Jones having had his usual large breakfast; "I'm a growing lad" he'd say, and Williams sat with his normal two slices and a large mug of tea.

Stokes was sat again, as usual, in the same place of his temporary Detectives Room, meaning the canteen, which was farthest away from Williams and Jones, the latter who he knew had been promoted six months before from the uniformed ranks, and was guessing he was chatting about the office murder to his older chum and partner Williams. He'd have been right. Though he'd also be telling Williams, that Stokes had told him they were going to see Miss Felliosi this afternoon, at 3 pm, and 'be ready'.

AFTERNOON: Stokes had arrived with the young wavy haired detective Jones, and having been introduced to Pasha, they'd both been asked to go into my office, and to 'please seat your-selves down.'

Jones had, I immediately saw, not been able to take his eyes off of Pasha, and she'd further tantalized him by giving him one of her big friendly 80% smiles, and a wink for good measure—not seen by Stokes of course.

It had then struck me, seeing the interplay between them, that Pasha would make a good foil to my obtaining

308

THE LADY DETECTIVE

any knowledge of what the police had so far found out about the murder that might be of use for me. Good thinking!

When the two detectives had sat themselves down, I'd made an excuse to leave the office, and having closed the door behind me to have a word with Pasha, had told her I needed her to help me find out from Jones, any positively known, if anything, developments on the murder.

'No problem, no problem at all,' she said, copying Jones' Welsh accent. 'You just leave it to me, see, I'll soon have him singing like a nightingale, you'll see.'

Smiling at her choice of words, I returned to my office, and saw Stokes had been, with his large frame, sitting very awkwardly in the armchair, which had, as usual, began to again protest and groan under his weight. I then asked politely. 'So how is the diet going, Sergeant?'

Giving me a look that said many things, some not nice, he eventually replied. 'Fine thanks', then still looking decidedly uncomfortable in the chair, had continued. 'I have some news about the solicitor whose details you gave Detective Jones here; for it seems that the solicitor was paid £2000 pounds, meaning £1000 pounds for each office contract that he signed as a Guarantor.' As if I couldn't have worked that one out. Duh!

He went on 'And after we'd put the squeeze on—humph, I mean after we questioned him, he revealed that his client hadn't been Brassy as we'd first thought, but a Jon Wainwrights'

He breathed in deeply, and continued 'Then we found from our criminal files, there'd been nothing known about this Brassy, however when we put in the name of Jon Wainwrights, it became a different matter altogether, because this Wainwrights, does have a criminal record as long as your arm.'

'And what were those crimes for?' I asked politely.

He paused as if waiting for me to say something more; before he coughed, looked at Jones, and then with a tired sigh continued. 'He was, as Wainwrights, particularly known

❧ 309 ❧

by the Customs and Excise, and the Home office, mostly for smuggling and gun-running, though our foreign friends in Interpol did think he was probably the brains behind some of the biggest drug deals that has ever occurred in this country.'

'Wow that's amazing!' I said amazed. He nodded, and then closed his note book, and with a slight movement of his mouth that could have been taken as a smile, said. 'So if this is true, it could mean it's not only good news for us, the police, but for you also, I would imagine, having tipped us off.'

Jones, had then coughed, and appeared annoyed at the 'hippo', for he felt that he should have told me that bit of good news himself, it having been Williams and himself who'd done all the donkey work in finding out the information that Stokes had given me, whilst Stokes himself had been either sitting around the canteen, gulping mugs of tea, or scratching his head, or crutch, and not being too sure what to do next.

Now Jones said. 'Although we're still not sure Miss Felliosi, how all this works of course, we feel sure that this Wainrights-Brassy character also has a partner who we believe goes by the name of Dubois, and he is also supposed to be a very nasty character.' He laughed. 'In fact he collects GBH's like we do stamps. Anyway, acting on your marvellous description of the 'second man' you saw leaving who had a limp, we feel that this Dubois, would appear to be the man who you saw on Sunday afternoon.'

He then looked towards Stokes, who'd merely grunted, and then continued. 'Problem is we still don't have enough proof to pin this killing on him, or anyone else at this moment.' Then realising what he said, added. 'Oops, sorry about that Miss Felliosi,' had smiled, then said 'because as the dead man's partner, this Dubois, if it was him, could always say he was entitled to be in his own office at any-time he liked, which is true.'

Stokes was now very animated with Jones explaining the situation, and after pulling his eyes reluctantly away from Pasha who had again entered the room, was now intending to out-do Jones in his knowledge of Wainrights-Brassy, as well as Dubois, especially having seen Jones ogling Pasha, if that was not too strong a term, and because he didn't like that, had said.

'Besides that, we've still no idea where to find the man of course, or even where he lives.' He then stretched out his long fat legs, and putting both hands behind his neck with a flourish, looked as if he had in some other time, been sunning himself on Swanage beach, then glibly added, 'that was until I found out where he hangs out, all thanks to a previous surveillance report by the Fraud Squad on Wainwrights.'

Having said what he'd said, and feeling well pleased with himself by making Jones look as if he had known very little about what was really going on, compared to him, he'd again sat back into his chair, making the sturdy leather chair complain its displeasure, and that had then given me my chance to have had a little chat with Stokes.

'Could I talk to you alone for a moment Sergeant, about something that could be important to your ears?'

I gave him one of my most appealing looks, which of course I didn't feel in the slightest, and then turned to Jones, and asked 'Would you give me a moment to speak with the Sergeant?' Jones returned a look that might have said—'I'll do anything for you' kind of looks, had looked at a bemused Stokes, before leaving the room to gratefully talk with Pasha.

Taking this moment as one of goodwill, I said to Stokes in a soft voice. 'So I take it with this visit, and with your sharing the facts of the case, Sergeant, you are perhaps trying to say that you've made a big mistake as far as I'm concerned, and I'm now off the hook, so to speak, for the murder?'

'I'm not sure I said that, Miss Felliosi, or so sure you are,' he said frostily 'even though you have probably given us the biggest lead we've had so far to help us solve the murder . . . because so far there hasn't been any other evidence of anyone else doing it. However I will admit that I may have been too hasty in my judgment when arresting you so quickly, and I will probably be made to regret my actions by no doubt being sacked when your father forces the Commissioner to give me the big heave-ho.'

The Big heave-ho would be deserved in this instance I thought. 'So are you saying, that you are now being forced to apologise to me Sergeant? Or is it something you are saying, and don't mean?'

'Well yes and no, and because I still haven't any real proof on who committed the murder as you know, or how it had been achieved. Meaning how could the killer have moved the body from one room to another, without showing us any forensic proof how they did it.'

He then realised what he'd just said, and had quickly recovered by saying. 'Besides our finding your fingerprints at the murder scene of course, which I might remind you, are still the only ones we have found.' He then gave me a look as if to say, *"Yes I do mean you, you stuck up little madam."*

'So that makes me a criminal in your eyes, does it? So what you're really saying is, that besides all of my own excellent detective work, and my passing over to you very juicy bits of info that I had personally found out, I will still need to prove my innocence—and all because you personally have no idea who the real murderer is, or how he done it. Am I right, Sergeant?'

Having left him open mouthed, I paused, and said, 'Will you excuse me for a moment,' and then went out to the reception area, to find Pasha and Jones chatting, and having a cup of coffee.

Looking at Jones I said. 'Detective, Stokes and I have now finished our little chat thank you, so now give me a minute to talk to my secretary if you please.' He nodded, and walked back into my office, holding his cup of coffee.

When he'd closed the door, and out of hearing distance, I enquired 'Did he say anything worth our knowing?'

'Only that there hadn't been enough substantial evidence to make any charges of murder stick against you . . . and whatever evidence they had on you, wouldn't have got you a one day sentence, let alone you being convicted for murder.

THE LADY DETECTIVE

He told me, that the whole of the station thinks Stokes is 'a twat', his words, to have arrested you, and that all the police could get you for, were petty crimes like Breaking and Entering, Trespassing, that kind of thing, as everything else at present, was circumstantial.'

'Thank you, and well done Pasha. Well done. That makes me feel a whole lot better, and it'll also match up to what fatso did 'almost' say to me! Right then, I'll now need you to come into my office . . . and make notes. Meaning I need your support and be a witness.'

Now feeling good, I sort of sashayed back into my office as if I had a ten ton boulder lifted off from my shoulders. And feeling light as air, I'd sat in my office chair, to say in a matter of fact voice.

'Well Sergeant, what if I can prove to you how this murder was done by this fellow Dubois, or anyone else who may have access to both offices. What would you say to that, Sergeant?'

Both detectives looked at me with eyes and mouths that were either wide open, or had been moving up and down. So I'll allow you to guess who did what!

The first to recover was Stokes, and he'd only been able to splutter. 'Well I must say that if you can do that Miss Felliosi, then you must be a very clever young lady indeed, because it certainly has baffled you, eh Jones!' Then he smiled, well sort of.

I gave him a look that said *Now why doesn't that surprise me*, before adding in a softer voice. 'Well gentlemen, what is your answer?'

Stokes had then answered none too happily 'Why not'.

'Right then, for me to give you the answers, I'll also need some sort of recompense from you, Sergeant, for all you have put me thru, prison and so forth. So by way of an apology, I would like you to say to the press, "Woman private investigator solves murder mystery", and I want this to be placed in all the best known tabloids of course, with your

❧ 313 ❧

highest praises. Now for that knowledge that'll be a start. So what do you say?'

Stokes I could see, wasn't at all sure about requesting my demand, then considering its implications if he didn't, had eventually growled a reply.

'I'd say don't push your luck Miss Felliosi, cos if you know, that could further implicate you as being the murderer.' I thought *"Oops he's right you know."* However he continued. 'If you really do help me solve this case, then I would, after getting my Guvnor's approval, be glad to share your glory in solving the crime.' Then he added, 'and I'm sure my detectives would all be equally as grateful to you in helping solve a crime that they would never have solved in a month's of Sundays, or got close to solving.'

Hearing this, Jones had given Stokes a quick look of pure venom, then said 'This murder may have got certain people completely baffled, though not all of us as, eh Sergeant?' Jones then smiled at Pasha.

And then adding further to Stokes' discomfort, seeing Jones looking at Pasha, I said. 'Now you haven't given your personal word, to my conditions yet, Sergeant. So what is it to be?'

Pasha had then smiled at the fat Sergeant, who was now looking as if he'd been forced into a corner, and saw relax a little, yet knowing the man would have hated to admit he'd been wrong about me, I'll still need to watch my back! Now looking wildly around him, he grudgingly mumbled 'Yes I suppose so.'

'Well I suppose you really hadn't much of a choice, Sergeant, because you are skating on very thin ice if you didn't know it.'

Stokes had of course realised that he was indeed skating on thin ice, re me and his arresting me, and he'd also known he'd given no choice but to change his manner, having noted that Jones and myself, and Pasha, could barely suppress laughing out loud over the thought of this grossly overweight man, wearing skates, and then to have pictured him skating

THE LADY DETECTIVE

on thin ice that would eventually crack and his bulk then thrown into ice cold water. Oh dear, my imagination has run riot!

He gave me a sickly sort of grin that I'd grown to hate, before he added 'and I was going to add thank you Miss Felliosi.'

'Well I thank you for that, Sergeant,' I said feeling pleased, 'though you could, I suppose, give your colleagues a bit of back-patting for all the work they've done, don't you think?' I looked towards Jones.

Stokes growled. 'Back-patting, or glory-hunting, is not my problem, or theirs at this moment, it is all about solving this murder. The problem being, how it was done, and who done it . . . ah, besides yourself Miss Felliosi.'

'Excellent. So now that we all understand your thoughts a little better, might I ask of you one more favour; and that will be to allow Detective Chief Inspector Ross, in on this case. For I wish him to handle all aspects of this case that has to do with drugs. So is that alright with you, Sergeant?'

'Drugs! Why are you now mentioning drugs and DCI Ross?' He growled. 'I don't see why DCI Ross needs to be involved in this case.'

'Well he will be, with or without your consent, though it would look better if it was with your consent . . . agreed?' I then looked at him. 'Are you seriously telling me that forensics have not informed you that drugs are also involved here?'

'Well no . . . not yet. No-one has.'

'Well then, the facts are, with this Wainwrights, and Dubois, now coming into the frame, and Wainwrights being into drugs, as you said, that surely should have warned you of this fact. It did DCI Ross fortunately.'

I was going to say *"especially with his being the potential head of the National Drugs Squad"*, and caught myself in time, and instead said. 'He does already know a lot about what's going on here.'

I thought then to say too much would give away the fact he had seen for himself the carpets, and said, 'DCI Ross is

❧ 315 ❧

also my friend, and his family are friends with my family, and I'd say it would be a good idea for him to have been brought in on this anyway.'

'And he's a dam fine officer, so I hear,' chipped in Jones, keen to show his agreement. Stokes then suddenly moaned. 'Oh I get it, it's the old pals act again is it? I bring him into the action, and he gets all the glory, is that it?'

'Not at all Sergeant . . . though didn't you say it wasn't the glory that you were looking for, it was only solving the crime?'

Stokes made a strange gargling sound in his throat, before saying. 'There is nothing wrong with wishing for a little glory is there? It's not as if it's often there to grab, is it?'

'Don't you worry, Sergeant, your lads will get most of the glory . . . just as you would I'm sure have wished.' He groaned again, and then glared at me as I continued. 'However as glory is not your only concern, as you say, you must really keep on thinking along those lines mustn't you? Otherwise if it's only glory you're after, then a lot of people, mentioning no names, will I assume have thought that was very selfish thinking.'

I let him reflect on what I had said, before teasingly adding. 'I personally think that Jones here, and his partner, ah Williams, and your team of detectives should get all the glory going, for actually spot-lighting the actual murderer; if it is Dubois.

And of course once the case is solved, I'll also be getting praises for my part in solving how the murder was actually done. DCI Ross will also be getting a certain amount of the glory, if he can catch the gang who have I believe been getting filthy drugs into the country—though that must be very hush hush, and not repeatable. So all in all, Sergeant Stokes, we'll all benefit in some small way for solving this dastardly crime of murder, won't we, although I'm not sure what glory you will personally deserve!'

It was so deathly quiet after my saying that, you could have heard a pin drop, before Stokes whispered hoarsely.

THE LADY DETECTIVE

'Oh, don't you think for one minute of your trying to make a fool of me!'

I feigned further surprise at his words. 'Sergeant, Sergeant, Sergeant! How could you possibly ever think that? How could you possibly ever think such a thing, after being so badly treated when I'd been a murder suspect! Oh come, Sergeant, what could have possibly made you ever think of that?'

Jones I saw was nodding his head in agreement, and smiling at Pasha.

'You . . . you know what I mean, when I say you making me out to be a fool,' Stokes mumbled.

'Heavens forbid Sergeant, me trying to make you look a fool! Please tell me how was that possible? How could I, possibly change what is a known fact?'

I pouted at him, wondering whether he now fully understood my total dislike for him, and waited to see if he had caught on to my acid sarcasm and see whether he'd react angrily or not; and as he hadn't said anything in his defence, I pressed on.

'I would like you to give me until tomorrow afternoon, Sergeant, say until about the same time of the day, to sort out a small matter. I will need until then, to fill in the only remaining piece of the puzzle that remains still missing to prove to you how the murder was accomplished. So shall we say that we all assemble here tomorrow?' He nodded.

'Oh, and Sergeant, please come with all of your team, for DCI Ross was quite adamant about that. So until tomorrow . . . agreed?'

He agreed, I thought, not happily.

Chapter 80

O nce they'd both departed, after saying a few more words of this and that, I punched the air in delight, and felt totally happy.

Pasha, with a smile, had then closed up the windows, and from her handbag produced and lit a josh-stick, which I'd thought was hilariously funny, and then left me to phone Stewart, for me to tell him everything that Stokes and Jones had said to me.

I told him that we were all to meet tomorrow at my office, and that'll include all his team of detectives, who'll be here with him. I then told him we should meet at the Dog and Whistle at 17.00 pm that night, had he wished, and he'd said he had a prior arrangement around that time, and couldn't make, but would see what he could do about seeing me at my place later that night.

That sounded very vague, although he did sound very pleased with the information I gave him—and with me of course, but said he'd phone me by 4.30 pm if he could make it. He didn't phone.

So at a little after 4.30 pm, I asked Pasha if she would like to accompany me to the 'Dog and Whistle', the little pub down the road, and after agreeing that she would, we locked up shop early, so to speak, then set off to walk the short distance to a small public house that was fast becoming my

THE LADY DETECTIVE

favourite local watering hole, for now with my feeling I was floating on air, had wished to share my joy for not being thought of as a murderess—though the Court hearing would make it official in the eyes of the Law—if it got that far.

On entering the pub, we'd both been greeted by the smiling landlord, whatever his name, oh Willie that was it, and by a couple of men who I'd previously seen in the pub having a pint at the bar.

The landlord commented. 'Well I must say ladies, that you certainly do brighten this place up for us lads no end.' The two men at the bar having heard him, then chipped in with. 'Dead right they do', and 'Smashin', really smashin'' That sounded Australian.

We'd walked through the Public bar and into the small Lounge, saying hello to a young couple and two men, before asking Willie for two glasses of champagne, and his menu card, to be told by the smiling landlord.

"I have a bottle of champagne that I keep for special occasions,' though "he couldn't sell it only by the glass, because I'll be left with the rest of the bottle, cos no-one else drinks the stuff." He'd apologised and said, "It wasn't a sales gimmick to get me to buy the whole bottle, just business."

So I changed my order to a whole bottle of bubbly, and then paid him to get another bottle in for another occasion, and then chose from the menu a plate of double prawn and lettuce sandwiches, and Pasha had ordered the same.

I said I'd like to buy everyone in the pub a pint if they'd accept a drink from two strangers, referring to Pasha and myself, or even a woman in particular; and to a man and one woman, everyone had immediately accepted my offer of a free drink, and that included the landlord, who'd then wondered if he should then introduce them all by name to me. Thank-goodness he didn't.

I explained to a bewildered Pasha that the champagne was my way of celebrating for my not being thought of as a murder suspect any more . . . . 'I am almost off the hook' I told her, 'for the murder of the man I didn't know.'

❄ 319 ❄

ROBERT H FELLOWS

I then told I had in the office taped the meeting with Sergeant Stinky, where he'd committed himself by admitting that I wasn't any longer the murder suspect, and subject to his Chief's ok, would be releasing a statement to the press to that effect, telling them of my part in solving the murder—if tomorrow went ok.'

Then I said. 'It wouldn't go kindly for him, if he were to ever make life difficult for me again, or even think about changing his mind.'

'Now that was really crafty of you Jessica to do that. Thing is, can you really prove how the murder was done, or are you just playing a game, you know, fencing for time.' She was now looking concerned.

'Both . . . I'm doing both Pasha. Oh don't you worry, I believe I can prove how it was done. I just need to tie up some loose ends, although at this moment in time, well until tomorrow that is, it's out of my hands.'

'Out of my hands,' you say, now that sounds a bit like 'maybe or maybe not?' Pasha groaned.

I'd sat back wishing and hoping what I'd said, would turn out to be true.

Oh boy, how I needed that office fireplace to give me the answers I needed. In fact, I felt the answer to the whole murder case was now resting on opening the fireplace, and my neck, otherwise whatever Stokes and I had verbally agreed, I knew I could again be back in the frame for the murder of Mr Happy guy, if what I thought might happen, didn't happen.

I'd also hoped the information I passed on about Dubois, and Brassy/Wainwrights, would be all Stewart would now need to have come up with a solution of how these two men now under investigation had been smuggled drugs into the country; and I was interested how he intended to put paid to the gang, or ring, or whatever they are called.

I'd also needed for more than my peace of mind, for Stewart to help me to come up with the answers, otherwise

❖ 320 ❖

he knew he could definitely be in my bad books for a long time. Well for a day at least!

Pasha had for the next hour, enjoyably chatted about her family and friends, and many times she'd made me laugh, and been the perfect tonic to my being concerned that everything in the end would not turn out alright for me.

After she left, I'd then gone home to have an early night, knowing it was going to be a long day to-morrow, not knowing that it would be in more ways than I had envisaged.

CHAPTER 81

FRIDAY

The morning had gone pleasantly by, though a little nail biting, for I hadn't had an opportunity so far, with Stewart, to get into the offices again.

Oh my missing person turned out to be a cat. The lady saying the cat would answer to the name of Thomas, Tibs or Tibby. It was grey with white paws, and had a speckled left ear and nose and there had been a large reward of £20 if found.

So I asked Pasha to phone around all the animal shelters in the area to see if she'd been admitted, and if that didn't get any results, to phone all of the local vets.

Half an hour later we found that Tibs having had a minor scuffle with a small boys bicycle wheel, been taken down to the local vet, and would soon be ready for collection, with a woozy head, from the local RSPCA.

We'd collected her, and called the lady back to tell her that we had found her 'darling' Tibs, and telling her about the accident, and after the delivering the slightly hurt little animal back to its grateful owner, had collected a quick £20 + £8 expenses for the vets bill.

THE LADY DETECTIVE

Our finding her beloved Tibs had made an old lady very happy, as it had for me; for the profit out of the money would pay one or two smaller bills for the week.

But for now I needed an early lunch, food, so I suggested Pasha come with me for lunch, and then discuss my 1.45 pm appointment for the following afternoon, and the further three appointments she'd now booked in for the following morning, and other office ideas.

The 1.45 pm appointment, she'd thought, 'sounded like it may probably be a Missing Person,' as they hadn't given her the fully details. Now that could be interesting! Well with four appointments booked, that would at least be a start to my career, and tomorrow would be a busy day if today went as planned.

Once we'd eaten, I told Patience that I would need to get back to the office to make a phone call, to check on something that was important.

Then after we'd finished the rest of our egg ham salad, and our second glass of bubbly, we'd said cheerio to any faces we knew, to leisurely stroll back to the office which had been something of a giggle, as every hot blooded male had ogled at us, or made wolf whistles, and one builder had called out, 'Come wiv me darlin', I'll show you what a good time is.'

His mates had laughed good-naturedly, before Pasha had answered back to him. 'Your good time mate, might be a good time for your normal girlfriend's darlin', but it wouldn't be good enough for a real woman,' then had crooked her little pinkie.

His smile vanished as quickly as we did, although we'd still been laughing over this double innuendo, right up until we walked back into the office. In fact I was still giggling, up to when I phoned Stewart at his office, who then answered in his normal cheery voice saying.

'Hello sexy, now you've found me, what is it you want to do for me, or me for you, lover girl,' he growled suggestively into the mouthpiece.

❀ 323 ❀

'Behave. I hope there's no one in hearing distance to hear you acting like a demented loony,' I said good-humouredly, adding. 'Stewart on a sensible note, I need to know when we are planning to get into Byways again? Also have you had anyone try to fathom out what that list of numbers we found in the drawer could mean?'

'Sorry I've had more pressing things on my mind Jessica, and I have already phoned Stokes and your office answer-phone cancelling to-day, and making it tomorrow.'

'What did Stokes say?'

'He grumbled something about 'being messed about,' yet he'd conferred—naturally.' He laughed.

'So tell me, did you solve the figures letters puzzle, yet?'

'I'll tell you everything later when I see you—ok?'

'God you're annoying. Well then I'll see if your answer to that particular puzzle is anything like mine!'

'Look, I'm busy Jessica, so I'll see you at your office, or anywhere else after work, even at the 'Dog and Whistle in a couple of hours, or less, if that's ok with you?'

I looked at my watch; it was 14.45 pm. 'Ok, fine.'

'Good.'

'Oh and will you by then have any further evidence that you can tell me about those samples?'

'All is in hand my dear, all in hand. So ask no more, and I will tell you what I know when I see you, ok? So bye for now.' I knew then he couldn't talk anymore, so I repeated his words, 'Bye for now', and put down the phone, having known he'd explain all when we met up later, and before my persuading him to take me to a Greek restaurant for a meal.

Then I'd imagined Stokes having been told the appointment for to-day had been cancelled until tomorrow, and had imagined his anger at the short notice to now make it for the following day at the same time. as he instructed everyone that the meeting was off, and tomorrow, unless instructed differently by DCI Stewart Ross.

Such is life of a Sergeant, eh, I thought with a smile.

CHAPTER 82

Later, I had left the office after taking two more enquires for my services. The first was nothing more than their wanting to use me as a debt collection agency, which I won't do. And the second was about someone wanting me to find someone, which I would do, even though they would eventually not turn up for their appointment—most annoying.

As arranged, I'd walked into the small Lounge area, and then seen Stewart sitting at a table in the far corner of the lounge, talking to a tall well-built man, and had sensed that whatever they were talking about, would be probably more 'important' than my interrupting them. So I'd left them to talk.

Ordering a small GT, with ice, from Mrs Landlord—I forget her name, which had I been advised of it, was not I thought a very good start to forget such things for a budding private eye.

'Getting to be quiet a regular these days, aren't we?' she said. 'Yea good,' said Willie with a toothy grin, 'cos it's always good to see new faces, particularly, if you don't mind me saying, when they're as lovely as you.'

'Well thank you kind sir.'

'Willie, have you got nothing better to do than chat up the customers. Common, I need a hand in the public.' She then

❀ 325 ❀

said to me, 'I'm sorry about him, he does go on something terrible if you let him.'

Willie tapping his nose moaned 'Always moaning my trouble and strife is.' His wife smacked his arm, and he just smiled and shrugged his shoulders at me.

Sitting down at a table facing Stewart, who hadn't appeared to have noticed me up to that moment, as he kept on talking with this other man, having never before seen him being so serious in the way he was talking, I definitely knew he wouldn't have appreciated my interrupting him.

Another five minutes had gone by before he'd at last acknowledged me with a smile, and then excused himself by saying. 'Sorry about my manners Jess, something big has come up, and it's all about to happen as they say. Well according to our reliable source, it is.

He saw me looking at the tall fair haired, passably good-looking man on his left. 'Jess I'm sorry, where are my manners. Jess, this is Detective Inspector Harry Stockton.'

Having said our hello's he paused, and then said. 'Now this is confidential, but as it you, it would seem that a large shipment of drugs is due to arrive tomorrow by way of a cargo boat tomorrow night, docking at London Docks at about 18.30'ish, although which one we aren't too sure about, though we'll know tomorrow.

Now because all this is very hush-hush, for only a few people are on a 'need to know' basis, and walls have ears,' I'd needed to talk to my second in command, Harry here, rather than at the office.

We had then spent a further five minutes talking about tomorrow and the cargo; and then a further very pleasant twenty minutes talking about the best holiday places we would personally like to visit, before he'd stood up saying, 'I've got to go. My wife is having a bit of a birthday bash for her mother, and I still need to buy some booze.' Adding 'It's been nice to meet you Jess, and sorry that I can't stay any longer.' He'd then nodded to Stewart, saying, 'Goodnight Sir', and took his leave.

THE LADY DETECTIVE

'Nice chap' I said to Stewart, and then said 'now I really do need to discuss a matter of importance to me and to you . . . ok?'

He nodded and said. 'Oh I don't know about you Jess, but I'm starved, and as I've haven't had time to have had anything more than a sandwich all day because of what is happening tomorrow; I'll talk to you over a meal, an authentic Thai meal, how does that grab ya?'

He saw my questioning surprise. 'Yes an authentic Thai food in a authentic Thai restaurant, would you believe? Which I saw has recently just opened close when I was coming here. Or perhaps you fancy having a Greek, or a curry, or maybe a steak? So what do you say, because whichever one you chose, will be fine by me, and we'll talk some more there.'

'Thai food sounds very exotic, and its food I believe is almost too good to eat! I know this from Lynda, who, as you know, has been to Thailand for a holiday. So Sir Galahad, let's go for a Thai.' And then realised that I was also hungry, as usual, and said so.

We finished our drinks, said goodnight to Willie and his missus, who I now remembered her name being Joan, and strolled down to the recently opened Thai House restaurant, which happened to be only 500 yards away.

The Owner had with a wide smile, welcomed us on our arrival, and when we'd been seated, told us of the 'Grand Thai Special' that was on the menu that night.

After looking at what the meal comprised off, we'd looked at each other and nodded, and told him that we would both like to try it.

Later, having finally ate all we could, having filled ourselves to bursting point with so many varied little dishes and delicious delicacies, we'd sat back and enjoyed a chilled white wine which the owner also recommended, and said it'll be paid for by the Thai restaurant, 'with compliment please'. He later told us that he'd thought his Thai restaurant was the first in all of the West End. And he could be right.

❄ 327 ❄

Later we vowed to the always smiling owner, we'd recommend him and his restaurant to our friends. His name had been difficult to pronounce, and as it sounded like Arthur, with his consent we called him Arthur. He was pleased, and we could hear him telling the staff that his new name was Arthur, although the way he said it, it sounded more like Arfur, which would go down well with the locals around the area.

'That was an excellent meal,' I said contentedly to him, and then addressing both Stewart and Arfur added, 'and now feel like I'm a bloated whale having been washed up on the beach,' and blew out my cheeks and stuck out my normally flat stomach, so both Arfur and Stewart had laughed, before adding 'and don't think I'll be able to move from here, unless you hire a crane.'

Arfur had then went off smiling to serve another couple who'd just walked into the restaurant, to leave Stewart saying, 'I feel the same as you,' pushing out his stomach, 'so I'll say this place is definitely worth mentioning, and not only to just our friends.'

Then taking another sip of his wine, he asked. 'Alright, so what was so important that you needed to see me about?' He grinned, 'or was it just another elaborate excuse because you always need to see me?'

'That's being a trifle conceited don't you think?'

He grinned again. 'Well I do seem to always know when you can't go a whole day without seeing me—it must be my charm!'

'I suppose the answer to that is both a yes, and a no. Yes, because you now know that I need your help very badly to prove my theory, and solve the murder, and,' I took hold of his hand, 'no, I don't want to always see you.'

I paused for any effect, and seeing he'd put on a sulky hurt look, added, 'silly I'm only teasing.'

Brushing away a imaginary tear. 'Well at least it's nice to know that I'll be helping you out,' he said glumly, 'besides what you said the other night, that I was a truly fabulous, and ardent lover!'

I smacked his hand and said 'Shush'.

I then repeated much of what I had told him on the phone about the meeting I'd had with Stokes at my office, and told him about the agreement that we'd made that I had on tape, and been witnessed, which told anyone that he no longer thought I was a suspect in the Brassy-Wainwrights murder.'

Stewart had only smiled, and nodded his head in appreciation when I said I would need now for him to get us both back into the two offices one more time to prove my theory on how the body had been moved into Byways from Rugs and Tings. He agreed

He winked when he told me that maybe he would need more evidence to prove his own theory about those samples we took from Rugs and Tings, being directly linked to the drugs smuggling racket that you suspected.'

At that he again smiled, when I said that Wainwrights aka Brassy, had possibly been partners with this Dubois, who I'd heard, was an out and out hood, and they all could be involved in the a drugs racket under the guise of their being an Import Export broker, and a 'Import Sales' firm.' He'd even nodded his head happily at what I said.

I continued, 'so I'm guessing that maybe this murder actually ties in somehow with this drugs business, or even the big delivery of drugs that you were earlier talking so earnestly with Harry Stockton about.' At this point, I was so exhausted by having said as much as I had, I'd drunk my wine, to have a rest.

Stewart had then gently begun to clap his hands together, saying 'Brilliant—just brilliant!' He continued. 'We, that is Harry and I, had also been of the same opinion as yourself dear Jess, about the drugs, though it being the cause of the murder we hadn't considered, cos that's your theory.' Then added, 'I wanted the meeting to be tomorrow at three o'clock, because I need to explain to the detectives what I know about

❦ 329 ❦

drugs, just in case we hopefully see loads of it tomorrow.' He then smiling said, 'Ok, what else is it you want to know?'

I thought of the list of numbers and letters. 'And those numbers and letters we found must also have something to do with the murder and the drugs mustn't they? Otherwise why would that piece of paper been hidden so carefully away to make it difficult to find it if it weren't?'

He put his hands up in the air before saying 'Shush. Calm down, and have another drop of wine, and I'll explain.'

'Calm down!' I told him, 'are you telling me to calm down when so much is at stake!' I bristled. 'You said your department has worked out what the numbers and letters had meant. Well, have they?'

'Not yet, to be completely honest old thing—we have only a theory.'

Then I told him that I thought I had come up with an answer to that problem, and if it helped I would tell him. He nodded. So I told him that I thought 'they had to do with clients, and orders. The letters would be the initials of the people they were getting orders from, like AF, Alfie Field, and the numbers would be the amount, money wise, that was ordered in £'s, like 30,000, and the smaller numbers, I thought had been the profit made from the deal.' Finally saying 'Although I wasn't certain that the theory was correct of course, I thought he needed to know.'

'Interesting, I also thought they might have something to do with sales figures.'

'Well if they are, then money-wise, it looks as if it is quite a profit making business.' I said.

'Very true, in fact there can be enormous amounts of money made if you are involved in drugs.'

'And all because of people who like to puff or blow on something that they already know will do them no good at all, and can be harmful to their health. It doesn't make any sense.'

'It's the way of the world, Jess. It really is a form of self-abuse, or weakness.'

THE LADY DETECTIVE

Then to change discussing a complicated subject, I said. 'Stew, now you know I really do need to solve the riddle of the fireplace, and was hoping that you might, with me, finally prove how it was done.'

I'd then pretence groaned loudly in exasperation, so much so, the owner had come over to the table and asked if the food had been alright, and Stewart telling him, 'It's not your food that's making her noisy, it's her mind.'

The poor man had nodded, and as he had moved away, had begun shaking his head. 'Strange people' he was heard to say to someone.

With Stewart just grinned across the table at me, I'd continued. 'Common Stew, you know those ashtrays on the mantle-piece were in the wrong office! Plus you've already seen that both the offices have fireplaces that look so alike they would defy anyone to spot any difference, agreed?

Steward again looked right at me, and I him, whilst I continued to sip the remainder of the wine, before he answered. 'My, my Jess, haven't you got it all worked out, however when it comes from your fair lips, it all seems perfectly logical.'

'So does that means we're going to break into those offices again, yes?'

'Of course it does!'

I let out a 'Brilliant', and leant over to kiss him, which brought a smile from Arfur.

Stewart said. 'Although Breaking and Entering is still breaking the law you know? And I . . .' we both said the next words in unison together, ' . . . could get sacked if I get found out'—and both laughed.

He added, 'Strange isn't it that I now need the answer of why two socks had not quite the same fibres on them, and one had shown fibres from two different carpets, being on either side of the fire-place. So that is something else that I haven't got my head around, yet, though I now agree with your theory about a hidden entrance.' Then smiling contentedly, he then leant over and kissed my forehead.

❦ 331 ❦

ROBERT H FELLOWS

'What's that for?' I enquired happily.

'Because it's thanks to you, that the massive tip off about Brassy and Dubois being probable partners, has helped me realize who it was bringing in the 'harmful' stuff as you call it. So I owe you, the police owe you, and hopefully, the country will soon owe you!'

CHAPTER 83

Half-hour later, and arm-in-arm, we'd strolled leisurely back into my office building, and had walked past a surprised Ben who'd been listening to a soccer match Liverpool versus West Ham, and West Ham were winning, at least it sounded as if they were, because he'd just let out a scream of delight and said. 'Now take that won't ya. Come on you Hammers, give 'em what for!'

I'd also noticed the desk with the radio was now facing towards the buildings main front door entrance. Good for him!

'Evening Miss Felliosi.'

'I've forgotten something, Ben,' I smiled happily at him, 'so won't be long. Enjoy your match.'

'Right you are Miss Felliosi. Mum's the word eh!' He'd then winked at Stewart.

What in heaven's name does this man think we will be doing up there? Whatever his imaginations are, beggars belief. Though thankfully he'll have no idea what we were actually getting up to. Though when he gave us both one of his almost toothless smiles, quickly followed by another of his all-knowing looks, that had made my hackles rise.

'Are you meant to be listening to the radio Ben?' I asked, annoyed, 'I mean, won't it distract you from doing your job, which is keeping an eye on the entrance, and the reception

❦ 333 ❦

hall?' Then thinking *"besides whatever your filthy mind is imagining is going on upstairs?"*

Having been chastised and maybe brought back to earth, he said as we left him to walk to the lift. 'Well it's never happened yet Miss Felliosi, honest.'

'Well someone missed a murderer walking in last weekend.' I said as I walked away.

Stewart questioned as we approached the lift. 'Bit harsh on the old chap weren't you?'

I'd smiled, saying. 'That'll teach him for making false assumptions on what we're up to . . . upstairs.'

'Oh he meant no harm by it.'

'And what of the wink, eh? Besides, that's a jolly good way to start rumours as to my debauched character, you know that. So being a bit harsh, no I don't think so. Besides, *he is* meant to be watching the hallway at all times, because he's being paid just to do that, and he could have quite easily missed someone walking casually straight past him last weekend, and someone did. On Sunday for instance— meaning a man has gone straight up the stairs to the fifth floor, and then murdered Mr Happy, and I was blamed for it.'

We were both laughing as the lift made its ascent, and I added 'all hypothetical of course—though it could have happened that way. Besides, whatever must he have been thinking for him to have said 'mum's the word'?'

With Stewart now coming up close to me saying, 'I couldn't even hazard a guess old thing.' Then he'd pretence growled, and making a grab at me, took hold of me, saying 'Even so, I wouldn't mind having just a little bit of whatever I'm now thinking.' and kissed me passionately.

'Phew, down boy. Control is what you need Stewart, you must learn how to control yourself,' I panted, straightening my clothes, 'besides, we've work to do you know!'

Sighing loudly, he made to grab me again, so I knuckled his hand twice before the lift came to a squeaky halt.

On alighting on the 5th floor, after a swaying ride up in the lift, caused mostly by Stewart jumping up and down

and moaning about his injured hand, we walked the small
journey of more than a hundred feet or so up the hallway, to
the offices of Byways Ltd and Rugs and Tings, to once again
break into these offices for what would now have been the
third time, for me.

'Remind me to ask Ben, had he known the owner of Rugs
and Tings, and had he remember seeing anyone leaving or
coming in who had looked anything like the same man over
the weekend?'

'Good thinking good looking. So now I'm meant to make
notes in my head to remember to tell you what you should
remember to ask Ben. I'm now your secretary, yes?'

'Ok, point taken smarty pants. Sorry,' and grinned.

We broke into the office of Byways Ltd first. At first, it
all seemed as if nothing had changed from either of the times
I'd previously been in here. The room may have been a mite
stuffier, and a little less smelly than it was before, obviously
needing some fresh ventilation, though I had immediately
noticed that the ashtrays and the cigarette butts had been
removed, obviously for evidence.

'Now to find some sort of secret switch to open up the
fireplace,' I said as much to myself as to Stewart. 'Perhaps
it's in or around the fireplace, or maybe on the mantle-piece.
So let's find it. Oh, and Stewart, don't you dare forget to say
the magic words 'Open Sesame' whilst you're looking . . . it
all helps.'

I'd then silently said the words in my mind as we both
began to search for a secret switch, and having prodded,
pushed and poked at everything in sight around the fireplace,
for fifteen or so minutes later, I had in frustration, kicked
and thumped at everything towards the end, having still not
found the answer of how to open the ruddy thing.

'We've got to be doing something wrong Stew,' I said
lamely, whilst still looking for the switch, now saying. 'I
would have thought to make it easily, it will have needed to
be somewhere around the fireplace.' I then moaned, 'I just

know the switch has to be around here somewhere, I just know it is.'

I paused, and taking another long look at the confounded fireplace, I said. 'Of course the ruddy thing could also have been anywhere in the other office, couldn't it?' I groaned. 'Now I know we haven't found it yet, but we will, otherwise my theory on how the mystery murder had been accomplished, has now flown completely out of the window.' I groaned again.

I looked over towards Stewart, noting he seemed to be un-impressed with my words, so I continued. 'Ok, let's have a break, and give ourselves time to think this one out. I mean it could be somewhere else other than in the fireplace of course, could it? I mean the switch might be hidden inside the desk, the drinks cabinet, along another wall, or even under the carpet.' I said hopefully to liven up his and my thoughts.

'Now that's a thought,' he said with an exasperated sigh that had not given me renewed hope.

So suitably un-geed up over this new thought, we'd spent a further ten minutes looking in the desk, behind the blinds, and banging around the walls. In fact having looked everywhere, I was on the point of screaming, when finally Stewart had leant tiredly against the wall saying.

'Sorry Jess I give up, we've looked everywhere, so a blasted switch can't be the answer, cos it just isn't here.' And on saying that, we had both heard a loud click.

Wide eyed now, I saw that Stewart had been standing some three to four feet to the left of the mantelpiece, and maybe two feet into the room, where he'd been leaning with his back against the wall, both in exhaustion and boredom, when the whole of the fireplace, complete with mantelpiece, had begun to move around in a clockwise direction.

Finally on reaching a ninety degree angle to the wall, it had stopped, letting us both stare in utter amazement into the office of Rugs and Tings next door, with both fireplaces sticking out into the room on either side.

With the whole thing remaining open, and having made the right assumption in the end, we'd hugged each other in

THE LADY DETECTIVE

delight, though we both had known we had oh so nearly given up on the idea of a secret entrance, and so it had been with a great personal relief for both of us to know I'd been correct.

And now feeling completely overwhelmed, I gave out a little yippee of delight, which I repeated, before finally saying. 'We found it Stewart. We finally found it.'

'You mean it found me,' he chuckled.

'Well who would have ever guessed the switch might have been there? Well I never will. Do you remember me saying something about the carpet?'

Stewart smiled, saying. 'Well your notion about a switch being in the room was correct, though even you I doubt would have guessed that it would take only my weight on that odd piece of carpet, to set it off,' pointing to the spot 'and solve the mystery.'

He continued. 'Do you know, I could have sworn one of us must have already stood there before?'

'Me too,' I agreed, 'however no-one thought it had needed your big ploddy feet to stand on it to do the trick!'

I went over to where he'd been standing, and bending over, I saw that on the small area of carpet that he'd stood on, and looking almost identical to the rest of the carpet laid in the room, there'd be a small piece with a minor difference in the pattern. So being careful not to ruin my nails, I had without any problem, begun to pull up the small piece of square carpet that had been nailed down.

After that, Stewart had helped me to expose the wooden floorboards to find that one of them had also been slightly different from the others, and it had brass nails to nail it down, whereas the others had been stainless steel.

'So the switch mechanism must only work when someone puts their weight directly on it.' He said.

I then asked him to stand on the switch again to see if it would, this time, close the entrance. Nothing happened, so he tried again, and again, and again, and still not the slightest movement of it wanting to do as I'd wished. So now suitably puzzled, again, for I'd expected another click, and for the fireplace to again return to its original position, I cursed most un-Lady like! Leaving Stewart jumping up and down like a yoyo on the floorboard, and getting more and more frustrated by the second, and finally exhausted, said to me. 'We can't leave the ruddy thing open can we?'

'Ok. How's about you standing on the right side of the fire place in about the same place, and see if that works,' I said with an air of false hope.

Stewart had then gone over to the right side of the fireplace, and about the same distance from the mantelpiece to where he'd been on the left side where it had worked, and then said. 'I've found another odd bit of carpet.'

He then stood on it, and heh-presto, there'd been another click, and the whole of the fireplace had started to revolve itself again to a face on position. Of course we hadn't known then until an hour or so after that it would have needed two more clicks for it to have returned the full 180 degrees to how it had originally been, after we had visited both offices, jumped and looked everywhere, until finally we were seeing the fireplace that had been in here, which I later thought, would have accounted for how the cigarette butts had been found in Rugs and Tings, the 'wrong' office.

For the present, you can imagine our surprise and delight when the fireplace had returned to its original position. So much so, once we'd worked out that it had needed another two clicks on the secret switch, it may have seemed when we'd been looking at each other, that we had been two people who had just broken into the impenetrable vaults of Fort Knox, US of A, and gotten away with millions of pounds worth in gold bars.

Looking back on it now, Stewart and I must have looked funny, with our jumping up and down on the switch to get it to close, and open, and close and open, like children!

And now, having shown my excitement by jumping up and down with glee having finally found all the answers to control the fireplace, had said excitedly. 'Well Stewart, it would seem we've solved the mystery of how someone

THE LADY DETECTIVE

could move one large body from one room to another without anyone seeing anything. And what's more, we now have the proof, with the boot polish samples of the floor marks in each office, of how it was done.'

Feeling more pleased than I'd been for a long time, I hugged Stewart, saying 'What say you, partner, that we mosey back to my place and celebrate? It'll be my treat'

'I don't mind if I do,' Stewart replied wickedly, 'though I'm not sure if it'll be only booze that we should want to celebrate with doing!'

'Cheeky! Well who knows, maybe after a glass or two, we could celebrate in another way—maybe!'

Holding hands, as we'd been about to leave the building, having passed Ben who'd again given us his almost toothless smile, had then blurted out whilst he was stood inside his office doorway, having seen our happy and flushed faces.

'So did you two find what you were looking for?' Followed by another one of his all-knowing grins—did the man ever learn? And when Stewart had quietly nodded to him, he'd seemed more than satisfied at this, and with a little laugh had added. 'It's good when that happens, isn't it?'

'Oh yes its good when that happens!' repeated Stewart as we walked away, and then teasing, added, 'And tremendously satisfying.'

I blushed, knowing exactly what he'd been referring to, but had still giggled never-the-less at his impasse. It was only afterwards I remembered that I hadn't asked Ben the questions I'd asked Stewart to remind me about, and as he hadn't, I'd slapped his arm.

'What's that for?'

'So the next time I ask you to remember something, you'll remember.'

'Huh!'

CHAPTER 84

The following morning, driving down town to my office at 8.40 am, with the top down on my convertible, and sun on my face, it made me wonder if it was the good omen I'd been hoping for, particularly after having had so many diabolical bad days prior to it . . . which you all know, I've had.

It appeared to be one of those days that most of us are always praying for, and for me the fine weather early in the morning, had meant a pleasant change from the totally diabolical weather we had of late been experiencing, so I'd driven to my office in a lighter, happier, more joyful frame of mind.

After last night, feeling light as air, I just knew this day, with not one cloud in sight, was going to be a totally glorious sunshiny day. This was going to be a day that was saying nothing was going to spoil this day for me.

And now, I was even enjoying the company of far too many cars on the road, with their smelly exhausts, who'd been all heading with their owners to their own workplaces.

*   *   *

Three hours later, having finally seen the last of the three appointments that had been booked in for that day, I'd been sat in my office, reflecting on two of the appointments being women, and one being surprisingly young, and very attractive; and the other being in her mid-forty's, and very homely looking, and both had thought their husbands were playing away from home, and wished for me to catch them 'at it'.

The third appointment had been a nice old boy of 78, who told me all he now wanted, was for me to find his long lost son! The old boy had told me that he was dying of throat cancer, and would like to find his son in time to pass on to him some of his wealth before 'he snuffed it', his words not mine.

Of course 'I will give your requests my very best attention' I'd told all three, yet I knew that I would in the old boy's case, try even harder, for that would, in my mind, be a goody for testing my skills in tracking someone down.

So having taken down all the relevant details of each case in my new personal note book, I'd told them all, I would inform them on a daily basis if necessary, as to my progress. I'd also asked them all for a retainer for my handling their case, and for any initial expenses, and taken £75 from the old boy, and £50 from each of the ladies.

And then because I hadn't had anything to eat since my having breakfast at 7.30 am, and feeling ravenous with my poor stomach doing flip overs and grumbling enough for me to have sympathized with it; and now with it being 12.45 pm, and lunchtime, I asked Pasha to go over to the local deli across the road, and get for me, a salt beef salad sandwich, with mustard.

Now have any of you ever noticed that on occasions when you thought you'd found the time to enjoy munching thru a sandwich, or been gratefully sipping a much needed cuppa, how you are so often disturbed by a phone call, or there'd been someone ringing on the front door that you just know you need to answer, or even when you are finally settling down to watch the TV, or listen to music, at the end of a long hard day, someone, or something, disturbs you. Well it's the same for me.

The phone call had been from Stewart saying 'He'd some brilliant news for me,' and 'that the news would keep for a few more hours until we meet up in my office,' which wasn't to be until 3.00 pm.

The swine, he knows I don't like to be 'tortured' that way, and now being too excited over what he was to tell me that was brilliant news, I couldn't eat any more of the delicious sandwich which I'd been so enjoying up to the phone-call, and thrown the remains into the litter bin. And what's more, my lovely hot cup of soup was now stone cold. Dam it!

And now I had slightly more than two hours to fill in until I saw Stewart and the Detectives, and having already seen the appointments that I'd had booked in for that day, those minutes were now going to be a problem to face.

At first, I'd started to make up new files for each new case I'd interviewed, and having put into each file all the relevant details and notes of the case, I then put them onto my in-tray on the long desk, before they would hopefully share the space of an otherwise empty cabinet, with the one solitary solved file that I'd completed. Which being the first case that I'd ever solved, good old Tibs the cat, would now always remain my first paying customer—well her owner would be.

It was then I stupidly realised that my conversion rate of solving cases was 100% so far; so maybe I should have a wall chart or something on the wall to show all the cases I had solved in bold letters; or in graph form, that should be easily seen by all my new clients, for a 100% success rate would certainly look very impressive to anyone wanting their own personal problem solved.

So I'd talked to Pasha about it, and she'd suggested the graph form 'was ok', but gave me a thumb's down to having a person's name on the board. That was now obvious; so I don't know what I'd been thinking of.

THE LADY DETECTIVE

And then for something else to do to idle the minutes away, I'd then spent time checking out the addresses, and any other relevant details about my two new clients husbands, and began making enquiries as to Ben's lost son.

Then I phoned my Mother for a chat, and after that, had a giggle on the phone with Lynda, and when she asked me 'what's new' I told her about the quaint little pub down the road, and also the new Thai restaurant that was also down the road, telling her that Stew and I had eaten there, and saying 'the food was delicious' and similar stuff.

Also I had in those minutes, a half a dozen tea's and coffees, and then had strolled aimlessly about the office to help pass the time away. Come on!

CHAPTER 85

PROOVING A POINT

Having finally, and anxiously, seen through those long, long minutes, Stokes and his detectives had arrived on time, at precisely at 3 pm, and he'd been accompanied by seven men and one woman, who'd been all greeted in the reception area by Pasha, who'd then been asked to make themselves comfortable, and told they could help themselves to any drinks from the machine if they wished, or she would do it for them. Considerate too!

A further five minutes followed, before a very happy looking Stewart, accompanied by D/I Harry Stockton came through the door.

Now Harry I now knew was Stewart's new side kick. Though I hadn't known that Stewart had, without my knowing, set up the National Drugs Squad, which would, once they became known, be called by everyone, as 'the Nods', or NDS.

Having been introduced to everyone who I didn't know by Jones, I'd asked Stewart into my office, and poured him out a small Scotch, for I knew of Stewart's dislike for vended tea or coffee, and had in the meantime, instructed Pasha to place a tin of assorted biscuits on the table for anyone to help themselves, and would you believe, in no time at all, the tin was empty baring a few biscuit crumbs, having been mostly eaten by, you've guessed it, Sergeant Smelly Stokes.

Also on seeing Stewart's preference for a beverage, had changed his mind from wanting a tea, and had also asked for a small Scotch, to be abruptly told by Stewart 'that he was on duty', leaving Stokes looking suitably puzzled.

The detectives had then for a few minutes stood about chatting about nothing in particular, similar I'd imagined, to attending one of the Prime Minister's 'I say, any new ideas chaps' cabinet meetings, that the PM had always banged on about was so important.

Of course I might have guessed that Pasha would enjoy being given all the attention by the men, for she really was a tease. Although detective Golightly, being a women of twenty four or so, and attractive in a masculine way, and being the only police woman present, was giving her a few—'Blimey what a show off'—type looks, mixed with an occasional smile to any man who had spoken to her!

I was, as many readers might have gathered, far more than being a little anxious to get this meeting on its way. And seeing that I was in charge, in a manner of speaking, and knowing I had the surety of this meeting being at least in my offices, I felt I was in the driver's seat so to speak, and had now wanted desperately to show them all what I'd discovered, and how clever I was!

Besides wanting the meeting to start, I had also wanted to hear the good news that Stewart had yet to tell me, and not knowing which should come first, my dilemma had been that I couldn't wait any longer to begin explaining how the murder had been accomplished, then hearing the 'good news'.

I'd eventually clapped my hands for attention, and found everyone had stopped talking, and were now all either settling back in their chairs, or standing patiently, waiting for what I had to say.

❦ 345 ❦

Thinking I would now close this murder investigation by my summing up the facts as I saw them, for I didn't intend to let my little moment slip by un-noticed, without my not being seen as another Miss Marple.

I saw Stewart smiling at me, and knew he'd also be enjoying my moment, bless. 'Gentleman, and lady, shall we get down to the business in hand?' Not wishing to disappoint, I'd smiled at the faces before me, and opened with.

'Now correct me if I am wrong Sergeant Stokes, for I don't want to make any stupid mistakes, or even make any hasty decisions that I may regret,' and heard a few titters of laughter, for they'd all known what I'd been referring to, and now having obtained their interest, they'd all been watching the fat man squirm in his armchair, which again was groaning its displeasure under his weight whenever he moved. I continued.

'So with that in mind, Sergeant, I believe you told me that you were more than a trifle baffled to understand how a murdered man's body could have been found in another person's locked office, which happened to be next door to the office of the murdered person. Am I correct?'

He nodded. I continued. 'And would I also be correct in assuming that you have also been wondering how on earth could I, being the murderer, (laughs) have moved the body from one office into another without being seen, or for him not to have left lots of blood stains in the hallway, or anywhere else for that matter, especially after I had caused the horrendous damage that had been inflicted to the victims face. Am I correct?'

Again Stokes nodded, slightly blushing. I continued. 'And, according to you Sgt Stokes, I had been physically strong enough to have dragged, or lifted the dead man into the other office after 'doing him in.' Would that be the correct terminology?

I heard a titter or two before adding. 'So assuming I'm correct so far, would I also be correct in assuming that you

THE LADY DETECTIVE

have still no idea who the real murderer might have been—
besides me! Is that also correct, Sergeant?'

He nodded and said, 'Yes' in a low voice.

Inwardly pleased at his admission, I smiled then and
said. 'So now you must stop me if there is anything I say
that any of you don't agree with, or you know is wrong, ok?'

The detectives, had with Stokes, again nodded, his jowls
again wobbling. 'Good. So as far as you are concerned, this
case has not been an easy one for you to solve?' Again Stokes
nodded, and I added. 'Which is hardly surprising, I suppose.'

This had bought a few more titters and smiles from my
listeners, 'Well not to worry Sergeant, for that is precisely the
reason why you've all been asked here to-day, so that I can
show you how the murderer could move the body from one
place to another, and not leaving any blood stains.'

I paused for affect before continuing. 'In fact Sergeant,
I'll even throw in the possible reason, for free, the motive of
why I believe this murder did happen.'

Now all the faces I saw were showing interest, including
the pretty lady detective who'd looked up to then, as if she'd
got out of the wrong side of the bed of a guy she hated. So
I'd paused for a moment longer, to give them all a little time
to mull over what I'd just said, before asking Stokes, after
giving him a No4 smile.

'I would like you to answer a question for me, Sergeant?
Which is, what is the latest news you have on this feller who
calls himself Dubois?' He looked suitably taken aback. 'The
reason I ask, Sergeant, is because we, that is your superiors,
DCI. Ross, DI. Stockton, and little ol' me of course, and
maybe one or two of the others in here, would like to know
what you know about the man.'

I noticed some of the detectives had been giving me
various forms of agreement, so obviously Stokes hadn't
passed on any of this information.

Now he cleared his throat before saying. 'Well Sir's, Miss'
addressing both Stewart, Harry and myself, 'I think that the
name you've just mentioned, could be Brassy's partner, and

❀ 347 ❀

they'd a falling out over something or other, which resulted in Brassy being murdered, although had it been by Dubois himself who did it, I'm not sure!'

'Now is that all you know Sergeant?' asked Stewart.

'Well Sir, I've come up with the last known addresses of where both Brassy also known as Wainrights, and this Dubois have been living, with a little help from the Customs and Excise. So we did early this morning, called on both addresses by way of a small raid, as you have no doubt been informed of, Sir.'

Then still looking at Stewart he'd continued. 'Now chummy Dubois and Brassy were not at either of their addresses a couple of hours ago, however there were a number of dubious characters living at each address, who we've taken into custody, and are now helping us with our enquires.' The fat man had then sat back, as if he'd said all he'd meant to say.

'Helping you with 'our enquires', Sergeant? Queered DI Stockton. 'So are you now telling us everything? Or are you perhaps holding something back?'

'No Sir.'

'Perhaps I should have asked, what those men had said to you, meaning those who were working for Brassy, and those who were working for Dubois?

Stokes sat forward again in his chair. 'Well Sir, the men we've taken into custardy from Brassy's address, said they call him 'The Fixer', and hadn't seen him for some days now. And not one of the men who'd been at Dubois place knew who Dubois really was, because he'd only been known to them as 'Mr Big'. And when I asked him why he was called Mr Big, they'd said they hadn't been sure why, but maybe it was because of his size, or because he was the big Boss.

Anyway, one man told us that this 'Mr Big', Dubois that is, normally handled everything himself, either by the phone, or thru a man he'd known as 'The Fixer', which was Brassy, and it wasn't unusual for any of them not to have ever seen him, 'unless we'd done something wrong, then he'd be vicious!'

THE LADY DETECTIVE

At this Stokes paused to wipe his brow before continuing on in an unhurried way. 'Also none of them could tell us anything about the business, cos they'd said, they didn't know anything. Besides, with most of the men being foreigners, they didn't understand English.'

Stokes then to clear his throat, had taken a large gulp of water that he'd asked someone to get for him before he continued.

'This man said, he saw to the men's comforts, living quarters and so forth, on the orders of 'Mr Big', and when I told him that he could now be an accomplice to a murder, bluffing of course, he said he didn't know anything about no murder, but did know of a warehouses that was owned by Dubois that he'd tell me if I was to make him a deal. And giving him the nod, he told me it was somewhere close to something green in Chiswick. Probably means Turnham Green.

The one of Brassy's men said he remembers there'd been a place in North London somewhere, and when I pressed him further, he said it was by some playing fields where the Rugby team Saracens played, which means it was Southgate. He said he knew that, because his father-in-law lives there, and watches rugby.'

He paused, and taking in a deep breath Stokes then said. 'And then he told us a funny thing, he told us that there were at least three or more extremely large commercial washing machines in this warehouse.'

'Like dry cleaning machines,' I asked, and he shrugged he didn't know.

'Oh dear. Oh dear. Oh dear,' Stewart exclaimed, looking concerned at Stockton. 'The fool could now have blown it. He's now pre-warned Dubois we are on to him.' He turned angrily to Stokes. 'I hope you haven't been to either of those warehouses. Well, have you Sergeant?'

'No Sir, I mean . . . yes Sir we haven't been anywhere near them, for I'd also been informed by the informant, they were always locked up and made secure, and both had dogs

❀ 349 ❀

to protect them, so I'd have required back up, and a go ahead from a superior officer to have done that, Sir.'

'Well then Sergeant, aren't you the lucky one, because had you gone ahead and visited either one of those warehouses without getting permission, you'd have got an instant dismissal from the Force with immediate effect, and probably no pension, especially had there been someone at either place to have warned Mr Big or The Fixer, or any other of the chiefs, which you may still have, now you've rounded up some of the gang.'

Stewart then paused before saying. 'So did you report your findings, or these facts of the gang's activities, to anyone higher in rank than yourself—your Chief Super or Inspector, for instance?'

'Well Yes, and no Sir, well not the Chief Super, though I did inform Duty Inspector Field, and he in turn said he would tell Superintendent Knowles, and as yet, I haven't been informed what to do.'

'Well isn't that fortunate for you, Sergeant, that Superintendent Knowles has contacted me, and I've asked him not to give anyone under any circumstances, the go-ahead to check out the warehouses. Go on.'

Stokes looked shocked; and breathing heavily, blurted out. 'Well Detective Jones here, had an idea that the machines were not for dry cleaning, but to launder whatever it was that they'd been bringing into the country. So as a joke I'd said, well if it wasn't clothes they were laundering, then it must be money they were laundering.'

Stokes had then smiled, and when he'd looked about him and seen that his joke hadn't worked because no-one had even smiled, at his attempt to lighten the dark cloud that was above his head, had then added, 'Jones and Williams also thought it might have been for drugs, though how the machines were to be used for that, I hadn't the foggiest idea.'

'No surprises there then, eh Serge?' quipped one of the detectives, getting smiles all around.

THE LADY DETECTIVE

Stokes ignoring the remark, took a large sip of water before saying 'I'd also been told by the man who'd been looking for a little leniency, that they were expecting what he'd called 'a biggy' coming into the country, whatever that meant, and it could happen very soon.'

DC. Williams interrupted. 'The thing is Sir, we, that is us detectives, are wondering if this Mr Big, who as Dubois, is known as a violent man, whether he could be involved with the murder of Brassy-Wainwrights?'

'And' said Jones, 'because we've also been informed by a friend in the C&E, that they are extremely baffled how large amounts of class 'A' drugs are coming into the country, which they believe has each time a street value of many £millions of pounds, they are suspicious of Dubois.'

Stewart questioned. 'Williams and Jones isn't it?' Both nodded. 'Well, we'll have something further to say on that subject, later on.' He then looked to DI Stockton, who said 'fine with me.'

Stokes said. 'I've got nothing more to add, Sir, other than to say that the SOC officers have again tested for more fingerprints and clues in both of the offices, and found nothing whatsoever to further tells us who'd killed Brassy, so must have either used gloves at all times or . . . ,' he mumbled, '. . . now here's a thought, not fact . . . had their fingerprints removed!'

CHAPTER 86

Stewart, who'd been quietly sitting in one of the armchairs looking relaxed and thoughtful, listening to what Stokes and the others had to say, had at that moment suddenly sprung to his feet saying. 'Now that sounds a bit drastic wouldn't you have said, Sergeant, but is nevertheless, it is feasible!'

He then cleared his throat. 'Well I must say it would seem, that you have all done very well to have found out an awful lot of useful information in a very short time. Although I might also suggest that some of you have certainly done more work than others, and therefore got better results from their endeavours.'

He now looked towards Stokes 'Although I am very surprised to hear that when you found out about this 'biggy' happening, you hadn't bothered to inform Customs & Excise of it being about to happen, eh Sergeant?' Then quietly, 'now that kind of important knowledge, must always be, ladies and gentlemen, passed on to your seniors, and never, ever, be kept to yourselves.'

Then giving a stern look around the room at all the detectives, he finally looked a deepening red-faced Stokes. 'So Sergeant, I now want you to inform Customs of this 'biggy' coming into the country, the one that you were informed about . . . how long ago was it?'

'Not long, maybe two hours ago, Sir.'

❉ 352 ❉

THE LADY DETECTIVE

'So when you were told about this 'biggy' about two hours ago, Sergeant, those hours may be vitally important! So now if you ask her politely, I'm sure Miss Felliosi will let you use her telephone to phone C&E; although I feel almost inclined to make you walk down the stairs and out to a police box, or to a public phone box to do it. Have I made myself clear?'

As I watched Stokes struggling to get out of the comfy armchair, and back onto his feet, I did feel just a little sorry for the fat man when he'd asked me if he could use my phone, which did leave me debating with myself, just for a second, whether I should also add to his discomfiture, and have him go outside the building to look for a phone box, having known, and felt, that these thoughts were a true reflection of how I really felt about the fat man, when thinking it might have been a small personal recompense for all the humiliation and worry he'd put me through over the past days.

Never-the-less I did approve his request for him to tell C&E, and we'd all been quiet as he made his call to the C&E.

After making the phone call, he sighed heavily, and turning back to us, his all ears audience, had said. 'They already knew Sir. They said you had already told them of this going to happen.' He resumed his seat, his face now a wet scarlet embarrassed red blob.

'Alright, now let no-one ever forget that any important information that's not within your scope must be immediately passed on before, shall we say, your own personal glory, ok!'

Stewart then turned to Stokes. 'Right Sergeant, about the murder, perhaps you can now tell me everything you know? And there's no need to be shy, and not speak freely in front of Miss Felliosi, being that it was she who you arrested for being the murderer. And what's more, I'll personally vouch for her not running away, Sergeant, while you explain your reasons why you arrested her. Although it's only fair to warn you that Miss Felliosi has already worked out a lot more about who the murderer is or could be, than I assume you have. This she will reveal after we've all visited the two

❖ 353 ❖

offices up the hall. Or am I perhaps being pernickety over this, is that's the right word I'm looking for, Sergeant?'

Stokes was now looking really annoyed, even angry, having heard stifled laughter in the room, his having been picked on again, and was now looking down at his feet, then hands, wishing he could be anywhere else but here in this room. He now proceeded to answer the question.

'Well Sir, besides Miss Felliosi' finger-prints found at the crime scene, and a scuffed fingerprint on an ashtray, both offices have been wiped clean as a whistle of any evidence.'

'Did you check the Champagne bottle in the fridge for prints?' I asked.

'How did you know about the bottle? Yes we did Miss,' I shuddered, 'ah Miss Felliosi' he corrected himself. 'Maybe the DNA on the cigarette butts in the ashtrays, might give us the answer we need, so it's now down to our friends in forensics, who are telling us, me, that they've been very busy with two other murders, and we need to wait our turn.' He sucked in large quantities of air, and said. 'Other than that, Sir, we haven't found anything of any consequence to help us with this investigation, and no blood stains.'

Jones then added. 'Though Miss Felliosi was kind enough to supply us with the address for the dead man's solicitor, didn't she Williams? And she was also kind enough, considering what you'd previously put her through, Serge, to tell us that this Mr Brassy, had in fact signed both leases in two different offices, which had in turn, then given us the name of Wainwrights, which you now know is Brassy's other name.'

'Oh' added Williams, 'and that information certainly helped us eh Jones, to then been able to place him as an associate in crime with Dubois, because we knew that chummy Brassy was his mate, and because Dubois was also a thug, and into prostitution, drugs, or something similar, that could only mean one or two things, one, that this had something to do with women or drugs, and two, the murder of Brassy!'

Stokes who'd been sat glaring at Jones and Williams, had after taking in huge gulps of air, and not to be outdone by these two, had spluttered. 'Well it was my finding out that it was Rugs and Tings who'd had the Import-Export License, and not Byway's Ltd.' Still breathing heavily, 'And there's more.'

Stewart growled 'Well get on with it man, we haven't got all day!'

Stokes continued, slightly shocked with the DCI's abruptness. 'Well I admit that at the time, I didn't think that Rugs and Things—Tings, could have had anything to do with drugs, as I thought the murdered man had been selling only imported goods . . .'

'. . . but not us, sir, cos we,' pointing to Jones, 'thought that drugs were involved,' said Williams.

'. . . however having found it was Rugs and Tings who'd had the license for Importing and Exporting, and not the other way around as marked on their office doors, probably to confuse people,' continued Stokes quickly, 'it meant that Byways Ltd, meaning Dubois, had been the Sales agent, which then meant, we thought they must have both had a hand in purchasing and distributing all manner of goods, drugs, around the country, without anyone suspecting who did what.'

Stokes had then sat back in his groaning chair, and with a soiled handkerchief in his chubby hands, proceeded to wipe away sweat from his fevered brow.

That function of the offices was interesting news to me, as to who did what in each office, though it didn't change anything else as far as I could see, although Jones was to tell us that once the goods, which he and Williams had suspected could have been drugs, had passed through the scrutiny of the Customs & Excise men, they had then suspected, according to Jones, they'd been doctored in some way.

CHAPTER 87

Although Stokes hadn't been at all pleased with his overall contribution to the murder case, and knew he'd underestimated those trouble-makers Jones and Williams, who hadn't helped by putting in their oar to make him look, and feel, even more of a fool in front of the DCI than he'd actually had been.

He now admitted to himself, he'd made far too many mistakes, and all of this, had been a calamity waiting to happen, and having now reflected it had mostly been all of his own doing.

Although normally a man of few words, Stokes thought his explanation of the case so far, had been the most words he'd put together for a very long time. In fact he'd been strangely pleased with all he'd said, and would almost certainly be telling his wife Ethel about it later, and in detail.

That thought made him now wish he was at home with her right now, for he could be telling her all about this meeting, and his horrid horrible day, and she'd have probably then sympathised with him, and offered to get him a nice strong cup of tea, along with a few of her delicious home-made cream cakes.

Then his day dreaming had unfortunately been interrupted, when he'd heard Williams saying: 'However after Sgt Stokes had suggested the rugs might have been to wrap around illegally imported guns, or things similar, we

❖ 356 ❖

THE LADY DETECTIVE

felt, that is the team felt, that from the evidence we'd found, the rugs almost certainly must have been concealing drugs, and we'd bagged up some samples for the forensic team, didn't we Jones? And it was because of that, that we, Jones and me, had thought that Brassy had been selling imported drugs, and then we found out where Brassy lived, after Miss Felliosi' tip off, and then where both his and Dubois warehouses were.'

Williams it appeared had certainly not wanted Stokes to get any credit at all for any of the ideas that he, Jones, or the team, had brought to the murder enquiry . . . and I couldn't blame him of course!

Now Stokes blustered. 'Oh yes . . . so it was . . . right, that's good, ah, so now it seems you're saying, that you were the only people who only had some good ideas, yes?'

'Yes Serge, at least many more than you ever had.' growled Williams. Williams and Jones had then given Stokes a look that might have killed a smaller and weaker person, and I reckoned I knew why that was, just as I was equally sure that Stewart hadn't missed that look either.

Stewart had then looked at me, then everyone in the room in turn, before saying. 'I think it's appropriate to say well done on having a good tight team, Sergeant. Wouldn't you say Harry?' Stockton nodded. He continued, 'especially when considering this murder, had, with its various intrigues involved within it, been extremely frustrating for your team, and especially for you Sergeant Stokes, being their leader. Am I right?'

'Yes Sir, it has been quite frustrating as you say, Sir.'

'So now you must all be wondering how this mysterious murder had been accomplished, eh!'

Heads were nodding as he'd walked to the window and looked out at nothing in particular, before he'd turned back to us saying. 'Well let me assure you, that everything should from here on in, get much easier to understand. So happier times ahead, eh Sergeant? Although I can equally assure you all, that it will not be happy times for Dubois and his merry men, because it will for them be less than jolly when we get

❦ 357 ❦

our hands on them. In fact the more I think about it, I can inform you as each minute passes, that it'll be getting far less jolly for them—don't you think Harry?'

Stockton nodded and smiling said 'far less jolly, sir.' I smiled, and then we'd all smiled, except poor old Stokes.

* * *

Walking back to his seat, he sat down again, then bent over his knees, before lifting up his face and smiled at us all again.

'I can now tell you that following a tip off,' Stewart said, 'the distinct probability of a load of drugs being delivered to our shores by boat is real. And its destiny I've been informed is our very own London docks. Also I've been notified as I speak, that this should happen anytime in the next couple of hours, and all we detectives will be waiting.' Two detectives had clapped.

Williams then said. 'That's fine Sir, but what's that got to do with Brassy being murdered?' he asked, 'as if I can't guess!'

'Well Williams, when we catch him, and you sit down with chummy Dubois, we'll all know more about that after he's been interrogated, won't we? Cos then, we'll definitely know whether he'd be charged for the murder of his partner in crime, a certain Mr Brassy aka Wainwrights, or be charged with drugs smuggling. So Williams, how does that bit of news grab you?'

'Sounds grabbing good, Sir!'

'But Sir, without our having any real proof that he did the murder, unless he squeals, how will you know he'd murdered Brassy-Wainwrights?' piped up Jones.

'Yes Sir, cos as far as we know, there aren't any clues, or prints that he conveniently left for us to find, to accuse him of the murder, un-like Miss Felliosi, 'sneered Stokes.

THE LADY DETECTIVE

Stewart smiling at that quick dig meant for me, and lent forward towards him. 'Well Sergeant, Miss Felliosi thinks she has the answer to that problem. And saying that, I think now will be as good a time as any, for Lady Jessica to now show us all, how she thought the foul deed was done. So without further ado, as they say, I'll now pass you over to Miss Felliosi.'

When all eyes had turned towards me in total expectation of my telling them the answers to what they'd spent many hours and days puzzling over, I'd felt like a celebrity at that moment, having been put under the spotlight, and being applauded for who they were.

Feeling slightly embarrassed, I gestured with my arm to everyone in the room whilst saying. 'Would you all please follow me,' and proceeded to lead everyone out of my office, and down the hall to the offices of Byways Ltd.

CHAPTER 88

On reaching that office, Stewart had with a wink at me, asked Stokes. 'Can I have the keys Sergeant . . . I'm assuming you'll have them on your person, with you knowing you'll be coming in here?'

Stewart had spoken these words in a much to a casual and gentle manner, I'd thought: "Oh, oh, Stokes you had better watch out," because knowing Stewart as well as I did, and because I could always tell his mood swings, I knew he would always continue gunning for Stokes over the grief he gave me.

The fat Sergeant looked at his superior officer, patted his pockets, and in surprise had said. 'They're back in the office, Sir,' and shook his large head to give his chins more exercise.

'Back at the office you say!' Stewart said looking aghast. 'Now is that what you would call bad-forward thinking, Sergeant?' He shook his head. 'Well Inspector Stockton, perhaps you'll oblige us with your burglary skills.'

Harry knowing it was a wind-up said. 'Well it's been a very long time since I was, you know, a burglar, but I'll try,'

He then bent down, and proceeded to fumble around the lock, sometimes jiggling the door-handle up and down similar to the way that Stewart had previously done when we'd broken in, to mask the fact that he was unlocking the office door by using his own set of skeleton keys.

❦ 360 ❦

THE LADY DETECTIVE

Harry had then straightened up saying. 'There's no need for me to unlock the door, Sir, because it's been left open all the time!'

Harry and Stewart had then looked at each other, leaving me valiantly trying to suppress a smile, though now they'd both been looking at Stokes with feigned amazement, and following his example, we'd all done the same.

Stokes was stood open-mouthed in surprise and amazement! And I couldn't blame him, for the feller had really been set up!

Stewart, pretending now to be angry asked 'Why Sergeant? Why have you left this office door open for anyone to have entered? If I may be so bold as to say so, that is totally un-satisfactory; and it's made even worse, in the knowledge that anyone, me, Harry, Jessica, Jones, or anyone else, could have entered here, and tampered with whatever evidence there might have still been in here which may have solved this mystery crime.' He sighed loudly. Then continued, 'And that Sergeant, could have meant, that any Court in the land on knowing this, would have immediately dismissed any evidence you've got, as being possibly contaminated and flawed. Am I right DI Stockton?' Stockton nodded.

'I mean what were you thinking of Sergeant? Was it not your responsibility to ensure that the door had remained locked at all times?'

Stokes mumbled something that sounded like it was an apology. 'I don't know how that could possibly have happened—honest Sir!'

*   *   *

Stewart was first to enter the office, and had casually strolled over to the fireplace, before turning around to look for the unfortunate Stokes, who had been trying to hide at the back of all the detectives to cover his embarrassment, perhaps knowing that more pain was to come his way, and considering his height and size, was impossible.

Stewart pointed to the faint brown marks on the carpet, and asked him. 'And what did you make of these marks on the carpet?'

Still flustered, Stokes answered. 'Well they look like something had maybe been dragged over . . .'

'. . . Very good Sergeant,' said Stewart interrupting him, 'that is exactly what I also think has happened. And that I believe might have also been the first sensible remark you've made to-day. So what do you imagine that 'something' might have been?'

'Well at the time I had wondered about the marks, and thought it could have been something dragged along the floor, a heel or the toe of a shoe perhaps, but seeing that it went up to the fireplace, a dead-end so to speak, I gave that idea a miss as being too fanciful.'

'Ah, too fanciful you say?' Stewart smiled at Stokes, 'A very good choice of word. However that was another one of your big mistakes.' Then pausing for a second continued. 'So allowing for that, what did you make of the cigarette butts? I mean, had you actually noticed them?'

Stokes was now looking as if he was going to explode with anger at the humiliation, and barely controlling himself, had mumbled. 'Yes I noticed them.'

'And after that, did you not think it was unusual that in there, in Rugs and Tings, there'd been ashtrays full of them, when all the evidence clearly points to Mr Brassy being a non-smoker?' No answer from Stokes, 'and the sign clearly stating "Please do not Smoke in this office" that in here, in Rugs and Tings, people should refrain from smoking, you hadn't taken a note of, and ignored.'

'Yes sir, though I did give it some thought . . . well we all did! However I can only say that at the time I'd assumed Brassy must have made allowances for who-ever the person who'd been smoking. Meaning it may have been a really

THE LADY DETECTIVE

important client that he'd been entertaining, and wouldn't want to upset that person, by telling them not to smoke.'

'Well that's a reasonable assumption, Sergeant. In fact, I believe it's the same assumption as Miss Felliosi had first thought of.' You could see a look of relief that had come into Stokes' fat face, short lived unfortunately, when Stewart he added.

'However, that was before she'd then thought, having seen the amount of cigarette ends in the two ashtrays, that the man must have spent quite a long time in here, and had chain-smoked . . . which she didn't believe had happened. And that leads us on nicely to the fact that they are the same brand of cigarettes smoked by this man Dubois, are they not?'

'Yes Sir, they are, he also likes Turkish, and Russian,' answered Stokes with a flourish.

Stewart then paused, and still looking and smiling towards Stokes, was I saw, thoroughly enjoying in his own quiet way, giving Stokes a roasting, a dressing down, and strongly suspected that Stewart was giving him payback for all the mistakes and trouble he'd caused everyone, particularly me, for his indifferent attitude to the case, which to be fair to the Sergeant, I didn't very much like to see, especially in front of his own men, for I'd have thought a quiet private word in Stokes' ear would have been preferable, regardless of how unforgivable the Sergeant' summarisation of the crime, and his treatment of me, had been.

Stewart continued. 'Ok, then what did you think when a similar stub was found in the fireplace, in there, by Miss Fellioso? I mean did you wonder why that was, or didn't you really care too much either way, thinking you already had your suspect?'

Stokes was shaking his head vigorously to again make his jowls wobble like jelly, before he said. 'I beg your pardon sir . . . I didn't care! Meaning what exactly?'

❖ 363 ❖

'Meaning Sergeant, that had I been your immediate superior, I would have wanted to have known everything about your handling of this case. I would have wanted to have known what you had regarded as important, or regarded as not important. I'd have wanted to know what did at least warrant your attention enough to have stimulated some spark of interest to finding out the truth. That's what I mean, Sergeant.'

At this obvious heavy slur, Stokes had bunched his fists, gasped, and was now looking physically drained of all his blood, and begun to make weird sounds as if he was choking, before he shouted out in anger.

'My superior did know the bloody facts of the case so far, had you bloody bothered to check. And sir, you needn't be so bloody insulting all the time. I mean what have I done to you for you to be so know-it-all bloody insulting, eh? Yes, I might have been foolish, made a few mistakes, but hearing them coming from you, in front of everybody . . . well it's . . . it's below the belt, and you should be ashamed of yourself.'

At that outburst, everyone stared at Stokes for a long ten seconds with a little more respect, before Jones, had surprisingly come to his rescue to cool things.

'Well you did find and check out the nutshells, didn't you Serge?' He said brightly, although you thought it had been said sort of tongue in cheek.

'Oh, and what sort of shells did you think they were, detective?' I enquired of Jones, whilst observing Stewart still looking at the fat man.

'Well I did hear that the Italians, or is it the Greeks, always liked to be always eating them. Just like that bald guy on TV, who plays a New York cop, and sucks on a lollypops, does. What's his name? Coj, no Koj, that's it, Kojac, now I know this because one of the men in the forensic team who has travelled a lot, says he knew them to be pasticcio nuts, although I wouldn't know if they really were to be honest, cos I've never bought or ate any.'

I said with a smile, 'In fact those nuts would have been another clue for you as to who the killer might be. It was a clue that appeared to have not been followed up with what you would call logical thinking; because none of you it appears, had actually thought when you found those pasticcio nutshells, that added to the clue of those smelly French Guilloise cigarette ends that were found in the room next door, and in here, that being both together, may have suggested to someone thinking of a suspect for the murder, without needing to use DNA testing.'

Turning to Williams, I asked. 'So what conclusion had you come up with, seeing those two pieces of evidence Williams?'

'Similar to you Miss Felliosi, and when we we've told by forensics this morning, that the DNA tests they've done on the cigarette ends, matched Dubois profile, we knew he must have been here as a partner, or not, and have ever since been trying to find this Dubois for questioning.'

I spoke gently to Stokes. 'What I believe I'm implying Sergeant, is that had you asked yourself the question of who you knew among the criminal fraternity who had a liking for pasticcio nuts and those horrible French cigarettes, you would have almost certainly come up with another suspect, besides myself of course, to have pulled in for questioning, on the Monday.'

I saw Stewart nodding in agreement to what I said, before glaring at Stokes and at the other detectives and saying.

'Call yourselves detectives, God help us, it has taken a private citizen whose been falsely accused of being a murderess, and had needed to solve the puzzle of how the murder was achieved to prove her innocence, and you lot had not done nothing to prove different. You even had her locked her up for murdering a man she didn't even know, based on the evidence of her fingerprints being found around the murder scene.'

He breathed in heavily and looking at Stokes. 'I believe, had you been concentrating on doing the job properly, instead of grasping at straws, you might have had another suspect in custody? I mean did it not occur to anyone, anyone at all, that her fingerprints could have been in the room for any number of reasons, any one of which would have been nothing at all to do with the murder. Or should I have said, had nothing at all to do with Miss Felliossi killing him.'

Stokes said defiantly. 'I think you are wrong. Of course we knew all that. We also knew that with her dabs being found all over the place, she was a suspect, and with her saying she didn't know the man, then coming up here, that wouldn't have needed a genius to think that doesn't exactly ring true, does it . . . sir? Even in your scheme of things, she would still have been a suspect.'

Stokes then gave Stewart a contemptuous look, and Stewart unabashed with a shake of his head, I thought angrily, had continued. 'A suspect yes, Sergeant, however a murderer not at all, and with you being the arresting officer, how for the life of me did you ever expect that flimsy piece of evidence to stand up in a court of a murder trial? Well?'

Then not waiting for an answer had growled, 'and what is even more laughable, is that in all that time, and right in front of your own eyes, you had all the evidence you had needed to point a finger to who the killer was, or could have been, which though not yet proved, should have of least told you it was possible that the murder might not have been done by Miss Felliosi, just as she'd been saying all along she hadn't been, and no-one had listened! Quite frankly it's bloody laughable.'

Now Stokes in particular, was looking down at his feet crest-fallen over what Stewart had said, as were some of the Detectives, for none of them had ever been given such a dressing down by a senior officer before, and now looked as if they were shell shocked. Yet the dressing down had all been said in such a quiet manner that it had almost seemed surreal, dreamlike.

Now feeling humiliated and made to look stupid, most detectives were looking towards Stokes, for hadn't he at

THE LADY DETECTIVE

times, refused to listen to anything any of the Detectives had to say on the murder . . . or me being of course his prime suspect as an example. knowing that had anyone of them run their thoughts past the fat Sergeant, he'd have probably, and did, poo-poo the idea, especially had that idea, or thought, opposed whatever the fat man had been thinking about the case at the time,.

Stokes was now saying 'However you know as well as I do, that someone saying that they weren't innocent of a crime, is as you know, very normal in the criminal world. And those two items being found doesn't necessarily mean it was this guy Dubois who had killed Brassy does it?' He drew in a big breath, 'I mean, because they were possible partners, and had offices which were next to each other, you cannot just naturally assume he was, or was not the killer until it's based on real facts, sir.'

I thought that was a sensible repost, and Stewart having taken forever to reply, had only said. 'True, but you did assume with Miss Felliosi here was didn't you?'

'Sir, I'm wondering if your personal friendship with Miss Felliosi, has made you un-fairly more interested in this case?'

Then seemingly oblivious to the sudden rise in temperature that Stokes had now created, I now sensed Stewart's humiliation of Stokes hadn't finished just yet. And sure enough he'd pointed towards me, saying.

'Fortunately that is correct, on hearing of the arrest with you controlling the case Sergeant. Now without Miss Felliosi asking herself some important questions, that you all should have been asking yourselves in order to finally come up with some correct answers, which she has to save your bacon, you might now have all been entered into the Metro Police's high jump competition, and might well have all been demoted down to the rank and file.

And you Sergeant Stokes, without any shadow of doubt, would have failed at any height, and been stripped of your stripes . . . am I right, or am I right?'

'You are right Sir,' some of detectives had answered.

❖ 367 ❖

Stewart nodded and said 'Ok . . . so now I have a small confession to make, which may come as a surprise to some of you, and has only come about because of Miss Felliosi being a friend, as Stokes has mentioned, having been put through the most disturbing and compromising of all situations—that of being thought of as suspect number as a murderess. At least according to someone, (some laughter) she felt that she had better do something about it, so by using her own initiative, she had to get herself out of the mess that she had actually put herself into in the first place by being a silly, and nosy woman, she had to save her own bacon, asked for my help as a friend, which I'd willingly gave of course, as I'm sure that each and every one of you men, would have no doubt done the same—eh lads!' Then he winked.

I noticed all the men in the room actually did smile or nod their heads, after doing that wink, and everyone, besides Stokes, had suddenly looked more relaxed. So with the detectives and Stewart looking at me, I blushed.

'Now it was Miss Felliosi who found a cigarette stub in the fireplace. It was also she who'd puzzled over the scuff marks and asked me to take samples of it from the floor in each of the offices. It was she who had even suggested that the cigarette butts and the pistachio nutshells could have been left by the same person. And it was she who came up with Brassy, so we're now assuming it could be Dubois, or at least someone else who has similar habits, who must now be our No1 murder suspect.

And all of that I might add, had come about from someone thinking to only save her own neck—from the possible noose!'

He paused for a moment. 'Now my part in all of this is, as Miss Felliosi will verify, was that I found the rugs in Rugs and Tings, looked highly dubious. In fact some of you may have noticed what appeared to be a small amount of dried powder in the corner of some of them. So having taken a sample of the powder, heh bingo, it proved to be heroin. So that was a big result you might say . . . and all because of her asking for my help!'

THE LADY DETECTIVE

Having then taken over centre-stage, I continued. 'Now from all the samples you also sent in Stewart, came another big result, for the brown scuff marks both in here and next door were analysed as being from the same boot-polish, and they'd been almost identical, except for one big difference, and that difference was that traces of both office carpets had been found on one of the heels of only one of the socks. Which then made it a puzzle of course, yet another clue as to what I am about to show you.

Now had you asked yourselves how come that there wasn't any blood stains on either of the carpets in both offices, or in the hallway, and then considered that the dead man had been found with his head almost entirely unrecognisable as a face, having been bashed in you might say, what was then your conclusion, detective Jones?'.

Jones having thought long and hard over the question, answered. 'Obviously it proves that the man had not been dragged or lifted from one office to the other, without something over his head. Yet the evidence now shows that the man had somehow been dragged from here to there, with those brown marks heading towards and from this fireplace, and the socks.'

'Correct in both details.'

He then pointed to Rugs and Tings, and shook his head. 'Then that bodes another question of how could that be? Which I certainly haven't an answer for . . . unless the wall opens up like some kind of Aladdin cave!' He thought for a moment, 'do you know what Miss Felliosi, we, that is Williams and myself, did previously think along those lines, but when we searched for a lever, switch, button, we couldn't find one, could we Frank?'

The older policeman shook his head before saying, 'No, though it was Jones who thought of that, and not me.'

'Well, well, so close, yet so far!' I said interrupting their self-praising.

◆ 369 ◆

'In fact you were both correct in thinking the dead man had been dragged from next door into here . . . and it would have been through this fireplace!

You would also have been correct in thinking there'd been a secret switch to open up the wall, or in this instance, the fireplace. So again well done, though shame on you that you gave up on that idea, otherwise very commendable!

With all eyes now turned on me, I was to put it bluntly, in my element, for I was now beginning to really enjoy being put into this Miss Marple/Poirot summing up situation, and pointing to the fireplace I said.

Ok, has anyone any questions?' I asked looking around me. 'No, then I will now continue to explain how I solved the mystery of how the murder was achieved, that all but two of you had found so difficult to fathom. Isn't that so?'

Some of the detectives answered 'Yes', with Stokes saying 'I expect so.'

'Now I'm assuming that you all noticed those marks before the fireplaces in here and next door, and noticed the direction the marks were going as well, and even some of you would have noticed that the end, and the beginning of the marks next door, when facing the fireplace, there was a sort of squiggly circle, and the rest going in a straight line to or from the fireplace, as you were. I would like you to look at those circle marks, because they were my clues that the man had been pulled thru the fireplace in Rugs and Tings.'

I paused for breath and to take in their expressions, and continued. 'In my opinion, I thought he'd been hit on the head, and when he crumpled back to his assailant, had then been turned around, hence the round marks made by his shoe heels, and holding him from under the arm pits, facing up to the killer, was then dragged completely into the fireplace, somehow losing one shoe, according to the socks, and then the killer, maybe with a cloth under the head, had literally smashed his face to pulp, hence there'd been no blood on the carpet.

THE LADY DETECTIVE

Then allowing for the blood to stop flowing, the killer had finally dragged him thru the fireplace into here, minus two shoes now, according to the socks, where he'd again turned the victim over again, hence there being a second round mark, though less deep, made by his heels in the socks this time.'

I paused again for breath and to take in their puzzled expressions, and continued. 'So ok, the killer must have removed both shoes, why I don't know, and then afterwards, now with only socks on, placed him as the chalk outline of the body shows, looking to the fireplace, and not out to the room.

'So why do you think the killer turn the body completely around again, to face the way he came?' asked Williams.

'Well I think that was purposely done so we'd all think he'd been hit from behind in here as he looked towards the fireplace this side, whereas he'd actually been hit from behind as he faced towards the fireplace on the other side.

I mean, would you have questioned had his body faced away from the fireplace and towards the room. Probably! You may have wondered how had he been surprised to be hit face on, so the killer had to confuse the police into wondering how the murder have been done, left him where there'd not been enough room to swing whatever it was. So my thoughts were the body had been left this way to confuse.

In other words the killer, a most clever, shrewd, and cunning killer you might say, had deliberately set out *to* confuse us, cos he could have left the body next door, instead of which, he had pulled it into this room, and even turned the body completely around, after coming thru the fireplace, just as he had intended.

I paused again, looked at the faces who were imagining the body being dragged into here face up, turned around and over, and finally left face down after the murderer had maneuvered the body into the position he'd wanted it to be found.

'Ok, if there aren't any questions? No, then shall we all now go next door?' Obediently they all followed me.

❖ 371 ❖

Chapter 89

RUGS AND TINGS

Again before entering, Harry had given another fine display of how to really open a locked door by using a skeleton key, and I'd quickly continued with my summing up of the crime from where I'd left off next door.

'Oh, if I may divert your minds away from the body for a moment, to something that had first got me thinking about how the murder was done. So now who can tell me how it was possible for a heavy smoker *not* to have needed any ashtrays available in the room?'

There'd been no answers. So I continued. 'Ok, then who can tell me why had there'd been ashtrays in here for a non-smoker? With two being found in here, Rugs and Tings, on the mantle-piece; so the logical answer that I came up with for both situations, was, what if this fireplace in here actually belonged next door?

I mean that would then give me the answers to all of my questions on how the murderer had made it look like an almost impossible murder to prove, re the body being in the wrong office etcetera.'

THE LADY DETECTIVE

And now I could now see new signs of interest among the detectives.

'So once you suspected that the fireplace held the answer, you then thought about how it had opened, or turned around, to leave an opening, like a secret door—yes?' questioned Jones.

'Yes, that's exactly what I thought Jones. So now all you now have to do, is to find the secret switch that you said you looked for. So for a few minutes, shall we all do just that, let us all look for the secret switch shall we?'

When they had all set to work, with me acting like I was a team leader, and with Stewart, really enjoying watching them all searching for the secret switch, until after ten minutes of trying, all but one had given up, their all saying that 'it was impossible to find.' So I had with a smile said. 'Ok, I'll now show you.'

Going to the fireplace wall, I looked for, and found, the slightly odd piece of carpet, and had stood on it thinking that would activate the switch to open the fire-place. 'It's here' I said stamping down on it, and nothing happened, so I stamped down even harder, and still nothing happened.

Now it was my turn to feel a fool, and as I felt my cheeks beginning to burn, being suitably puzzled, I called to a smiling Stokes to come over to me. 'Sergeant would you mind placing your foot just here,' I said pointing to the spot.

He did so, and immediately the fireplace began to make a whirling sound as it began to turn itself in a clockwork direction, just as it had done the previously day for me and Stewart.

With a small 'yes' to myself, I could now see into the office of Byways Ltd through the opening, just as my guests were now doing.

Jones appeared to be the most excited of them all, saying. 'Brilliant, absolutely brilliant,' in his lovely accent, and pausing said, 'or as they say in parts of the Rhonda, 'Well I be nevered, who'd have thought it eh?'

❦ 373 ❦

DI Harry Stockton, with a nod of his head towards the fireplace, said. 'Now that's clever. That is very clever indeed. I am impressed you having to find it and solve this mystery all by yourself, then I will say that congratulations are in order.'

'Thank you.' I said, not sure whether "all by yourself" had meant because I'd been a woman, but chose not to think on it, when the detectives had begun to look at me and the fireplace with awe and astonishment.

'Well, well, well!' I heard one of them saying, obviously astonished at seeing a real fireplace opening up as if by magic, and exposing the room next door! And others had begun to murmur their congratulations.

'Well I did need the help of DCI Ross,' I said, with a smile towards him, 'because this switch was obviously meant to work for people above a certain weight to have stood on it, meaning people a lot heavier than I am,' and looking towards Stokes, got a small titter from the female Detective, who then added.

'It has probably a counter-weight of some sort that can be adjusted when needs be, to different weights!' She murmured.

Jones uttered. 'Now that is brilliant, truly brilliant Golightly, you working that out all by yourself.' He looked at me. 'I have a question, how do you close it Miss Felliosi?'

Was he being a cheeky sod, I thought not. So I went to where the second switch and showed them. Then was saying, 'Right, as we are focusing on the fireplace, with the way the victim had his head beaten in with such considerable force and rage, and yet no blood stains were evident, that also made me wonder how that could be. So I figured that the murderer must have done that, sometime *after* he had murdered him, and cold-bloodedly used some weapon, and covering over his head with a cloth or something, had done it in the fireplace, making sure he only used the tiled space in between both of the fireplaces, whilst he'd been bashing in his face—gruesome to say the least!'

I continued. 'Though I suspect there'd been another reason why he'd battered Mr Happy in the fireplace itself,

THE LADY DETECTIVE

was to also confuse the police with no blood . . . because you'll find evidence of that in between the tiles, which the killer has attempted to clean up, but couldn't completely.'

'So all this was a game to the killer, you think?' said DI Stockton.

'The killing . . . not at all. However with the body facing towards the fireplace in there, with his head smashed in, the killer would not have considered that position as being normal, even considering there'd not been enough, or very little room, to swing the killing instrument to kill him had he faced towards the fireplace, to warrant the damage to the face, so yes, that was very cunning, and meant as a game.'

I continued. 'So it was in here, Rugs and Tings, where the murder was done, and not next door, and with his placing the body as he did, it would never have got you guys thinking, no slur intended, of the murder being accomplished anywhere else, although some among you, had thought of that possibility—but failed to understand the fireplaces secret.'

Having known they would all have wanted to walk back and forth through the opening like a bunch of school children playing a game, I had needed to tell them not to, 'until samples of the blood on the tiles were taken, as we still didn't know for sure, who the victim had been.'

I continued summing up. 'Incidentally, my thoughts had also been that the killer had maybe wanted the murder scene to be a kind of smoke screen in order to make you think of it as being a straight forward killing—in there,' I pointed towards Byways. I continued, 'by why that was, I have no idea!

And finally, the killer must have then come back thru the fireplace to this side again, after he'd placed the body so-so, and then left by this office, not needing to lock it, or even re-lock the door next door . . . as I found out to my cost,' I laughed looking to Stokes 'so again fortunate for the real murderer.'

I heard murmurs of approval, 'Oh, and maybe he hadn't noticed, or hadn't cared, that he'd left the light on in Byways, or the body being found much sooner than I believe, he'd even anticipated.'

'Do you think the murder was planned?' asked Williams.

'Yes I do.'

'Why is that? Was it because of the office light being left on? Did you think the killer had arrived at dawn for instance, when the light would have been a dull grey?' Williams asked.

'Well it's a theory of course, without specifically knowing the victim's time of death. Besides he could have switched on the light with no worries, being he was a partner.' I said.

'Frank, are you saying because the light had been left on, that the killer may have been waiting from early in the morning to complete the deed,' said another detective.

'And with it then being daylight, to leave the scene after killing, hadn't then anticipated seeing there'd be any people around the hallway, with you working on your office, so had not been able to walk away quietly un-noticed,' suggested the woman detective.

"Yes, all that also probable! Though I did think whilst extending o that idea, that maybe the killer hadn't known that I'd been working on my offices that weekend, and having previously killed the victim on Saturday or Friday, had for obvious reasons, needed to make those face changes particularly, and then thought to re-arrange the body to complete his deception, and had come up with the brilliant idea of acting the part of two men on the Sunday, and had walked past me looking like Al Capone; and making me think it had been the owner of Rugs and Tings I'd spoken to, by his telling me that.'

I thought for a moment then said. 'What had been so clever about that act, was that he'd been a wonderful jovial flirtatious un-seen face wise American/Canadian, with his phony accent, and brilliant clothes choice, and in the next hour or so, had changed his whole attitude and physical look, with a limp and grumpiness, when he left the building.'

'So you were fooled?' Asked DI Stockton.

THE LADY DETECTIVE

'Not completely, although I still can't grasp why he had to go through this marvellous charade of events when he really had no need to—that is still baffling me.'

'You meaning, had he previously killed Brassy, why should he need to come back here when he really hadn't needed to?' The young woman detective said. Then asked, 'and the other man, the dead man, when did he arrive?'

'Good question. I've thought about that as well, and can only assume that the killer, or the murdered man, and we can't confirm which one it was, had sneaked past the reception office when they weren't paying attention. I mean the murderer, as the owner of Rugs and Tings would have been recognised by reception, though could have fooled me, and anyone else who might have seen him walking in or out of the building with the same coat and hat on, and I might have also given him the benefit of doubt had it not been for his wearing black shoes making me wonder why that was.'

'Meaning what?'

'Meaning I might have still thought of him as being that same jovial man by his wearing the same clothes, yet I was concerned over his changing his shoes from brown to black ones, which had completely intrigued me, as DCI Ross can vouch for! (My meaning that party-night on Sunday, when my incoherent mumbling about them, had everyone in stitches of laughter, and me wondering why)

I continued, 'which I will now assume may never be found, because he'd have walked away with the brown ones in his pocket, and most likely have thrown both pairs in a bin somewhere.'

I looked around at the detective's faces and still saw slight confusion on some faces, and could hardly blame them, for I too, was finding the murderers motives difficult to understand, and un-orthodox to say the least!

I was about to tell them all as modestly as I could, that all this intrigue on the Sunday might or might not only have been to deceive the police, or me, when Stewart had looked at his watch saying.

❧ 377 ❧

"That was marvellous Jess, however I'm expecting a phone call in your office in half-hour Jess, and I still would like o tell you all a little about drugs. Will that be ok?'

I nodded somewhat reluctantly, as I was enjoying being the centre of attention.

*   *   *

In a very quiet voice he began to say.

'Now for some of you who don't know anything about how this drug's thing works, so I'm going to tell you what I know, due to what might be happening later on. I might take a few minutes, but I feel you all could benefit from the knowledge, so be patient.'

A groan was heard from the detectives, and Stewart had smiled and nodded. 'Ok, listen up. Now these rugs you are now looking at,' pointing to the one's on display, 'have travelled many miles overland in airtight containers, and have, un-fortunately for us, finished up here in England, having previously left, as you might have guessed, the docklands and security of France—where else eh?' Some laughter followed.

He continued. 'Now Customs have been aware, having been previously informed, that there were drugs coming in from Afghanistan, via Turkey. Though I must inform you, that besides drugs coming into the country from these two countries, there'd also been Burma supplying, and the Golden Triangle, which is along the Chino-Burmese borders near Laos, who are now reported to be, at this moment, the second biggest drug supplier in the world, and all because the CIA had seen in their wisdom, to support anti-communist Chinese Nationalists, which in fact, helped the development of the Golden Triangle, as it's called. Ok so far?'

We all nodded.

'So then because of the on-going Soviet and Afghanistan problems, again with America's involvement, that again had helped the growth of the Golden Triangle, and increased the production of opium on the Pakistani-Afghan border. They was done mainly to buy or sell arms in exchange for these drugs.

So now this second largest supplier of drugs nationally, next to Afghanistan itself, especially after they'd begun trading with the Mafia in Sicily, who have now shifted to them as a supplier, due mostly to demand, and because the various criminal Mafia organizations in Italy, had been fighting violently with each other over the heroine trade.'

He looked at our faces. 'So there you have it, my simple run down of the suppliers of opium and heroin trade, as we know it today.'

He smiled, 'though that's not the end of it, because now I'll try to quickly explain how heroine is made into different products, with of course its derivatives.'

He paused for a moment. 'For example, these rugs that you see, have had their pure wool immersed into heavily impregnated water, with the heroine powder, prior to their being exported. Now this heroine will become refined to an opium or crude opium, once it's been isolated from its morphine content.

Ok, so having carefully dissolved this crude opium in hot water, it now has lime added, so impurities that it has, such as slithers of wood etcetera, are its washed and filtered again, those impurities are discarded. Ok so far? So now it has chloride added; ammonium chloride, that will now make it into a crude morphine.'

He looked at his black book, and continued, 'now something called acetic anhydride, whatever that is, is added, and then they are all heated together for I believe six to seven hours, and at a temperature around 85C, allowed to cool, before its finally diluted again with pure water, to make it an alkaline.'

He paused before continuing. 'Everyone ok so far? Stokes?' Some had nodded. 'Right, so that means I haven't lost any of you in not understanding what I have said so far—yes? Though I can stop here if it bores you.' No-one says anything!

Stewart had then taken out his little black book again, opens it, and with 'Ah yes', then continued. 'Now this alkaline has sodium carbonate added, which then becomes a crude heroine when mixed with hydrochloride salt. And this is again filtered and washed.'

He paused. 'Now here is where this very long process becomes much more interesting for at least those people who are using it. Why? Because this crude water-based soluble, has now become a white, or yellowish powder, known as opium, or crude opium, and is now usable for smoking—like a cigarette.'

He then stops again and asks, 'I've noticed some of you are looking a bit puzzled, maybe too many funny names to remember—so shall I go on?'

Someone said 'Go on sir.' And Williams with a grin said. 'It does all seem to be an awful lot like hard work, sir.' Stewart smiled and nodded, then continued.

'I agree, yet it doesn't finish there, cos this powder can be further processed and then purified further using hot alcohol, charcoal, and filtrates, which you have to dilute with ether and other things, to become heroine, or China White as it is known, or No 4, or even a No 3, which in appearance looks browner, having had a small amount of caffeine added to it to help it vaporize more quickly.'

He took in a deep breath before saying. 'So there you have it, guys and girls, these forms are the most commonly used in Europe, although No 4 is the least used, and to complicate matters further, you can get black tar in this country, that is mainly used in the US of A, and produced in Mexico. I should say, by substituting fertilizers for pure chemicals in the initial stages of making opium, this has made the refining process relatively easy for the less scrupulous criminal to make, so they say!

I should also add if any of you are thinking to try doing it, that in the latter stages, when a large amount of chemicals

THE LADY DETECTIVE

and solvents are used, this process does require extreme skill and patience, and as for removing the highly inflammable ether, well one mistake and if it ignites you can say hello to your maker.

Harry added. 'It does appear to be from the start to the finish, a very slow process, and very hard work, as Williams has said, but to make the best, the purest drugs, however long the process takes, is I can assure you, worth all the trouble, for the enormous money it earns.'

Chapter 90

THE RAID

Stewart then suggested we wound this up, and all get back to my office to receive the phone-call he was expecting. So we did.

In my office, when my phone had rung, Pasha having answered it, had then passed it on to Stewart, who'd began to excitedly talk to the person on the other end of the line.

'Yes . . . yes this is DCI Ross speaking.' And then had listened to whatever was being said by the other person, until he began to grunt excitedly.

'Yes, Yes, I understand all that,' and 'Yes, all that is perfectly understood, thank you. What's that? Yes, we'll get down there as soon as we can. Oh, I should say in approximately twenty-five minutes. Bye!'

He then phoned someone named Sergeant Haynes, telling him 'it was a go', and then gave him a description of a lorry, its reg number, and which dock the boat was berthing at. And finished by saying, 'Ok, send a couple of cars with eight men down to the docks immediately, and I'll see you soon as.' And then put down the phone after saying 'Good-bye.'

❦ 382 ❦

THE LADY DETECTIVE

He put the phone back into its cradle, and with enthusiasm said to us all. 'Righto ladies and gentlemen, now it's time for us to all go and catch ourselves some real villains.'

When I asked him who it was who had phoned him, he replied. 'That was Customs & Excise informing me that a boat with a consignment of goods for Byways Ltd, was due to berth quite soon at South docks to be unloaded.'

So now it would appear that whatever I thought was going to happen re this drug consignment, appears to be happening.'

He turned to DI Stockton. 'Harry and you have just heard, I told Haynes to get up to speed, and send men to the South docks, as then be on alert until further instructions, and here's the details that the C&E gave me.

And now people, we will need to also get ourselves moving down to the docks as well, so those of you who would like to see a bit of action, you had better follow me.'

CHAPTER 91

Pasha, who'd previously been preparing to go home, was startled to see a whole load of people suddenly rush into the reception, and then I noted, it was 17.34 pm on my watch when we'd all rushed out again after Stewart had received the phone call, and we all heard him say a few words to whoever he was talking to, before she heard little ol' me shouting towards her as we had again all hurried past her. 'Sorry Pasha, can't stop, we've got a boat to catch that's about to dock.'

And as I left the office, I hurriedly added, 'so I'll leave you to lock up for the night if that's all right with you, ok? Goodnight.'

I had then waved to her, and had half running, half walking, continued down the hallway to the crowded lift, catching up an already panting and puffing Stokes, before realising that Pasha wouldn't have had a clue what I'd been talking about with my mentioning a boat, for I hadn't told her anything about the drugs or anything like that, all hush, hush you see, and in the lift I'd begun to laugh after having remembered her puzzled face.

It was there that I saw a sign saying it would take a maximum of five people at any one time. And as I had counted we were six, with three people actually preferring to run down the stairs, I'd kept my fingers tightly crossed during the downward trip to the bottom, having known that

THE LADY DETECTIVE

Stokes had been the last person to force his massive bulk into the lift.

In fact we had been seven people, when smelly Stokes had wedged himself in between me and the steel gate, before one man, who I now know as DC Blacksmith, had hastily got out, and gave Stokes a look that said it all, before saying. 'It'll be a lot safer using the stairs that being in here with you, fat man!'

On reaching the ground floor, we'd all hurried past Sydney, the startled receptionist, and out onto the street, when Stewart had yelled back to the detectives who were now all bunching together on the pavement. 'Get to your cars, and follow me.'

'I'm coming with you' I said, jumping into the backseat of Stewart's car, to sit alongside DI Harry Stockton. Stewart having previously been sensible to have requested his driver to park right outside the building, and wait for him.

Stewart had nodded ok with a smile. Then seeing the fat man looking wildly around him in every direction, having been left behind by his faster moving colleagues, who'd now rushed off to retrieve their cars, before returning here to follow Stewart to the docks—Stewart had called out the window.

'Ah Sergeant, whose car are you in?' Then Stewart, not waiting for an answer said, 'never mind standing around man, just hurry up and get into anyone's car, will you.'

Poor Stokes, I saw was now as harassed as he'd been in the offices, and I could see he was now fervently hoping that DCI Ross, would take a running jump over a cliff—or worse, and then hoping that one of the other detectives would give him a lift to wherever, now that DC. Blacksmith, who I now understood to be a very good man to have on your side when the going gets tough, had been upset by him on the way down here to see me.

It appears that the fat man had refused him time off that Saturday coming, so he could attend his favourite cousins wedding and reception. The Sergeant having told him: 'You must be bloody joking aren't you Blacky? Surely you've had

❦ 385 ❦

enough time before now, to arrange time off to go to any shot-gun bloody wedding! And now with our having to solve this ruddy murder; it's more important than you going to a wedding. So the answer is no.'

Not knowing of this ill-feeling, Stewart had in the meantime been saying loudly, so we could hear him over the engine. 'That dressing down I gave him,' meaning Stokes, 'will hopefully teach him not to be so ruddy work sloppy in the future . . . if he has one.'

And having still seen the fat man panting on the pavement, then added 'And perhaps I should have also mentioned for him to have gone on a diet.'

"And to see to his BO" I thought. Oh nasty me!

CHAPTER 92

S oon after, we were driving down crowded streets in a four vehicle procession, all heading in the direction of London South docks, from my place in the West End, and driving at a fairly high speed of fifty to sixty miles an hour, with all or car bells ringing loudly, to tell people, and other cars, that we were coming, and for them to get out of the way, as this was, and we were, important.

Then a message had come over the intercom soon after leaving to head for Trafalgar Square, from a Customs & Excise man, telling Stewart that the boat was about to dock in approximately five minutes, and was told that the consignment was to be off-loaded onto a waiting lorry with a XPB126B number plate, which after checking, Stewart had been told were false number plates.

Stewart then told C & E, 'that we are on the way with extra police,' and to 'continue letting me know what is happening.'

A further five minutes had passed, before the C & E man, who had a high-pitched voice, told Stewart that the boat had now docked, and preparations were now being made to transfer the crate on to the lorry, and said that the manifesto had it down as rugs for Byways Ltd, and that he would as instructed, now delay the lorry for a reasonable time, by doing a 'slow' search before it left the docks.

❖ 387 ❖

Stewart had told the man off for not giving them an earlier warning of the docking, then asked the man. 'What back-up was there in place that the C & E were supplying?' And been told that when the lorry leaves the docks, it would be accompanied by three Customs & Excise men in one black Ford Zephyr, and a further two undercover NDS Police cars who had just arrived, meaning a total of eleven men would be following the lorry, plus us of course!.

Stewart had now been given a secure line, and had told the eight detectives travelling behind us, all the latest news about the boat arriving, and others were now in place and on full alert.

A few more minutes of tense silence had passed, before the car's intercom again burst into life as we headed past Trafalgar Square to the London Embankment, with the line crackling like a number of fire crackers being let off. Then a new caller told us, his voice sounding as if it had been put through a clothes mangle, that he would now be the one giving Stewart 'any further news as it occurred.' And informed Stewart minutes later, that the lorry would soon be departing from the docks, and to stand by.

With Stewart now drumming his fingers on the dashboard and humming the theme tune from 'Bridge on the River Kwai', as a further five minutes had gone by, before 'Mangle voice' told us that the lorry was now leaving the docks, and heading towards Rotherhithe tunnel.

Minutes later, he told us the lorry was heading towards Mile End, or Commercial Road on the A13 and now onto Commercial Street, and then onto the A10, and for us to head in that general direction, which was obvious, and he'd continue to inform us as to the lorry's progress.

With a great deal of beeping of car horns and bells jangling, all our cars had at high speed, all headed towards the Bethnal Green area, before being told that the lorry had now gone onto the A10, and was heading towards Tottenham.

By now I felt as if I should have been biting my finger nails, something I hadn't done since I'd been a young girl of

THE LADY DETECTIVE

12 or 13 years old, but would have found that impossible, as I'd been hanging on for dear life onto the passenger strap-handle all the time, whilst the driver had sped onwards, as if he were driving in some god-dam motor rally, with me enjoying the thrill of it all.

A further three more minutes had gone by, and still no further news had come thru on the intercom. 'Where are they?' enquired a calm Stewart to no-one in particular, and then as if by magic, had been informed by Mangle Voice. 'Now they've gone through Tottenham, and heading towards the North Circular.'

'We're not that far behind them, sir,' said Bert, our highly skilled 'Special Squad' police driver, so if I cut across to the north of the A10, I'll get nearer them much quicker.' More nail biting minutes had gone by before Mangle Voice had said amidst a lot of screeching noises made by the inter-com. 'They've turned off the A10, and now on the A406 to Palmers Green and Broomfield Par, over.'

Then another minute passed before he said. 'Hello, hello, hello, now they've turned off at Junction 6, and are on the A1004 to Southgate, hold it, now they've gone over the bridge into Kings Road and Sterte Avenue.'

And a minute later said. 'They've now gone onto the Purbeck Industrial Estate. Hold on . . . they've pulled up outside a warehouse that's got 'Bridges Transport' in large faded red letters on its fascia.

'Bridges Transport!' Exclaimed Stewart with a growl. 'Well they won't be crossing them for quite some time, (meaning bridges) if this goes down as well as I hope it does!'

Bert told us. 'Ok, we're about three or four minutes away from Junction 6, and the Purbeck Industrial Estate, sir.'

And then after some more extremely fast driving, and luckily not having had any traffic problems; we pulled off the A12, and onto the A11, when Stewart had then enquired over the tannoy.

'Sgt Haynes, is everyone now on site, and in place?' He'd then received an 'affirmative' from his team leader.

❧ 389 ❧

At last our driver Bert told us, after he'd driven like a bat out of hell since we left my offices. 'That sign means we're now only a minute away from the Estate, sir.' And then asked, 'shall I turn off the bells?' and having been told 'yes', then had by intercom, informed all four detectives cars that were following, to do the same.

Stewart, was now looking in complete control of himself had then spoken on the special line to Sergeant Haynes, who said 'everything was in place at the business park.' Adding 'all exits had been closed, and no-one, and that includes any person or vehicles, are being allowed to leave or enter the Estate, whoever they were.'

I had previously been told that Haynes was an ex-commando, and was 'a tough, no shit, no nonsense, kind of character', and Stewart had told by him, 'I should be with you in approximately two—three minute's—tops.'

I could barely contain my excitement, and at one point during those minutes, had even urged Bert to drive faster. He'd just grinned.

Stewart now turned around to Harry saying, 'Well Harry, here we go, so best of luck.'

And then looking directly at me, he said. 'If this comes off, and it's as big a drug bust as I hope it'll be, then we'll all soon be part of being involved in the biggest haul of illegal drugs to have ever entered into this country of ours judging by the weight om the manifesto. And soon, very soon, we'll have hopefully cracked wide open, the biggest drug smuggling gang to have ever been known in England.'

He gripped my hand saying, 'And a great deal of this is down to you Jess, for being such a ruddy nosy blighter.'

'Yea good for your nose, Jess,' grinned Harry. Cheeky sods.

Seconds later, we'd finally arrived at the Estate, and going over the bridge, Stewart had got Bert to stop out of sight of the warehouse, and then been immediately greeted by a thick-set, strong looking man, who I pre-supposed to have been Sergeant Haynes.

THE LADY DETECTIVE

Having had a brief discussion with both Stockton and Haynes, Stewart had given further instructions by intercom to the Customs men, having known that some of his Elite Drugs force, had been up to this time, deployed in keeping vehicles, or people, from leaving or going into the Estate, and was now saying 'that Stokes' detectives, and the Customs men were to take over their positions,' which they did, 'whilst everyone else,' which meant all the armed police, were told 'to move in on the warehouse in three minutes—from now.'

CHAPTER 93

The Nods, Stewart's men, would as part of an elite armed Police Force could instantly be deployed to any potentially violent situations, always drug related, and had all been given, if required, a license to kill. These men had also been equipped with protective body armour and the latest weaponry.

However this particular new elite force, was the first, and under the direction of Stewart, and would be after this raid, not onlt called the National Drug Squad, his little baby, but also be known at the Nasty Drug Squad, or Nods.

Some weeks later I'd be informed that this special elite force, the newly formed Nods, had been the brain child of Stewart, yet Stewart hadn't blown his own trumpet about this, and hadn't even told me that this was his idea. I must be losing my allure!

Three minutes later, the raid on the warehouse had begun, and from where I'd been standing, I saw lots of people running here and there. There'd also been a fair amount of swearing, and people shouting at people I couldn't see. Certainly tough measures had been employed, having heard guns being fired, and shouts of 'Get yourselves down on the ground—now!' by the NDS men, the best being—'Get those bloody hands up in the bloody air, and grasp clouds, now', and 'Spread those bloody legs wider you bastard son of a bitch . . . now!'

As I had been watching all this going on, I'd seen an armed man jumping out of a rear warehouse window, and I'd time to pass that knowledge on to an armed policeman near me, before the man having run towards us, had spotted us, and begun firing his gun towards me, when he'd stumbled and fell with his gun flying thru the air and out of his reach, and been quickly set upon by two husky looking Nods in combat uniforms, frisked, and dragged unceremoniously to a waiting vehicle that had been reserved for any captured villains. They would after a court hearing, be sent to a prison for a very long sentence.

During the time the raid had lasted, it had all been very exciting for me to have witnessed, until finally, ten minutes or so after Stewart's men had first been ordered to move in, most members of the gang had been arrested and thrown into one of two of the meat wagons.

It was then the NDS had come across a reinforced shell of what had once been a thirty foot boat, this had all of its windows and entrances reinforced with steel.

A NDS police officer then had quietly told me, 'Now we've come to the 'difficult' part of the raid. This will not be an easy job to crack open,' Which had been obvious, then adding 'so probably the Guvnor, (meaning Stewart) will have to employ extreme measures to gain entry and get whoever has locked themselves in there, out of there. So you might not want to see this, cos it could be gruesome!' He'd then given me a big grin to tell me he'd been teasing me!

He actually meant, that for some, to break into 'fortress' would be the hardest part of the raid, and for others, like myself, quite exciting minutes of the raid.

But get them out they did. Having first tried for twenty-five minutes, to bash open the steel doors, and using other methods, unsuccessfully, until Stewart had finally told his men to use the gangsters own lorry to push the boat around for a bit, and having done that a number of times, and still no joy, had then ordered for it to be rolled over, and probably more than was necessary, had them doing that a few times, until the men inside had called a truce by opening a door, and Dubois and the remaining three men of his gang, had then shown their cut and bruised faces to be arrested. They'd quickly been given their rights, photographed, and again quickly taken away, separately, to Cannon Row Police Station.

On Stewart's instructions, all the other gang members, having initially been taken away in the meat wagons, would later be separated, and sent to different local police stations for questioning. The thought behind this, was that the prisoners had no chance on conferring with each other, for various reasons.

Still on site, Stewart had his men quickly look through the boat for any evidence. 'The thing is,' DI Stockton told me, 'they (meaning Dubois or his management) might have been stupid enough to leave some details of other gang members, warehouses, contacts, or the guys names who'd finance all of this, putting this in a safe or something. You never know.'

After that, Stewart had instructed for the villain's lorry and the 'boat', to both be taken to a special Police pound to be kept safe; and allow forensics to do their work.

Harry hadn't guessed correctly, cos after Stewart had everyone searching the warehouse premises to look for further evidence, knowing he'd done this more in hope, for he knew there'd be little chance of finding anything incriminating. And so it proved his thoughts were correct, for the warehouse had been emptied of any evidence.

He would also later find that all the other warehouses owned by Dubois, and his dead partner, had also been cleaned out, and been clean as a whistle of any other incriminating evidence.

At these police stations, the villains had all been asked questions by the interrogation team about what they knew, or "Who was backing Dubois," and "where are the other contacts, warehouses, and whose running them." They had been threatened with all manner of punishments, all legit of course, and the questioners had quickly found out who'd been the money-men involved in fronting up the money for the purchasing of the drugs, who'd been looking for a quick return on their money, with no questions being asked, and been told of other warehouses, contacts, and who was running them—no honour amongst thieves comes to mind.

Although with the other warehouses being 'clean', I did ask Stewart had he thought that maybe the other gang members had perhaps been pre-warned, or even tipped off from someone on the inside, meaning the cops, or Customs, and he thought that was possible, but un-likely, but never-the-less would certainly be looking into it!

He thought it most likely that precautionary measures had been taken by the gang after hearing of the murder of one of their bosses; for it had been fully reported on in the Nationals, and been on the News, about the mysterious death of a man being found on another man's office, which Stewart had said 'was a big mistake' and in the future, 'any details that had to do with any drug cases, would not be spoken of until I want that kind of information to be released to the media.'

CHAPTER 94

Once the gang had been taken away, all Stokes' detectives, including myself, were taken into the warehouse, and been shown five massive washing machines that had been found on site, each one neatly tucked into its own separate cubicle, and each one having a pile of wet or damp rugs stacked in piles at the side of the machines, and many more dry ones that were still to be 'washed in front of them.

These rugs were of a slightly different quality to those I'd seen in Rugs and Tings. For a start they were much thicker, and their colours I thought were much brighter, having been probably made in different regions of Afghanistan, or somewhere else, say Turkey, who also made colourful rugs, before I'd again thought, "What a waste of a jolly fine rug to have had them filled with a load of white powder, washed, and then probably discarded as second-hand goods!'

I'd then noticed a pile of clay garden gnomes that may have accompanied the rugs to keep them company. The Police would later confirm that Customs & Excise had been given a short sharp lesson, of how it had been possible for the Dubois/ Brassy gang to have got away with 'smuggling' drugs into the Country for such a long time. By using such innocent looking items as these.

Later still, once the gnomes, and carpets had been cleaned of heroine, bagged and tagged, this raid had been confirmed

THE LADY DETECTIVE

to have been the biggest drug bust that the British Isles
had ever known, and that had afterwards left all manner of
people, mostly unjustified by some, who only craved for media
attention, congratulating each other with much back slapping
and hand-shaking.

Stewart had I admit, from what I had seen of him, been
nothing but thorough during this raid, almost like he'd been
placed under a spotlight, and even outshone it—and that I'd
been pleased to see!

Although once the criminals had been taken away, he had
in fact shown everyone his fun side, for he had afterwards
been acting with almost school boy pleasure over the success
of this raid, and had shown himself to get as excited as if he
had been given his first bicycle at Christmas, complete with
a stainless steel bell that he could ring, ring, and ring.

And now when he, and we, had barely calmed down,
he'd called for our silence, and said he ought to now quickly
explain to us detectives, the function of these special washing
machines stood before us, as we might never again see the
like.

Whilst he was looking very proud and pleased with life,
as he was entitled to be, considering what had been achieved
this day, he somehow had seemed to now look taller than
he normal did, my being excited maybe, until I noticed, cos
everybody had started to use them, he'd been wearing a pair
of new high heel shoe for men, that had a two inch heel, that
were now all the fashion. Oh come on you guys, men and high
heels. Whatever next?

In a very quiet voice he was saying. 'Now listen up. Now
these rugs are similar to the ones you saw in Rugs and Tings,
so have travelled many miles overland in airtight containers.
Now for those who remember how this drug's thing works
that I told you about; well now I'm going to tell you, now
with you all being together, how this works. It might take a
few minutes, but you'll benefit from the knowledge—I hope!'

'Can't we do this later, sir,' said one detective 'I'm
cream-crackered?'

❧ 397 ❧

Stewart only smiled. 'As I said, it'll on take a minute. Now our sources, as I've previously told you, had informed us that a container would be coming overland from Afghanistan, via Turkey, to France, which proved to be the case, according to the shipping documents, and having slipped through France's dock security, then finished up at our South docks. (Which had formerly been part of Surrey docks, which with others in the docklands, were to be filled in after being closed last year, and I heard were to probably have houses built upon them.)

'So now these rugs have arrived here to be 'cleaned', because we think that a liquefied heroine, mixed with water, has been mixed with the wool in one large vat at the suppliers end, and after the wool had been left to soak for some time, and then probably dried out in a heated kiln—something on the lines of how fish are smoked in an enclosed corrugated shed, so that when the rugs did eventually arrive in this country, all the gang this end will have to do, is to wash out the heroine from the rugs by putting them into these very large machines, and give them a thorough wash. Then the water and heroine mix will spurt out, and then finally be separated by using strong very fine filters that will catch the heroine before it's washed away down the plug hole.'

Stewart pointed to the two large stainless steel containers standing behind the washing machines, 'Then this liquid will then be put in those, and when the last of the water is evaporated, dried out, then he-ho presto, they are again left with the original drug once again in its powdered form again. Dam clever really, don't you think?'

I was amazed by how much effort, time and money had been needed to have gone into producing the finished powder product, albeit now in bulk, and could only utter. 'And if anyone sniffs around this warehouse, all they'll find is machines filled with rugs, or already 'cleaned' rugs, which to the unsuspecting eye would seem harmless enough, especially if they thought they'd walked into a dry-cleaning business!'

'That's right,' agreed Stewart.

'Now that's clever, although I suspect these rugs would have been 'cleaned' during the night hours, and because of that, as you pointed out, was another reason why some of the rugs look a little washed out—haha.' I said to make a joke and receiving some laughter.

'Like those in the office of Rugs and Tings,' added Williams, laughing.

Stewart continued. 'Which had been in my opinion, what I would call being very stupid. I mean to have already processed rugs in the office, probably to demonstrate to drug buyers how it was done, although all it has done was to alert us how those rugs with the drugs had come into the country. Although' he said, 'besides it all being really rather clever the way it was done, had they not done this, then this operation might have gone on undetected for a lot longer than it did, had it not been for the murder.'

He laughed, then added, 'no doubt all will be revealed at some stage in the future, why Mr Grumpy killed Mr Happy—those are the names you call them isn't it Jess?'

A little laughter, until a surprisingly pensive Stokes continued. 'Well regardless of the money, it still seems like a lot of hard work to do to earn your money. You know, with setting up heroin suppliers in Afghanistan, then finding different ways to get it into the country without arousing suspicion, arranging the transport, then paying off people to keep a blind eye, and finally to have the headache of distributing the stuff all over the country—even after you've washed the rugs!'

I must have not been the only one who thought he had a point, because a few people had nodded their agreement.

Harry Stockton had however knowingly said. 'A headache it might be you say! However I would have thought that once it's in the country, by careful organizing its distribution, and taking those risks, the amount of money they'd be getting out of it, the bosses, Dubois, would have said that it was all worthwhile!'

He continued, 'It might appear for some of you to be a very slow process from the start to the finish; however with it being very hard work, as someone said, to have made the best, and the purest drugs, I can assure you, money wise, it's worth all the trouble, however long the whole process takes.'

Stewart after looking at his watch, 'And that is why it's becoming so popular to do. Now with it being late, for those of you who I've accepted in the interrogation team, I'll now suggest you get a few hours kip, though I will start these interrogations with Dubois and his management, the rest can wait, for it won't do them any harm at all if they are left to ponder over their fate, if we were to start interrogating them from around 1 am.'

He laughed. 'And thereafter, be interviewed on and off every hour until we get the last of the info from them.'

Stewart had thought that to do early morning questioning, would be fun when the gang were tired, and have less resistance, because you never know, non-stop hour on hour off interviewing of Dubois and the lesser small fry, without their getting any sleep other than quick naps, would maybe get them to tell us about other territories and gang members, and other warehouses, much quicker than they would have.

Which was to be the case, because the villains did blab all they knew, and when other villains and distribution places/warehouses, had all been finally caught in his net, that would have put paid to Dubois and his gang, and got this case put to bed, so to speak.

Stewart, with me, then appeared to walk away before turning back again to face the detectives.

'Oh, and I suggest, once we've done with the interviewing, whenever that is, and obtained a full statement from each of the villains, and you have nicely written your account of these events tonight in your little note books, and statement,' he smiled, 'then tomorrow night, might I suggest, we all hobnail it down to the Cellar Bar, (Police off duty bar)

THE LADY DETECTIVE

where you'll meet up again with the lovely Miss Felliosi here, myself, Harry, and of course all the NDS lads, who I'm sure will be particularly keen to help you celebrate this splendid bust . . . no offense to the ladies present! So shall we meet at say at 7 pm tomorrow?'

He'd then taken my arm again, and begun to walk away from the detectives, before turning once again to them and saying.

'Oh, and might I also suggest that all the drinks are on me tomorrow night, not literally you understand, unless you of course disapprove of that idea?!'

'No of course not, sir,' was the unified answer.

CHAPTER 95

SATURDAY

After yesterday's marvellous and most exciting evening raid on the drugs warehouse, I'd gone back home after the raid, had a small meal, then managed only a few hours' sleep, having been excited by the day's events, which had been I suppose, more than most of the detectives would have had, including Stewart I imagine, with all the interviewing they had needed to do!

And then to-day, having been greeted by Pasha at 9am'ish, when I returned to my office, and had checked to see if there'd been any messages of importance of people wanting my services, and as there'd been none, other than a load of well-wishers who had phoned in to congratulate me on opening the business, and some wishing me good luck at the trial, I thought better late than never, don't they say!

Then for the next hour, I'd needed to explain to Pasha what all the excitement of yesterday had been all about. Though I hadn't elaborated on it too much, orders from Stewart, so I told her loosely all that had happened both before and after we met in here, and had afterwards busied myself around the office, before going out to lunch between

❖ 402 ❖

THE LADY DETECTIVE

1-2 pm with Pasha, and there I told her I was due to meet with all the detectives and the new NDS that night, so again it should be an exciting time.

And finally at 5 pm, I'd gone home, showered, changed my clothes, and then found myself heading towards Westminster again at 7pm, and within a few minutes of entering the Police Cellar bar, which had been in the basement cellar of Scotland Yard, been enjoying a celebratory drink with Stewart and the lads, in what you might have called, an already lively atmosphere.

Then Stewart gave me another reason to make me feel happy, when he told me that he was going to treat me to a slap up meal afterwards, and that Harry Stockton and his wife Sharon would be making up a foursome. That, I surmised, wouldn't be until say around 10 pm.

CHAPTER 96

In the Cellar Club bar, I'd again met up and been greeted by Stokes' detectives, and by members of the NDS elite force, and been introduced to Sharon, Harry's wife, who was a petite lively soul, and we had begun to enjoy the hospitality of Stewart's free bar.

During the next hour, I was to hear stories about how all the villains had after they'd been arrested, separated from each other, and then been locked up in the cells of various Police Stations within a radius of three miles around Westminster—and after some very serious cross-examining by some seriously hostile interviewers, after they'd been cross-examined a number of times at various times of the night, the police had got hold of some very useful information, before the prisoners had been allowed to smoke and have cups of tea.

This idea had been at the request of Stewart to avoid any complicity among the prisoners, which it would seem, had proven worthwhile doing, with the prisoners not being allowed to rest.

The use of these slightly dubious strong arm tactics, had been, shall I say, beneficial, as other warehouses had then come to light, belonging to Dubois or Brassy, and had been 'visited' during the night, and day, by some of these men here with us, and that had resulted in many more villains being arrested and taken away for questioning—which was now extending around the country, and still more information was being acted on.

Whatever methods the Nods had used, they seemed to have worked, and it had saved an awful lot of time, and tax payer's money, than using the softy-softly approach as advocated by the politicians!

And now those men, having said their piece, were now all nicely tucked up in bed, and will have been all staring at those horrid plain whitewashed walls, for maybe months, or years to come, and have to listen to other prisoners insane chattering, which unfortunately, I had been made to experience a sample of, during my one night's bed and breakfast experience of police hospitality; which had been quite enough to have completely put me off for life, from ever wanting to listen to that insane form of chatter again.

Though having heard of those prisoners 'mouthing off', it had crossed my mind, that this 'insane' behaviour, with its aggressive tendencies, should have been listened to as an ideal situation to be noted by psychologists, who could have then either offered them help in a form of a mental institution, or at least have had them sent far away from me as possible.

Now most of Stewart's Nods, other than those who were still interviewing those villains who had remained stumm, or had nothing to say, or been the newest bunch of the arrested, had left their mates to have had a glass or three with Stokes' detectives, who had also been having a glass or three of whatever free drinks was their tipple, so were now all beginning to relax and enjoy each other's company, when Stewart had un-fairly been asked by one of the detectives:

'How long had you known about that drugs consignment, sir?'

Stewart answered with a smile. 'Well detective, I'm not allowed the liberty of divulging that knowledge to you of course. However, with the goods and the gang now being safely under lock and key, I can tell you, I have known about this particular very large consignment coming into the country, I forget when, though on what date, or even where it was being delivered to, I hadn't been notified.'

What he also deliberately failed to mention, was his contact had informed him that the goods were to be delivered to an organization who he'd previously known had many subsidiaries throughout Great Britain—some small, some large, and that was why the aggressive interviewing, having desperately needed to know of their whereabouts in the Country of these outlets, and this had all come about after having got the names of Brassy-Wainwrights, and Dubois into the frame, then that had been the last piece of the puzzle he'd been looking for, as he had known it was being run from London, and they had also both lived in London.

So prior to all the raid's that had taken place, and knowing who was probably behind the organisation, he'd known the chances of the drugs being delivered to anyone of the London docks, were high, though he hadn't then known, where the drugs were to go to, or the distributers were.

Of course, with Brassy or Dubois not being involved with the manufacturing of the drug, only the cleaning of, it would be far less of a risk doing it that way, with rugs or whatever, and a lower risk of detection by our Customs men using containers, than taking the higher risk of bringing in loads of already made up drugs in packets into this country, however lax the European Customs and border guards are!

Although without any means of any sophisticated detection equipment, which was still in its infancy, customs would now need to tighten up in a number of ways.

Now he smiled, and said. 'Although as I speak I've been reliably informed that after the raid, two senior Customs Officers in France have been arrested for their part in this smuggling racket; as others are to be at various other borders on the way here.'

He now told us that three officers in our C & E had also been arrested after the raid for their involvement in the operation. He also mentioned a covert operation, or sting, was now being carried out, arising from the 'interviewing',

THE LADY DETECTIVE

by various Police Forces in other countries, as it was here in the counties. Many of whom had been on people who'd been watched over for many months, who'd been known to be involved in importing, selling, or making of drugs, that were to eventually be distributed around the British Isles.'

He was to tell me at a later time, that 'the new NDS' thought up by us English, (meaning him) would be established in most European Countries, and they'd be, hopefully, particularly severe on any border control officers, or people, who for money, had allowed vehicles to return to this country knowing they were being used for drugs.

Though now he was to tell us. 'And make no mistake about it, in the British Isles, we will be severe with our own, because with this drug business now becoming big business, if we don't try to control it now, it will become a massive problem in ten, twenty years from now, when the criminals methods of bringing in drugs, becomes more sophisticated, and less detectable.'

He paused for a moment, and said. 'Although we have now at least, made a big effort to control the suppliers of the stuff coming in from Afghanistan via Turkey, and all those crooked border guards on the borders coming towards us, can only hope for any leniency when they're arrested, knowing that normally they'd be severely dealt with, unlike here. But we all know that money speaks louder than words, and we also know of the authorities in some Countries will always turn a blind eye to what is going on if given big back handers. So who knows what the outcome will be!'

With a frown Jones asked. 'So you are saying the suppliers and buyers of the stuff will be thinking of many more ingenious ways to get it into the country?'

'Exactly, which will mean, as I've said, we'll need to have more sophisticated equipment, and be even cleverer to catch them, and also being much more aware of how it's being distributed, if we can't control it being used.' He shrugged. 'Drugs are big business, and are going to be very big business, if it's not controlled, and this particular gang we caught, may

❈ 407 ❈

have gone on completely undetected for quite some time had it not been for a certain little lady whose inquisitive nose led us all into a pile of washed out . . . rugs,' laughter ' . . . and her being initially motivated because of another individual murdering his partner for reasons known to himself; which may or may not be divulged at a later time to us when he is questioned.'

'Do you mean when Jones and Williams again have a little word in his little pinkie, don't you?' added Blackie, making the detectives laugh, and Stokes looking even more miffed, because he'd not been asked to be one of the interrogations—interviewing team!

'Thank you Blackie, we'll do our best,' both Williams and Jones said, not having seen Stokes looking at them, and Stewart, with nothing less than pure hate behind his eyes.

Chapter 97

Stewart hadn't mentioned that he'd also got some of the names of the people who had been running the subsidiary branches for Brassy and Dubois, with his form of interviewing, and further criminals were arrested, and these arrested people had told Stewart's men of even more subsidiaries, from which they would again obtain more names, and now I'd been told, arrests were happening now all over the South of England, and in the North.

Asked the young woman detective, who was looking quite lovely out of uniform, and surrounded by the men, whose inquisitiveness would I imagine had meant she'd have quite a future ahead of her in the police force. She questioned. 'So how did you suspect it was Brassy and Dubois?'

'Well, we'd already known of Brassy and Dubois knowing each other, however what we didn't know was they'd been connected to each other, business wise; however all that changed, thanks to the inquisitive nose of one very lovely lady, and the rest, as they say, had all fallen into place very nicely. So now, all we need to do now is to tie up all the loose ends, and make this one very interesting case to be heard in Court.'

'And the drugs, Sir, what would have happened had the delivery been, say in Liverpool?' Stokes asked.

'Well fortunately that didn't happen, did it, Stokes? So there's no point thinking about it. Although to answer your

❦ 409 ❦

question, I am sure another police force would have handled the situation let's say . . . almost as efficiently as we did . . . ah joking! As I've said, we only knew that something heavy was imminent, as I've previously explained, though we didn't know when or where it was going down, or even how big it was, we certainly didn't know who was behind the business, until you guys found out that Brassy was Wainwrights, who was a mate of Dubois, who was especially known for his drug activities—and that was the missing piece of the puzzle being put together.'

'And we now know that piece of knowledge, had come by Miss Felliosi, having discovered, through her own private investigations, that both offices in the same hallway, were rented by Wainwrights.' Williams said.

'Exactly,' Said Stewart, 'and that, with knowing Wainwrights was connected to Dubois, was the icing on the cake, and was all it took to crack wide open this drugs gang . . . with some outside knowledge of the container delivery of course.'

'So had you not known about Dubois being involved with Wainwright/Brassy, then this wouldn't have happened, eh?' Jones said, who'd been enjoying this little chat, 'Now that's amazing!'

'True Jones . . . very true. So now this little free boozy is all due to Jess and her being such a good Wilhelmina Gumshoes.' He looked over to me and smiled, before raising his glass and saying, 'So here's to you Jess.'

I felt so very proud of myself at that moment, particularly when everyone had said 'To Miss Felliosi', or 'Jess', and all had raised their glasses to me, for I must admit I was quite proud of what I'd achieved by my sleuthing.

Williams having taken another large mouthful of his third pint of Whitbread bitter, because he began saying 'It's all for free lads,' and would repeat the same words to himself, and colleagues, many times during the evening to anyone he spoke to, or saying: 'This beer is all free, thanks to DCI Ross, whose a jolly good sort.'

THE LADY DETECTIVE

He now enquired. 'Sir, during Dubois confession, has he given you any hint as to why he killed his partner?'

Standing beside me and Stewart, Harry and his wife, at the end of the bar, we'd now been surrounded by Williams' colleagues, when Stewart had smiled and answering his question by saying, 'It'll be the same old story Williams, greed. It was because of Wainwrights greed.'

When he'd been asked to elaborate on that, he said. 'Well Dubois claims that his partner 'was fitting him up'. He claimed that Wainwrights had been importing on the side, and selling his 'extra' drugs, and hadn't told Dubois anything about it . . . meaning he hadn't cut him in on the profits. Though there is no proof of that.'

Stewart then quickly related what a miffed Dubois had told him. He said 'that Brassy had broken the faith hadn't he,' meaning his word, bond, whatever was binding, and said, 'that Brassy could have very easily jeopardised the whole sodding business by his offering our buyers a choice of two suppliers,' which he'd explained, 'would have meant our buyers, who are incidentally a crafty lot of bastards who need to be controlled', his words, 'would then be forever always looking for a better deal from either him or me. Now I couldn't have that, could I? I mean, my very good and true friend Brassy, (he then spat on the floor) would not only have earned from the buyers, who couldn't care a toss who'd they bought off, just as long as the deal was right, ultimately mean less wages for me, and from business we'd done together, so more for him. Plus it would also have spoilt a perfectly good little business because of his being a twat, and that I couldn't allow—could I, so he needed to be topped!'

Stewart told us that Dubois went on to say.

'Unfortunately for him, what happened was, and what did him in, was he'd been doing a bloody balancing act trying to remember who he'd previously done the business with—prices and such, well he began screwing up what deal he'd offered them, and that did him in, didn't it? Cos for him, it was like lifting weights, and when they'd become too heavy

❈ 411 ❈

for him to hold over his head, they'd all came crashing down on his bonce didn't they?'

Stewart then said he'd laughed, before saying—'Just like somefink else did, eh!. Not that any of this matters any more now anyway, 'cause he's gone to fairy land, and good riddance to the bugger as well, cheating sod! Cos in the end he got found out when his punters came back to me, cos there's no accounting for fools and idiots is there? No brains you see— just muscle Stupid sod!'

Stewart told us, 'though he didn't say whether he did or did not personally murder him, though he did say "he'd been very angry that the bugger could have eventually copped the lot had he any brains bigger than a pasticcio nut, and then there'd have been no commission to share with me, would there—so he had to go?"

I'd wondered where the expression of 'cop the lot' had come from.

CHAPTER 98

'It would appear that your glass is empty Williams, oh and yours Stokes, so hadn't you both better go and get them filled before the glass forgets what it's for, eh? Now don't be shy.'

At once Williams had gone directly to the bar for another 'free pint', before Stewart had turned to Stokes before he'd also gone to the bar, and then saying to me.

'Jess, that list of numbers you'd found in Mr B's office, and passed to Stokes here, I bet they has a tale to tell. Didn't you say you thought those letters and figures were the people that Brassy had supplied, the sale price, and the profit that he made from the deal.'

I said with a chuckle looking at Stokes. 'Stewart I've already told you that, haven't I? Because I remember saying, "If those numbers had anything to do with what was being earned, it certainly looked like a lot of money—so it was no wonder Dubois was peeved!' And then gasped, 'Of course that's the motive and the evidence of why Wainwrights was murdered. You've got the proof Stokes.' I'd then punched into the air and said, 'Yes!'

'So Stokes I want you mark that piece of paper as the motive exhibit for the murder, ok?' Stokes had nodded, and he asked Stokes 'so what did you make of those initials and numbers, Sergeant? For I'm assuming that would have been

❦ 413 ❦

something you'd have looked into. So please tell me your thoughts?'

Stokes had at first said nothing, for having previously telephoned his wife Mabel, and promised he'd go straight back home after having had a couple of pints out of courtesy to his Guvnor, wrapping up a drugs bust, and now for Miss Felliosi solving the murder, had in the meantime, changed his mind when he'd thought.

"Why the heck should I only have a couple of pints? I mean the bloody man has been rubbishing me off, so why shouldn't I help him to spend his stupid money if he wants to throw it about willy-nilly."

So having had another pint of bitter, his third, he'd then started on drinking double brandies, so by the time DCI Ross had spoken to him, like now, he'd already sunk quite a number of doubles, and was feeling slightly sloshed—drunk—inebriated, and had giggled before answering.

'Oh very good Sir,' he said, slurring heavily now, (does that remind you of anybody?) but had thought by speaking slowly he'd not slur his speech, or so he thought, he'd then said abruptly.

'Whatever you say to me is fine by me . . . . Ok? So now I will say to you, why don't you forget about work for the day, eh, be a good chap, and let's just enjoy this evening, ok, because I've had . . . because of you, person . . . personally had, had . . . a rotten stinking lousy couple of days, and now I fully intend . . . to now fully intend, to avail myself to . . . to, with enjoying your hos . . . hos . . . hospitality to the full, by drinking your booze. Though not, not to your health, ok! So respect . . . respectfully, sir, let's have no . . . no more talk about business, murders, or drugs today eh, there's a good chap.'

Though I saw Stewart had nodded his compliance, and had looked amused at the Sergeant, he had in a slightly sinister way, then laughed.

It had then been that I knew Sergeant Stokes' time at this Police Station, and perhaps in the job, was well and truly numbered. For not only had Stokes made far too many unexplainable bad mistakes in his handling of the murder case, which had upset a lot of people, me and my father in particular, which I knew Stewart would never forget; having had me imprisoned because of his stupidity, he was now being disrespectful to a superior officer, which was something I'd knew, Stewart would also not forgive.

So food for thought eh, cos booze and parties don't mix, especially if you have your bosses present to have a go at about your grievances. It never works, and is silly!

Having said what he'd said, Stokes had gone to the bar, ordered another large brandy, and had begun to fully realise who he'd been talking to, so had hastily gulped down this his umpteenth brandy, and having further indulged in having many more of the same just to cover his embarrassment, the fat Sergeant had, twenty minutes later, left this little happy gathering to go home, after saying 'Goodnight' and 'Thank you', and 'Plish cuse my, my manners,' to Stewart.

Then having had no response from Stewart, Williams or Jones, or anybody else whom he'd said goodnight to, that had left him with no doubts as to their thoughts about him as he left, and he wondered whether his good wife would be any less a cold comfort when he got home.

CHAPTER 99

I for one had not been sorry to see him go! For earlier in the evening, before his having many double brandies, and his final disappearance from the gathering, I'd asked Stokes.

'That crooked solicitor—has there been anything done about him?'

I'd asked him that, more to change the subject of his moaning about his having to work from the canteen, and to save him from further embarrassment, which I felt Stewart may have been contemplating towards the fat Sergeant, even though in terms of embarrassment, he had yesterday seen to it, that he'd been already been torn apart by himself, Stokes' colleagues, or me.

'No Miss,' he'd said. There he goes with the Miss bit again, 'not yet. Although please believe me when I tell you, I've had more important things on my mind to do . . . besides that.' He added sarcastically, before he began to vigorously shake his head, giving everyone another opportunity to see how many chins were now having a chance to get some exercise.

'And not very well at that,' said a voice in the crowd behind him, sounding very much like it was Williams.

'Fine,' I said angrily, 'then for your information, Sergeant, I suppose I should tell you, that having told my father about this non-important matter, and the office probably now being

❖ 416 ❖

THE LADY DETECTIVE

empty, and his saying he would look into it, he has now told me that he would be asking for the full four month's rent due to him on both offices, at £40 per week each, for the required two months' notice that hadn't obviously been paid.'

And seeing he wasn't much interested in what I had to say, I added. 'And my father has told me that with the lawyer acting as the main guarantor for both offices, he'd be definitely asking him for a further month's rental that is now also outstanding on both offices. So you see Sergeant, Brassy' solicitor will now be out of pocket on his dubious dealing with Brassy, plus my father's costs could be substantial, which daddy has told me could amount to be around £3,000.00 that was owed to him.'

The Sergeant still looked as if all this wasn't of interest to him, so I continued. 'And if it could be proved the police didn't handle this matter correctly, or the solicitor had been not straight up, then he could even find himself without a license to act as a lawyer, so both could be in trouble.'

And when Stokes asked me what I meant by that, I told him 'My father has told me, that by his meaning the police, and their not handling this solicitor matter correctly, the implications of that,' I added, 'could serve the Solicitor right for being such a fool, and the police for being so stupid. Don't you think so, Sergeant? Because I know, he really had meant the police being you. I wonder why that is Sergeant?'

At which point Williams, who'd been listening, had laughed, then said. 'Did you hear that Skip? And Dubois thinks there's no accounting for fools and idiots, and it was here all the time. He also said 'there's no honour amongst thieves, and he's right, 'cause some buggers would nick anything if it wasn't nailed down. And that includes other people's ideas and glory, eh Serge!'

He then took another large gulp of his beer, looked at Stewart, smiled, and then raising his glass to me, downed the remains of his drink, and had again looked at Stokes holding a half empty glass, and that had made me laugh having then seen the different expression on his face.

❄ 417 ❄

Stewart had also laughed, having noted Williams' angry expression towards Stokes, and Stokes had permitted himself a small smile, for he'd also known that I was also referring to him as well as the solicitor, as "being stupid", and then had afterwards imbibed stupidly with drinking many more double brandies, and more than he had intended, before he later stupidly had said those idiotic insulting words to Stew, before leaving us!

Chapter 100

SUMMING UP

The successful Drugs bust, had I'd later been informed by Stewart, had reached an estimated £12 million pounds, with a street value of being over five times that, which was a massive amount of money for 1970's. And the stupid part of all that, had been the gang would not have probably been found at all, well at least not as quickly, had it not been for the greed of two, and another man's stupidity in arresting me—namely Stinky Stokes.

Which reminds me that after both court cases, Sergeant Stokes had been offered early retirement, or be transferred to another division somewhere in the country 'out of harm's way', and had retired himself, as had Williams, who'd been given a choice of a promotion and to stay on, or an early retirement on Sergeant's pay as a thank you.

And the last I heard of him, he was as happy as a sand boy attending to his large garden, just as he'd always wanted to do, and would soon be winning prizes for a new type of rose, appropriately named—Jessie's.

Oh, as for to the money men who had fronted the purchases of the drugs, two had been prominent businessman, and two, high standing politicians, and all four had been charged with being an accessory to importing drugs for the selling thereof, which had created such an uproar, that it would be difficult to explain—so I won't!

After the court cases, Stewart had been promoted to a Chief Superintendent, the youngest in the Force by a considerable margin, so I'm told; and with his heading up the NDS, Nods, they would under his guidance, eventually have tentacles in every Police Force, and Police Station in the country.

He'd also coined the phrase 'ALL TO DO' that would become a motto for all the different Police forces in England, who would now not be deliberately vying with each other for the big credos, but work together for the betterment of all. Nice touch!

*   *   *

Finally it was two months later, once the NDS police and the detectives had spent many hours of hard work, by pen-pushing, foot-slogging and asking thousands of questions to everyone associated with both cases, they had eventually, and separately, sorted out all of the evidence and statements, relating to the drugs bust and murder.

Then it had been a further two months before there'd been a trial re the Drugs; and a further month after that, the murder trial.

The Drugs trial, had seen Dubois given a custodial sentence of six years, and then he'd been told weeks later, at the murder trial, that he'd also been sentenced to another 20 years for killing his partner in crime, Wainwrights.

*   *   *

At the trial, it had also appeared that he'd acted both parts in the hallway of being Mr Happy and Mr Grumpy, and then after being sentenced, had said that he was not Dubois, and that his name was Fletcher. Moreover, he said he could prove it, which, as you can imagine, had put almost everybody in as state of flux, before he had actually proven his name was Fletcher, and that Dubois had been an alias.

Of course that had led to his having an immediate re-trial, and then worse was to follow.

*　　*　　*

Confused are we? Well no-one had, including me, been able to identify for sure who the murdered man had been, because of his face being smashed in, and totally unrecognisable.

The dead man also had no identifying marks, teeth, scars, tattoo's, or fingerprints, that could prove he hadn't been either Dubois or Brassy/Wainwrights, and now with Fletcher saying in court that "as a partner, I was obviously entitled to have been in either offices to leave my fingerprints," the police had found that Fletcher had none, having been surgically removed.

Before his re-trial, this Fletcher/Dubois, who we thought had been the partner with Import Export license, had told Stewart "that his *partners* were bastards, because he'd hadn't expected either of them to have had an Import Export License," and in court during his trial, had repeated that he hadn't expected "his partners to be two-faced scheming bastards."

So that had confused things even more, particularly when he said, "And when I found out that both of my two-faced partners had been using my rugs idea to import further drugs into the country, without telling me what they were doing, well that I can tell you, had really pissed me off."

He continued, 'and when those two son of bitches (Brassy and Dubois) had told me they'd been selling drugs, and not splitting the profits with me, well then the bastards had then got their tuppence worth didn't they, after all, they were only supposed to have been selling for the firm, and me doing all the importing, so I had to teach the greedy conniving bastards the error of their ways, didn't I?'

*   *   *

'It had been then that the penny had dropped,' Stewart had said, when he realized after he re-read Fletcher's statement, with Fletcher saying that 'they were supposed— his partners—to have done all the selling for the firm', that Dubois or Brassy, weren't the only partners of this supposed Import Export and Sales outfit.

Also, Dubois office, which we thought had been Byways Ltd, and been the Import and Export Consultant, wasn't, because it had been Rugs and Tings who'd been that, so they'd been the real Import Export Agency, and not the Import Sales Consultants. Or did it?

Either way, both Fletcher's partners were not supposed to have been importing drugs, or even have even been supposed to have had a license to import goods, cos Fletcher/Dubois did that!

Which also meant, that the office signs on both office doors, were also not what they seemed either, having been deliberately exchanged to confuse anyone, who, shall we shall say, were being a bit nosy—the law I suppose.

So if Brassy, or his other partner, had been imported the rugs, how had they managed to do this for so long without being found out by Fletcher? That question had meant an all-around the clock questioning by the detectives, and many sleepless nights for Fletcher, before he'd at last confessed "That I'd found out about my partners misdemeanours, when someone had a word in my ear as to what was going on, cos my two partners were cocking up the prices—the thick gits," though he hadn't named who the partners names he was referring to, "and having noticed that she (meaning me) was having work done to her office, I realized that she could be the alibi to my getting rid at least of one of the cheating gits, so had then devised a plan whereas I would be mistaken as the murdered man, (meaning Mr Happy) and then I'd smashed in his face even more to a bloody mess in order to confuse matters even further for the police."

And when he'd been asked which office he'd done this, he said. "In Rugs and Tings didn't I, and after I smashed his face in, in the fireplace, I put his body into my partner's office, Byways Ltd."

The thing is, was he again lying about that also to confuse, by his saying 'my partner's office,' meaning which partner, Brassy/Wainwrights or the other secret partner?

He went on 'I thought I'd done a blinding job in messing about with the evidence, and my creating two different characters to fool anyone.' And I would have had to agree with him there, for the man had been a brilliant actor, and you would have thought the same had you met Mr Happy, and then seen Mr Grumpy.

He had been full of himself in Court, and said. 'That swapping identities on the different offices had been my idea, and after I'd murdered the scheming git, I had "for a laugh" thought to remove and replace some clues from one office to the other, hence the French fags being in R&T's office, cos he didn't smoke did he? And then the pasticcio nuts, which I'm addicted to, into Byways, and so forth from one office to the other, as well as cleaning off all fingerprints off of everything, even though I needn't have worried re my own."

He'd then told the Court. "Oh, and with my name not on anything to give me away either, I knew I could do what I wanted, for I'd got one of my stupid partner's (Not mentioning Brassy) to sign for both office leases at separate places, which he'd done, cos he was that stupid.'

And then to explain that brilliant double person deception, he said. 'Well on that Sunday, having already done in my other partner that week, I had on the Friday night, knowing my other partner liked to have a bit of a quiet time to mull things over, have a drink, and have a chatter, after I'd slipped in, then went up the stairs to the 5th, and killed him, and then out the building undetected, cos the old bloke at the desk was reading something and didn't see me, not that it mattered cos I wouldn't be who I said I was had he asked.

Then later, I'd thought I'd have a bit of fun, cos I like fun, and as I had nothing to lose, so had deliberately gone out on the Saturday morning, and bought myself a large brimmed hat and a full length fur overcoat "down the Portobello market", though the "tassel shoes I already had."

Then on the Sunday, having first observed that lovely lady Investigator in the hall by looking through the steel lift from the top of the stairwell, I had deliberately pretended to come up by way of the lift, having previously ran down one flight of stairs, climbed in to present myself to her in the hallway, This was again to mess up the evidence she'd give when to give myself another false identity I'd introduced myself as the guy who worked in Rugs and Tings."

Stewart said he'd laughed when he told the Court how he had fooled me with his acting skills by doing both the Mr Happy and the Mr Grumpy guy parts to create a witness, thereby giving him an alibi if he ever needed one, even though he'd known he wasn't mentioned anywhere.

At court, he went on to say. "I particularly wanted to confuse matters, and wanted her (being me) to not be sure that I wasn't the same geezer coming into the building, as the same one who left. It was a game. I was playing a game, because I really do love mind or dare games, especially had any-one thought I'd been Brassy, it'll have been perfect."

When the Barrister told him that it was his wearing different shoes that had made me suspicious of who he was, or wasn't, he said. "Now that wasn't intended to be part of the act. The reason she saw me wearing different shoes, was because there'd been so much blood from my having given the two-faced lying git, his face a further bashing to be different than his real one, that's a joke, two-faced, get it?' He laughed. 'Anyway, lots of his blood had splashed onto my brown tasselled shoes, and ruined them, and as the stains on them would have been too obvious for anyone not to have noticed, particularly had that girl still been in the hallway, I'd used his."

And to explain why only one sock had fibres of it from both office carpets, he said. "Well when I turned the man around the first time, one of his shoes caught, and came off. Then after I completed dragging him thru to the fireplace, I'd taken of the other shoe to wear, and put both his shoes on, gone up the hallway with me own brown shoes in me coat pockets." He laughed "which I bet would have confused the law, (meaning the police) I expect him having no shoes on!"

Which would also explain, why fibres had been on only one sock from both carpets!

Stewart said he'd made the court laugh we he added 'besides how was I to know the silly sod was wearing shoes two sizes smaller than me? I mean it's not as if you go around asking people, even your mates, what size footwear they wear, do you? Truth was, I was crippled for days after that!'

I'd been intrigued with his saying that about his being crippled, for that limp I'd thought had been a brilliant addition to his looking like another character, even though different shoes had not been his intention. Or were they, could you ever believe anything this man says?

Strangely at a later time, we did hear that Brassy did in fact have a slight limp—or was it Dubois?

Stewart said, he said. "Just my luck eh, there was me wanting to deliberately confuse things for a laugh, to be seen as someone slightly different, and to then be ear-wigged as a killer by the little lady, well I hadn't planned on her being so smart, cos other than the shoes, it have been a brilliant murder!"

Stewart had said Fletcher had sung like a bird in Court, and was full of his self, and had been pleased with murdering his partner, and had explained what he done on the Sunday.

"After I had sorted that bastard, I turned up on Sunday, and then after smacking him some more for the hell of it, I pulled him into the other office, (meaning Byways) because he obviously wouldn't be using it anymore," He laughed "and then turned the bastard around in front of the fireplace for a laugh," and again had laughed.

When asked why he did that, he said "because then there police would have then be chasing their tails in wondering how was it that a body had been in an office that wasn't his own. Get it? Remember the girl would tell them that he—or me—had worked in Rugs and Tings, having told her I did," He laughed with no humour in it "and here I am because of my wanting being stupid and too cocky over setting up a false trail to myself."

Stewart told me that after his not coming up with anything else that was meaningful, he'd then been told of my visiting both of those offices that Sunday night, and my being arrested the following day by Sergeant Stokes for his partner's murder, and been asked had he anything to say about that? And Stewart said he'd laughed and said: "Now that is one very smart and very lovely lady, and I'm sorry for her being inconvenienced, and sorry that I had needed to deceive her."

He also asked the Court to pass on a message to me. "That he thought of me as a bright young lady from that first time of meeting me," and then told the court. 'It would seem that this Jess Felliosi has even been too dam smart for me, cos I've been charged with murder and in here, and she, the clever little darlin', was charged with murder, and is out there, ain't she?' Then he'd added, 'besides it's all fair in love and war don't you think, and it'll all turn out fine for her in the end . . . you see."

And in the end, whatever that likeable killer had thought and said was proved right in the end!

CHAPTER 101

Pasha and I had, over a matter of a few months leading up to both Court cases, become firm friends, and she'd quickly become both my life-line to reality, and my blessing in disguise, for now only months after we'd first met, she was handling everything to do with the office, making my appointments, and seeing to the people who called in with an ease and an efficiency that was a joy to behold.

Pasha had also prior to and after both court cases, been wonderful, which allowed me to earn mega bucks for my sins, for I had been in big demand for my doing TV work. Also there'd be my biography published, as well as endless amount of articles written about me in magazines all over the world.

I'd even been asked to do a film for one know famous company, and offered the lead role, which to be frank, I'm wondering whether to do or not to do—and probably will.

So, having all that to cope with, besides my having own work at the agency to contend with. And because of all the extra work that had come into the agency, due to 'The fireplace murder' and the 'Biggest Drugs' court case ever known in England, Pasha had become very important to me.

The publicity had also forced me to employ three more helpers. Two had been females, who I'd employed not only for their brains, but because they were both also very attractive and bright, and had the desirable proportions that most men would slaver over whilst they had just sat nylon legged asking

❦ 427 ❦

questions, and getting the desired answers to their questions, the person willing to talk even to keep them there a little longer.

There was the lovely Tracy Styles, who at the age of 27 was a gorgeous ashen haired brunette, who was exceptionally brilliant in finding lost people, especially husbands, and was soon to be known amongst us, as 'Trace 'em' Styles'.

Then there was Sharon Barnaby, 26, who was also brilliant, and had red hair similar to Pasha, and had a brilliant mind when it came to being devious to get her answers. Both ladies stood over 5'10 inches tall.

I'd also employed a 6'4 inches hunk man mountain called Rick 'Chubby' Chambers, called Chubby because of 'his baby face', who also had been, thank goodness, blessed with having a similar high IQ to the two ladies, and all three had most importantly, a decent background, and had all attended well-known public schools, which was particularly important, now we are having mega-rich women and men among our clients. We also had snobs of both sexes wanting our services.

Chubby, at 31 years old and single, had thought he knew everything there was to know about crime, having studied the subject for a number of years, and had a diploma in criminology, though Sharon would out of the three, emerge as the best of them in the months ahead, and would then become my understudy in this business of solving crime without it becoming a court case, which gave my lawyer friends some work, had it done—less my commission.

The three were all found to be honest and trustworthy, and for me to have them in my small firm, had been great, and I'd been very fortunate to have found them.

Now with Pasha being 'Head of Staff', I had the complete package. She had before Sharon took over the job, helped me in controlling the three new Investigators, especially when it came to the office side of things, typing reports, sending letters, invoices and so forth, and having had so much work to do, she had been forced to take on, for herself, two part

THE LADY DETECTIVE

time staff to help her, who would after the Court hearings, both become full time staff.

As you can gather, crime and sex was big business for me! And as a Private Investigator firm, we were as a team, very good in solving or sorting out our clients problems. No let me change that to, as a team we are exceptionally good, having 98% of our clients saying that we were, having been very, very, satisfied with our work.

Which meant for as long as men couldn't behave themselves, then I was happy, because whatever they got up to, now accounted for over 50% of our business, and the money had just kept rolling in.

My three 'helpers' would, whenever necessary, do their own investigating or fact finding, by using local libraries, museums, or delving into the nations archives at Somerset House, and so forth, as I did when I'd needed important facts for any case I was working on—besides using Stewart and friends of course!

I employed the best, expected the best, and got the best from them. So whenever I charged a client my premium rate, it was as a result of their good work, and it reflected as such in their wages.

Oh, and another fact was that two months after the two Court trials, I had un-surprisingly, needed to rent both of the now vacant offices that had started the ball rolling for me, namely Byways Ltd and Rugs & Tings. Then I had them both completely re-vamped, and the hallway and office floors covered with a new carpet, that in the offices, hadn't given any clues as to where the foot-switch was to open the fireplaces.

Needless to say, I never told any of the staff where the switch was hidden, though I knew with them being all ladies, they must have searched for it, or had even stood on where it had been, not knowing they'd have needed to bulk up more weight to have made it work.

Maybe one day, I might surprise everyone by getting Stewart to go from one office into the other, thru the fireplace,

❧ 429 ❧

just to scare the living daylights out of the typists, or whoever was in there, although I couldn't really see that happening, so maybe that secret will now always remain mine and Stewart's special secret.

CHAPTER 102

FINALLY

During, and after the drugs and murder trials, Sergeant Stokes and his team had been praised for their involvement in both cases, and there'd been a particular mention given to DC's Williams and Jones.

Special praise had been also mentioned in the drugs trial, for DCI Ross and to the new National Drugs Squad, for his organising the capture of not only this drugs gang, but many other leading drug gang suppliers throughout Great Britain who had bought from Dubois.

Certain members in Customs & Excise had also been praised for their diligence in their handling of the Drugs bust, whilst others had been arrested and given jail sentences for their part in allowing this and many other consignments of drugs to be imported into the country, and for their turning a blind eye—for money.

*   *   *

FINALLY, FINALLY

As for me, well what can I say, other than I'd been awarded two Police Commendation medals for my part in providing the evidence on how the murder was achieved, with my solving the mystery of the 'fireplace' murder, and providing the evidence to have apprehended the 'bad' drugs men.

I'd also received a substantial amount of reward money for my helping to break-up this dangerous drug gang; money which I had put into a 'No drugs' charity.

Though I suppose best of all, was my having a photograph and name plastered all over the daily newspapers, and having it banded about in all the society columns, glossy magazines and so forth, all of whom had written such wonderful articles about me, of how I had single handed solved a puzzling drugs related murder by pitting my wits against dangerous criminals.

There had been headlines such as: Jess solves the 'Moving Fireplace Murder', and 'Mystery Murder solved by Lady Dick', which I didn't feel was in good taste, and 'Police out-thought by Lady Sleuth', although the headline I had personally liked, was: 'Lady Jess gets off to 'crack'-ing start in drugs murder' (crack being a drug), and 'Frustrated cops given a hand by beautiful detective!' As if!

I suppose smutty headlines like these, might have caused a fair amount of good humour, and it certainly had got me a lot of business.

Another good thing was that I'd been labelled as 'Lady Jess-tigator' or the, 'Now don't ask for less, get Jess' fame. The rhyme was not very good I know, but the 'Lady Jess-tigator' instead of Investigator, had stuck with the media, and would be remembered. I'd thought perhaps I should change the name on my door again—but hadn't!

The enormous publicity I received, with my having appeared as a witness in two separate and now famous Court cases, had obviously done me or my business no harm at all, for it had meant that I was now known to almost every woman in Great Britain, and beyond, and more importantly, among the monied woman in our society, who would now have felt they had at least a 'friend' in a detective agency, who they could confide to, or feel on equal terms with as women, to share their problems!

Also being that I was born into one of the most privileged and richest families in England, and being a very beautiful lady; and known sportswoman, had made my social profile blossom ten-fold. I'd suddenly been put under the spot-light, and glowed. And with my being the Lady 'Jess-igator' or The Lady Detective, the fame had come easily with me, and was getting me a lot on prime time TV in documentary's, chat shows, and such, to allow me to tell people what I did for a living.

The best part of all this, had been that most of the money I'd been paid to do these shows, had meant a lot of money would be going to various charities, and deserving people.

Oh, and perhaps I should tell you that my father did in fact win a lot of money with his betting on me getting off the murder wrap, which he'd said I would! He told me he'd bet heavily at various betting shops; on whether I would or would not get off, and then with all of the money he'd won, with some of his own, had set up a home for deprived children.

Of course the biggest problem for us women was, as we all know, our men folk two-timing on us, which for business, had of course been fine by me, for all I had to do then, was to come up with the evidence of their men's infidelities, and that as they say, would be like taking money from a baby!

Of course there'd also been many cases when men had felt sure that their wife, or girlfriend, had taken advantage of them by cheating on them! Which made a change from the norm—or did it?

CHAPTER 103

FINALLY.
FINALLY. FINALLY.

As you can now gather, my being involved in both a murder and a drugs case, had been a most satisfactory beginning to both my career, and business, and I was now far removed from that frightened young woman who'd been watching her name and occupation being scripted onto a new panelled door by a little man with wispy hair, with trepidation.

From all the publicity I'd got, my investigating business would continue to get busier, and the money would just keep rolling on in, partly due to all those lusty men who couldn't keep themselves to themselves!

Though the rest of my business had come from missing persons, nasty disputes over who owned what; debated wills, sour relations, and so forth, and I'd even, would you believe, been hired by a friend to help solve as the 'Jess-tigator', a murder of a friend's relative, which I must inform you, had been a very simple case to solve; being a son who had turned murderer, because of a mean rich old woman, his mother, who because he was an invalid, had even refused to often

❦ 434 ❧

THE LADY DETECTIVE

change, or buy him, new sheets for his bed. So for revenge, he had arranged to have her murdered by people who had left so many clues as to who they were, being the two gardener's, a child could have solved it.

Well that's it for now, except if you recall, my telling you about that nice old boy who was dying of Cancer, who'd wanted me to find his long lost son. Well I did find the son, and he'd lived only three miles from my offices. Well it appears that the son had done well for himself, by becoming Head man for a National car park firm, and when I found him and told him that his old man was looking for him, he said that the old man had been evil to both him and his mother when he was a young boy, and had been forced out of his house, when he continued to bring many younger versions of his mother to his home.

He also told me that right up until they'd both left, they'd often been beaten by the old boy over silly things, and when he'd been thirteen had ran away. That was over twenty-five years before, and in all that time, hadn't wished to see his father ever again, though he'd always known where his father lived.

He suggested to me, that as his father was rich, that I should get as much money out of him as I could, and give it all to a charity for beaten up wives and children. Obviously because of the ethics involved, I couldn't do that, although I did tell him I'd tell the old man that his son had never wanted to see him, and that I would personally put the money that I earned from the case into charity. He'd agreed, and even added a bit of his own money to the amount.

The son also told me, he'd never found out where his mother had gone to after he'd been put into a home. So I had given that some thought, and found out that with her trying to cope with the stress of it all, she'd been institutionalized, and had recovered, and continued as a nurse, to work at the same place. And so I'd been a witness to a successful and tearful re-union, though I won't bore you with the details.

◆ 435 ◆

Well as I have said, that really is it for now, except to tell you that the young Detective Jones, pops into the office every now and again to see Pasha, and have a cup of coffee, and that she told me one day, that she thought he was a really nice chap, and intelligent, and they were both going to see his parents on their farm back in Wales before it was sold, and they'd came to live in Muswell Hill. London. Make of that what you will!

And then to top it all, month's after Fletcher had been convicted of the murders of both his partners, he had confessed in prison, that he wasn't Fletcher after all, or Dubois or Brassy, because all the documents on them all had been forged, including birth certificates, and he could, had anyone wished, prove who he really, really, was—again!

Anyway, the uproar his statement had created, had needed to be heard to be believed, because the newspapers were stirring the pot by saying that when he was released, he could use his 'real' name, or even another fictitious name, and because he'd then have a clean criminal record, and with having no finger-prints, could re-offend again and again, without anyone knowing he was a convicted murderer! Or, he could assume the role of a businessman, and an honest citizen.

Fletcher did say. "As I've already been banged up for doing in, either Dubois, or Wainwright, it means when I'm released, I cannot be tried for the same murder again.' His meaning it was 'Double Jeopardy'

'It's a funny old world, isn't it?' Stewart had said, hoping his statement wouldn't amount to anything. Or would it?

*

Oh, and as for my own court case re the murder of a man who I'd supposedly murdered, who according to Stewart could never be named by his real name, well that never got to Court, as it was thought in light of the trial above, there'd

THE LADY DETECTIVE

not been a case for me to plead 'not guilty' for, so the case had been scrapped and dismissed even before the trial, though I had later been awarded damages for unlawful arrest by Stokes, instigated by my father.

Oh, there's just a little more I need to tell you, which you may find boring, because I need to tell you in all honesty, cross my heart and hope to die if I'm lying, that I really hadn't a clue about my behaving like a proper idiot in the hallway, like I was some kind of nut-case not having one of their better days!

I suppose, the point I am trying to make is, seeing as I'm not normally one of those women who are forever looking around for a sympathetic shoulder to cry on when a problem occurs; or had I been offered one, would rarely have taken the opportunity to use it, it really is for me now so red facing to have to tell you how frightened and scared I'd felt at the time; and now, having weighed up the pros and cons, obviously seeing it through your eyes at what happened to me, I am completely surprised that I hadn't been carted off by one or two white men in short white coats, who I'm told, did immensely enjoy taking people away that acted like I had, to be locked up and even worse—have had their head examined. Yoicks!

I suppose I had acted completely bonkers, and being in my own little world, I did think I was being hypnotized, controlled, by the little man, who'd only been working on my new office door, who I of course now realized had been nothing more than he been employed to do as a sign writer, so should have known he'd know who I was, because I'd have already ruddy well given him all the information that he needed to put my name and occupation on to the door. Fool I'd been!

So now I can only offer you my sincere apologies, even though you really hadn't witnessed the strange goings on in the hallway, with the foot-shuffling, hair-swishing, and my generally acting like I was a moron.

Of course, having returned to the here and now, you might now say, hypothetically speaking, that it had been therapeutic.

I might laugh at myself now, being the Lady Detective, the Jess-igator, but not then, for my thoughts had then been very real, and very, very scary. Even frightening!

As I've said, it certainly is a funny old world—isn't it?

THE END

CPSIA information can be obtained
at www.ICGtesting.com
Printed in the USA
LVHW091942260319
611839LV00026B/1/P